A Life Cut Short

A Life Cut Short

Relle Bateman

Write My Wrongs, Co., United States
www.writemywrongsediting.com

To my husband and three beautiful children, for the sacrifices they've
made for me to achieve this goal.

Where there is great love, there are always miracles.
—Willa Cather

PROLOGUE
Nine Months Ago

"Do you believe in miracles?" Professor Gomm asked. "What is a miracle anyway?"

Students offered answers to her questions in a technical way. This group of students rarely held back, unlike me. But my thoughts echoed theirs: *A good thing that happens that no one can really explain.*

The lesson was supposed to touch on the idea of miracles from both traditional and somewhat spiritual points of view. Professor Gomm trod lightly with the concepts of the latter, knowing religion could be a touchy subject. I wondered if she'd had a sensitive student in the past, causing her to be extra cautious during the current go-around. I glanced at the other students in the room who didn't seem to even care, no one repositioning themselves uncomfortably in their seats or looking down or away.

The young-looking and heavy-bottomed woman who stood in front of the small classroom continued along the traditional route. "But what defines 'an extraordinary event' or 'something amazing' for one person may not fit what another person defines as such." She walked along the front row of students, making eye contact all over. "Maybe miracles are more of an everyday occurrence for everyone than we think. A woman giving birth to a baby could be the same kind of miracle to one person as finding an awesome parking spot when they're running late is to another."

I tried to keep up and process her words, not knowing what to write for my notes yet.

"After all, people have different priorities, different needs, and different points of view. The flip side of the birth coin is death. Most times we view death as awful and sad. Sometimes it's 'good the person isn't suffering anymore.' But the death of someone could also be a miracle when viewed by, say, someone who needs a kidney, a liver, or a heart. So viewpoint matters in terms of lots of things, including miracles. Who knows? There may be a ripple effect from a death that only the universe understands. Maybe we can't always see what we need to in order to appreciate it.

"We're going to circle back to life and death and the universe, but first…" Professor Gomm returned behind her desk. "There are only two emotions we truly have. A lot of people think they are love and hate, but they're not. Hate stems from fear." She held up two fingers. "The only two emotions we have are fear and love. All other emotions stem from these." She turned and wrote the two words on the whiteboard.

Okay, I've heard this before, and it makes sense.

"So here's a different take on miracles according to Dr. Helen Schucman's *A Course in Miracles*. It's a hefty book that, honestly, I have mixed feelings about, but for all intents and purposes with today's lesson, we are going to take a look at one little bit of it. She talks about a miracle as a change in perception from thoughts based on fear to thoughts centered on love." The marker squeaked as she drew an *X* over "fear," an arrow, and a circle around "love." "Again, maybe miracles are more of an everyday occurrence than we think. If we can change our fear-based thinking to love-based thinking, if we can make all of our day-to-day choices out of love instead of fear, then that is a miracle in and of itself and will open the door for more miracles. We're supposed to work miracles—that is, change perception from fear to love—in our lives and others' every day."

Well, wouldn't that be nice? Miracles every day.

"Why?" she asked, then immediately went on. "Because love is the only real thing, and everything else is a delusion."

The word *delusion* was a bit much for me, but the answer of love being what mattered most wasn't. Stories, movies, even dance routines that emphasized doing the right thing or the meaning of life emphasized *love.*

Professor Gomm continued, stating we should also believe that through "miracles" and "love," anything was possible.

Really? Anything?

Students had held back before, but at that point, a few let loose. The class became an open debate that lasted at least fifteen minutes. I was torn between following along with the back and forth of it all or just taking a catnap until it was over.

Finally, the professor held up her hands and announced we needed to move on. She was able to circle back. "Okay, so, another take on miracles. And again, an everyday occurrence for everyone. Everything that happens, *especially* life and death, are tools for the universe to adjust and normalize itself. If it didn't do this, the universe couldn't guarantee its existence would continue on a safe path."

Hmm, the old "everything happens for a reason" saying?

She went on, elaborating on that concept for a few minutes, then prompted the class with questions. "So, if the universe is continually self-correcting and self-organizing, does that mean the universe itself is one miracle after another? That it's one moment of brilliance after another? That it's an everlasting world of opportunities for life to fulfill itself?" It wasn't an assignment, just a subject for thought.

"A tree comes from a little seed," Professor Gomm said, holding her forefinger and thumb just an inch apart. "Its greatness is already encoded. And it doesn't say no to this miracle. It can't. Humans come from an egg and a sperm; the embryo's greatness is already encoded. You. You can grow into something great." She opened her arms wide to show us just how great she thought we could be. "Don't say no."

Is the point to always say yes? I thought.

It was as if Professor Gomm read my mind because she clarified, "Now, don't go crazy saying yes to every little thing. Remember, this is just a lesson, just an idea." She closed the book on her desk and added in a soft tone as if she believed the next part, "But own your everyday miracles, however you want to view them. Create them however you possibly can. Think about what would happen if you changed your perception"—she pointed to the board—"and focused on love. What would happen if you said yes?"

Little did I know I would take her advice in the near future, and things would get really complicated.

Saturday, July 31

So here I am, standing on the edge of a cliff, ready to jump. Red dirt coats my old Skechers. I never thought I'd be someone who'd do something like this. And, technically, I'm not. I peer down into the red-streaked slot canyon—three hundred feet down, at least. It makes me light-headed, so I pull back, but the image of jagged rocks at the bottom stays in my mind's eye as if it's been painted onto the backs of my eyelids. I turn my gaze straight ahead instead of imagining my broken, bleeding body at the bottom.

There's another cliff about one hundred feet across the way. Actually, there are two across from each other, with an opening of possibly fifty feet between them. It seems like a space the daring Evel Knievel would relish jumping. I imagine the man in the white jumpsuit on his motorcycle, cape flapping behind him in the wind as he accelerates up a ramp and over the gap, landing easily with a spray of dirt as he stops.

I blink. *Enough of that.*

The bright sky is clear of smog, and even though the breeze is warm, it feels pleasant blowing against the sweat on the back of my neck.

I've lived in Utah all my life but have never been to Zion before. It really is something you have to see for yourself. The rock formations and canyons are almost something to worship, but the colors are a wonder in their own right. The rust-colored stone against one of the bluest skies I've ever seen and the whitest of white clouds give me a sense of pleasure I wasn't expecting. There's even color in the air I breathe; it's fresh and free of toxins or chemicals—it's green.

I'm not alone. I'm with a bunch of people I've never met before today except for the girl inside me. But to say I've met her is a stretch. We're all here for this one purpose, this one thrilling adventure, with which almost nothing else can compare. Almost.

The girl inside me must be anxious as well because she hasn't taken control of my legs to make the jump yet. I'm appreciative of this, needing another minute. Although, on the other hand, it really is just dragging out my own anxiety. I could take all the first-day-of-school jitters I've ever had and mix them with every awful dentist's appointment plus that horrible gyno appointment I had last year, and I don't think the resulting anxiety concoction would even come close to making me as nervous as I am right now.

I'll put up with it, though, because I promised her. I *am* waiting for *her* to move my legs, though. I'm leaving that up to *her*. That was the deal. And I'm loyal to the deals I make.

I'm Camry. The girl inside me is Cassia. She's the entire reason I'm here. She's had me visit new places and do crazy things. Well, crazy for me. I am not a thrill-seeker; I'm a safe-seeker. I'm cursed with seeing the danger in almost everything. Don't get me wrong; it doesn't completely rule my life, but it does take over a lot of my thoughts. So if not for her, I'd be home in my cozy little Salt Lake City apartment, probably watching a cheesy romantic comedy. If not for her, I wouldn't have overlooked the risks in driving to Las Vegas in May, taking a mud bath, eating octopus, and riding the coaster on the top of the Stratosphere. Essentially by myself. If not for her, I wouldn't have overlooked the hazards in going to Yellowstone in June and being chased by bison just to get a photo. Twice! And more or less, again, by myself.

This, though—today, here on this cliff—this is by far the craziest thing Cassia has talked me into doing. The dangers of this trip exceed the others.

In my head, I have an exchange of encouragement for Cassia and somewhat for myself also. I tell her she's brave enough to do this. I tell her, as much as I don't want to do this, I do want to *for her*. I want to be the body she doesn't have any longer. I want her to feel the nerves of "before the jump" the way we feel them right now. I want her to feel my heart—our heart—thrashing as brutally as it is in this moment. I want her to feel the fall, feel the wind against us, feel the rush. And I'll do my best to keep visions of my broken, bleeding body at the bottom of this canyon out of my mind.

She doesn't say anything, and I don't know what she's thinking. I never do.

Finally, she shuffles my feet; because there are two kinds of people in this world: the ones who have the balls to jump and the ones who walk away with their tail between their legs. Obviously, Cassia is the former.

This is it, I think. *Oh God!*

We both clutch the rope attached to the harness; *that* is a mutual desire. The guys with us clap and cheer. She jumps, and we begin to fall. Down, down, down. The rope catches (and doesn't snap, thank goodness), and we start to swing toward the other cliff, the one about a hundred feet across the way.

I scream at the top of my lungs, then Cassia screams at the top of my lungs, then the canyon walls echo our screams back to us. The wind whips around my face as we cut through it like a pendulum. I close my eyes tight, but she opens them back up. It's difficult to breathe from the force of the air. I never knew my heart was so strong; I'm surprised my ribs can contain it. *Is it possible for a heart to actually explode?*

We've now passed the bottom of the swing, and my stomach lurches as we fly between the two cliffs and slice through the air up to the other side.

Once we reach the top of the upswing and pause slightly before falling again, I make the horrible mistake of looking down. The freeness of it all scares the crap out of me. There's nothing but this thin rope for me to grasp, so I clutch it and squeeze my eyes shut again as my body flips over and we fall facedown back to the other side.

My ponytail is pulled back by the wind, and with a heavy smack, I crash into something huge. With my face!

Oh heaven above!

I want to grab my nose but don't; I don't want to let go of the rope. I've opened my eyes now. I'm still falling—well, swinging.

What the hell just happened?

I search for a clue, and there it is.

A bird!

A *big* bird.

It's falling now too. Probably wondering, like me, *What the hell just happened?*

Oddly, I think of the video clip of the bird who flew directly into the path of a one-hundred-mile-per-hour baseball pitch. The batter never even got a chance to swing; all that was left was a puff of feathers.

What are the odds? I watch the bird swirl to the ground. *What are the odds of falling into a bird's path while swinging through a slot canyon in Zion?*

Am I one in a thousand?

One in a hundred thousand?

Less?

Lucky me, I think. My eyes are watering now, the wind forcing the tears horizontally into my hair. I think my nose is broken. It's definitely bleeding; I can taste it as it runs between my lips. I heard a crack, but then again, perhaps that was just the sound of the collision. Perhaps that's just the sound made by a bird beak smacking against a human nose.

Then I'm hit with something else, a sudden realization Cassia isn't with me. *Did the impact knock her out of me, or is she just avoiding the pain of the break?* I feel terrible; this was supposed to be for her, and she didn't get the full experience. I continue to swing, having no other choice, but as I start to slow, I'm brave enough to take one hand off the rope and feel the damage. The skin isn't split, nor does my nose feel off-center. This is the silver lining. *It'll be fine*, I tell myself.

By the time I'm mostly just dangling between the two cliffs, the rest of the crew have come to the end spot and are waiting for me at the top. They holler down to me to be sure I'm all right. I wave haphazardly and give two thumbs up. The motor begins to pull me up.

When it's all finished, when the last two of the group that signed up for the swing and had the balls to jump do so, I climb into the front seat of one of the three Jeeps that drove us here. I'm still trembling, and my nose is still oozing blood. I hold tissues under it and position a cold pack the driver gave me on top of my face.

Cassia still hasn't come back.

I felt weird signing up for this, coming alone, and being paired with strangers, but it's even more awkward as the guys in the back of my Jeep are still talking and laughing about my jump. A smirk is glued on the driver's face, too, although he doesn't go on and on about it as the two numbskulls in the back do. I think they're names are Miles and Murphy. They're thrill-seeking twins from Kansas that I wonder if they'll make the age of thirty. They're beginning to get on my nerves.

Whatever. My one-in-a-hundred-thousand bird collision will be online in no time; he recorded everyone's jump.

Back in Salt Lake City, I don't get to a doctor until Wednesday. The doctor confirms my nose is broken, but it's a clean break and doesn't need surgery. *Whew!* He likes my story and says he's going to look me up on YouTube.

Great. That's just great.

I'm unaccompanied right now. Cassia didn't come with me to the doctor visit. *Why would she?* She did come check on me the night it happened, though, easing my worry about her and telling me how sorry she was for the whole thing. It's not like it was her fault, but I get it. She's sorry it happened.

I don't know where she goes when she's not sharing my body. A while ago, she told me she can't stay inside my body all the time; it wears her out. It takes a lot of energy for her to talk through me and move my legs and arms, and it still takes some strength even to simply accompany me while I do all the talking and moving. I don't quite understand it, but there it is.

I've tried to learn more about her, but she's like a vault, and I don't have the slightest idea what the combination is. I've been trying "nice" and "patient" but maybe her combination involves something other than that. I have a fear the combination includes a threat, which goes against the grain of my character.

Once, in the beginning, I lay on my bed and cleared all my thoughts and waited and waited. I finally began talking to the empty room, just asking her to come and visit. Every time she joins me, my entire body tingles just a little bit, like when a person's hand or foot falls asleep. It begins in my chest, then travels to my stomach, then to my extremities, and finally moves out through my head.

One of the first times we actually had a conversation with each other, I asked her to tell me about who she was, her family, her life, and even her death. She didn't answer any of my questions. She left me when I asked about her death, and in her absence, I blinked her tear down my cheek.

Before Cassia, I was going to school at the University of Utah. Although I was only two semesters in, I like to think I was earning a degree. The truth is, by the time Cassia came along, I was starting to question my aspiration of having a career in dance. The original idea had been to teach dance. I don't think I'd be good with little kids, but possibly high schoolers. The musicals were a blast.

But in January, at the beginning of last semester, I began to feel that wasn't the path for me. I'd sprained my ankle the second day of school and, surprisingly, didn't even feel too bad about dropping out of the dance-centric classes after only a week. I signed up for more general studies and decided to just focus on finishing those and figure out a degree later. For a nanosecond, I had the wild thought I should be done with school altogether, but something told me to keep going. So I did.

When Cassia found me in April, after finals and the car accident last semester, I was lying in my bed waiting for the headache to go away, and I just decided I was supposed to help her.

Well, don't get me wrong. It took some convincing. This was after I thought I was crazy for about two weeks due to the uncontrolled movements, random words that would come out of my mouth, and dreams where it was like I was someone else.

But eventually, the random words became sentences that made sense. Still, they came out of nowhere. One time, I wasn't even thinking about going for a walk, but all of a sudden, I blurted out, "I want to go for a walk."

Of its own volition, my body stood up and took me for a walk around the block. My eyes searched and took in the everyday sights of the neighborhood as if they were brand new, despite the fact I'd lived in the city for the past year. The calm expression of wonder on my face certainly wasn't a reflection of the thoughts and feelings going on inside of me. The thoughts of losing my mind and feelings of general freaking out were pushed far back, and I was forced to notice the yellow flowers in the flowerbed at the apartment building next to mine, the Victorian trim on the houses around the block, and the sheer awesomeness of the giant mountains. I even noticed the FedEx pickup on the corner, which had never caught my eye before.

Another time, I spelled my name with my right hand even though I'm left-handed. I marveled for a second at how good the handwriting was before I switched the pen to my dominant hand.

And the dreams—I was a different person in them. The feeling was sort of like watching a movie and taking the place of the main character. I thought for sure the car accident had rendered me cuckoo. The last resort would be to call my parents; I didn't really think I could deal with them. The second-to-last resort would be to go to a doctor, but I didn't really have money to do that. So I called in sick to work and began

Googling concussions, which then turned into a search for a psychiatrist before my fingers typed, "You don't need a psychiatrist."

I gaped at the words and wondered how and why I'd typed them. My right hand picked up the pen on my desk and wrote, "My name is Cassia."

I stared in disbelief at those words for a long time also. I spoke aloud, "Cas-ee-uh? Cash-uh? No. Cas-ee-uh? Yes. Cas-ee-uh." Dropping the pen, I went to my bed. Cuddling a pillow, I tried to wrap my head around everything while actively thinking, *I'm not crazy, I'm not crazy.*

I spoke aloud, "No, you're not crazy, Camry."

After another week or so, Cassia began to gain better control of her words, helping me understand she was a ghost that could somehow be part of me at times. I didn't know how to feel about it all. *How was it possible? Why me? Should I go to a doctor? Should I call my parents? How could either of them help me? Did I just let this ghost girl come aboard so we can ride my crazy train together? Come on, Cassia. Meet the conductor. His name's Ozzy. Let's go!*

Around the twelfth day of being aware of Cassia as a ghost who could communicate with me, I hadn't made any decisions. I was home, waiting for my headache to go away. I was trying to process it all and found myself thinking of the lesson from Professor Gomm's class about miracles, changing fear to love, and saying yes to more things. Cassia had told me she had a bucket list and asked if I'd be willing to help her fulfill some of it. I decided to try to drop the fear of it all and explore this new world of body sharing to see where it led me, hoping I didn't end up in the loony bin.

Ultimately, I didn't schedule any classes for the summer semester. I promised the next few hot months to her, except for work. After all, I need money. But I'll do what's in my power (well, my budget) to do her bucket list for her. I'll push fear away as much as I feasibly can. I'll say yes to as much as I feasibly can.

Yes.

Cassia has been with me for three months now, and I haven't told anyone about her. I mean, I don't *think* I'm crazy, but I recognize this whole thing as *sounding* crazy, so I don't feel comfortable telling anyone. A normal parent-daughter relationship might say that one could speak to their parents about something like this, but I certainly don't have a normal parent-daughter relationship. My parents retired last year and decided to pack up and move to Florida. It was the strangest thing ever! People who live in Utah all their lives don't just pack up and move to Florida. St. George, maybe, but not Florida. The humid climate of the southeast is a complete one-eighty from the high desert dryness of Utah, not to mention the culture.

I'm an only child. They *left* me.

Somehow, that's not unexpected. They've never told me so, but I think I was a mistake. I know they love me, but it's as if I'm the "redheaded stepchild" for each of them. I don't know how to explain it. I always had good clothes and plenty of food. I was always tucked in and kissed goodnight. And they've paid for and supported everything that included the word *dance* in it. But once I hit thirteen, I was on my own for a lot of things. It got worse when I turned sixteen, able to work and drive myself places. Then the magic number of eighteen was another level of worse—worse than stories of classmates I knew who were getting kicked out and trying to find roommates to live with. My parents sold my childhood home, kicked me off to the U, and said "cheerio" to me and everything else they've ever known about Utah. For Florida!

So, as I sat alone in my apartment after I'd just moved in, I realized there was another *always*. There's always been something missing in the parent-daughter relationship because, just like an unplanned pregnancy, they have no plans for me now either. Like I said, they *left* me.

And I haven't told my friends about Cassia either because I've lost almost all contact with them—this is what tends to happen when you move two hours south to go to college in Salt Lake City. They're all busy back in Logan, working and going to school as I am. Not to mention they have boyfriends, which technically makes them busier than me. Plus, I don't have Facebook; I deleted it after the Joe Incident (I don't want to talk about it). The point is, how can I tell my friends about the spirit of a dead girl who randomly enters my body to enjoy a life she lost prematurely when I don't even take the time to tell them "hi"? I mean, Kayla is good at keeping in touch with texts, I guess. But it's all superficial stuff. I can't get deep and personal with her about the craziness going on with me. Our once "tell-all" relationship has shifted to a "tell-about-10-percent" relationship.

I've also lost track of my high school boyfriend, Ashton. He got into UCLA, and I thought we'd agreed to still call each other, but he never answers, and I find I just don't give a hoot anymore. We had what I'd consider a typical high school relationship, but I guess it was time for him to move on. An official talk about it would have been nice.

So, yeah, not that what's going on with Cassia and me is something I *have* to tell someone about (again, I'm uncomfortable with that idea), but the bigger point is, I don't really have anyone *to* tell. I hang out with people from work now and then, but that doesn't really count for anything. It's weird how it's just slowly become this way. I mean, before I knew it, it was fall semester midterm, and I hadn't gotten together with my friends. Then it was Christmas break, but my parents went to Italy. *Italy!* Same thing for spring semester; here and then gone. You'd think summer would be easier, but it's not. My parents are still traveling, and because it's summer now, so are some of my friends. I'm no different; I've been traveling too. Vegas. Yellowstone. Zion. Kayla's the glue of our group, but she took summer classes and hasn't been in touch as much as usual.

Coming up on a year without my parents, my friends, and Ashton is getting lonely, I have to say. I lost the people closest to me and my comfort zone all within three months last summer. It's nice to have Cassia, even with the creepy dreams.

Thursday, August 5

Here we are, back in the bowling alley today. Cassia's goal is to score three hundred, but she'll settle for one spare. We've come on weekdays for the past month, with the exception of missing the first three days of this week due to the bird incident.

We're getting better, though. Wait, I should say she's getting better. She's gone from mostly gutter balls to only one or two a game. The deal is only one game per day; she can't handle much more than that anyway. Hopefully, there's only another month or so of this. Not to say I don't enjoy it. I've actually started to like it a lot. It's just the money situation is beginning to take its toll on my diet. I'm down to ramen noodles every day for lunch so I can accommodate bowling, among other things. I mean, I rotate the flavors, but it's still getting old.

The last roll of the game, she gets a strike. I hold up my left hand, and she jumps to high-five it with my right hand. "Yeah, baby!" we both scream. We walk away with a score of 208—the best score thus far. I'm proud of her; she really does most of the work.

The only reason I could get out of Cassia for this whole bowling thing was something about it being for her dad. Again, she doesn't usually answer me when I ask her questions like this. She goes into her vault and turns the handle, so I just assume her dad loved to bowl and she's trying to honor him or something.

I go to return the shoes, and the guy behind the counter is laughing at me. His name tag reads "Benson." He wasn't here when we got the shoes today, but he's been here more than half the days we've been coming. I've caught him doing homework at the counter before, so I assume he's going to the U as well. I guess him to be a year or so older than I am, so nineteen or twenty, possibly. I think how he needs a haircut; it's getting to be shaggy. I imagine Scooby next to him, paws on the counter and tongue hanging out.

I blink. *Enough of that.*

He doesn't hide his laughter when I set the bowling shoes on the counter and scowl at him slightly. "Did you just high-five yourself?" he asks.

"Yeah. So?" I reply harshly.

He lifts his brows and looks away from me. I feel like he's thinking I'm a snob. Spraying the shoes, he places them on the shelf behind him. "Thanks," he says without turning back around to me.

"Sorry," Cassia says from my mouth.

I think to myself how she didn't need to say that. I've wondered before if she likes him, and I've wondered what I'd say to her if she ever asked me to go out with him for her. I wonder about it again because *this* is where it gets difficult to say yes (you know, the whole say-yes-to-everything, miracles-happen-every-day thing).

Guys.

Guys are the difficult part of that.

It's not a matter of fear-to-love. It's a matter of moral values.

He turns around and stares at me inquisitively.

Cassia grins, and I try to turn to walk away, but she won't let me.

The small physical fight with my legs makes him eyeball me curiously. "It's okay," he says.

I pinch my right arm. The deal is she has to let me have the left hand at least. She can control my right arm and hand because she's right-handed, and I control the left because I'm left-handed.

She gets my hint and says from my mouth, "See ya tomorrow."

Benson opens his mouth. His eyes scan my face as if he wants to ask something about my bruised eyes and nose, but instead, he says, "See ya tomorrow."

My bruises weren't that horrific to begin with, and now they're just that yellowish-green color, but still, it's obvious I was injured.

Cassia lets me walk away, and I feel like he's staring at me, so I look back. He gives a small wave, barely lifting his hand off the counter. I wave back before I'm blinded by the sun when opening the door.

Home is an apartment on A Street and South Temple. The door—number 123—sticks a little as I open it and wave to my neighbor before entering.

Mrs. Halman is old, old enough to favor being called Mrs. Halman instead of Gaylene. Or maybe it's because she was a teacher. Or maybe she has a distaste for her first name, Gaylene. I sure as hell wouldn't go by Gaylene if I could help it. Her muumuu is a dated green and pink and hangs from her thinning body. She waves back from the chair she sits in outside her door. I think she enjoys the breeze that comes through the outside hallway. I don't understand it. It's too hot for my liking.

My keys clank as I hang them on the decorative hook/mirror combo my mother gave me for a housewarming gift when I moved in. Cassia isn't with me; she left when I began driving home from the bowling alley. This has come to be our routine. She sometimes comes back to chat before I go to sleep.

I set my purse on my small countertop and open the fridge. It hums and displays the vacant shelves for me. I let it close and open the large cabinet I placed in the small dining room and consider my pantry: crackers, cereal, microwavable popcorn, ninety-second rice, and, of course, ramen noodles. I decide on the rice and watch a movie in bed.

Halfway through the movie, I'm relaxed and all cozy when I feel the tingle of Cassia joining me. She takes my right hand and squeezes my left.

"Hi," I say.

She squeezes my hand twice for her greeting back to me.

She's early. Ordinarily, she comes after I finish whatever I'm watching. We usually talk about my day, or I share a memory with her. All I have to do is think about it (looking through my pictures helps me, though), but she's come on her own this time. I turn the TV volume down.

"I heard what you thought about Benson today," she says.

I'm trying to remember which thought she's talking about. It somewhat bothers me that she hears my thoughts and I can't hear hers. I mean, that would bother anyone, right? Not that I have big secrets or evil thoughts, but still…they're mine. They're private.

"I *would* like to go out with him, but I won't ask you to do that," she continues, clarifying which thought she meant.

"Okay," I say, not sure of what else I *should* say.

"There *is* something I'd like to ask, though." She talks slowly as if she's nervous to ask me.

"What is it?" I ask sincerely.

"I'd like to go to a rock concert, like, really rocky."

I think how she has a strange bucket list. *Would a rock concert be on my bucket list?* I also consider how the bowling is adding up and wonder if she's trying to think of "bucket list items" that aren't too expensive. I feel as though she's considering danger as well, knowing my constant worry about that. I was glad about bowling being an item on the list; I mean, it's not only cheaper than a vacation, but what dangers can come from bowling? Concerts can be pricey too though, considering it's only a couple of hours of entertainment. I'm still trying to recuperate from going to Zion. That *really* was the last of my savings.

"If it's less than forty bucks, I'll do it."

"Thank you, Camry." Every time she says it, I feel in my chest how much she means it.

"Hey, I'm having a good time too. But…you're welcome. That was a good game today."

"I know, right?"

"I bet if you put up the bumpers, you could get your three hundred."

"No, Camry! I'm not cheating."

I laugh at her. "It's not cheating. There's three hundred with bumpers and three hundred without bumpers. You're just choosing the first one."

She pinches my left arm.

"Hey!" I pinch her back, which really is just pinching myself.

"Ow!" we both say, then laugh.

"So how was work today?" she asks.

I tell her how I worked with Ty today. It was his last day, so I signed the card Trish had left for all of us to sign and gave it to him with a cake pop I'd bought from Starbucks.

"Where's he going again?"

"Nowhere. His classes are just getting too busy. He had to quit."

"Wasn't someone moving?"

"You're thinking of Zach. He changed his mind."

We chat more about nothing really. As I've shared random memories and opinions with her in times like these, I've learned tiny bits about her too. Not kidding, *tiny* bits. Like her favorite color was blue, and she hated any candy that was a gummy. Like I said, I wish I could learn more, but she doesn't usually answer direct questions. It's almost midnight when she goes.

Whenever she leaves my body, it's the reverse of her joining me. My head tingles, then my fingers and toes, and the sensation travels up my arms and legs and out my chest. I feel like my heart skips a beat at the moment of separation, and I'm left a bit breathless, having to inhale deeply. It's a bit annoying but not painful.

In my mind, I turn over how being with her and doing her bucket list is much more awesome than going to school for the summer semester.

Tonight, I dream…

I'm in a long baby-blue dress. I feel beautiful. I feel young. But my dad is arguing with me about going to the dance. We're in the kitchen. I scream at him across the island that he never lets me do anything.

"We do things all the time, sweetie," he says with his deep voice as he makes dinner.

"Yeah, you and me. You never let me go out with my friends!" I whine.

"Your friends aren't good friends," he says, a bit more serious.

"What do you know? You don't even know them." This is the typical teenager/daddy argument. And I'm not going to win. I'm almost sure of it. "It's not like I'm going with a guy!"

"But there'll be guys there. I'm sorry, sweetie, but the answer is no."

I begin to cry. Not garishly, but tears flow down my cheeks that I can't stop. I could have slipped out and avoided this confrontation from the start, but he got home early and caught me.

"Senior year. Okay? Senior year. Not now. We've talked about this."

I storm off to my bedroom and slam the door.

I wake up, knowing instantly the dream isn't mine, not just because the gourmet kitchen isn't from my childhood house or because I never had a dress like that, but because "Dad" isn't *my* dad. It's one of Cassia's memories, and it felt undeniably real. I can't pinpoint how I know it's hers; I just feel it. Her dad loves her and will protect her at all costs. She knows this. But she's correct. He hardly ever let her do things with her friends. Hence, the rock concert.

Rebelling much?

Friday, August 6

At work the next day, it's the boring old standard. The campus bookstore is always a little bit slower throughout the summer, but fall semester is right around the corner, so it's out with the old and in with the new. I'm working with Zach today. I don't mind Zach. He's a political science nerd who loves card tricks, but more importantly, he's a good worker. He doesn't doodle at the cash register like Ashley or have his eyes glued to his phone like Chloe. He anticipates the customers' needs, and he's nice. His only downfall is the political conversations he tries to have with me. I don't enjoy politics, which translates into I don't enjoy talking about politics, but he doesn't always seem to understand this. Like right now. I'm looking at his slim face and crooked teeth, trying to convey with my I-have-no-idea-what-you're-talking-about expression that I have no idea what he's talking about. Luckily, a customer enters, and Zach is more than happy to help her.

I go back to cleaning and arranging the shelf I was working on before Zach came over to chat with me. I frequently sing to the radio as I work; it helps pass the time. I don't sing loudly or obnoxiously—well, I don't think so, anyway. I have a soft, whispery type of voice. Working here, I've learned there are two kinds of people in this world: the ones who look oddly at me when I sing and the ones who begin to sing with me. I love it when the latter happens. It's rare, like witnessing a butterfly coming out of its cocoon, but I love it.

After my shift, I head over to the university gym to run five miles and lift weights. I like to do this Mondays, Wednesdays, and Fridays. I do love a good routine, you know. I skipped Monday and Wednesday this week, though. The inside of my nose was swollen still, and it felt as if I were breathing through a straw. And not like a regular straw—like, one of those coffee-stirring straws. It sucked. Well, not literally, but you know what I mean. Today is the first day I feel like I can breathe adequately enough to exercise.

I prefer to shower after my workouts at my apartment so I don't catch some disease that'll turn my toes green or give me hobbit-looking feet. *Camry Baggins? No, thank you.* Coming out of the gym, I'm blasted with 102-degree heat. This summer is especially, terribly hot. I get in my car and turn the air conditioner on full blast. I adjust the blowers before I buckle up and begin to drive home to shower.

My Civic is two different colors now, thanks to the accident. I ended up replacing a third of the car after the drunk driver ran the red light. The original silver is now complemented by a red door, front fender, bumper, and hood. If you ask me, it was an unfair fight, my little coupe up against his lifted truck. *Who needs a lift that high?* It was like Grave Digger coming to run me over as I sang to David Archuleta, yielding to turn left. Silver lining? It wasn't my fault, no bones were broken, and he had car insurance. That's enough; I can't ask for a paint job too.

After my gloriously long shower, I'm off to the bowling alley. I pull through the parking stall so I don't have to reverse when I leave and turn down the radio.

"How was work?" Cassia asks as she joins me.

I leave the car running so the air conditioning still blasts me as I greet her. Cassia came to work with me only one time and didn't love it. It's fine; she distracted me anyway. I've concluded she doesn't enjoy exercising either since she never joins me for that. Then again, it's feasible it all just wears her out too much.

Her tingle fades away. "Eh," I answer, then move to turn off the engine.

"Wait." She pulls my hand back.

"What?"

"I want to stop bowling."

"What? Why?" I discover I'm reasonably sad about this. I didn't realize I liked bowling that much. *Perhaps it's just the routine I like. What will we do if not this?*

"I feel bad you're spending so much money on me."

I understand her feeling bad. Money is on my mind probably more than danger, so I know she hears about it often. But I tell her, "Well, don't. I told you it's fine, and I'm having fun too." But I get the sense that's not quite the real reason she wants to stop bowling. "Cassia, you can't lie to me. There's already so much you won't tell me; the least you can do is be honest."

She hesitates, tapping my fingers rhythmically on my thigh. "I *need* you to save your money," she corrects herself. She's candid now. I feel it.

"For what?" I ask apprehensively.

She's mute.

After an eternity, I deduce she must not want to discuss it now.

I have an offer in mind. "Today is Friday. How 'bout I give you today and all of next week?" I feel this is a decent compromise. It'll give her time to talk to me later, time to still try to get a three hundred, and time for me to phase out rather than quit cold turkey.

She grabs my left hand and shakes it up and down. "Deal."

That Benson guy is working again today. He grabs the size eight bowling shoes for me, and I pay with cash, like always. I grab the shoes, then hesitate. It's not Cassia hesitating; it's me. He's staring at me with an odd expression. I stare back. His eyes are blue—ocean blue, surrounded by long dark lashes.

His lip curls up on one side a bit. "Why do you come here?" he asks.

I think about telling him it's none of his business, but I don't. Instead, I admit, "I'm trying to get a three hundred." He chuckles, and I glower at him. "I'm getting better!"

"I know." He chuckles again, and I think about how he's probably watched me every time.

The thought annoys me a bit, the same annoyance I had for the Jeep guys laughing at me. I feel like it should embarrass me too, but it doesn't. It could be because I know it's not me bowling. It's Cassia. Why should I be embarrassed for Cassia?

I leave his counter and go to my assigned lane. "How come you didn't talk to him today?" I ask Cassia as I sit and put on the uncomfortable shoes.

"Saving energy," is all she says in return.

I assume because I've only given her six more games, she wants to center all the energy she can. "Let me do *all* the walking this time then," I tell her.

A male voice interrupts, "Who are you talking to?"

I jump and squeal as I look behind me.

It's Benson. He has a soda and a straw in his hand. One of his eyebrows is raised to match his question.

"What're you doing?" I ask, a little irritated he made me squeal. My right hand pinches my left arm.

Cassia.

I try to soften my expression for her.

"I brought you a Coke." He points to the drink with his other hand.

"I don't…" I pat the nonexistent pockets on my skirt to finish my sentence, then add, "I didn't order a drink."

"I know." Benson steps forward and sets it on the small white table in front of me. "And don't worry about the…" He pats his pockets mockingly. "It's on the house." He smiles and nervously puts four fingers of each hand in his pockets, then starts to leave by walking backward.

I open my mouth to thank him, but Cassia takes over instead and asks, "Why?"

He smiles bigger and steps forward. I consider him, looking him up and down. He's tall, at least six feet, possibly more, and well-built with broad shoulders. Probably played football. He sort of has a big forehead, but overall, he *is* good-looking, I decide. With his dark hair and light eyes and a sweet smile that quirks to the right, I suppose I can see why Cassia likes him.

I try to think what it is about him I *don't* like, what has turned me off about him. I flip through the pages in my memory to the day we began coming here, and I do remember overhearing him talk rudely about someone with another coworker of his. He's nice enough in his job duties, I presume, but he never goes out of his way to make customers comfortable. I feel like this is just a stupid job to him that'll help get him through school. Nonetheless, the conversation I overheard rubbed me the wrong way, I guess. Ever since then, I haven't really bothered with him. I could try to get over this now, but I think it'll be an obstacle for a while. The first impression lasts forever, right?

He answers Cassia's question slowly. "Because…" He's thinking and breaks eye contact. "Because you're a loyal customer, and we appreciate your business."

It's a lie. I know it's a lie, but still, I have to give him credit for trying. Both Cassia and I grin and say, "Thanks."

I add, "You didn't have to do that." After unwrapping the straw paper, I shove the straw through the lid with a squeak.

"May I make a suggestion?" He's still nervous. He takes his hands out of his pockets and rubs them together as if they're clammy.

I watch him with confusion as I take a drink.

"Stand a little more to the left." He points to the lane.

I squint my eyes and bite the straw. I'm a little bit annoyed by the advice. I tell myself I shouldn't be, and honestly, I don't know why I am. He's just trying to be nice.

Wait!

There it is.

He's trying to be nice…to *Cassia*. She's the one who's bowling, not me. She's the one he likes, not me. She's the one he gave a Coke to, not me. I'm *jealous*, and I'm taking it out on *him*.

Oh God, I suck.

I let Cassia take over, and she changes my expression from annoyed to interested. "Let me try that. You watch and tell me what I do wrong," she orders.

She's a little bossy for my liking, but the order makes him noticeably happy as he sits and she grabs the pink ball. She goes to where she normally stands, then takes a small step to the left.

Looking back at him, he nods his approval. He's leaning forward with his elbows on his knees and hands together in front of him.

She pulls my arm back and walks forward as she hurls the ball. It smacks against the wood floor and spins as it curves to the right and back to the center of the lane. It hits the center pin and—strike!

She jumps once, and I remind her in my thoughts to save her energy. Also, I'm in a skirt, one that doesn't quite reach my knees. *We don't want to give him a peep show.* She turns and walks cheerfully back to the chairs. To Benson.

He stands and smiles big. "See?"

"Yeah! Thanks!" she says with a little too much enthusiasm, in my opinion. "Any other suggestions? I'd be happy to have them."

His smile hasn't faded all the way, and I think he's actually giving her question some good thought before answering. "No, that was great." He winks at us. "You'll be at three hundred in no time."

She smiles and picks up the Coke for another swig. "Thanks again," she says, gesturing to the drink.

Benson's expression falls flat. "Oh damn! Your nose is bleeding." He rushes for the napkins at the center of the table just as I feel the tickle come out of my nose.

I barely have time to set the drink back down before he's shoving napkins in my hands. I dab at my nose. The napkins are half soaked; it's much worse than I thought. "Crap."

"Here, sit down." He grabs my elbows and directs me to sit. "Lean forward a bit." He grabs more napkins. The ones in my hand are all soaked through now. My bright blood drips on the white floor. "Shove the napkin up there and pinch your nose." He throws some more napkins in my hand. "I used to get nosebleeds all the time. I'm gonna go get some ice. I'll be right back." He does a skip/jump thing before jogging away, hollering behind him, "Pinch your nose!"

The sixty seconds he's gone feel like he went home, had a microwave dinner, and took the long way back before returning to me. My face must be a bloody mess because he scoldingly says, "You're supposed to be pinching!"

"I *am* pinching!" My voice sounds nasal.

He grabs more napkins, takes the used ones, and discards them in a small trash can he's put between my legs on the floor. Then he pinches my nose so hard my eyes water. After all, it isn't healed all the way yet.

"*Ow!*" I shoot him a dirty look, and he smashes the ice against my face. I hold back a second groan from that. *Really, dude?!* "Eww…I'm swallowing it," I gurgle. My stomach churns with a heavy threat of something more. "I'm gonna throw up."

Benson points to the trash can, and I heave forward, spewing the bloody contents of my stomach into it. More napkins are shoved into my hand, and I wipe my mouth. He doesn't let go of the death grip on my nose.

After a couple of excruciatingly long minutes, it's under control. I take over the pinching and apologize to him, observing my blood all over his hands. I can't bring myself to thank him, though. He was too rough.

"Let's go wash up," he says, snatching the trash can and leading me to the restrooms.

As I enter the women's restroom, a pair of middle-aged ladies coming out offer me help. I insist I'll be fine.

Looking in the mirror, I thought it'd be worse. There are a couple of smears on my cheek and chin and, of course, under my nose. My nose is bright red from the pinching and hurts like a mother, but overall, things are quite reasonable.

I wonder if it was the workout that did this. Perhaps I should lay off for another week. I wash my hands first, then move to my face, making the mistake of putting my head down and starting up the nosebleed again. I grab paper towels and press the ice back on my face until it slows down. I switch to cold water so I can wet a corner of the paper towel, keeping my head up as much as I possibly can, when I abruptly realize Cassia isn't with me.

"Cassia?" The bathroom offers only a small echo in reply. I can't believe I was so engrossed I didn't feel her leave my body—or notice it until now. I make use of the bathroom while I'm there and, feeling stupid about the whole thing, think about dodging out of the building without Benson noticing, then see I still have the bowling shoes on.

Suck!

With a new paper towel bundled up under my nose, just in case, I return for my shoes. When I take the bowling ones back, I have to wait a minute. Someone different accepts them, sprays them, and thanks me. His name tag reads "Chip." I consider asking the balding middle-aged man to leave a message for Benson but decide against it.

My eyes loosely search to find Cassia, which I realize, after a second, makes absolutely no sense. *What am I doing? I just need to go home. Maybe she'll come visit me later.*

I'm almost free and clear of the completely embarrassing situation and almost to the doors when he calls out from behind me, "Hey, damsel! Wait!"

Cassia quickly joins me as I turn around. *Whoa! Was it the turn combined with blood loss that made me dizzy just now or Cassia whooshing in so quickly?*

I don't think my dizziness is perceptible, but Benson's eyebrows come down as he asks, "Are you okay to drive?"

"I'm fine," I insist with a flick of my wrist. *Did he just call me damsel?*

"I see you're not planning on finishing." He points over to my lane.

I want to look at him like he's an idiot, but Cassia giggles at his joke and says, "No."

"And you were gonna leave without saying goodbye? How rude!"

I let Cassia keep speaking for me. "Sorry, I didn't see you."

He waves me to walk with him as he passes me, resting a hand on the bar to open the door. "Let me walk you to your car."

Summer brightness and heat pummel us as we come out of the bowling alley and walk toward my Civic. I tell myself to thank him for the gentleman he's being right now, but Cassia does it for me. She says it with much more meaning than I'd have done anyway, so I guess that's good. Then she adds, referring to the blood, "We don't have AIDS."

I shake my head, humiliated. *Really, Cassia?*

"I mean, *I* don't have AIDS," she corrects, but that's not much better.

He stares at me oddly. "I…wasn't worried about that. But that's good to know. I don't have AIDS either, in case you were wondering." We've reached my car. He gives it a once-over but doesn't comment on the dual colors. Instead, he fixes me with a look.

"I'm fine to drive," I assure him.

He nods slowly, then cocks a brow. "See you on Monday?"

"Yeah." I hit the button to unlock the door, and Benson opens it for me.

"Your money today will go toward Monday's game."

I stop, one hand atop my door. I'm not going to lie; that'd be nice. "Are you sure?" Cassia asks.

"Yeah, it's no problem."

"Thanks." I turn to get in my car.

"Hey."

I turn back around again.

"Sorry, I gotta ask. How'd you…" He points to his nose.

Instinctively, I touch it, and Cassia laughs. "Oh. Well, you should see the bird," she says.

He pulls his head back, all squinty-eyed and puzzled.

I manage to sit in my car and start it, still with the door open and one leg out, though.

"You're gonna leave me hangin' with *that*?"

Chip opens the door to the bowling alley and hollers, "Hey, Benson. I could use your help."

"Yeah, man. Just a sec," he calls back to Chip, then to me, "Hey, wait."

I squint in the bright sun as I peer up at him. I'm starting to feel annoyed. His face is expectant—for what, a quick version? I roll my eyes. "Ugh!" I say aloud, not meaning to. Cassia pinches me.

I open my mouth with the intention of telling the stupid story, but Benson stops me with a chuckle. "I was just gonna say 'drive safely.' You can tell me on Monday."

I misread him. *Suck.* Now I feel bad. Still, I lift my other leg in, he closes my door, and I drive away. I actually don't feel that well. How much blood *did* I lose?

Cassia doesn't come visit me tonight, but I dream again…

My dad is spending more and more time with this girl. I'm not exaggerating when I say girl. She's only a hair older than I am. I instantly dislike her. I sit in the kitchen, eating my bowl of cold cereal (the perfect dinner sometimes), and watch them go out the front door for their date, him in a tuxedo and her in a skimpy nude gown.

Ugh! Nude. That's what they'll be later, I'm sure. I gag on my cereal as I think about them in bed together.

The dream shifts, and I'm in a car. I've ditched the last part of school to drive around with this boy, Travin. We've parked in an underground parking lot and have started to make out. I think about going all the way with him, but I don't want to lose my virginity to Travin in a parked car of all places.

I wake up, having the thought that Travin resembles Benson, and I can't help but wonder if that was the entire point in her giving me that dream. She really did like him—Travin. I don't know if they were exclusively dating each other, and I don't think her dad knew about him, but they *were* "dating." She would've gone all the way with him if it weren't for the car and the location. She just wanted a tad more romance than that.

Unfortunately, Cassia never shows me anything that gives away *where* she lived. Underground parking doesn't really help me.

Monday, August 9

All weekend, Cassia doesn't visit me. She's done that before, but still, I worry about her. I go to work and am greeted by Chloe, the texter. Don't get me wrong, I like Chloe, but unlike Zach, she's a terrible worker. I wonder if she has more than one conversation going on because every time I look at her, she's texting, and there can't be *that* much to say to one person, right? I sigh at the fact I'm going to be doing most of the worklist today. I've tried to get her to do things, but she rarely does them well. I usually end up fixing her mistakes, which only adds more work to my overall load. It's not worth it.

She hasn't seen me since the bird incident. Her blue eyes look me over through narrow slits. "What happened to you?" It's a curious question with some hidden care, but mostly, she's trying not to laugh.

"I broke my nose," I answer.

"Obviously. How?" She sets her phone on the counter next to the cash register.

Okaaay, she's interested enough to put her phone down. I don't like the story, but more so, I don't like the attention the story is bound to get me. I give her the same answer I gave Zach: "Just an accident in one of the slot canyons down in Zion." I shrug like it's no big deal and trace a finger down the worklist for the day.

Zach left it right there. "That's a bummer," is all he'd said, but Chloe keeps going with a flip of her blonde hair off her shoulder. "That doesn't really answer my question. What happened?"

I shift my weight and keep my eyes on the worklist.

"Did a rock fall on your face?"

I can't read her tone. Is she trying to be funny, or is that a serious question? My finger lands on "Discount the white hoodies 10 percent." I'll start with that. "Something like that," I tell her.

"Really?" She half laughs. "I was totally kidding. Are you going to get a nose job out of it?" She perks up like this is a cool thing. Chloe has nice features; she wasn't a cheerleader but fits the bill for one. She's a head shorter than I am, her figure is shapelier than mine, and even though her eyes seem squished and her lips are thin, her appearance is cute, including her nose. It's a normal nose that fits the size of her face just fine. I guess noses are a common thing to be self-conscious of, though.

So I say, "Do I *need* a nose job?"

"Hmm." She scrutinizes my face while I feign offense. "It could make you more social."

What?! Now I really am offended. "A nose job could make me more social?"

She nods enthusiastically, then laughs at her own joke.

"I'm not *not* social."

"You've totally been antisocial lately."

I'm immediately on the defensive. "Nuh-uh." *But have I been?*

"What's up anyway?" she asks, actually sounding concerned. "Because I know it's not school, and I know it's not work." She gasps, slapping her forehead. "Oh my God! I'm so stupid. It's a guy." She tightens her thin lips so they basically disappear; she's confused. "But it must be like a creeper guy because you're not giddy; you're"—her eyes grow round—"antisocial."

"How about you keep up with checkout, and I'll work on the worklist?" I tell her, changing the subject.

"No, seriously. We haven't hung out since like…"

She can't think of it, but I remember. We went to a small house party after finals in April. "Since you ditched me at that party," I finish for her.

She shuts up, knowing it's true. But she's already apologized for that, and I'm not looking for another one. And I'm not looking to blame her either because it's not her fault, so I don't know why I said that. I mean, yeah, she ditched me at the party, but it's not her fault we haven't hung out since then. And yeah, I'm sour toward her a bit for that, but…

"No. Since your car accident."

What's the difference? They were about the same time. She's just trying to blame me instead.

I'm saved by the bell—or, rather, chime. Her text message alert signals her to immediately engage in a fast-finger conversation. I walk over to the white hoodies.

I skip working out after my shift, instead heading over to Smith's. I need more ramen noodles, but they also have a ticket counter, so I can maybe see about tickets for a rock concert. I don't buy stuff online anymore if I can help it, not since my credit card information was stolen last summer; I try to pay cash for most things now. I don't know who might be performing; I don't think it matters to Cassia.

She's abruptly with me, causing me to trip over my own feet. I catch myself but seem like an idiot to a woman walking out with her groceries.

Crikey, Cassia! Walk much?

Knowing my intentions, Cassia says, "You don't have to." She wants me to save money and still hasn't told me why.

I think about trying to dig it out of her again, but I'm not in the mood for guessing the vault combination right now. And honestly, I'm curious about a concert. I remind her, "If it's less than forty bucks, we'll do it."

She doesn't respond.

Jeez, it's hot. I've walked through just the parking lot, and I'm sweating in all the wrong places. For some stupid reason, I don't mind sweating when I work out, but this kind of sweating irritates the crap out of me. Possibly it's because I can also feel my skin melting off. I imagine myself melting completely right here in the parking lot like the Wicked Witch, featuring people stepping over me with faces of disgust as I reach for their help.

I blink. *Enough of that.*

Once inside the store, the air conditioning instantly soothes my skin, but it still takes me a minute to cool down. Marching over to the ticket counter, I see no one is there, which sort of flares me back up.

After I stand for a minute, looking around dumbly for someone to help me, a guy walks up with a Mountain Dew in his hand. "Sorry, I had to go get a drink," he says. His voice is deep and doesn't really match his face, which is pretty attractive.

What is it with good-looking guys behind a counter lately?

"What can I do for ya?" He stands a little taller than I do, with the greenest eyes I've ever seen looking back at me. He finishes taking a swig and sets the bottle down, waiting for me to speak.

I pull my eyes away from his, glance at the board, and ask, "Um, how much is a ticket for Korn?"

He tries to hide it, but I see the fleeting look he gives me. He's surprised I asked for that ticket. He searches it and asks, "Just one ticket?"

"Yeah." I pull out my wallet from my purse and set it on the counter. I notice his name tag reads "Jake."

"For you?"

"Yeah."

He scans me judgingly again. "The cheapest ticket is fifty-nine ninety-five." His dark-blond hair is styled carelessly in every direction as if he got sidetracked getting ready this morning and didn't quite finish. He doesn't seem like he belongs in Utah; he looks like a surfer, tan and fit.

I wonder if he was born in California but moved here like Californians seem to be doing these days. It's a bit annoying. Then again, if they all look like this Jake guy, maybe it wouldn't be so bad. I bring my thoughts back to what he said. I can't help it; my immediate reaction is, "Suck."

"It's worth it," he says. "They put on a really good show." As he looks at me, awaiting my decision, I see he's not looking me in the eyes. He's looking at the bruises underneath my eyes. Again, instinctively, I touch my nose. He glances away and clears his throat.

I can only imagine what he thinks happened to me.

"You're seriously going alone?" he asks, scratching his jaw. My eyes follow the motion, noticing how his square jawline complements his features.

I blink. "I would be. Why?"

"I just don't think a girl should go to a concert like *that* alone." He looks me over. "Especially a girl like you."

I'm wearing a salmon-colored shirt collar dress that comes to my knees, and even though I can also agree I don't fit the bill of someone who'd go to a rock concert, I don't appreciate him judging me so outright.

"People get crazy. People *are* crazy." He lifts one brow.

"Well, I can't afford it anyway." *Sorry, Cassia,* I think in my head.

"I have to say, I'm surprised you like them. They're kind of hard. But if you like *them*, you'd probably like Chevelle. They're playing next Friday. Only twenty-nine ninety-five."

I ponder that for a second. "That could be cool," I say, more to Cassia than to him. I'm waiting for her to answer.

After another second, she says, "Okay."

I take cash out to pay for the ticket. Instead of taking the money, the ticket guy's eyes and mouth fly open with alarm. Out of nowhere, something stabs into the curve of my neck and shoulder.

My body jolts as I grab at the familiar sting of a bee. "*Ow!*"

He was too late to warn me. Thoughts race through my head as quickly as the annoying little bug came at me. I'm allergic to bees. Like, anaphylaxis-within-minutes allergic. I have an adrenaline shot at my apartment, which would be faster than driving to the hospital and dealing with the emergency room.

Suck! My car is across the hot parking lot. If I run, it'll spread through my system even faster. This cannot be happening!

I can feel it starting to swell already. The reaction seems as quick as ever, and since it's on my neck, it'll inevitably reach my throat next. "I'm allergic to bees," I manage to croak in horror.

I turn to jog out of the store. The wheezing begins. I hear the ticket guy say something behind me, but I can't make it out for the rushing heartbeat sound in my ears. The reaction is building so fast.

Abnormally fast.

It zooms through my body at Mach speed, spreading its venom generously throughout my system. I'm panicking that I'm not going to be able to get home before it's a full-on breathing problem, and I'm right. My vision tunnels, and I black out, collapsing just outside the front doors on the sidewalk before I even reach the parking lot.

Tuesday, August 10

When I start to wake up, I first *hear* I'm in the hospital. There's a soft beeping of machines. Then I *feel* I'm in the hospital—an IV is in my arm, and a nasal cannula's in my nose for oxygen. And then there's that *smell*, the smell of a hospital. It's dark, but I see there's a glowing digital clock above the door. It reads 01:24. My vision is blurry, but I can make it out.

I try to envision what happened between the last thing I recollect and now. Stupidly, I think, *I hope my dress didn't flip up as I passed out and fell down.* I feel my hands. They're scratched—from falling, I decide. I think about my knees, and yes, they ache and throb. I probably landed on them also. I touch my neck, lifting the IV line with me. It feels slightly inflamed and tender. As I make my way up to the top of my head, where I feel a pull of pain, my fingers find a small section of shaved hair and stitches in my hairline above my left eye. My next thought is, *I can't afford this.* And then I wonder about Cassia. She's not with me, and I can't recall if she was with me when it all transpired. Thinking of her makes me think about how I didn't make it to bowling.

My head hurts.

I adjust myself, fiddling with the bed controls to lie down more because my butt is numb. I eventually fall back to sleep and dream I'm in Smith's, only it doesn't look like Smith's. It looks like a hospital. There are beds everywhere with nothing to separate them. A bee rapidly turns into a bird and begins attacking me. It pecks at me with its beak, then stings me all over my body. I jolt awake with anxiety.

As I attempt to slow my breathing, I wonder, *Where's Cassia?* I really thought she'd come to me by now. I recognize I have no control over getting her here and focus on falling back to sleep. And honestly, my eyes are heavy, and sleep is tugging pretty hard.

I'm feebly aware of a nurse or assistant coming in to check my vitals around five in the morning. She takes off the cannula, and I want to ask her questions about what happened but can't seem to form the words. I blink weakly, just once, and she rubs my shoulder, telling me to rest. When I completely wake up, the clock reads 09:04.

I'm gawking at the ceiling, trying to focus my eyes and clear my dry throat, when someone opens my door. It's gentle but still startles me. I jump, which makes my neck ache.

It's the nurse. "Oh, you're awake," she whispers. She walks over to me. "How are you feeling?"

I look at her, unsure how to answer. Thinking is difficult at the moment.

"Can you rate your pain for me on a scale of one to ten?" She pushes the button that causes the blood pressure cuff on my arm to inflate. She's short and round, pushing up her glasses and waiting for my answer.

Somehow, "five" comes out of my mouth. *Why'd I say that?*

She starts typing on the computer next to and a little behind me. Then she turns to me, still whispering. "There's a gentleman waiting to see you."

Huh? Did they call my parents? Did my dad catch a flight? I guess he could've flown here that fast.

"His name is Jake. Is it all right if he comes in?"

What the H-E-double hockey sticks?! What is Jake, the ticket guy, doing here?

My blood pressure is finished, and she types some more.

"Yeah," I say hoarsely. *Why'd I say that?*

"Okay, hun. I'll go get him."

The hospital has dressed me in a gown, and I feel exposed, so I pull the sheets up a tiny bit more. I lift the head of my bed and try to fix the messy hair I'm positive I have. I almost certainly look dreadful, but whatever, I guess. I try blinking rapidly since my eyes still aren't focusing. It doesn't really help. The window shades are closed, making the room dim, which isn't helping my poor vision either.

Not long after she closes the door, it cracks open again. "It's me, Jake. From last night. Is it really okay if I come in? Are you decent?"

"Yeah," I try to holler, but it's barely anything other than a croaky, crackly whisper.

It must've been adequate because Jake enters and pushes the dimmer switch enough to light up the foot of my bed just a bit. "Hey," he says softly.

I know it's just a dimmer switch, but it's like the brightness of a noonday sun just arrived to get my headache going.

"I wasn't sure if she made it clear I'm not a relative. Are you okay with me being here?"

I squint. He looks tired but still damn good. "What're you doing here?" I ask, thinking this situation is especially bizarre because *it is*.

"I was worried about you."

He doesn't even know me.

"It's visiting hours; I thought I'd check on you."

I offer only silence. I can't seem to gather my thoughts, and my head is beginning to throb more.

"My mom's a nurse here," he adds as if it validates everything, then seems to realize with a shake of his head that it doesn't. "I'm sorry. I can go." He turns, hand on the doorknob, but stops to say, "I just…wanted to know you were okay. I mean, they told me you were stable. But I've been waiting all night to see how you're doing."

I notice he's in the same clothes as yesterday: shorts and a T-shirt sporting a Panic! At The Disco logo. "You waited *here* all night?"

There are two kinds of people in this world: the ones who'll wait all night at the hospital to see you're okay and the ones who…won't. I feel like Jake is in the minority category here. I mean, Cassia isn't even here. I'm not sure how I feel about either of these realizations.

He slowly turns back and points toward the door. "Well, out there." He then gestures to my face. "It looks *a lot* better. It got pretty scary there for a minute. I was kinda freakin' out."

I rest my head. "Dare I ask what happened?"

He takes a breath and leans against the counter next to the door, palms on the edge. "What do you remember?"

"I remember going down just outside of the store."

"Yeah, you passed out on the sidewalk, hit your head, started bleeding everywhere. I'd started to come after you because you left your wallet, so I saw you fall, but…" He repositions himself, crosses his arms over his chest, and sucks his bottom lip between his teeth. I wonder if he's nervous.

I press, wanting to know and not wanting to know at the same time. "Then what happened?"

"I called nine-one-one. You were so swollen, your neck and face, and you were turning blue. People had started to gather around; an old guy gave me a handkerchief for your head." He breathes, letting his hands fall. I wait patiently. "Someone heard me on the phone say you're allergic to bees and luckily had one of those things that give you a shot, you know?"

I nod. There's one at my apartment as we speak, in a cabinet, collecting dust. He seems shaky even telling me the tale. I can't imagine how shaky he must have been at the time. His nerves have got to be done for.

"It took the ambulance like twenty minutes to get there." Rolling his eyes, he's visibly aggravated by this fact. "I ended up doing another shot thing after a few minutes because they weren't there yet."

It's a lot for me to absorb, and I feel bad that he had to go through all that. I'd have been freaking out if I were him too. "So…" I begin. "You saved my life?"

He chuckles softly. "Yeah, I guess I did." I think he's still picturing it all in his mind because he shakes his head slowly with his gaze fixed on nothing. "There was so much blood. Seriously. And you were blue and…How do you feel anyway?"

I shrug. "I have a headache, but I'm okay." It's an understatement; my head is thumping like a bad drumbeat. I feel him regarding me, and it puts me, to some extent, on edge. I can't bring myself to look at his face, but I accomplish a "thank you." It feels utterly inadequate.

"You're welcome." We sit soundlessly for a moment. I'm trying to process what he went through for me. He pulls himself away from the counter. Then, maybe feeling awkward, he says, "I'll go now."

I stop him, saying, "Wait. Do you know where my things are? My wallet?"

He points to a chair in the corner. "And I put your money back in your wallet." He steps over toward the foot of my bed. "You all right?"

I think my face must be giving away how much my head really hurts. I try to blink it away, but who am I kidding? The silver lining here is at least I'm not throwing up; I can't ask for a pretty face too. "Yeah. I'm Camry, by the way."

He steps closer and offers his hand. I lift mine, and we shake. His hand is warm. I didn't even realize I was cold. "I know," he admits.

I squint at him, befuddled.

"I looked at your driver's license."

"Ugh! I hate that picture," I comment, rolling my eyes a bit.

He releases my hand, and I miss the warmth straightaway. "It's better than how you looked twelve hours ago." He smiles. "But you're right—it doesn't do you justice."

"Wait! You went through my wallet?"

"Well, I sort of had to. I helped check you into the ER so you wouldn't be a Jane Doe." Then he chuckles. "Chill out. I'm not a bad guy. I promise."

"If you say so," I joke weakly. But I didn't think about *that* whole process. I think about it now—imagine him talking to the paramedic people, the ER people, the doctors. *Oh...my...God!* My eyes grow wide before I close them and steeple my fingers around my nose and mouth. *Yeah, how could he be a creeper if he did all that, Camry?* "I'm so sorry. I totally ruined your night. Like, worse than I thought."

He huffs a small laugh. "You didn't ruin my night. I was happy to help you. I mean, it's not like I was gonna go back to work and just forget about it all. Go home and go to sleep like nothing happened. I wanted to make sure...you were okay." He scratches his jaw and changes the subject. "This hasn't been your week, has it? Can I ask how you broke your nose?" Pulling the doctor's stool over, he sits next to me, down by my knees.

I laugh inside, thinking about Cassia's response to Benson. "I ran into a bird."

He seems confused but chuckles again. "What?! How'd you do that? And how big was this bird if it broke your nose?"

Where's Cassia to tell the ridiculous story? Sometimes I hope thinking of her will somehow summon her. Like my thoughts are a whistle only she can hear, she'll suddenly be here, giving me that familiar tingle and talking through my mouth. But she doesn't show, so I have to tell it myself.

He stifles his laughter throughout my story. "Oh my God, that was *you*? My friend was telling me about that. It's on YouTube."

"Yeah, I know," I say, a little annoyed, but I'm chuckling too.

"*You're* on YouTube." He says it like it's the most unbelievable thing ever.

"I know," I repeat dully.

"I'm *so* gonna look it up. Did you kill the bird?"

"I don't know. I think so." I picture the bird swirling down to earth.

"You sure you're okay?" he asks. "Your eyes are all glassy."

"Yeah."

"Okay," he says, apparently trusting me. "Well, I'm glad. I'd have issues and need therapy if you, like, died in my arms." We laugh together, then he seems to have a thought. "Hey, do you need a ride? I can stick around or come back if you need me to."

I'm already shaking my head. *No way. He's already done way too much. And wouldn't that be weird?* "No. No, I'm fine. Thanks, though."

"You have someone you can call?"

I rub my eye, thinking how I have absolutely no one to call, but I nod anyway.

His mouth does a twisty pucker thing like he's doubting me, but he says, "Okay. Get some more rest before they come in and start bugging you again."

"You too. I mean, they're not gonna bug you, but go get some rest." I slap my forehead. "You know what I mean."

He laughs. "Yeah. Bye."

I give a small wave and watch him go. He leaves me feeling odd about the whole thing. I somewhat wanted him to stay, but then again, my mind is fuzzy and not working properly right now. I need massive doses of Tylenol and ibuprofen and possibly even need to puke.

An assistant comes in and checks my vitals again. They're respectable. She gives me some ibuprofen. Whether they're standard orders for her or if Jake pulled some strings, I don't know, but I'm appreciative. She informs me I'll most likely leave in the next hour. I succeed in falling asleep for that time.

The nurse who comes in afterward is eager to see me. My headache is considerably less but still lets me know it's there, just with a subtler drumbeat. "Oh my goodness!" she exclaims. "You look so much better!" She places a hand over her chest. "I've never seen Jake so worried."

Ah, Jake's mother. The badge clipped to her scrubs reads "Caroline." While the photo on it shows her as a brunette, she's blonde now. I like her hair blonde better; she looks younger. Her laugh lines are deep, though, reaching from her eyes down to her cheeks.

I grin in reaction to her comment, then yawn, still waking up.

"I hope it was okay he came in," she says, checking my eyes with a light.

I shrug because I don't know what else to do.

She moves to the computer, clicking, typing, more clicking. "Good. Good. Everything is looking good. Do you want to list someone as your emergency contact?"

I look at her, confused. "My parents should be on there."

She shakes her head. "I can add them."

I give her their names and cell numbers while wondering if that's part of why Jake stayed and asked if I had a ride. *Did he think I had nobody?*

"Well, you can give them a call while I go fetch the doctor. He'll take a look at you while I get your discharge papers ready." She stares at me, smiling and deepening all her laugh lines. I fear she wants to say more about what happened, or about me, or her son, but I stop her with a "thank you."

I watch her leave, and soon enough, the doctor is standing next to me, telling me what happened and everything they did to help me yesterday. I'm not sure what makes him think I can follow this; he's talking fast and using doctor language. He also mentions expensive-sounding stuff, like "imaging of your brain" and "x-rays of your face." But I suppose I catch the gist of it: no broken bones, mild concussion, lots of rest. He checks my eyes again and has me do a series of little tests, then tells me to see my "regular doctor" in a week to remove the eleven stitches in my head. He hands me prescriptions for an adrenaline auto-injector, a steroid, and pain medicine. He also tells me to continue taking Benadryl and keep some handy for the future.

I think to myself how there was no way Benadryl would've had time to absorb into my system to help with anything. The reaction was so *oddly* fast. I take the papers from him and thank him for his time. He leaves, and I'm relieved; he was overwhelming me. *Good. Now I can just be regular whelmed if that's a thing.*

I don't intend to fill the pain medicine; Tylenol will do. No intentions for the steroid either; the last time I was on that, I couldn't sleep. I want to fill the auto-injector and give it to the person who offered theirs, but I have no clue who they are.

Caroline returns cheerfully with the discharge papers as promised. She explains them briefly, and I sign them. It's almost as if once they're signed and I'm not in her care anymore, she can speak freely.

She says, "You're just such a doll, really. Jakey would love to see you again, I'm sure." Her smile is as hinting as my head was pounding an hour ago.

I stare at her without blinking. I'm uncomfortable, and, in a different way than the doctor, she's a bit much for me to handle right now. It takes me a second to choose a response. I decide on the most polite and easy one. "I will."

And perhaps…I really will.

"Did you call your mom for a ride?"

Suck! Is that what she meant? "Yeah," I lie.

She smiles kindly and leaves me to get dressed and go. I quickly call my boss, Trisha, to let her know I won't be coming in. She's irritated but tells me to bring my discharge papers in tomorrow, and she won't write me up. It would be my first write-up, which I don't consider a huge deal, but it still bothers me. It seems like my stitches would suffice, but whatever. I hope I haven't upset her by missing work lately. I've always given plenty of notice when I want time off, except for the broken nose and this. Maybe she's stressed because she hasn't been able to replace Ty yet.

I walk the fifteen scorching blocks back to my apartment, take a Benadryl, and immediately get in the shower. I feel absolutely disgusting—like, as bad as the mud bath Cassia talked me into, or worse. She joins me mid-shower, scaring me.

Feeling me jump, she apologizes. "I didn't mean to startle you."

"It's fine." I wonder where she's been, but I don't ask. I know she won't answer me. I don't know if she doesn't *want* to tell me or if she doesn't even know *herself* where she goes.

"Are you all right?" she asks tenderly.

"Yeah." I don't want to grumble about my headache, but then again, I don't have to; Cassia can feel it. After a second, though, I understand she meant the question to ask if I was mentally all right. "Were you with me when I passed out? I can't remember."

She answers softly, "Yeah."

Something in the way she answers makes me wonder if *she's* all right.

She hears my thought. "It felt like dying all over again." Tears form in my eyes. They're hers. "I got stuck," she explains. "I mean, I wanted to stay with you at first. I thought if there were two of us, we could make it back to your apartment, but I was scared. I'm sorry. When I finally managed to leave, you fell, and there was nothing I could do."

Even though I can't hear Cassia's thoughts like she can hear mine, I do get emotion from her, and right now, I feel her sincerity, fear, and grief about all she's just confessed. And even though I have a ton of questions, it's the thought she started with that takes the front seat for my reply to it all.

I wish you'd tell me how you died, I think to her. She leaves me at that point with nothing but her tears for me to blink away.

I rest the remainder of the day—well, physically, anyway—I'm on my bed staring at the ceiling. Mentally, though, I'm racing the afternoon away. It hits me just how close I came to dying yesterday, and although it all happened so quickly, I still had time to freak out. I can't imagine feeling that feeling *again*. I understand why Cassia wanted to get away from it. It also makes me think if she's comparing my experience with hers, she must have died unexpectedly. A car accident is the only thing I can think of.

My mental race continues with the fact that I collapsed *after* she managed to leave my body. What does that *mean*? *Could* we have made it if she'd stayed with me? Logic tells me no—if my throat is swelling shut, then there's no oxygen to support bodily functions. She's not superhuman. *Is she?* I squint at the ceiling as if the answer is written for me there in tiny lettering.

My mind drifts back to the bee sting. I was beyond lucky. What if Jake hadn't been so quick about calling 911? More importantly, what if one of the bystanders didn't have the adrenaline shot? I'd still be in the hospital right now—only not in a patient room, in the morgue. I close my eyes. I can't keep going over this; I'm going to drive myself crazy.

I gasp. *Drive!*

Suck! I still have to go get my car. Ugh!

When I fall asleep that night, Cassia's memories fill my mind again…

I'm at a wedding. My father's wedding to Miss Gold Digger. Of course, I've put on a happy face, though I couldn't be more dismayed. I've learned throughout my life how to do this happy-face thing. I think Dad knows I don't really approve but hopes I'll come to accept it all. After a while, my cheeks hurt from all the phony smiling.

I catch myself daydreaming about moving away to college. I was going to try to stay close, but now I'm thinking the other side of the country would suit me just fine. I'll have to check into that when I go back to school on Monday. I'm snapped back into the present time when my dad kisses Bridezilla. I mean Gold Digger. I mean…what's her name? Tiffanie.

After the ceremony, I watch them drive away, thinking how things will never be the same again. I lost my mother when I was five. I'm eighteen now, but it feels like I'm losing my father too.

But just like after my mother left, life will go on. Because I am resilient in my big-girl pants, I am fine being alone, and...because I have no other choice.

Wednesday, August 11

It's all I can do to get through my shift because I still don't feel well. The day seems like a week. And for some reason, I'm irritated with customers today. I mean, they're just asking where things are, but if they'd open their eyes, it's right there! *Ugh!* I'm blaming the headache. I'm still taking Tylenol for it, and my face and neck still feel swollen, even though Trisha keeps telling me I look fine. Still, if I didn't need the money, I'd have called in sick.

Trisha is a ninja-over-the-shoulder-type boss. Suddenly and without warning, she's just there, over your shoulder, watching you and your work. If I'm singing or at all distracted, it takes me a while to notice she's behind me. It's spine-chilling. But today she's worse than normal. Maybe she's worried about me; I've complained about my headache more than once. More than ten-ce (that's not a word, but you get it). Or maybe she heard me being snippy to the last three customers. Yep, I was wrong to do that.

Putting the kibosh on bowling tonight, I leave work to head home. It's another one-hundred-degree day, and I failed to remember to crack my car windows and put up the sunshade. Again, I blame the headache as my distraction from that. My car is boiling hot when I get in; I bet I could cook a whole little spread on the dashboard. For some reason, I imagine breakfast foods: eggs, bacon, pancakes. I must be hungry.

I've missed bowling for three days now. My routine has been shot. Cassia tells me to give it up, then backpedals because she wants to see

Benson. I tell her to shut it—it's been shot, but it isn't dead—I owe her five more days.

As I pull into my apartment parking stall, she teases in a high pitch, "So when are you going to go see Jakey?"

Jakey? Unbelievable! "Were you there? At the hospital?" I ask, dumbstruck. *Was she there the whole time, the opposite of what I thought? Was she there like a good friend would've been?*

Silence. Then she says softly, "Yeah. I stayed with you. And so did Jake. He…" She trails off.

I wait for the end, but she's not giving more. "What about him? Do you know something, Cass?"

She takes what feels like ages to respond. "The only thing I know for sure…is that life is too short."

This hits me like a slap in the face. Not a rude one—a friendly one, if that's possible. I mean, you hear it all the time, but when Cassia says it, it takes on an entirely new meaning.

She leaves me as I enter my apartment, but her comment stays with me. It stays with me through my Frosted Flakes dinner and as I start to get ready for bed.

I stop undressing and put myself back together again because life *is* too short. I'm going to Smith's to see the handsome Utah surfer with green eyes.

Disappointment yanks my shoulders down as I see Jake isn't working today. There's a chubby twentysomething guy standing where he should be. *How dare he?* Still, I approach and ask, "Is Jake working tonight?"

"Clark?" he asks, eyeing my stitches.

I eye his patchy beard in return. "No. Jake."

With just a hint of a grin, he says, "Jake Clark?"

I catch up. "Yeah."

He picks up a pen and starts to fidget with it. "Nope. I don't think he's scheduled to work until Saturday." He eyes my stitches again and halts the fidgeting. "You're the girl," he says.

I cover the stitches and dip my head. *Of course, he'd tell people. Of course, it'd be news to share around the store.* I'm embarrassed.

"That was crazy." He holds out a hand, gesturing to me overall. "Guess you're okay now, yeah?"

I make an agreeable face and shrug.

"I can text him if you want." He pulls his phone from his pocket.

"No, that's okay. I just…was here. I'll catch him some other time."

"Did you get the tickets?"

A quick squint. "No. And I can't afford it now. It's okay." I shrug it off.

"No. I mean—" He squints back, now confused like me. He points to my purse. "Aren't they in there?"

My hand reaches for my little bag as my squint continues.

Chubby, patchy-beard guy—he has no name tag—gives me a wry smile. "Check your purse."

I unzip it and flip through it but see nothing. Then, looking closer, I discover a paper sticking out of my wallet; it's just a hair longer. I haven't opened my wallet since the hospital, so, *Nope, didn't see it.* I unfold the paper, and butterflies twitch in my stomach as I find two tickets inside; they're the tickets for the rock concert I almost paid for before going into anaphylactic shock instead.

I read the note: *Meet me at Smith's at 6:00. We'll get dinner before the show. Hope you're feeling better. Jake.* His phone number is under his name. I'll have to remember to put it in my phone. I can't help the smile forming on my blushing face.

"See?"

A small chuckle escapes me. "Yeah. Thanks."

"Glad I could help," he says.

I tuck it back in my purse and step away, but curiosity gets me. "How'd he…?"

He smiles and leans on the counter. "I was called in to work for him that day. I texted him after a while, asking if things were okay. We went back and forth for a minute, but he asked me to get the tickets and bring them to the hospital when I got off work."

I nod, feeling the thoughtfulness tug at my heart as I picture Jake in the hospital, texting, and this guy meeting him there with tickets. "That's like…really nice."

He lifts himself off the counter. "That's Jake for ya. He's one of the nicest people I know." The phone rings. He glances at it. "I gotta get this."

"Of course."

"See ya later."

I wave and start to leave, still with pictures in my mind of Hospital Jake formulating this plan to leave a note with the tickets in my wallet, happy to know I'd find them and be surprised.

I veer over to the ramen noodles. *Might as well get some while I'm here.* But like Jake, the ramen noodles are missing too. I scowl at the empty section where the cheap food should be. Well, at least this little trip isn't a total bust; I found Jake's note.

I sigh. Time to go home and go to bed early.

<h1 style="text-align:center">Thursday, August 12</h1>

I'm feeling 80 percent better today; I slept a good fourteen hours. Work wasn't necessarily a breeze, but it was a manageable storm, especially since I worked with Zach today. It didn't hurt that most of my thoughts were focused on Jake and the upcoming concert, so time just zipped on by. I was struggling to switch into Benson and bowling mode, but Cassia is with me now, which seems to help. We stroll into the bowling alley, and I approach the counter, prepared to pay.

Benson turns around. "Hey! Where have you been?" He notices my stitches, and his eyes grow wide. "Whoa! Wait. Let me guess. Another bird attacked you?"

I shake my head, and Cassia laughs, saying, "A bee." I hand him my money.

He seems perplexed as he grabs my size eights. "So a bird broke your nose, and a bee cut your head open?"

"More or less, yeah," I tell him.

"You're the strangest girl I know."

"You don't know me." I don't mean for it to bite, but it does. Cassia pinches my left arm.

His comeback is speedy, though. "I'd like to." His long eyelashes reach out and take hold of me, it seems. I can't believe I didn't really notice them in the past. I don't breathe or blink for a number of seconds as we have a staring contest.

What are we, eleven? I think. *Wait for it.* There…the crooked smile makes its glorious appearance.

I finally seize the size eights, thinking that's the end, but he pushes my money back to me. "You don't have to pay today. Remember?"

The memory of us by my car with all his kindness pushes through all my other trivial thoughts. It bobs on the surface of the rough waters I've been in for the past couple of days. Pocketing the cash, I smile in thanks.

I attempt a turn to leave, but Cassia won't let me. She bats my eyes at him and gives her own version of a crooked smile. Again, the physical fight I have with my own legs makes him curious. I must look like an idiot to him. I *am* the strangest girl he'll ever know. I triumph, and we walk away.

Walking over to our lane, I say to her, "Please remember I don't feel well. No jumping."

"Got it," she says back to me. Then, in a singsong voice, she says, "You're starting to like him too, though. Aren't you?"

We're sitting now, and I've taken off my shoes. "No," I respond. "He likes *you*."

"He doesn't like just me. It's not about you or me separately. We're together, one person."

I blink. *It doesn't feel that way sometimes.*

Cassia's first three rolls are gutter balls. Maybe we should ask for the bumpers. Then the ball could bounce around like the thoughts in my head.

"Your wrist hurts," she says.

"I noticed. Try holding it differently."

"Like how?" She's annoyed.

"I don't know; just try something different, Cassia!" *God, it's like we're sisters.*

"You're talking to yourself again. Cassia."

Scheisse! Benson. And he thinks my name is Cassia. Great! Have I never told him my name before? No. There's been no reason to, and he's never asked. How would *he know? Ugh, whatever!*

"My wrist hurts," I say as if it's an explanation for the conversation with myself.

"Because of the bee fight?" He sets down two Cokes.

I picture myself fighting with a bee kung-fu style and chuckle. "Yeah."

"Where does it hurt?" He picks one Coke back up and takes a swig.

Why two Cokes? He's going to hang out and watch me?

"Over here." I point to the outside of my right wrist.

He comes close with both hands out, bringing a spicy man-fragrance with him. "Let me see."

Cassia doesn't think twice about putting my right hand in his left.

His eyes meet mine, then shoot quickly back to my hand. He grabs my left hand and compares the two. "It's not swollen." He drops my left hand. He drops *me* but hangs on to Cassia.

My five-foot-eight stature isn't necessarily short for a girl, but as I peer up at him in my bowling shoes, I certainly feel so. He seems like a friggin' skyscraper. Ashton was five-eleven, and I feel like Benson has got three inches or so on him.

He rotates my wrist inward slowly. Then outward slowly. "Ow!" I pull back, but he's quick, snatching my fingertips. That's the second "ow" I've screeched at him.

"Sorry," he says. "You sure it's not fractured? I mean, with your luck—"

"Hey!" I scowl, then admit, "Well, you've got a point, I guess." *But they did x-rays, it must be fine. Except, what if they didn't do x-rays there? What if it is broken?*

"How's your grip?"

"Fine. I think." I flex my fingers.

"Don't throw underhand so much. Try not to twist your wrist. Keep it straight; just let the ball hang and throw it that way."

I glance at the two Cokes.

"I'm off now," he explains. "Can I hang out and hear all about your good luck?"

I shrug because I can't think of a reason to say no. "Sure."

His suggestion helps. Cassia hits six pins, then two, but it still hurts.

She dawdles, watching the machine clear the lane, and whispers to me, "I don't think it's broken, but I don't want to make it worse. Let's just stop."

I walk back and take the Coke with my good hand, *my* hand. "I'm done."

Benson sits leaned back and legs apart. I notice he's not nervous any longer. He's at ease. "Really?"

"Yeah." I rub my head. The ache is coming back. Taking the Tylenol from my purse, I swallow it with the Coke and deliberately sit two seats away from him.

"You all right?" Benson asks.

"Yeah." I shove the Tylenol bottle back in.

"Can I hear about the bird and the bee?"

Cassia laughs and repeats, "The birds and the bees, huh?"

He gets the joke and laughs too.

I pipe up. "They're dumb stories."

"Dudes dig scars." He points to my stitches.

I shake my head and correct him, "The expression is '*chicks* dig scars.'"

He shrugs. "Guys do too."

I sigh and let Cassia tell the bird story. As she does, I think of my dream. Benson looks very similar to Travin. Or the other way around. Whatever.

"Oh man," he says. "That poor bird!"

I'm appalled. "Poor bird! Ugh! How 'bout my poor nose?" Cassia and I are laughing. Benson is too. He's funny, I decide. I'm starting to get over that whole first impression thing. *Only starting. Let's not get carried away.*

"Did it die?" he asks.

"I think so," I say.

Cassia adds, "I mean, if the hit didn't kill it, the fall would have."

I think how that's true. Can't believe I never thought of that before.

"Don't you feel bad? I mean, seriously." But he's still laughing. "Imagine you're flying all peaceful-like"—he extends his arms like a bird—"and then *bam*!"

Cassia and I can't stop laughing. "No," I answer. "I don't feel bad. It's a stupid bird. I mean, how could it not see me? I'm pretty big, flying through the air. They're supposed to have good eyesight."

He holds on to his stomach and shakes with silent laughter. After a minute, he slows down. "Are you, like, gonna have a bird phobia now?"

I glance around. "I don't think so." But then I bring to mind the other dream where the bird/bee attacked me. I hope I don't have a phobia. *Would I know about it now if I did, or do I have to be faced with a bird to know? What situation would constitute panic? A quaint bird chirping in a tree or only a large one flying toward me? Ducks? Geese? Chickens? Do they count?*

"Damn, that was funny." Benson sits forward, his laughter fading but not his wide smile. Then he says, as casual as ever, "I'm hungry. You hungry?"

Cassia answers, "I could eat."

What the hell, Cass?

She softly rubs my left wrist. She means to say sorry.

"Cool. Let's get somethin'. What do ya feel like?"

Neither of us answers. *Sssuck! How can I go back on this without being a complete snob?* I shift my eyes as if I'm thinking. Well, I *am* thinking, but not of a place to eat. Cassia's words repeat in my head: *Life is too short.*

Did she put the words there? Should I say yes to this? I can't think of a reason to say no to this either, so, ugh! Okay. This one's for you, Cass. "Subway is just across the street," I propose.

She grabs my hand and gives it a tender squeeze. I truly hope she doesn't get too tired.

After ordering two foot-long meatball sub sandwiches and getting our drinks, all of which Benson pays for, we sit in a corner booth. I didn't want to argue about who pays in front of the employee, but I pull out my wallet to reimburse him for my share. I find myself in a battle, which involves him slapping my hand away eventually. I laugh but beg him to take it.

With his mouth full, he says, "You can get it next time."

Argh! I should've just let it go. Now I don't know what to say. Benson chews his food and grins at me with a wad of it bulging out his cheek. He knows he's got me. I'm going to be forced to go on another date, if that's what this is, if I'm determined to pay him back.

"How's your headache?"

"Getting better."

A single nod. "Good." Then he adds, "I know it was just a matter of convenience, but this was a good choice. I haven't been here in a while. I've been on a Jimmy John's kick lately."

"Oh yeah? I've been on a ramen noodles kick lately," I reply sarcastically.

He laughs one hearty time. "The diet of a starving student?" he guesses. "You go to the U?"

I scratch my cheek, pondering how to answer this question. I'm not currently going, but then again, a lot of people don't go for summer semester. I plan on going in the fall. *Don't I? Do I answer yes?* I end up shrugging.

Benson's eyebrows come together. "What do you mean you don't know?"

"I…don't know what I'm doing," I confess. It works for so many things: school, my life, this…date.

"Hmm," he nods, understanding. "Starving and lost. It's a good thing I found you when I did," he jokes, then takes a bite so big I fear he's going to choke on it.

I smile and take my own small bite. As I chew, Cassia taps my finger three times on the sandwich, reminding me she's here (as if I could forget) and would like to be part of things. I still don't know about all this, but I suppose I did say it was for her.

I relent, and she asks, "So what's your favorite thing to do here—in the city?"

That's the first thing she has to say? Is she fishing for ideas because she's running out of them, or she thinks I've run out of them? I've actually just run out of money. I mean, my money tree is alive and well; it just isn't bearing much fruit right now.

"Well." He tongues some bread from between his teeth. "It's not quite in the city, but"—he nods toward the mountains—"hiking and camping. Totally."

A small smile appears on my face, courtesy of Cassia. "I've never been camping," she confesses.

He blinks wide eyes. "How is that possible?"

"Because…I grew up in Manhattan."

What the hell? I didn't know that! Then I wonder how much more she'll tell him. Perhaps all this will be a good thing. I mentally rub my hands together, excited to possibly learn more.

He's surprised. "Really? Why'd you move here? It's so different from New York."

I have a small worry she's going to get too tired and have to leave me, and then what? I don't think I can keep up with this topic on my own. *And yeah, why* did *she move here?*

She hesitates. "I…needed to get away. Took the first plane out. I like it here, though." I feel my eyes welling up with her tears and wonder why this is emotional enough to make her almost cry.

He moves past what I really want to know—why she needed to get away—and asks, "How long have you been here?"

Yeah, I want to know that too. Did she die here or in New York? I'd always assumed she was from here and died here.

She sniffs quickly. "Three months or so."

Hmm, this doesn't really help me.

"Oh, not long. What do you like about it?"

"I think…I'm not a city girl," she says, scrunching my eyebrows down.

He makes a face. "And yet, you're living in the city."

She smiles. "I mean…this isn't *The City*."

"For Utah, it is."

Now *she* makes a face.

"I know what you mean," he admits with a small chuckle.

"No, I mean…the people are nicer here. And it's beautiful, really beautiful. The sunsets. The mountains…"

"Wait till winter. Best snow on earth. You snowboard?"

I answer quickly, "No." Even if I did snowboard or ski, I can't have him thinking we're going to be an item when snow is on the ground four months from now. Don't get me wrong, the snow *is* awesome, and the mountains *are* incredible; it's just the avalanches every other week kind of freak me out. Super dangerous!

"I'll take you. It's awesome up there." He shoves the last bite of his sandwich in his mouth.

He's like a friggin' vacuum.

He adds, "And don't worry. The birds fly south for the winter."

"Shut up." Cassia and I laugh.

He also laughs and chokes on his food for a second. He takes a swig to clear it. "What's the bee story?"

I let Cassia tell him the bee story. She leaves out anything about the rock concert and anything about Jake and ends with, "I fell on the sidewalk outside the store." I point to my stitches.

"Holy shit," he says.

"Yes, the bee died, and it's *so* sad." I'm being heavily sarcastic.

"No!" He shakes his head. His eyes are big. "Who helped you? How'd you get to the hospital?"

I lift my shoulders. "Someone called nine-one-one, and an ambulance came."

"Damn! I've never known anyone *that* allergic to bees. That sucks!"

We discuss how bizarre it is that bees die after they sting you. Benson and I, that is. Not Benson and Cassia.

"I'm glad you're okay," he confesses thoughtfully, fixing me with a gaze and changing the entire mood of the conversation. His ocean-blue eyes are like the sea; they seem to rock from side to side as he looks into both my eyes. "I'm glad you didn't die." His sea is gentle, and his smile swells to match the waters, big and wide.

"Yeah. Me too," I say, almost in a whisper. Cassia's probably thinking, *Me three, for the second time.*

The mood shifts back when he asks, "So is your family still back in Manhattan?"

"Yeah, my dad…and my stepmom."

"Oh, what about your real mom?"

"She's in Syracuse."

Cassia is keeping her answers simple, I notice. But still, I didn't know that. I push away the annoyance that I've been trying for three months to get information like this out of her, and she's seemingly telling Benson with incredible ease. I'll just accept it as a good thing. Silver lining of going on a date with Benson: I get to learn about Cassia.

"Oh, Syracuse, Utah?"

"No, New York. I didn't know there's one here too."

"I forget there's one there. Do you like your stepmom?" Benson's elbows are on the table, and he's leaning forward. I think he's *truly* interested. I once read you can tell if a guy likes you if he asks questions about you. Benson's doing that and more. He's leaning in. He's making fantastic eye contact. He's listening to the answers.

"Not really, but whatever," she replies. I'm guessing she wanted to say more because she opened my mouth but closed it a second later. I wonder if he noticed.

"Is she why you wanted to get away?"

Cassia waits to answer. She must be thinking. "I guess so. In a way."

"No brothers or sisters?"

Cassia shakes my head.

Hmm…we're both our parents' only children. Just a girl.

"Well, that explains some things," he says jokingly. Cassia hurls a chip at him. He catches it and eats it. "Do you think your dad misses you?" he says through crunches.

My eyes begin to water again, and she nods my head.

"Are you going to stay out here? Like, live here?"

Cassia shrugs my shoulders. "It's…complicated."

She's almost crying now. I feel the sorrow in her. In me. It's distracting. I forget for an instant where we are, that Benson is even with us.

"Ah, dang. I'm sorry." He reaches for my elbow across the table and gives it a gentle squeeze.

Cassia wipes at her tears.

"I'm an ass," he says.

"No." She waves it off and smiles big as she changes the subject. "I'm going to go back for Christmas."

Wait! What? Does she mean her spirit or me too? Ah, suck! Is that what I'm supposed to save money for?

"Ah, I've always wanted to be in New York during Christmastime," Benson says. "And New Year's Eve. It looks so cool."

I'm feeling drained of energy all of a sudden. *Cassia?*

"What about you?" Cassia asks. "Where'd you grow up?"

Cassia?

"Not far. North Salt Lake. I'm the oldest. They still have four at home." Benson goes on about his two brothers and two sisters. He speaks highly of his parents and says he goes to their house for dinner at least once a month, more if there's a birthday or holiday. Then there's something about lacrosse and guitar. I'm feeling weird. Something about his sister's cheerleading.

Cassia?

"And what about you? Bowler?" Cassia asks.

He chuckles. "Nah, I mean, I like bowling. But it's just for fun. I'm in the civil engineering program."

"That's cool. My dad's an engineer. Architectural and structural."

Benson and Cassia talk for an extended time about architecture and bridges. It's all stuff I know zilch about. I find I sort of zone out. Before I know it, the sun is on the horizon as I look out the windows and past the city buildings. The Subway staff is beginning to clean up, and we're the only ones left.

This is the longest Cassia has remained with me. Why am *I* the tired one? She must feel it too. I try to tell her she needs to wrap it up.

She must have heard me because she interrupts him mid-sentence. "What time is it?"

He peeks at his watch. "Nine thirty."

"Sorry, I need to go."

"Yeah." He sounds bummed. "I didn't realize we'd been here that long."

We stand up, and I remind her to behave herself as we walk back to my car. Luckily, he hasn't asked for my number yet, not that I know of anyway.

He's nervous again. His fingers make their way into his pockets with his thumbs sticking out. "Thanks for havin' dinner with me. That was fun, gettin' to know you."

Cassia smiles. "Yeah. You too."

He points to the bowling alley. "See ya tomorrow?"

Cassia nods my head. I take over and shake my head, ending up with a comical circling motion. "Probably not," I say, focusing to force my right hand up to remind him my wrist hurts. It feels like lifting a fifty-pound dumbbell; I think my forehead vein is bulging. Taking back control from Cassia is way more difficult than it should be.

"Oh, right. Duh." He thinks for a few seconds. "I might have a brace you can try if you want. If I can find it, I'll bring it tomorrow. You can stop by at least. I hope." He looks shy by the end there.

I drop her arm—wait, *my* arm. This is still all my body. I'm exhausted from that just now. I think I hear Cassia tell him, "Okay."

He backs away from me with a grin before turning around to go to his car. As soon as he does, Cassia leaves. I inhale a deep breath. When the tingle fades, some of my energy returns, but I still have to focus on staying awake for the short drive home. I can't shake the feeling something else isn't right.

What's happening to me? Is it because she was with me for so long? I don't feel like myself.

I'm sure she was tired as well, but now I wish she'd stayed a little bit so I could talk to her. I'm uncertain what her intentions are with all this, and I'm worried I did the wrong thing.

I arrive at my apartment just before ten o'clock. I don't like getting home when it's dark; it creeps me out. The dangers double past dark, possibly triple. I check behind me more than a few times as I walk from my parking spot up to my door.

My meatball sandwich doesn't have to fight for space in the fridge; I set it on an open shelf and go into my bedroom to get ready for bed. I don a unicorn pajama top that says "Just keep dreaming." I chuckle to myself because I don't want to dream. If I dream, I'm pretty sure it'll be about everything that's bothering me. I'm worried things are going to turn from this cluster of confused feelings and stories into a massive knot of mixed emotions and conflicting conversations. *Argh!* All right, I guess I'm glad she's not with me right now. I can have my own time. Time to be all wishy-washy. Time to think.

Although, I wonder (I've always wondered) if she's next to me, following me around. After all, she always joins me at the same times. Like after work or just before I arrive at the bowling alley. Before the temperature spiked, I'd eat lunch outside, and she'd usually join me just in time. And I know it sounds strange, but she enjoys the feeling of the hot water when I shower. I mean, who doesn't? And she never joins me when I'm at work or the gym, or when I'm reading a book in bed, or when I practice ballet. I know she doesn't like my job, and it's possible she doesn't like reading or dancing. It could be they wear her out, and she'd rather save her energy for the good stuff.

Still, I wonder.

And since I wonder *this*, I also wonder if she can still hear my thoughts even when she's not sharing my body.

And when does this stop?

Strange. I haven't thought this before now.

Possibly because it was just Cassia and me, and I've enjoyed our time and adventures together. I guess I thought I could keep up better. Financially, I mean. But those three big trips cost more than I expected. I didn't intend to begin a relationship, either. But now there's Benson and possibly Jake. Having other people involved is wrong. Benson, specifically, is wrong, on more than one level. I'm beating myself up for allowing that to happen the way it did tonight. I wanted to give that to her. I wanted to say yes for her, for that, but when—and how—does it all stop? When she's finished with her bucket list?

Is a boyfriend on her bucket list? *I think not!*

And when do I go back to school?

When do I move on?

Get a boyfriend (of my own, Jake or not), get married, have kids? I can't live a double life for her.

It was odd tonight, sitting on the sidelines and yet not. I was excited, at first, to learn more about her. But it didn't take long before I felt…out of control. I mean, she gave me my left hand, of course, but I found I couldn't really use it. I zoned out for a while too.

How long? I don't know. *How can I control how much control she has?* I stop myself. I just need to go to bed, relax, and see if she'll come and talk.

Cassia doesn't come.

But I dream…

I dream of Benson and the things the two of them talked about at Subway. The things I don't remember. They talked about all the bridges in New York and the buildings her dad has completed, and they talked more about his school. He has three years left to go. And her school: she's taking a break but may go to school here in Utah.

And she shared memories of the holidays in New York, starting with the Macy's Thanksgiving Day Parade to New Year's Eve in Times

Square. She shared how her mom left her and her dad when she was five, which happened to be the first Christmas she ever remembered.

It's all there, everything I missed at dinner (at least, I think it is). But more important than the things I missed in conversation is that I feel how happy she is. It's the happiest she's been in a long time, with the exception of finding a new friend—me.

Then I dream of a future with Benson: he moves into my apartment, we go to school together, we kiss, we make love, we get married...

I wake up with a deep breath.

Friday, August 13

I'm still disturbed about what happened last night with Cassia, and work is doing nothing to help me with that. Trish is in the back switching out books, and Ashley is doodling at the register, her new lob haircut hanging in her face. She found out through Chloe and Trisha about my accidents, so I luck out not having to repeat the embarrassing stories. She's talking about a girl she likes as I fix the pens and highlighters that fell off the shelf when I bumped into it. I'm trying to listen and let her story distract me, but it's not enough. I need something more to help divert me from the knot in my stomach I've named Benson. He's twisting my insides and worming through my gut.

"I've tried to hang out with her a couple of times, but she's always working," Ashley says.

"Uh-huh," I reply, but I'm thinking, *I can't decide if I'm mad at Cassia or just extremely worried about everything.*

Ashley goes on. "I guess I could ask when she *doesn't* work and see if she wants to hang out then."

"Uh-huh." *I feel like she just got a little too excited and ended up taking over a little too much.*

"Or I could stop by her work. Would that be weird?"

"Uh-huh." *She's been cut short of a potentially great life. She's not necessarily wrong to want more.*

"It would?"

Suck. I have no idea what Ashley just said. "Huh?"

She's stopped doodling and is looking at me with her dark chocolate eyes, a little displeased, like I've snubbed her. "Would it be weird if I stopped by her work?"

I think. "To ask her out or to pretend you just happen to be there?" I think she said she works at a clothing store, so the latter is totally doable.

Ashley presses her red-lipsticked lips together. "Pretend I just happen to be there."

I push the other world I live in to the side and try to give Ashley my full attention. Well, at least 75 percent. I think about telling her to ask Chloe; she knows more about this sort of thing. But I realize I do actually have advice when it comes to relationships. Well, it's Cassia's advice, but whatever. "Life is too short. I don't think it's weird. Go for it."

She seems satisfied with my response, even delighted. Returning to her doodling, she says, "Thanks."

After my conversation with Ashley, my other world sucks me back in, as much as I don't want it to. I wasn't planning on working out today—the doctor advised against it—but I need to for my mental health right now. And I miss my routine, so I go after my shift. I just hope I don't get another nosebleed.

By the time I finish running and lifting weights, two things haven't happened: I haven't gotten a nosebleed (of course, I didn't work out as hard as I normally do), and I haven't gotten rid of this unsettling feeling. I want the hot water of my shower to wash it away. I don't even know how to describe it, only that I can't stand it.

Cassia hasn't joined me yet, and my routine tells me she should be here. I'm getting antsy. We should be driving off to the bowling alley soon, even though I don't want to go; I just want to talk to her. But I'm standing in front of my closet with my towel wrapped around me instead, trying to decide what to wear. I roughly flip through my choices of dresses and skirts while my mind flips through my choices of what to do about all this.

I really don't blame her for wanting more, but at the same time, I have to set boundaries. This is *not* an ordinary friendship. This is *so* the opposite; there's no place to find rules for this kind of relationship. There's no Googling *What to do if your friend who shares your body starts to take over your body,* or *What to do if your friend who shares your body wants to date someone you don't want to date.*

But am I overreacting? She took over a little too much, but she didn't give him my number, she didn't kiss him, and she promised nothing really for the future. I sit at the foot of my bed and fiddle with the corner of my towel. I consider bowling. I'm not sure why; I don't want to see Benson's pretty ocean eyes today. *So why am I considering going there? To try to correct the mistakes? At least my name? But what would that matter if everything else is a lie? Would Cassia come if I started to drive there?*

I make a quick decision—I'm going. Because I'm almost positive Cassia will come if I go there, and if she doesn't…well, then I'll tell Benson the truth. I have no idea how that'll go, but I'll figure it out. I'll officially be the strangest girl he (or anyone else) has ever known, but I'll be done with this icky garbage feeling. I choose a long purple shirt with a belt over some white leggings. Like yesterday, I need something to conceal my scabbing and bruised knees. I pull my hair into a ponytail and put on my platform sandals.

I grab my keys and get in my car, but Cassia's still not with me.

I drive all the way there and park, but she's still not with me.

"Come on, Cassia," I say aloud.

Silence.

I huff out a breath, get out of my car, and walk tall up to the doors of the bowling alley, but she's *still* not with me.

Here goes, I think. I open the door and march toward his counter when she suddenly joins me, gluing my feet to the floor halfway there. I almost face-plant but windmill to save myself. "Really, Cassia?" I spit.

Benson starts cracking up and asks, "Are you okay?"

Cassia has somehow become a ventriloquist, and I'm her puppet. "Please don't do this," she tells me through my unmoving lips.

I slap my hands over my face. "*Argh!*" It comes out louder than I want it to. *Now is when you decide to come?! I got this far before you'd come talk to me?!* I look down at my feet, then back up at Benson.

Laughter still consumes him as he leans over the counter for support. "Seriously. Are you okay? What are you doing?"

He got a haircut. I squint at him. *Ugh*, he looks good. "Nothing!" Then I point at him accusingly. "You! Stay there! I'm going…to the bathroom."

Benson watches me storm off in the direction of the restrooms with my nose in the air. "I'll just be here then," he hollers with still a hint of laughter.

I quickly make sure no one else is in any of the stalls before I take the last one and open my mouth, ready to whisper-yell at Cassia.

She beats me to it, talking low. "I know what you're going to say, but before you do, I'm sorry. Okay? I'm sorry. I didn't realize how much I took over until after I left you. I swear I didn't."

I sigh and rub my forehead. *Okaaay.* "We're getting *way* sidetracked, Cassia. This isn't what we agreed on."

Her trademark silence. *So frustrating.*

"And you know it's wrong, right? *Really* wrong. Think of Benson." I can't help it. I think about what I thought of last night, about living a double life.

She hears my thought. "Whoa," she says, a bit louder, my voice echoing off the stall door back at me. "I'd *never* ask you to do that."

"Yeah, like we weren't supposed to go out with Benson?" I hiss with an eye roll.

"That was like…a gift."

"Well, I'm regretting giving it to you."

"Please don't," she says sort of whiny. "That's why I gave you that dream. So you'd know everything you missed and how happy I was for that time. Really. I can't thank you enough."

I know she means it, but I still can't help thinking, *Maybe this is all a mistake.*

"No, Cam, don't think that!" She's almost frantic. "Please," she begs.

"If you can talk to Benson, you can talk to me. No more secrets, Cassia. You have to tell me *everything*—about you, about what you intend for New York." I hesitate. "And how you died."

More silence. I mean, crickets are chirping, for goodness' sake.

"I mean it, Cass." My voice is stern. I'm the mom, and she's the little girl who's been misbehaving. This is as much of a fight as Cassia and I have ever had, and I don't like it. I don't like fighting. With anyone.

"Okay, okay." My right hand shakes my left hand. It's a deal.

I can't believe demanding anger is part of her vault combination. Maybe there's a little bit of guilt in there too. *Whatever.* "Okay. Let's go home."

"Wait. Can we try bowling? Since we're here." She rotates my right wrist, testing it out. It feels all right, but that's without seven pounds hanging from it.

I sigh obnoxiously but think how I promised her five more days and only gave her like four rolls last night.

She negotiates. "How about just one more day? Then we'll talk tonight?"

I fiddle with my earring. I suppose it's a fair compromise, but…

"It's a lot, Camry. And I'll probably make you cry. Can we just do something fun first?"

I loosely think, *What could it be if it's "a lot?"* I give in. "Fine."

Coming out of the restrooms, I once again march over to his counter. Benson watches my every step with a smirk I sort of want to smack off his clean-shaven face. "Everything all worked out?" he asks.

I think he's referring to my legs not working properly since he glances at them, though I don't know how that could've been fixed in the bathroom. But everything between Cassia and me *is* worked out now, so I say, "Yeah." I reach his counter and pass over my cash for a game.

He pushes the bills back to me. "Oh no, you don't. You can't bowl. Remember?"

I set my hand over the money, trying to tell him with a look that I think I can.

Benson does away with his name tag, then hollers, "Hey, Chip! I'm outta here."

I don't see Chip, but I hear a faint, "See ya later."

Benson walks around the counter and waves for me to come with him. His eyes sparkle like he's a man with a plan. I make no move, so he stops next to me. "I got somethin' for ya."

I begin to protest by shaking my head. His mouth twists into a knowing smile, then he grabs my hand and pulls me out of the building. I'm not going to lie—the touch of his hand on mine feels nice. I'm taken back to the time I dated Ashton; he loved to hold hands. I didn't realize how much I'd missed that.

Benson pulls me to his ten-year-old Silverado, opens the passenger door, and hands me a box. It's a wrist brace, size small.

My mouth drops open, but I'm speechless. *How the hell does a wrist brace make me so dumbstruck?*

Of course, it's the thought behind it. I barely know Benson. I don't even know his last name, and yet he went to the store either last night or sometime today, stood in the aisle looking at the options, and bought this.

It's ridiculous!

Benson chuckles. "It's not like it's a diamond ring. It's a wrist brace. Put it on."

I blink up at him. "Thank you."

"Of course." He takes it out, throws the box in his truck, and helps me strap it on.

I snap out of it and reach for my wallet to pay him back. "Here."

He stops me, insisting it's a gift.

Don't argue with him, Camry. That didn't work so well last time. I glare at him, though.

He sneers in response, shuts the truck door, and shoves his keys back in his pocket.

Good. Now I can go home and try to forget about this ridiculously nice guy. "Something fun" just isn't going to work out right now, Cass.

I back up toward my car and fumble for my keys as he reaches for me. Directing me with a hand on my shoulder blade, he says, "Let's walk." He points down the street.

"No. Where?" I protest with a hint of a whine.

"I'm gonna show you around the city a bit"—he points at nothing specific—"in a different way," he says with a wink.

I'm reminded he thinks I'm Cassia. It's half past six and, surprisingly, not too warm today. Still, I'm not overjoyed walking is his notion of showing Cassia around the city. Thankfully, she's staying out of the conversation so far, letting me decide my own answers. "Really?" I ask, glancing down at my platform sandals. I contemplate how I can get out of this.

"Oh, don't be such a Nancy. It's just a couple of blocks. We'll eat first, then you'll see."

I shake my head. *I really shouldn't spend any more date-like time with this guy.*

"Come on. I know you've got at least a half hour; you were planning on bowling just now."

I continue to hesitate. *"Something fun"* rings in my ears.

"You can buy this time," he negotiates with a grin.

Argh! He's got me. But then that's it! We're going home.

Side by side with him, I'm glad I picked the two-inch platforms, and if it really is only a couple of blocks, they shouldn't hurt my feet.

We're outside of the little café Benson has selected. Even though he said I could buy, I literally had to hip-bump him out of the way in order to purchase the sandwiches. He opens the umbrella at the table, and I make sure not to sit in the bird excrement.

"Okay. Question." He talks with his mouth half full. It seems to be a habit of his.

Cassia and I watch him. I realize she's going to have to answer; I can't be mixing up our opinions.

"Would you rather…go without your cell phone for a day or without your car for a day?"

Cassia answers, "Uh, my car."

Of course Cassia would say car; she's from New York. I'd have said cell phone. Nobody calls me anyway. "You?" I ask back.

"The same. Would you rather win against your dad or your stepmom?"

Cassia is doing well at not taking over too much. I clarify. "Bowling?"

He nods. "But don't overthink it. Just…answer quickly. Raw emotion. It's more honest that way."

Cassia blurts out, "Stepmom."

It makes sense. She doesn't like her stepmom; of course she'd want to beat her…at anything she could. Jumping rope. Race car driving. Bowling.

He nods. I think he also understands this about her. "If you could play against anyone in the entire world, who would it be?"

I ask, "What kind of questions are these?"

He gives us a glare.

"Anyone?" she asks.

"Yeah. Anyone. Famous. Not famous. Alive. Not alive." He snaps his fingers.

She squeals. "Aaagh, I don't know."

"Okay. You can think about that one."

As Cassia thinks, famous names run through my head—good and bad, alive and dead. Abraham Lincoln, Adolf Hitler, Michael Jackson, Brad Pitt, Lady Gaga, Mark Zuckerberg—

"Serena Williams," she answers.

Benson's eyebrows rise. "You like tennis?"

She nods. "What about you? Who would you choose?"

He offers no hesitation. "You, of course."

Oh, I should've guessed that. The perfect answer to win a girl over.

Is it working?

I feel myself grin.

Me. Not Cassia.

Scheisse!

I try to dispute the surprise Benson has in store but struggle to come up with a good reason not to go with him. Cassia is of no help; she remains silent as if whatever she might say could be used against her in a court of law. The fact Benson grabs my hand again and doesn't really give me an option doesn't help either. I guess I'm turning into a sucker for physical contact.

We walk around the corner, and the temple is revealed. I think about how he likes architecture, and I have to agree the temple is architecturally stunning. It's positioned in the center of beautiful gardens and paths. Its spires and pinnacles reach up to the sky, threatening to pop it open, and I'm envious of the view that the golden angel has on top there. The battlements are ready to take on the worst Salt Lake City has to offer, and I wonder if the All-Seeing Eye at the top of the center tower can see through me.

Probably.

I suddenly feel the judgment—as if I could go to hell for this—for what I'm doing to Benson.

Although I live only two blocks from the temple, it's been a long time since I've admired its beauty. I don't even notice the horse and carriage until Benson stops us and gestures to climb aboard. They've been parked on the street waiting for us. Cassia and I can't help but smile. Again, like Zion, this is something I've never done, and it's even closer to home. *I am so lame.*

"Ever done this before?" he asks.

I pause for Cassia to answer, thinking, *New York has something like this as well, don't they?*

"No," she says eagerly. I wonder if that's true; it seems unlikely.

"Good." He holds out his hand to help us into the bright-white carriage.

The driver grins politely at us. It takes me a minute to get accustomed to the horse smell from the lovely light-brown Clydesdale that's pulling us on our excursion—and the fact I'm shoulder to shoulder and thigh to thigh with Benson. I'm startled at how small this seat is. We settle in, and he puts his arm up on the back of the seat behind me.

The driver announces his name is Bob, and he'll be our tour guide for the next hour.

The tour begins here with the temple. As we enter the gate and follow the pathways large enough for the carriage, Cassia moves my eyes all around, taking in as much as she possibly can. My posture is erect, and my lips are parted as she tilts my head. The driver comments on the forty years it took to build it, finishing and finally opening in 1893. I barely register what he's saying. I'm more focused on how Benson is staring at me…us…her.

Her.

I mean, I'm also looking at the building, but she's the one with the eyes-full-of-wonder gaze that he's admiring.

Cassia points and says something about the towers and spires. Benson points out the reflection pond, and she gasps.

"It's better after dark with the lights," he remarks.

"I'll bet," she says breathlessly.

I can't help but wonder how many other girls he's done this with. Cassia recoils and turns away from him. *Crap. She probably heard my thought.*

Sorry, Cassia.

He takes his arm off the seat behind me and brings it back to his lap, seeming to sense her sudden discomfort.

After about a fifteen-minute ride around the temple, Bob says, "Now, we'll make our way up to the capitol. Relax, and enjoy the ride for a bit."

The horse clomps its way uphill now.

Poor thing. At least night is coming, and it's cooling down.

Cassia relaxes. Finally.

I side-eye Benson. He doesn't turn away or cover the fact he's been staring the entire time. "So how do you know Bob?" I ask quietly.

He smiles. Well, he smiles bigger. "What makes you think I know Bob?"

"He gave you, like, a little smirk when we started."

"Okay then, you really are a Nancy, huh? Like a little Nancy Drew over here." He repositions himself. This seat is about as comfortable as a bear hug. "He's a friend of my dad's."

I can't help it. I'm too curious. "And how many other girls have had this pleasure?"

Cassia pinches my left arm.

He adjusts himself again and angles his head at me. "Are we…going to do the whole past relationships thing now?"

"Yeah, why not? I'm curious. How many?"

He scratches his head and holds up two fingers. "Only one had the pleasure of this, though. But it was a different tour. It was for senior prom. We dated all of senior year. And the other one—" He sucks in a breath. "We broke up back in January. She just…wasn't the path for me."

Sounds familiar. "So does that make me a rebound? What's the timeframe on that?" I smirk. *Did I just say "me?" What am I doing? Shut your pie hole, Camry.*

"No, no," he says quickly, then smirks back at me. "That's only, like, within thirty days or something."

"Ah."

"Wait!" He points to his chest. "Am *I* a rebound?"

I giggle. "No. We broke up almost a year ago." *Seriously. Stop talking. Now.*

"Any more before that?"

I shake my head. "No. Just—"

Cassia says, "One."

Suck. I'm screwing up our histories. Getting caught up in the moment. Wading around in that damn ocean.

Not really wanting to but also not trusting my suddenly rambling mouth, I try to let Cassia have a little bit more but not too much. She shifts my body to lean my back against him just the slightest bit. He returns his arm to the back of the seat behind me.

The ride lasts an hour. It's twilight when we finish. Benson and Cassia have had a good conversation, mostly tour-related, Utah history and whatnot, which she honestly knew nothing about. Luckily, there was no talk of anything too personal, and she didn't cut me off to the point where I couldn't remember anything. *Thank you.* Benson helps us out of the carriage and goes to thank the driver. I step forward to admire the temple one more time. It's beautiful all lit up.

Without warning, the horse bites the back of my left arm.

I yelp, causing pedestrians to look in my direction. The driver jumps down and gives the horse a little slap. He tells the horse he's bad, then comes to me to be sure I'm okay. Benson has beaten him to it.

"It's okay," I say, rubbing my arm. *Eww, horse spit.* "I'm fine."

Cassia left me for a moment but is back now.

The driver insists that Sir Walter has never acted that way before; he's normally a really good horse.

Yeah, I'll bet he is, I think skeptically, shooting the horse a dirty look. He's probably going on strike for this whole "tour" thing, but I don't know why he had to take it out on me.

Bob keeps apologizing, and we end up getting a free ride for another time because he feels so bad. Or because he doesn't want to be sued. I realize if he's offering us a free ride, it probably means Benson paid for this one. It could be they're not as good of friends as I thought.

We begin walking back. Benson asks if I'm really okay, if my arm's bleeding. He's trying to look at it, but I'm clenching it with my other hand and won't let him pry it off.

I wait until we're out of earshot of the driver. "That hurt like a mother," I say. "It's not bleeding, but it's definitely gonna bruise."

He stifles a laugh, covering his mouth. "I am so sorry."

"It's okay," I say, rubbing it. "I'm getting used to it."

Now he laughs aloud. "Just one more animal to add to your list of attacks."

I laugh as well. "Pretty much. Better not go swimming in the ocean."

He grabs my hand and laces our fingers. It threatens to be a heartwarming gesture.

Ugh! This is horseshit! I cannot be doing this. Let go of his hand, Camry! Let go!

But I don't.

We've made it back to the parking lot and begin to walk slowly over to my red-and-silver car. "So I have something to tell you," Cassia says, implying bad news.

Oh suck! What's she going to say?

I hear Benson stop breathing. Like, he's *actually* holding his breath. He's going to pass out if she doesn't answer him soon. *How long can he hold his breath?*

"I'm not going to come bowling anymore," she says regretfully.

There's a very audible sigh from him as his shoulders relax.

"With my wrist…and I can't really afford it anyway with the trip to New York and everything."

I'm afraid Benson having the knowledge she's not coming bowling anymore means he's going to ask for my number. I mean, I can't believe he hasn't already.

"I thought you were gonna say something else." He exaggerates his relief while scratching the back of his neck.

"Like what?"

"Like you had a terrible time tonight and you never want to see my face again."

Cassia rolls my eyes. "No! The horse biting me was *not* your fault. Don't worry about it."

We've reached my car, but Benson is two strides away from me, rocking back and forth with his fingers in his pocket. Heel. Toe. Heel. Toe.

I throw him a questioning stare.

With a crooked smile, he answers my unspoken question. "I'm just…fighting the urge to kiss you."

I cock my head. There are two kinds of guys in this world…

"I feel like you may think it's too soon, but I…" He breathes. "I feel like it's been a month because from that first day I saw you…I'm kicking myself for not…"

There are two kinds of guys in this world: the ones who jump in for a kiss because *they* want it and the ones who care enough to wait until you're ready. I like that Benson's the latter, that he cares enough.

I take the two-stride journey, grab the back of his neck with *my* hand, and smash my lips into his.

Are Cassia's feelings impressing on me?

Am I lonely—a year without Ashton?

Has Benson become a comforting routine?

I don't know the answer to any of these questions. Only that his neck is smooth, his hair is soft, and his lips are easy. The heartwarming threat from before has turned into a full-on melting of my insides.

Benson pulls me into him with both hands on my back.

Cassia places my right hand on his chest and hijacks the kiss. *Or did I let her?* She's more forceful than I am and quite talented at it, I decide.

I pull back. "Okay. Stop."

Mechanically, Benson apologizes.

I shake my head. "I was talking to…myself."

"You do that a lot."

"I know." I realize my left hand is still behind his neck. I hastily remove it, regretting how much I enjoyed the kiss.

"No. I like it. It helps me know what you're thinking." Then he adds, "But there're still times when it's like you're fighting with yourself. Like you're holding yourself back."

I don't smile. I stare and think, *You have no idea!*

The sun has dipped all the way, and it's dark outside. The lights from the parking lot illuminate us though and light up Benson's blue eyes. That damn ocean blue. I feel like I could get lost in it and in the lashes that are like hundreds of long fingers pulling me in. There's a little brown spot in his right eye.

It's like a boat.

A boat to carry me in.

Into him.

"Don't." He brings his lips back to meet mine.

"Damn it," I whisper. I believed I only thought the curse word, but then I felt my lips move against his, and he's separated us by an inch, or a mile, I don't know; my eyes are closed.

"Why 'damn it'?" he asks.

I breathe, "I like you." There's a hint of a whine in my voice, like when you get a paper cut. I think it's me talking, not Cassia. Or maybe she's talking, and I'm just adding the whine to it. I don't know why I can't tell sometimes.

He huffs a small laugh and pulls me in for a hug. Rocking us, he says, "I like you too. We should do this *every* week." I don't comment, just breathe him in. Then he adds, "Why'd you say that like it's a bad thing?"

"Because for me, it is."

He breaks the hug and opens his mouth. Probably to ask why.

Can't have that! I quickly stop him with, "Tell me something bad." I need a reason. A reason to walk away and not care if I ever see him again. *There has to be one, right? Otherwise, how am I going to deal with this?*

"Something bad?" he questions.

I look at him eagerly. *Yes.*

He thinks. He's going to play along, like all the silly questions he asked me earlier. Well, it's his turn now. "Um. There are starving kids in Africa. With AIDS." Then he beams. "But you don't have AIDS, and I don't have AIDS. I'm glad we covered that. It's an important thing to talk about at the start of a relationship."

I can't help but grin a bit, but I grab his shirt and shake him a bit too. "No. About you."

"Oh." He glances around, then back to my eyes with an intense expression. "I fart a lot."

Now I can't help but laugh aloud.

He smiles all the way, ear to ear. "Serious. I need to fart right now, but I'm holding it in out of respect for the first date rule."

I begin laughing so hard it's silent. I wave at him to stop.

He laughs as well, shoulders shaking. "If you're serious about the whole 'bad' thing, I'll let it rip."

"I can't take it. Stop." Still laughing, I shake my head.

He's still holding my waist, but I've let go. I need to wipe away my tears of laughter with both hands. After a minute, a long minute, I compose myself.

He adjusts his hands and cocks his head. "So is that a deal breaker, or can we go out next Friday?"

I shake my head for the first question. Wait, for both questions. The rock concert is next Friday.

"No?" he asks. "No, it's not a deal breaker, or no, we can't go out next Friday?"

I twist my face, feeling bad. "I can't next Friday." Cassia pinches my left arm.

He presses his lips firmly together as his eyes narrow. He's staring at me, thinking intently. "Since you don't have any friends or family here, I'm assuming…"

I look away. My face is giving me away; I'm a rotten liar. This whole scene just got really serious. I shouldn't have to explain my dating situation to him. *What? Does he want details?* I wonder if he's the jealous type. I touch my stitches. They're beginning to get itchy. I think of Jake. *How can it be I've been alone for a year, then meet two great guys at the same time? Why does it have to be like that?*

Benson sighs. "Now I'm *really* kicking myself."

This hits me the wrong way. I push myself away from him. His strong-but-gentle hands plummet to his sides. "What do you expect me to do?" I say with an irritated tone.

He's shoved his fingers in his pockets again. "It's fine, Cassia. I just really like you."

I talk over him. "Don't—!" I wanted to say, "Don't call me that," but I stopped myself. *Thanks for the reminder I'm "Cassia" to you.* I continue, "You could be going out with someone tomorrow, and I wouldn't know—or care."

Would I care?

"I'm not going out with someone tomorrow." His voice remains composed despite the irritation growing in mine.

"But you could."

"But I'm not."

"But you could!"

He holds his hands up as if I've pointed a gun at him. "Okay!"

Am I trying *to sabotage this so I don't have to deal with it?* In that same moment, Cassia leaves me. She takes my breath away, as always, but somehow, she's also ripped out part of my chest this time.

It hurts.

I try to hold back my wincing, but I can't help but grab my chest and squeeze my eyes shut.

"Whoa. What's wrong?"

I try several times to take a deep breath, leaning over a bit.

"Cassia? You okay?" Benson has stepped forward and grabbed my elbows…and called me *Cassia* again.

I finally manage to shudder in a breath and open my eyes. I whisper to his feet, "Yeah."

"Are you sure?" His thumb and forefinger pull my chin up to meet his worried gaze, but a look of confusion blinks onto his face. "Your eyes are hazel now. They were blue before."

"No. My eyes are hazel," I answer, confused.

He shakes his head. "No, they're not."

I squint at him. "I think I know my own eye color. They're hazel."

"Well, they've been blue every time *I've* seen you," he says.

This hits me like a ton of bricks; it almost takes my breath away again. Every time I've been with Benson, Cassia's been with me. She must have blue eyes. I'm more Cassia than I ever realized. I gasp and try to think back, try to think if I've ever looked in the mirror at myself while she was with me. Nothing stands out.

Surely, I've caught a glimpse of myself in the rearview mirror when driving, haven't I? What about the bathroom?

Then again, maybe this is something newer. Something within the past month. Something for Benson.

Then Benson adds, "They must change with your mood or something."

My mood?

My mood!

Is it possible to want to cry *and* punch him in the throat?

I slap his hand away from the tender hold on my chin.

His face suggests, *What the hell?*

I take the opportunity to turn and open my car door.

He's swift to grab my elbow before I get in. "Wait! I'm sorry." I truly think he's being genuine in trying to figure me out.

Ha! Good luck with that one, Benson.

I pivot and shift my weight to one hip, a universal sign of annoyance.

His eyes grow wide. "What is going on? How am I the bad guy here?"

I look to the sky, although I don't know why—Cassia's not coming back. Not like she's from above anyway. Who knows where the hell she comes from?

I stare up at him, collecting myself, and slowly exhale. I *am* the strangest girl he'll *ever* know. When I speak, I'm calm, and my tone is smooth. "You're not. That's the problem," I tell him. I needed something bad, but he's great. Amazing, actually.

His forehead creases. "I don't understand that. At all."

I scoff. "I don't expect you to."

We stare at each other for a long five seconds. His eyes have become hard. That ocean *can* get rough.

Then I move forward and kiss him.

Softly.

With eyes open.

We're not touching anywhere else, just our lips.

Cassia's not here. Will he kiss the hazel-eyed girl back?

Although his expression has softened, he does *not* kiss the hazel-eyed girl back. And that's exactly what I need. I pull back.

"Explain it to me," he says.

"I don't…It's…" Tears are forming in the corners of my eyes. *Don't do it, Camry.*

"Complicated?"

I was thinking *unexplainable*, but complicated works too. "Yeah."

He hesitates. "Can…I have your number?" He asks the question awkwardly as if he's never asked a girl for her number before. Actually, I wonder if he ever has. After all, he was a gentleman about the kiss; maybe he waits for the girl to offer her number too.

"No," shoots out of my mouth.

His expression says, *Really? Are you kidding?* Then he says, "So I'm just supposed to let you go? Let the most beautiful girl I've ever met walk away? Forget about the most incredible date I've ever had?" He flings his hand each time he asks a new question, and each time the waves in his eyes crash, I can feel it in my chest.

He really thinks those things? I want to apologize, but it'd be a slap in the face, and I already slapped his hand. I have no answers to his questions, and I feel like I'm not only the strangest girl he's ever known but the most horrible.

His eyes begin to plead as he examines my expression, waiting for *something*.

I stare back. Normally a situation like this would make me shy away and want to flee. Maybe Cassia is close and somehow keeping me here and staring back. I don't know. I'm mesmerized, though. Benson isn't acting how I'm used to a guy acting when things get heated. He's begging me without words. Ashton would be arguing back. He'd be raising his voice and saying the word "stupid" a lot. Benson doesn't only want to understand, he *needs* to understand. It'll affect the rest of his night if he doesn't. In fact, it'll probably affect the next week for him. And it'll be all my fault. I don't know what I can say to help this, so I drop my head and turn to go.

His response is an exaggerated sigh. Then he says, "Gimme your phone."

I turn back. *Huh?*

"Give…me…your…phone." His hand is out.

I place my hand on the little square pocket of fabric that rests on my hip from a thin strap across my chest. It holds my wallet, some makeup, a tampon, and my phone.

"I want to give you my number." His fingers wave upside down.

I hesitate but give in. It'll be better than leaving the way I was going to a second ago. His fingers brush mine when he takes it.

As he inputs his number, he says, "And I want you to call me and explain it to me whenever you sort it out."

He's relaxed enormously in the last ten seconds. Me relinquishing my phone must give him unsurmountable hope. At his kindness, I feel a grin creep up on my face, but I whip it back into shape before he lifts his eyes off my phone.

He holds on to it when I try to take it back. I look up to see the crooked smile has made its appearance once again. "I'm allowed to be a *little* jealous, ya know."

I yank it back. "It's not about that." *Didn't he listen to me?*

He cocks his head, and I get in my car, leaving him in a puzzle. A puzzle he'll never complete. He doesn't have all the pieces.

On the drive home, I don't feel Cassia around me. I'm pretty sure I ticked her off. But I let her have most of the night as far as conversation, and I let her partake in the kiss. I can't let her have total control; that was way too bizarre when she did that before. I didn't enjoy that at all. I feel bad, but I shouldn't. I shouldn't be sorry. I was doing her a favor. Well, I sort of got roped into that whole thing, but it has to end now.

"Something fun first." Look how that turned out. *Oh, how I hate feeling like this.*

As I replay the night, I realize a small part of me really does like Benson. But I can't get over the fact he doesn't like *me*. Yeah, he said I'm beautiful, but that's not all a relationship is about. What he knows is Cassia's *right*-handed when *she* bowls, Cassia's funny in a way that I can only *wish* to be, Cassia knows architecture terminology, and Cassia has *blue* eyes. And what about Jake? I want to give that a fair chance.

I walk into my apartment. I can't even recall the drive home. Apparently, I pushed the autopilot button. *Did I even fasten my seatbelt?* "Come on, Cass. Where are you?" I scan my apartment as if I'm going to see her.

I *feel* her, though. In a different way. She *is* here. I can sense her. I'm getting better at that. Or maybe she's becoming more obvious on purpose; I don't know.

"Seriously, Cass!"

I toss my purse on the counter. It slides off, and everything falls out. *Suck!* I kneel to pick it all up. Standing, I set the purse and the stuff that was in it on the counter.

I feel Cassia pass through me. Slowly. Slowly enough to give a thought to me: *You need time to cool off. I'll come back later.* And then she's gone; I'm alone in my apartment.

I heard her without her speaking through me. That was odd and remarkable and chilling all at the same time. I stand there absorbing the minutes. I do need time to cool off. Replacing the items in my purse, I find the note from Jake again. This'll help me simmer down.

I'm sitting up in bed, watching Netflix and struggling to stay awake. I started off tall; now I'm slouching and leaning on my pillows with heavy eyes.

Where is Cassia? It's almost midnight.

Suddenly, I feel her, as if my thinking of her did summon her this time. She's simply in my room, but I sense her, like when you notice someone coming up behind you. (Unless that someone is Ninja Trisha.) I guess this is how it is with Cassia now.

I turn off my TV and tell her, "I'm not mad." I tingle as she settles into my body.

She says nothing.

"You were right, though. I did need a minute. I'm sorry. I thought a lot about this while you were gone. I went too far. I got caught up in the moment. I do like him…but you're the one he likes, and I can't be you forever."

"I know," she says.

"And it'd be weird to tell him now all the stuff you said isn't true."

"I know."

"You have to let him go."

"I tried. And then you kissed him."

"What?!" I screech.

"That's why I started telling him we weren't going to keep bowling. I was trying to let him know things are…stopping."

I roll my eyes and tilt my head to the ceiling. *Oh boy. How'd I miss that?*

She laughs. "But then you kissed him, and I thought, 'Okay, I guess we're kissing him. I can go with this.'"

She keeps laughing, but I'm embarrassed and don't want to laugh about this, so I cover my face with my pillow to shut her up. *I feel terrible. What have I done?!*

She pulls the pillow off, tossing it to the side. "What you've done is…enjoy a kiss with a guy you like. And you also broke his heart." She says this almost matter-of-factly, but at the end, there's a hint of *How could you?* "I mean, I was going to crack it, but then you went and totally broke it."

"Whoa, whoa, whoa. You think whatever you would have done would have been any better?"

She's got nothing.

"And I didn't *totally* break it," I argue. I really believe this; he gave me his number and said he was jealous. He gave me my stupid girl-drama moment, and he's letting me have some time. Because he's a decent guy who, apparently, is familiar with girl drama. I add, "He's just *totally* confused."

"*Pfft.* You have no intentions of texting or calling him and no intentions of seeing him again, so it *is* broken."

She's right, I have no intentions, but I say, "No matter what, tonight wasn't going to end well. I thought you could see that." I don't want to play the blame game with Cassia. We could go back and forth all night. If she had come to visit me, I wouldn't have even gone to the bowling alley. If she had told him at the beginning of the date instead of the end, maybe we would have avoided all the stuff in the middle—all the stuff that, to him, made it the most incredible date ever. If I hadn't gone as far as kissing him, we'd maybe be fine now. On and on and on…

It's all pointless. What's done is done.

We quietly sit for a while. I feel like she does want to argue these points, but she's holding back. I ask, "Are we good?"

She rubs my hand. "Yes," she says in a tone you give your parents when you have to agree even though you don't want to.

I toss the covers off me, fling my legs out of my bed, and start walking to the bathroom. I *have* to see Cassia's eyes, the eyes that Benson sees whenever he looks at us. Flipping on the light, my reflection reveals myself in my pajamas with my hair in a bun on top of my head and blue eyes looking back at me. *Oh. My. God.* I lean toward the mirror and really study them. They're a touch lighter than Benson's, with lots of wavy lines and dark-blue edges. "Did you know this was happening?" I ask her.

"No," she says with amazement. She lets it be another few seconds and then adds, closing my eyes, "It's freaky."

I pry them back open. The eyes are the window to the soul, they say. What do I see when I look into the eyes of my friend, the dead girl? They're beautiful, but they're missing something. A sparkle. A light. Maybe it's there when we're having our adventures or when we're with Benson, but it's not here now. Still, there is a kindness and softness to them, along with an intelligence I can't put my finger on. A sensible type of intelligence, maybe.

I stand erect again and just observe myself. *Do I still look like me, or does this change my entire look? Am I still Camry, just with blue contact lenses or something?* Hmmm, I can't decide.

"Can we go back to bed?" Cassia asks. "This is weird."

"No," I tell her. "Leave my body and come back." I want to see the change.

She purses my lips but accommodates me.

Whoa! Just, whoa! Things don't change in the blink of an eye. It reminds me of oil spilled in the ocean. My hazel spreads from the pupil, not quite as thick looking as oil but somewhat slow and uneven. My right eye takes longer to complete the change, finally meeting all the edges after almost ten seconds; it aligns with the tingle sensation I get. As Cassia comes back, the transformation is quicker, still starting from the pupil, though, just spreading in probably half the time.

"Huh," Cassia says.

I agree. "Yeah. Huh." I exhale, commit her look to memory, then hit the light.

Entering my room, I hesitate with my next question, but a deal's a deal. "Will you tell me your full name?" I seize a pen and paper and lie back in bed with my pillows propping me up.

She lets me settle in, then answers, "Cassia Jane Simonsen." I write it down, thankful I don't have to ask everything. She knows what I want to know and continues, "My father's name is Terrick. He's well known in the architecture world, especially in New York. My mom's name is JoAnna. She left when I was five. My dad told me she couldn't handle the city or…raising a kid." The last part is said with sadness.

"My stepmom is four years older than I am. Twenty-two. Honestly, four years, Dad! I was mad because he was spending all his time with her. And I didn't like her. I mean, I still don't." She scoffs.

"What's her name again?" I ask. She said it in the dream, but I'm not thinking of it now.

"Tiffanie."

I write this down, spelling it with a *Y.*

She corrects me, "It's with an I-E."

I fix it, and she goes on. "I ran away. Well, I didn't run away really. I was going to come back, but…" She pauses. There's a heavy hesitation here—a reluctance I've never felt from her before. "Maybe just Google my name."

I've wanted to Google her, but this entire time she'd never tell me her last name. That should've been one of my stipulations a long time ago, but anyway. I stand and step over to my computer. My bedroom shares space with my office, which is really just my desk and a two-drawer filing cabinet, but I like to say "office." I wiggle the mouse and click on the internet icon. I type her name, and there it is, article after article after article.

"Missing teen, Cassia Simonsen…"

"Daughter of Terrick Simonsen, world-renowned architect, still missing…"

"Still no trace of missing Manhattan teen…"

"Police searching Syracuse, New York, for missing teen…"

"Remains found are *not* the world-renowned architect's daughter…"

I didn't anticipate this. I thought perhaps a careless car accident or a freak case of pneumonia. I thought I'd be reading an obituary. Not…*this.*

She was murdered. *She was murdered!*

It had to be murder. What else could it be? Anything else would've had obvious evidence, like…a body. They haven't found her body.

There're video clips of her father as well. He's tall and fit and handsome with salt-and-pepper hair. He's the man from the dreams. He asks for his daughter to be brought home—swears he'll pay any ransom. A young and pretty blonde a little behind him sobs into a tissue. This is the stepmother; I recognize her from the dreams too.

As I read the articles and watch the video clips, my eyes start to water. It's partially me and partially Cassia. She leaves me. I don't think she likes listening to me read in my head. I can still sense her, though.

I turn to look behind me at my bed. There's no indication of anyone there, no dent in the duvet, but again, I sense her. The room feels sad. The sorrow bounces off the walls, giving the air a melancholic quality. My heart sinks into my belly, threatening to destroy me, churning my stomach. I don't have words for her. I don't know what to say. Her outcome is one of the worst things that can happen to a person. I think about my parents and what they'd be going through if I went missing and they had no clue what happened to me. I see why she delayed telling me, why she just wanted to get lost in the bucket list, why she can't even really tell me now; I'm looking on the internet for this part.

I think, *I'm so sorry, Cass.* It feels inadequate, nowhere near enough. I decide that was a lot for her *and* me. There's no way I can ask more of her tonight. In fact, I could use the weekend without her, and I think she could use the weekend without me. I don't mean to sound rude; I just know I'm the type of person this sort of stuff lingers with. Maybe after a couple of days, my thoughts won't be so off-putting for her. "Thank you. We'll talk more on Monday." I feel her energy through my center, and a sense of warm love overwhelms me. Then she's gone, leaving a feeling of emptiness not only in my room but a little bit in me too.

I start to skim through the articles. Antony Masterfield, doorman of her building, was the last person to see Cassia. On January 6, he reported he saw her leave the apartment building the day before at approximately 7:30 a.m. She was dressed in black slacks and a white blouse with a long black overcoat. She entered a taxicab and drove north.

Kate Matthews, best friend. An article also from January 6 quotes, "I've known Cassia all my life. She'd never run away. Something's not right. We just—we want her home. We love you, Cassia."

Travin Tucker, high school friend. The same article quotes him: "It's not in her to run away. I mean, she won't even go past ninety-sixth street. It just doesn't make sense."

Tiffanie Simonsen, stepmother. A different article from the same date has more of the same types of comments Kate and Travin gave.

An article dated January 7 states an unnamed woman reports she thought she saw a girl who matched Cassia's photo on the same Greyhound bus she was on, headed to Syracuse, New York. However, after a particular stop in Castle Creek, New York, she was no longer on the bus.

Ryan Waters, police chief. Video clip also dated January 7: "With this new evidence, we're searching Castle Creek and the surrounding areas. We're doing everything in our power to find Cassia Simonsen. We ask that you respect the family's privacy in this difficult time. We don't have any suspects at this time. We're also working with the local police department in Syracuse…"

Terrick Simonsen, father. Video clip from January 8: "I want my daughter back. Please bring her back to me. Bring her home. Name your price, and I'll pay it. Just, please…"

JoAnna Simonsen, mother in Syracuse, New York. No quotes. An article states she left her husband and daughter thirteen years ago and has been living in Syracuse ever since. She has been and is currently being treated for depression. She hasn't remarried and has no other children. She is recently unemployed.

I'm getting the gist of it. I click the images tab, and there she is. My breathing halts as if it's been stolen from me, and goosebumps appear all over my body. I click on several of the photos to enlarge them. Cassia, surprisingly, looks a lot like me: slender figure, long dark hair, oval-shaped face, and almond-shaped eyes—except hers are a brilliant blue that Benson sees every time he looks at us. They have the wavy lines and dark-blue edges I just stared at in my own bathroom mirror. I rub my arms, but the goosebumps remain. This is "freaky" and "weird," just like Cassia said. I see now why she said it. *How come she hasn't ever mentioned how much we look alike? What does that mean?*

I print off a portrait of her and tape it on the wall next to the window so I can see it from my desk *and* my bed.

There are two Camrys in the world: the one with hazel eyes and the one with blue eyes.

I regard the photo for a long time before reviewing the articles again. Her smile is more brilliant than mine, I think. It's part of what makes her so beautiful. I force myself to read all the articles in their entirety and in order. I even print them off, staple them, and highlight the dates and names of family and friends.

I don't sleep until after four o'clock in the morning.

Saturday, August 14

I wake up with a kink in my neck from sleeping on my desk and see a note from Cassia.

I won't be going to the concert with you and Jake. It should be a time for just the two of you, and I want that for you. Please don't be upset. Just enjoy yourself. Love, Cassia.

I'm stunned.

Then I have a strange thought. If she can write a note to me in my sleep, why didn't she sleepwalk me over to my comfortable bed so I wouldn't have a kink in my neck? But back to the point. *I can't believe she's not going to come to the concert! Is she going to come at all before then?*

I left the lid off the highlighter, and now it's dried out. I chuck it in the garbage and get ready for the day, watching my hazel eyes in the mirror longer than normal as I put on my makeup.

Finding myself trying to solve Cassia's case, I realize I need to talk to her. *Where's her body? What happened? Who killed her, and why?*

Just like most stories such as hers, there are several articles the first couple of weeks after the disappearance, then it becomes old news, and not much follow-up can be found. I think the difference here is her dad has the money to continue a high-profile investigation. But maybe it's not like movies and television. New York City is a busy place with multiple murders and kidnappings in a day, I'm sure. Why would Cassia be any different?

And what about Christmas in New York? We didn't get to that either. Until we actually talk about it, I can't even bring myself to start looking at prices on the internet.

In a way, I regret telling her to take the weekend off. I sort of want some more answers now. *Pace yourself, Camry. And give her more time also. Remember, it's for her as well.*

The afternoon is coming to an end, and all I've done is catch up on my shows. Well, I take that back; I went for a jog this morning—like a real, actual jog—before the outside oven reached its maximum. Because I was going crazy thinking of Cassia, and because *damn my routines*. It was time to make a new one. An inconsistent routine. Boom! Done! Jogging outside on a Saturday. Just like that.

But looking at the mountain made me think of Cassia. And even though there aren't as many as in Manhattan, lots of people walk in Salt Lake, which made me think of Cassia too. And as I passed people, I wondered if they had a spirit of a dead girl in them, needing them too. And every dark-haired guy I passed made me think of Benson. It wasn't the point of going for a jog, to say the least.

Mrs. Halman was sitting outside when I got back home. She stopped me with an arthritic hand. "You all right, dear? You seem troubled."

"I'm fine, Mrs. Halman. I just went for a run is all."

"You haven't been dancing like you used to."

"No." I rested my hands on my hips, taking deep breaths. *She's noticed that? Interesting.* "No, I haven't. I've been helping someone."

"Well, that's all good and fine as long as you take care of you first. You're no good to anyone if you're not good to yourself."

She made sense, but I told her, "Running is still good exercise, maybe even better."

"Yeah, but up here is what I mean." She points to her head. "I'm an excellent listener if you need one."

"Thanks, Mrs. Halman."

So now I'm sitting on my bed, watching TV but not really watching TV. *Because how could Mrs. Halman notice something was off with me?* She was a teacher, which I suppose gave her a keen eye; she's very practiced at noticing a troubled student. *But am I that obvious?*

Ugh! How did this whole thing start? I think back to the beginning. Not just Cassia and all the weirdness, but me. What was *I* thinking?

Once I started to understand Cassia was real and I wasn't totally insane, I literally was thinking how I genuinely wanted to help her, but also how I wanted to be the person to say yes. That's sort of been my motivation through all this, that stupid lesson from two semesters ago. But there was more to that lesson. More than just "change your thoughts and do things out of love." *What was it?* Something about the universe.

Self-correction, that was it.

Everything happens for a reason. *Do I believe that?*

I know I'm supposed to help Cassia; I can feel that in my bones.

But why have I met Benson? I don't know that one.

Jake, on the other hand, saved my life. That *has* to mean something. I was planning to go see him today anyway. I just was feeling sort of weird about it all, considering all the Benson crap. But Mrs. Halman's words echo in my head. *You're no good to anyone if you're not good to yourself.* Every once in a while, I need to be the girl who says yes for me and not for someone else. I *am* "troubled," and I'm pretty sure Jake can help get my mind off all this "troubling" crap. I haven't texted or called him. I thought about it, but I'm going to be the girl who unexpectedly surprises him at work like I originally wanted to do on Wednesday. I need to thank him and tell him I'm doing better in person. Also, I should confirm our date; it's one week from yesterday. Jake did more than he needed to in making sure I was all right, and I can't help but feel like he's a *yes* I definitely shouldn't pass up.

I realize I'm not sure of his shift; I didn't ask the other guy what time he works. I make a purchase and take my chances. Walking over to the ticket counter, I find he's there. He does a double take as he sees me approach.

His smile shows off his perfectly straight teeth, something I didn't notice before, perhaps because he never smiled at me that first day, and the next day, I was out of it. He extends his arms as if he's speaking to the entire store. "You're all better!"

I smile as well. "Thanks to you." I toss a bag of individually wrapped Life Savers to him, and he catches it with one hand. I know it's a lame attempt, but how do you thank someone for saving your life? How do you ever repay them? I'll owe him forever. Every day that I wake up and breathe air is a day I have because of Jake. This fact makes me feel strange. I'll always be in debt to him. The only way to get out of this kind of debt is to save his life too.

I'm at the counter now. He chuckles at my gift and thanks me excitedly. "And you look beautiful. How *are* you?"

I shy my eyes away and think how *I'm* average; *he's* the beautiful one. "Good," I respond. I reach for my head. "Stitches come out on Monday."

He glances at my hairline but doesn't comment, then he stares at me. It's a thoughtful stare but long enough that I begin to feel uncomfortable.

"What? Do I have a booger?" I ask, sniffing.

He chuckles, his eyes lighting up. "No, I'm just…glad you came to see me. I wasn't expecting you to come. I thought maybe you'd text. This is a nice surprise."

"Well, I promised your mother, so…"

"Ah." He nods.

"Thanks for the tickets. I feel like it should be the other way around; I should be buying *you* a gift."

He pulls open the bag of Life Savers and takes out two. "You did," he says, gesturing to the bag and offering me one; they're the mint kind.

I take it but shake my head at his comment. "That's just a token of my appreciation, as they say." For some reason, I shy away again. "I don't know how I can ever do enough…"

"Camry, don't worry about it."

At the sound of my name off his lips, the butterflies in my gut flutter around and tickle my insides.

"I wanna go with you, and like I said, you shouldn't go to a concert like that alone. Just"—he points a finger at me—"don't get injured between now and then. Please."

I think about how I've chosen a three-quarter sleeve shirtdress to conceal the nasty purple bruise in the shape of a horse's mouth on the back of my arm. "I'll try not to. It's just been…a crazy summer."

"Well, I would think so. After your story about the bird and then what happened last week. I can only imagine."

Something about this exchange triggers a memory of what Benson hit me with the other night ("your list of attacks"), but it's not until now I'm feeling the effect of the blow. It's not just strange animal incidences; I've been getting hurt a lot lately, considering I've never broken a bone or needed stitches in my life. I mean, there's the bird and the bee and the horse, but before that, I sprained my ankle and tore myself up falling down cement stairs on campus—the reason I cut classes. And after that, I cut my hand slicing cheese; it probably needed stitches, but I didn't want to go to the doctor. Then there was the car accident—the first concussion. I'm so thrown off by these thoughts I have to consciously pull myself back into the conversation. "I'm excited about the concert. It'll be fun."

"Yeah." He stammers a little bit. "I can pick you up at your house if you want. I just wasn't sure if I'd talk to you before then. Thought meeting here would be easier."

"Meeting here's fine," I say. He nods, and it's awkwardly silent for a second. I'm still a little lost in my thoughts. "Well, I just wanted to thank you again and let you know I got your note." I pull away from the counter.

"Hey, wait. I get off in a few minutes. You wanna get some food? What're you doin' right now?"

"Oh, sorry. I'm going bowling with my friend, Ca—" I shake my head. "Wait! No, I'm not. Not today. So yeah." *That was odd. Was I seriously going to say, "with my friend, Cassia"? I never talk to anyone about her.*

He smirks. "Cool. Well, chat with me more while I wrap things up. Watch out for bees, though. I think there's a nest somewhere around here," he jokes.

I laugh. "Shut up."

Smiling to himself, he moves some papers to a drawer, then clicks around his computer. "What kind of food do ya like?"

"Um, I like most things. Except octopus." *He needs to know that's a "no."*

He side-eyes me but doesn't get a chance to ask about it because a customer comes up behind me.

I move out of the way for a man who fits the bill for a rock concert. "Sorry. We're just chatting." Then I look at Jake. "I'll come back."

He smiles at me with a "'kay."

I decide to busy myself looking at magazines until I can meet Jake back at the counter. As I skim articles about Lady Gaga and the latest Kardashian tiff, I catch myself thinking back to the articles about Cassia, which makes me revert back to the odd timing of my injuries. She disappeared on January fifth, and I swear I sprained my ankle, like, the eighth. *Did my injuries really begin after Cassia's death? Does that mean anything, or am I just having a stream of bad luck?*

Argh! I so need to avoid this disturbing topic in my head right now and focus on something I think I can understand—Jake. I glance from the magazine over to his counter. The customer is gone, and Jake is talking with a coworker, the one from the other day. I waltz back over to him.

"There she is," he announces to the guy next to him, or possibly to no one in particular. "Camry, this is Jake." He motions to his coworker. "Jake, this is Camry."

The other Jake nods to me. "Hello again," he says, then turns to Jake with comically wide eyes. "Was gonna tell ya. That girl visited you the other day. You know, the one whose life you saved." He nods sideways in my direction.

"Your name's Jake too?" I ask.

"You came to visit me the other day?"

The other Jake nods to me, and I nod to my Jake. *Huh. My Jake.*

"Bet that's confusing sometimes," I say, waggling my finger between the two of them.

"Yeah," they say in unison.

Then my Jake grins at me in such a sincere way, like I've pleasantly surprised him. *Go, me.* He pats his pockets, checking he has all his things. Then he grabs a small handful of the Life Savers out of the bag and leaves them on the counter for the other Jake, taking the rest for himself. He looks at me. "You ready?"

I nod, and we both say goodbye to Jake Number Two.

He barely touches the small of my back to guide me from the store. The oh-so-gentle connection sends a shiver up my spine.

"No other accidents, I see. Good job."

"Not in the last ten minutes, no." I'm not going to tell him about the horse; it'd mean explaining how it happened, which would mean telling him I was on another date with another guy just the night before.

Jeez, was that just *last night?* I feel like a mountain of things has happened since then. I was on top of Cassia's pile of information (which was only half of it), having no idea what to do with it and feeling way too unstable up there as it was. Like I said, I was going to come visit Jake anyway, but it's all very fortunate timing because I'm halfway back to level ground now with him. I'm feeling better already.

Jake leads me outside. He has a truck too—a Tacoma, newer than Benson's. *Stop it, Camry. Don't compare him to Benson all night.*

He opens the door for me, and I climb into the truck as I mentally climb down more of Mount Cassia. Forcing Benson's Silverado out of my mind, I take a deep meditating breath in through my nose and out my mouth. *Get off that mountain.*

Jake gets in, and I ask, "Where are we eating?" I only had a snack for lunch, and I'm absolutely starving.

"Do you like Mexican food?"

"Yes."

"I thought we'd go over to The Mayan and watch the divers."

"Oh, cool. I haven't been there in a while," I say. "Last time I went there was for my sixteenth birthday."

"How old are you now?" he asks.

"You looked at my driver's license." I side-eye him with a smirk. "I'm eighteen."

As he twists his body toward me with his left hand on the steering wheel, his eyes light up, and he says mischievously, trying not to smile, "Happy birthday tomorrow."

My face falls. *What's today's date?* "Oh my gosh! That *is* tomorrow." I laugh at myself. "I totally forgot." *Yeah, I'm so distracted, I totally forgot my own birthday. What is wrong with me?*

He laughs, too, as he studies me. "You seriously forgot your own birthday?"

I cover my eyes, embarrassed, not only because I forgot, but because *he* knows…and we're going out to eat and…*Argh!* "In all fairness"—I hold up a finger—"I probably would have remembered by tomorrow."

"Probably?"

I rock my head from side to side and shrug. "Okay, maybe not. I've got a lot on my mind." It comes out defensive at the end.

He snorts. "You mean more than just stitches?"

"Oh, ha ha." I glare at him teasingly.

"No, I know. You've had a rough couple of weeks."

He's talking about my accidents, but that's not what I was thinking about. He's right, though. There's that too. Again, a mountain of stuff! Unstable Camry!

"So let's get your mind off it a little bit." He shifts his truck into reverse, and we go. "What day did you come to visit me?"

"Uh, Wednesday. Jake Number Two helped me find the tickets."

He turns onto the main road from the parking lot, chuckling. "How 'bout Jake Miller? Number Two sounds…gross."

"Got it. And you're Jake Clark."

"Yep. You didn't see them?"

"The tickets? You kind of hid them."

"Ya think?"

"Yeah."

"Oh. Sorry."

Embarrassment hits me. I'm not only the girl he had to save, but I'm the girl who's too mindless to notice the gift he gave me. "Thanks. Again."

He comes to a stop behind traffic at a red light and peers over at me. "Camry, you don't have to keep thanking me."

My gaze falls to my lap. "I just…feel weird about the whole thing. And it doesn't help I don't even remember my birthday and you do and…" I don't know what I'm saying. I don't want it to sound like I'm feeling sorry for myself. I'm just seriously weirded out and don't know how to act.

"You suffered a concussion. You're allowed to forget a couple of things. But you remembered to come see me. Twice." I can hear his smile. He leans a bit, pulling his wallet from his pocket. He hands it to me as the light turns green.

I take it, uncertain of why he's giving it to me.

"Look through it. Maybe it'll help you feel less weird."

I hand it back to him. "I'm not gonna look through your wallet."

He doesn't take it. In fact, he shifts his weight, leaning his elbow on the door panel and changing to his right hand for steering. "Come on. At least my driver's license." He quickly reaches to open it up within my hand and points to his license.

I glance at it with a deep inhalation. "Jake Mathew Clark," I read. "Blond hair, green eyes, five-eleven, one fifty. December fourteenth, a year and a half older than me. Donor? Yes."

"Feel better?"

I close the wallet and hand it back to him but don't know how to answer. I'm not sure how I feel.

"Are you a donor?" he asks.

"Yeah."

"It's kinda weird, huh? The thought someone else might have one of your organs in their body if you die."

Maybe for the first time, I really think about this. "It is," I agree. I've never known anyone who died. I mean, my grandparents on my father's side passed away when I was little, so I barely remember it. My mom is estranged from her parents; I think they're still alive. There was a kid I went to school with who had cancer and passed away, but he was two years older than me, and I didn't really know him. Cassia's situation is odd, but it's the only thing I have that makes me really think about death in a way I haven't before. She was young, healthy, and perhaps had the capital *Y* on her driver's license, just as Jake and I do, signifying she was a donor. I think about Cassia's organs; they'll never go to someone in need. They're lost with the rest of her. They're gone. There's no miracle to be had there, or maybe I'm just not able to see it, according to Professor Gomm.

I'm distracted in my thoughts again, a little annoyed that almost anything can bring my thoughts back to her.

"I realize you literally almost died the other day. I don't know why I brought that up. I'm sorry." His face flashes a look of concern in my direction.

Huh. He's right, but I wasn't thinking of myself. "No. No, I'm fine. Are you going to school for something medical like your mom?"

"Nah. That's not really my thing. I mean, I could go that direction; I took a lot of classes for that path, but…it's like a plan B." He thinks about what he just said and adds, "Or C or D."

"Ah," I reply. "So what *is* your thing then?"

"Music. I love producing music. It's one of those things, though—if you don't know someone already in the industry, it's kind of hard to succeed."

"I can understand that," I comment.

"Right now, I just work with locals. New ones, mostly. People who maybe have written a song or have an idea they just need help with. I have a studio in my basement. Word of mouth seems to be keeping me busy enough."

"That's amazing." I try to say it with meaning because I *really* think it's amazing, but I'm afraid it comes out ordinary. I move on, saying, "So do you go to school for that? I don't know anything about that sort of thing."

He shrugs. "Yeah. Well…I've taken some online courses. What about you? Are you going to school? What's your thing?"

I peek out my window at the passing buildings and traffic, unsure of how to answer his questions. "I…Well…I'm a dancer, but I'm taking some time off from that." He glances at me but doesn't comment. "I've done two semesters at the U and…I don't know. I can't decide, I guess."

He nods, understanding, then asks, "What kind of dance?"

"All kinds. Ballet. Modern. Jazz. You know."

His eyes amusingly pop open. "Break dancing?"

I laugh. "Technically, I *can* do some of that, but I don't love it."

We arrive at the restaurant. It's reasonably busy, but with a whisper and, I suspect, a charming smile, Jake manages to get us seated quickly. He softly pushes the small of my back to follow the hostess, who leads us to one of the best tables in the restaurant. It's directly in front of the beautiful pool of water and the cliffs from which the divers will be diving. It's humid, being so close to the water, and a bit loud, but I know it'll be worth it. The pool glows a soft sea green from lights below the surface, and the cliffs are illuminated with red lights, creating a warm radiance. Green foliage hangs off the rocks next to the numerous mini waterfalls. It strikes me that The Mayan is a somewhat fancy restaurant. This is more than just getting a quick bite to eat. It may have been spontaneous, but throw in my birthday, and this is a full-on date.

They mess up my order. I have no intention of complaining.

"Didn't you order a steak burrito?" asks Jake, poking his fork at his rice.

"Yeah, but it's fine. I'll eat chicken too."

"Are you sure? I can totally grab the waitress." He begins to raise his hand.

I stop him. "No. It's fine. Really."

The divers begin, and I cringe almost every time they jump, thinking they're going to smash their heads into the rock *this* time.

No, *this* time.

Maybe *this* time.

Such a dangerous job.

I finally pull myself back to my food. Even Jake was distracted for a minute. "It makes me nervous to watch them, but they *are* incredible," I remark.

"I know, huh?" Jake responds. "My friend used to dive here. He loved it."

Hmm, maybe that's how we got in so quickly, with a great table to boot. I ask, "Were there ever any accidents while he worked here?"

"Yeah, he hit his foot one time on one of the rocks. There was a girl who slipped and hit her head, but she was fine. Nothing really bad, but it's kinda one of those things where…it's like eventually, *something* is gonna go wrong, ya know?"

The old "if you play with fire, you're bound to get burned" saying. I nod and mentally apply this possibility to Cassia and me. *Are we like that? Eventually, something's going to go wrong? Is it already going wrong?* I shake the thought away. *Why does she keep popping into my head?* She's like Whac-A-Mole.

I hammer her down and ask, "So what sort of music do you like to make?"

"Well, when it comes to producing music for a customer, I have to go with what they want." He halfway rolls his eyes as if he doesn't always love that part of the job. "But for myself…" He twists his fork in his fingers, thinking. "I'll have to let you listen sometime. What kind of music do you like to dance to?"

I've taken a bite and have to swallow before I answer. "I'll dance to whatever is on the radio. The type of dance, though, depends on my mood." I think about this. "I usually end up with a mix of ballet and modern."

"So you could end up dancing ballet to…Neon Trees?"

I nod.

"The Used?"

I nod.

"Chevelle?"

"Yep. Whatever's on the radio. It's sort of a thing I do."

Jake and I talk excitedly about a lot of music, the types of music we like and the types we don't like. I talk about songs I've performed to; he talks about people he's worked with. We talk effortlessly and have similar tastes. I never had a conversation like this in the nine months I dated Ashton.

Jake and I have a startling connection. It's a connection I don't have with Benson. Bowling is supposed to be the connection there. *Benson* thinks it is. And it *is*, in a way. He also thinks there's a connection as far as architecture, but that is also with Cassia and not me. I do love his sense of humor, though. Thinking of Benson makes me think of Cassia again. I wonder if she's nearby, eavesdropping as I sit and enjoy a meal with another guy.

Jake interrupts my thoughts with a question. "Do you sing?"

I'm a little thrown off. The question seems to come out of nowhere. Did he run off to left field? I curse myself for letting my thoughts wander. I guess I was the one in left field. *What was he talking about before the question?*

He starts to repeat himself, probably assuming I didn't hear him.

"No," I say, then correct myself. "I mean, a little, I guess. For fun. It's been a while."

"What? Like high school choir girl or somethin'?" His lips curl a little, and I bet he's imagining me on stage singing Christmas carols to an audience of supportive friends and family.

"Yeah." I cut a bite. "And the musicals."

He gazes thoughtfully and guesses, "Mezzo-soprano?"

I raise my eyebrows. "Very good. But aren't most people?" I lean toward my straw and take a swig of my lemonade.

He shrugs. "You should come sing for me. I've been looking for someone like you. I wrote a song, a duet, actually."

I set my fork down, incredibly impressed. "Really?"

He takes a bite and nods.

"That's so"—I pause to search for the best word but can only think of—"cool."

"Mmmm." He takes a drink. "Only if I have a mezzo-soprano."

"How long have you been lookin'?"

"Just started."

I shake my head. "You meet so many people who can sing; chances are one of them's a mezzo-soprano."

"True. I know other people. But…"

I stare at him. "But what?"

He brings his hands together in front of his chin, elbows resting on the table. He stares back. "I don't know. Something tells me I should ask you."

I fork the bite but leave it on the plate. "Seriously. I'm out of practice. I'm probably not the one for you."

"Or…" He's thoughtful again, bringing his arms to cross in front of his plate. "You could be perfect for me."

The butterflies dance in my stomach again, and I can't help but shy away with a grin.

"Just practice your voice. You can come over to my house sometime, and I'll play the song for ya. You can say no if you don't want to sing it. It won't hurt my feelings."

It's an invitation that makes me both uncomfortable and excited. I was a fair singer in choir—only got one solo because Kayla was absolutely amazing—but still…fair. *Good thing Jake doesn't know Kayla. She'd be perfect for his duet.*

With little shrugs here and there, I see he's attempting to downplay his passion for music, but it shines through in his eyes and in his smile. A career in medicine *would* be a plan B. Or C or D.

Fear to love. I decide yes. After all, that's what I'm supposed to be doing, right? I tell him, "Okay, but don't get your hopes up."

He appears to be holding back a comment with a grin. Instead of sharing his words, he peers up at the next diver. I don't look, though. Even his profile, which completely shows off his amazing jawline, makes the butterflies flutter again. His eyes dart to mine and startle me into looking at the diver too. Just like my stomach, he performs a twist and three flips. But while the diver hits the water, smooth and perfect, my stomach continues its acrobatics every time I look at Jake.

As we finish, some waitresses bring over a plate of fried ice cream, complete with whipped cream and a cherry on top. They proceed to sing me a birthday tune while Jake claps along, and my humiliation grows. They leave us with two spoons, Jake's huge smile, and my flushed complexion.

We each scoop a spoonful. He holds his up in my direction. "Happy birthday," he says.

I bump his spoon with mine for a "cheers" and reply, "Thanks."

"Let me pay for mine, please," I say as the waitress takes our plates. I grab my cash.

He stares at me and huffs a breath out his nose. He takes the cash from me and drops it on the table for the tip. "Okay?" he asks.

"Okay." We stand, and again, he taps the small of my back to push me on, the point of contact recalling the memory from before and sending another shiver through me. I like it.

When we come out on the cement terrace, the sun is still high in the sky, with extra leverage for a beatdown of heat. Large cement cubes rise up on either side of us, and we walk down the path they've made. They display a multitude of colorful flowers…that, unfortunately, attract bees.

I don't even really think about it until one of them flies directly in front of my face, stopping me in my tracks. I hold back a squeal, only making a small squeak, and freeze solid as it circles my head repeatedly. It takes a moment for Jake to realize I've stopped walking with him and turn around.

I squeeze my eyes shut as he walks back to me. "Okay. Stay calm. It's going to be fine. Do you have your…injector thingy?" He begins shooing the nasty insect away, but it is re*lent*less.

I slightly shake my head. I can still hear it buzzing around me. It's all I can do not to run away, flailing like a deranged monkey.

"Well, why not?"

I want to shout, "*Because I'm a dipshit*!"

Eventually, he pushes against my back and tells me to walk. I do so, peeking out of one eye, but the buzzing is still torturing me. After several steps, it suddenly stops. "Hold on." Jake stops me.

I close my eyes again and hold my breath. He comes around to face me and blows a gentle breath on my collarbone. I realize there was a tickle there. The bee zips away, but I still can't move a muscle.

His fingers wrap around the backs of my arms, and he whispers, "Camry?"

I don't even want to move my mouth muscles. "Hmm?"

Still whispering, he says, "Breathe."

I peek again out of one eye, then look up at his stunning green gaze…and his smirk. Releasing my breath, I mutter, "Damn these beautiful flowers."

"Duly noted, I'll never buy you beautiful flowers." We both laugh. "You okay?"

"Yeah."

He puts a hand on my back. "I've gotcha." He walks me to his truck and opens the door for me. I'm so glad chivalry isn't dead. Both Jake and Benson have it. Their parents need a special trophy. But is it just something that's a thing when they're newly dating? Ashton was gentlemanly at first, too, but then it died off after about three months.

On the drive back to Smith's, he side-eyes me inquisitively and says, "So, after getting to know you more, you're not the type to like Korn. Even Chevelle is pushing it. Why do you want to go? And why would you go by yourself?"

"Well," I say, an octave higher than my actual voice. "That's a long story."

He watches traffic for an opening he can turn into. After the right-hand turn, he peers over at me in anticipation of the nice long story.

Yeah, right! "Ummm…how about we save that one for another time?"

"Oh." He sounds disappointed. "Would you…rather do something else? You know, other than the concert."

I think for a minute. I *would* rather do something else, but somehow it seems like I'd be betraying Cassia if I did. *And who knows? Maybe she'll come with me anyway.* "No. I think I still want to go."

He nods once, slowly. "So you've never been to a concert?"

"I've never been to a *rock* concert."

"Ah. Well, think about a place you want to eat because it'll be your choice next time."

We continue on the topic of what concerts he and I have been to, which gets us through the fifteen-minute drive back. I direct him through the parking lot. "Don't make fun of me, but it's the one that's silver and red," I say, pointing out my car.

"And maybe you can tell me why your car is two colors next time too." He chuckles, looking out my window at it.

I rub my head, thinking of that first concussion. "That one's easy. Drunk driver ran a red light. Unlucky me."

His eyebrows come together, worried. "Were you hurt badly?"

"Not really. I hit my head and was a little sore, you know, but…"

"I'm gonna have to keep my eye on you, huh?"

I shake my head with a small laugh. "I'm fine." I've stretched the truth about the accident. Memories of lying on my bed with a concussion-headache fill my mind. That's when Cassia found me. I open the truck door. "Thanks again for dinner. I'll see you on Friday."

He hesitates, then stutters. "Uh—or tomorrow. If you wanna go bowling with me."

I'm halfway out but turn abruptly and cock my head.

"You had talked about going with your friend. Thought maybe we could go. My cousin, Ben, works over there." He points in the direction of the bowling alley. "Haven't seen him in a while, but…"

In an instant, I feel my weird little world come crashing down with the force of tsunami waves as he says "Ben."

What are the chances there's a different Ben who works over there? Not like Jake and Jake at the ticket counter. Ben and Benson at the bowling alley? I don't think so! And cousin?!

"You okay?" Jake asks.

Suck, Camry. Lie better than you did last night with Benson. Don't let your face show any more than it already has.

No, I'm not okay. I'm absolutely far from okay. The distance is Pluto at this point. I do my best to come back to Earth, to correct my face back to normal, or as normal as it can get with this new knowledge. "Sorry, I really can't tomorrow." *Or ever, for that matter.*

"Oh." He shakes his head at himself. "We'll just stick with Friday."

"Okay." I fake a smile. "Thanks again."

I've heard the expression "Small Lake City" before, but I haven't encountered it until today. The thought consumes me as I drive home. *Benson and Jake are cousins.* That pretty much seals the deal—I can't be with either one of them.

Suck! I really like Jake. Do I still go out with him on Friday? Ugh!

I imagine a Christmas get-together and my two worlds colliding just as I collided with that good ol' drunk driver. I'd probably walk out of that collision the same as I did after the car accident—single and with a concussion.

No wonder they're both chivalrous. They're raised by the same type of people, the same blood. Is that the silver lining here? *That they'd be chivalrous while the whole thing went down?* That can't be it.

The small echo of my completely empty living room greets me. I never have company, so I don't need a sofa, and I prefer to watch movies in bed, so no TV either. Excitement filled me when I moved in because this apartment has hardwood floors throughout, except in the bedroom. It's perfect for my dancing. I bought a few cheap full-length mirrors and hung them low so I get the visual when dancing and can see that my form's correct.

My favorites to dance are ballet and modern. I *really* need to de-stress. I was doing so well, right up until the end there. I was nicely distracted from everything that's recently been stressing me out. I was feeling good about the start of Jake and me. And then it all went to pot. Hopefully, Mrs. Halman and the others won't mind the music. After stretching, I turn on my little radio in the corner, I vow to dance to whatever songs may come, like always. And like always, the warm wood welcomes my toes; it doesn't creak or groan as I jump and spin. It doesn't oppose me or deny me. It accepts me and allows me all the graces and mercies I need. It supports me in the strongest possible way.

After an hour, I wipe the sweat off my forehead with a small towel and call it quits. The dancing helped; I'm not thinking about *the cousins* as much.

I'm getting ready for bed after deciding not to even *look* at the articles on my desk. I'm not going to learn anything new. The only thing I know that the people in New York don't is Cassia *is* dead. For sure. And the only way I'm going to know more than that is if she tells me. So I climb into bed, relax, and ask for her. I don't expect her to come, but I'm almost asleep when she does.

"How about we talk about going *home* for Christmas?" Cassia doesn't want to talk about the articles, so this is what I've moved on to.

There are three kinds of people in this world: ones who can talk about something difficult, ones who need more time, and ones who can't at all. *Which is Cassia?* Definitely not the first one.

I sit up and go to my computer. After an hour of searching different travel sites, I'm discouraged. I don't see how I can budget in time for Christmas. The round-trip ticket is enough to max out my credit card, let alone a hotel, taxis, food—Cassia lived in Manhattan, for crying out loud. Hotels in Manhattan don't come cheap, or at least not cheap enough for me.

I don't know why, but the flying part makes me nervous. Maybe because I've never flown before. I haven't even been to Florida to see my parents' place. With my school and their vacations, it just hasn't worked out.

I sit back in my office chair and ask, "Do you want to see your dad, Cassia, or just be in New York for the holidays?" The more I mull over this, the more I just don't know.

She stops tapping my foot. At long last, she says, "Both, but…there's more too."

"More? Okay," I say and hold up a finger. "One thing at a time. You want to see your dad. How do you suppose that's going to happen? That's a long way to travel to stalk someone and see them from afar because I can't just ring the doorbell and have Christmas dinner with him, ya know." *Not only because I'm a stranger, but I look just like her, for Pete's sake!*

"I don't expect that," she says.

Another finger. "And second, be in New York for the holidays. A crazy busy time with obscene weather and a girl traveling by herself. I'm not sure how that's fun for either of us." She opens my mouth, but I stop her. "And what's the 'more'?"

"You've never been there, right?" She's avoiding my question, asking a different one as if she's trying to sell me on the whole idea.

Doesn't she understand she's already sold me? I'll do anything I possibly can for her, even after all that Benson crap. But what's the point of this for her? *No.* I answer her question in my head.

"I could give you the *best* tour," she argues.

"I'm not the one with a bucket list, Cassia," I argue back. It's not logical to go there for myself. And I don't want her to expect too much. She may be disappointed if things don't go as she plans, *whatever* her plans are; I'm still not clear on that.

I'm feeling overwhelmed between Cassia and all the websites. I switch gears, having a thought. "There's a travel agency down the street from the bowling alley. We can go there to see if they have better deals."

I hold up a finger. "But *only* when you tell me how you died and whatever the 'more' is. Okay?"

Again, another long wait. "Right now?" she asks.

"If you want." I sense the unwillingness. *Okaaay. Is a threat really not part of her combination?* "Or…whenever you're ready, I guess."

"Thank you, Camry." She's downright and thoroughly sincere.

People have told me I have the patience of a saint—really, I just don't want to argue. I rub my forehead, wanting to ask more about her dad, but I won't. I tingle upon her leaving, then fall asleep and dream about a plane crash. Waking up from it, I think how stupid our minds are.

Once I fall asleep again…

I'm in a taxicab. I'm dressed attractively, and I feel expensive. I pay the cab driver with cash.

The dream skips, and suddenly, I'm paying cash for a ticket at a bus station, and then I'm sitting in the back of a bus looking out the window. We pass through Pennsylvania and back up to New York. I enjoy glancing out at the smaller towns, but even Scranton and Birmingham are eye candy for me. They're something different from the cement jungle I'm so used to.

Eventually, the bus stops to get gas in the small town of Castle Creek. We've been on the road for almost four hours, so I take the opportunity to get out, stretch my legs, and buy a snack.

There hasn't been much on this stretch of I-81. For a while there, I had a view of the Chenango River, but that gave way to more trees. There's a small red house and an extra parking lot across the street with trees beyond that.

I find a spot on the other side of the bus to snack on my bag of dried mango slices before we have to go again. There's a large boulder I wipe snow off of and lean against. It's cold outside, probably only twenty-something degrees, but I don't care; I'll be warm again soon. For now, I just want to take a moment with some fresh air. There's half a foot of snow on the grassy areas with slush and pockets of ice in the parking lot. I regard the quaint little road as I pop another mango into my mouth.

Approaching footsteps from behind startle me. It's a man. A man all in black. He's dressed for business. He walks with purpose.

Does he need directions? I'm not the best person to ask. Does he think I need help or a ride?

He comes within inches of me, fast enough I don't have time to register he's a bizarre stranger entering my personal space, to register to get up and step away from him, like immediately. He pinches my backside.

What the hell?

I look down at the syringe. The wooziness comes a second later, and then I black out.

I jolt awake, sweating and heart pounding. I try to hang on to it: Castle Creek, gas station, the man dressed in black. The witness from the article was right. Cassia was on that Greyhound and never got back on after that stop.

What?

It takes me a minute to calm my breathing.

"Cassia?"

Nothing. My room is empty of her.

I realize Cassia is never going to be able to *tell* me what happened to her, but she can show me. I don't feel like that's the end. What's the rest of it? She cut it off, or maybe I was disturbed enough that *I* cut it off. I replay it in my head, upsetting the balance of my nerves and blood pressure. Who the hell was the guy? Just some sick sicko? Some whacked-out whacko? What did he do to her and why? My mind boards me on an unwanted train of thought of the twisted things that twisted individuals will do to a person. Eventually, I'm so completely unsettled I turn my TV back on and land on old episodes of *Friends* so I can derail my runaway train. It takes me three hours to fall back asleep, and when I do…no more dreams.

Sunday, August 15

I try to sleep in, but today is my birthday, so my parents call me. "Happy birthday!" their voices ring through the phone. It's 8:30 a.m., and I should be grateful they waited until 10:30 their time, but I could've easily slept until 10 or 11.

"What do you want for your birthday?" my mom asks.

"Ummm," I say groggily.

She continues, "I'm sorry I didn't plan better and have a package waiting on your doorstep. Time just got away from me. Sorry, your gift will be late."

I read between the lines. My mother is a procrastinator, and my father left the birthday shopping up to her because he doesn't see it as his job, and neither of them has any clue what to get me.

"You sound tired," my dad says. "Did you party late last night with your friends?"

"No, I just didn't sleep well. How was your trip?"

"Which one?" my mom asks.

They've taken another one? "Georgia."

"Oh, it was good," she says as simply as if I were asking her how her weekend was.

"Yeah, it was really good," my dad puts in with not much more emotion than her.

Okaaay then. "Where else did you go?"

"Washington, DC, which turned out to be really neat," she says, a notch more excited.

My dad adds, "Yeah, lots of cool history. You should go there sometime."

I ignore this comment because…*yeah.*

"Well, what do you need, kiddo?" my dad asks. "For your birthday, I mean."

"Food," I reply.

"Well, that's boring," my mom says at the same time my dad says, "Done." They begin to argue, and I close my eyes.

My mom doesn't understand how food can be a present. "How would we give food to her?" she asks.

"It's basically just giving her money. She can just go get what she needs."

More bickering about it being boring. Practicality doesn't seem to matter. This might be funny if I weren't *so* over this like five years ago.

My dad wins. Finally. "I'll transfer a couple hundred bucks for you to go shopping with."

"Thanks, guys."

They tell me, "Love you. Bye," and I do the same.

I try to get comfortable to fall back asleep again, but now the text messages have begun.

My friends have group texted me. It picks up from the Fourth of July when they tried to get me to come up for the festivities, but I actually hung out with Zach and Ashley from work instead.

Kayla: *Happy Birthday!*

Sienna: *Happy b-day! We love you!*

Lindsey: *Happy day you came out of a vagina!*

Me: *Thanks.*

Kayla: *We know you never do anything on Sundays or your birthday, so we're coming down.*

I think about arguing this point, but she's correct. I have no plans today.

Me: *What time?*

Kayla: *We'll be there by lunchtime. So don't eat lunch.*

Me: *Do you want me to meet you somewhere closer to you? I don't mind driving up to Ogden.*

There's a long pause.

Me: *We'll have more time to do stuff if I meet you halfway.*

Kayla: *OK. Meet us at Olive Garden at 11.*

Me: *OK*
Sienna: *Yay! I'm excited to see you.*
Lindsey: *Me too. I've forgotten what you look like.*
Lindsey: *Facebook hater.*

When I arrive at Olive Garden, Kayla and Sienna are already there, standing next to Kayla's blue Corolla. I'm right on time. Leave it to Lindsey to be late. It's her infamous trademark. We three have always joked about her being late to important future events. We'd create entire scenarios. Late to her own wedding, so late the groom leaves with me or Kayla or Sienna. Late for the birth of her kids, ending up delivering at home or in a car or at the grocery store. And of course, late for her own funeral, walking in like a zombie, crawling into her casket, and blowing everyone a kiss as she closes it. Yes, we were goofballs in high school.

Kayla comes in for a hug after tucking her blonde hair behind her ears. "Happy birthday to you!" she sings to me in a mocking opera voice, then notices my stitches. "What happened?"

I touch them. "Oh. We'll wait for Lindsey."

She rolls her eyes. "I even texted her to meet at ten thirty so she'd be here on time."

"She knows you do that," Sienna says. "She knows it's actually eleven." Sienna hugs me next and asks how I'm doing as we start toward the entrance.

"Good. How are you guys?"

"Well, *that* wasn't convincing at all. What's going on?" Sienna asks. *Why wasn't that convincing?* "What? Nothing. I'm good."

We enter, and my saliva glands kick in from the fragrance of sauce and noodles and garlic. Kayla announces she's buying my lunch as the hostess leads us to a table, then she agrees with Sienna that I'm not acting normal.

"Seriously, what's up?" Sienna asks again, flinging her frizzy dark hair off her shoulder.

"Seriously, I'm good. How are you guys? What's new? How's Brody?" I ask Kayla. "And Andrew?" I ask Sienna.

My deflecting works for a bit. Kayla and Sienna enlighten me with what's new in their worlds, and I feel so far away from them, from high school, from my old life. I feel as if I'm just nodding and trying to care. I mean, I *do* care, but I can't focus, I guess. Instead, I'm focusing on trying not to give anything away about my new life and not to think about Cassia's dream; I don't want to distract myself so much that I miss what they say. But now they think something is up because I'm terrible at this, apparently.

Lindsey arrives her usual twenty minutes late with her poofy red curls bouncing happily along with her. "What'd I miss, suckas?" she says, sitting next to me, her eyes glued to my stitches.

"Absolutely nothing," Sienna jokes in a passive-aggressive tone as she rolls her big brown eyes. "We still know nothing new about Camry's life."

"There's nothing really new to talk about," I say.

Lindsey points to my head. "That's something to talk about."

I tell them the quick version, leaving out anything about Jake and even leaving out the whole hospital/ambulance thing.

Somehow, though, with that story, Lindsey sees through me as if she has telepathic powers. "You met a guy!"

Kayla and Sienna drop open their mouths excitedly as they instantly believe her.

I lift my hands and make my eyes big. "No. I'm *not* dating anyone."
Where did this come from? How did she know?

We go back and forth on that until they finally believe me. Either that, or they just decide to let it go. I eat my fettuccine alfredo in a rushed fashion. I don't know why. I must be nervous.

Lindsey's starting to complain about her boyfriend, Gideon, who both drives her nuts and who she loves to pieces. She's annoyed he doesn't seem motivated to move out of his mom's house, or go to college, or try to get a better job than Chick-fil-A manager. (Which isn't really a terrible job. He makes better money than I do. Lindsey just has a thing about fast food.)

Kayla and Sienna chime in with their own mini stories of things that annoy them about their boyfriends.

As they talk, I think about Ashton. The only complaint that comes to mind at the moment is that he ghosted me. Ugh, that word...*ghosted.* There's that Cassia reminder again. I change gears and compare Benson and Jake to my friend's boyfriends. Not that I know Benson and Jake in a long-term-relationship kind of way, but I don't see in them any of what my friends are talking about. Would I get to the point with either of them where I just sit and complain when I go to lunch with my friends? Or does viewpoint matter? Is my viewpoint completely different from my friends'? I interrupt, a little too rough. "I don't know why you guys are complaining."

Lindsey stops, looks at the others, and then back to me. "I'm just venting."

"Sorry," I admit. "I just think…you're never going to have perfection, but…they all treat you well. They've all got jobs." I think of Cassia. "They could die tomorrow, and you'd have *this* on your conscience." I gesture to all of them, meaning this ridiculous conversation.

"God. When did you get so dark?" Lindsey asks.

"It's living in Salt Lake, isn't it?" asks Sienna.

I shrug and scoff with a bit of a chortle. "Maybe."

Kayla folds. "You're right, though," she says to me. "Like, Brody always brings me that banana bread I love when he works out in Eden."

I point at her. "See! Now you try," I say to Sienna.

She thinks. "Andy is *so* good with my mom." Sienna's mom has multiple sclerosis, and I know Andy helps her with projects around the house.

We all look to Lindsey. She finally rolls her amber-colored eyes, giving in. "Gideon makes me laugh every day. He's such a dork!"

She says "dork" in a loving way, so I don't give her a hard time about name-calling. I feel better now. I feel not so nervous.

I cave and tell them about the bird incident too. I even show them the video from the internet. This gets me a lot of attention, which, of course, I don't love, but I'm able to handle it from these three better than anyone else. They're my best friends.

"Who'd you go with?" Kayla asks with a hint of jealousy like she wanted to be invited.

"Just a friend from work," I lie. "She's adventurous like that."

"Well, obviously, that wasn't *your* idea." Lindsey points to my phone, which no longer has the video on it. "You're too safe to sign up for something like that on your own."

"What's her name?" Sienna asks.

I can only lie so much. "Cassia," I tell them. "She's from New York." I confess that she invited me to New York for Christmas and I'm considering going. This gives us a lot to talk about without going into too much detail about my personal life. After all, New York has limitless things to see and do. And we all have opinions about what we would like to see and do if we were to go there. Like I said, great topic of conversation without actually telling them about anything really.

We finish lunch and head over to the movie theater to see the new Julia Roberts movie. Sienna buys my ticket, and Lindsey buys my popcorn and soda. All I'm going to end up paying for today is my gas to drive here. My friends know me well. I don't need material things. I love this present.

All things considered, it's a good day. But as I bid their familiar faces goodbye with bittersweet hugs, I find I'm giving them false promises to be better at texting and keep in touch. Because I'm feeling like a different person than who I used to be with them. It's strange how much can happen in a year, how different things are now. I'm still close with them but also so removed. The days of just assuming we'd meet here and hang out there are gone, and I don't know how to get them back. Maybe if I moved back, or at least moved closer. But I signed another six-month contract for my apartment, and it's not up until the end of December.

I decide to grocery shop now rather than closer to home. My dad texted me a couple of hours ago when the money was transferred. After that, I crank up the radio and sing until I hit the freeway.

The speedy traffic on I-15 forces me to turn down the radio and drive cautiously, though. Thoughts of Cassia's dream start picking at me like a relentless vulture after about ten minutes. By the time I'm in the city, I'm twitching with anxiety about it all. Having to push it down the entire time I was with my friends has completely backfired. I have heartburn.

I get home and take five trips back and forth to bring all the groceries in. My pantry and fridge are officially stuffed like a turkey. I smile, so grateful for the gift, then head back to my bedroom, not preparing a meal because I'm still full from Olive Garden. Actually, maybe that's why I have heartburn.

No Cassia at all today. It's a little early, but I'm ready for bed and begin watching TV. I try to stay awake for her, but she never does come before I tumble into a much-needed sleep.

Once I'm out, a dream begins…

I've regained consciousness in the back seat of a luxury car. I'm on my side, and my body rocks as the man in black stops the vehicle. With hazy vision, I notice the tan leather around me and him opening the door to get out. I feel weak and nauseated.

The door thumps as he closes it and comes around to get me. He drags me out by the shoulders of my overcoat, pulling my hair as he does. I notice we're in the woods.

I don't have enough energy to fight him, so I collapse defenselessly on the frozen dirt of the dead forest floor. I'm not sure if we've driven far enough away to somewhere where there's less snow or if the trees are simply dense enough here that snow hasn't really accumulated on the ground.

All the typical questions one might have are going through my head, but I don't have the energy to beg for my life, let alone ask anything. I didn't notice earlier, but he's wearing a pair of black leather gloves. It could be that he just donned them.

I glance up at him with heavy eyes, and as he treads around me, I see a gun in a holster under his jacket.

He seems foreign to me, with dark hair and deep-set eyes, possibly European. His face offers no emotion. Nothing whatsoever. His expression would be no different if he were getting gas in his car or, say, doing the dishes.

I may be eighteen, but I'm not stupid. Someone hired him to kill me.

My senses perk up. "Tiffanie," I moan.

Still no change in the man's expression.

It has to be Tiffanie. She's the only one who'd benefit from me dying.

I place my hands behind me; they unsteadily hold me up. I feebly dig at the ground to try to throw dirt at him, but the earth is cold and unbreakable and useless. Internally, I'm frantic, but my breath is just performing a slow dance in the cold air, unable to be frantic with me. I slur, "Whatever she's paid you, my father will pay more."

He snatches me by the neck with one hand and slogs farther into the dense trees with me. I pathetically grab his wrist for support; he's squeezing hard. I try to stand and pull free to run away, but he's walking too fast, and I'm still too weak. I try to kick him but can't reach. I try to grasp the gun but end up only scratching his stomach. Then he's hurling me down, knocking the wind out of me, but he doesn't let go of my neck. Instead, he sits on my chest, forcing the rest of the air from my lungs, squeezing even harder with both hands now.

I'm absolutely petrified I'm going to die, and it hurts so bad. I can't believe this is it. I think about my dad and how he'll never know what happened to me. I didn't leave a note or anything giving a clue where I was going. I look into the man's dark eyes one last time, anger matching the level of my fear, then...I black out.

I shoot up out of bed and grab my neck with both hands, panting like a dog. Again, I'm covered in sweat.

I try to hang on to it like before, but who am I kidding? I don't think I can ever forget this. The car. The forest. The gun. The choking. The fear. *Tiffanie*.

"Cassia?" I ask the empty room as I did last time.

And, same as last time, there's nothing but silence while I replay everything over and over in my head. The difference this time is I don't sleep the rest of the night. I don't turn on old episodes of *Friends* to pull me through this funk. Instead, I nosedive into all the details. The car, and how I could somehow smell the leather of its interior. The nauseous feeling that was eating at my stomach. The sound of his footsteps and the cold hard ground. The fact that Cassia was very set on a single thought: Tiffanie had hired someone to kill her. And the sinking memory of my own asphyxiation when I got the bee sting and she was with me, having to relive the feeling of choking. Her telling me that it felt like dying all over again and how scared she was.

Monday, August 16

It's one of the most ridiculous things, trying to get through work. I've only slept like six hours the past two nights, and my mind can't stop replaying Cassia's memory. And all the hows, whats, wheres, and whys are making me go certifiably insane. Just check me into the asylum already. After the fifth mistake I make, my boss asks me for the fifth time if I'm okay.

"I'm so sorry, Trish. I just…I just haven't slept well lately."

She sends me home at lunchtime. Trisha thinks I need sleep more than I need the hours, which could be true, but I need to know more from Cassia most of all.

I stop at the doctor's office a bit early to get my stitches out. The scar looks good, and my hair is growing over it. The physician talks a lot about the importance of continuing physical and mental rest. He also gives me information on post-concussion syndrome so I can "be aware." I don't know why, but I don't care about this. Perhaps I'm just too distracted to care right now. Don't worry, the irony isn't lost on me. I shouldn't let myself be distracted. I shouldn't be overworking my brain thinking of Cassia. I should be mentally resting. I toss the pamphlet on the passenger seat and don't give it another thought.

The doctor said I shouldn't work out; I don't feel like it anyway, so I bail on that. I think about heading over to the travel agency just to sate my own curiosity, but I stop myself on that one as well. I'll wait for more from Cassia before I get too much into that. And even though I'm done with bowling, it's Monday—the routine still lingers in my mind, so bowling creeps its way there also, along with Benson's crooked smile and ocean-blue eyes.

I play a conversation between Benson and me in my head. Me trying to explain why I acted that way on Friday, and him saying "it's okay" but still wanting to know what's wrong.

Suck! Do I owe him an explanation? What the hell would I say? Every version sounds ridiculous, the truth being the most utterly ridiculous of them all.

I decide, out of all my silly scenarios, my boss was right; I do need to sleep. And despite the fact that I'm not so sure I want to dream again, I go home with intentions to do so. Shoving worry aside about what images might fill my mind, I flop onto my bed, and (surprisingly, or maybe not) am out within minutes…

I see Tiffanie; well, the back of her anyway. She's on the sofa talking on her phone. I'm hiding down the hallway, hidden enough that she doesn't know I can see and hear her. It's late. I should be in bed, but I need to get a drink.

Her irksome voice stops me, though. "I know. I know. I'm just impatient. You know me and money."

Who's she speaking with?

"Will you just call the guy, Mother?" Her voice is bratty.

Tiffanie's mother was at the wedding, and Dad and I haven't seen her since. I instantly didn't like her. Just as I instantly didn't like Tiffanie. I don't know why I'm surprised they're speaking. Perhaps because I never speak to my mom. Don't even know her address—only that she's in Syracuse somewhere. Dad still seems so sad if I bring her up, so I don't anymore.

I walk out to get my drink of water and startle Tiffanie on the sofa.

She grabs at her fake chest. "Oh! You scared me."

"Sorry," is all I say, taking my glass and walking back to my bedroom.

"Goodnight, sweetie."

Ugh! "Night!" I holler.

The dream shifts. It's the next day, and I'm talking to my dad, trying to tell him she just wants his money.

We go back and forth, arguing for a long time—until he yells at me, "Enough, Cassia! Accept the fact that I'm happy. You will stop this. Do you understand me?"

I finally just shake my head in disbelief; he's too blind to see it. How can such a smart man be so stupid? I leave, hurt he raised his voice at me.

I wake easier than after the past couple of dreams. Cassia is with me. I roll over onto my back and try to release the sleepiness from my eyes by holding them open really wide. They start to water, so I relax.

Cassia starts, "It's a simple memory, but a relevant one." She pauses. "The '*guy*' she asked her mother to call is the guy she hired to kill me. I didn't think anything of that nature at the time, obviously. It wasn't until it was happening that…I just knew. And the next day, after I spoke with my dad, was when I decided to go find my mom. It was such a quick decision; I didn't tell anyone I was going."

I brave *the* question. "Is there more?"

She sighs.

I wait for her to tell me or make me sleep so I can see it, but instead, she closes my eyes and breathes slow and deep. I begin to feel weightless, featherlike. My thoughts are muted and imperceptible to me. There's an undemanding restriction with my body; it's gentle, delicate. When she opens my eyes, my room no longer looks like my room. There's a bright light all around me. It's welcoming, not blinding, but I feel irritated by it—or Cassia's irritated by it, I'm not sure which. We sit up.

After a few moments, the white fades out, apart from a tiny spot to my right. I have a bird's-eye view of a man standing over a body, pouring gasoline on it. It's Cassia's body. But *God*, she looks like me. I look like her. It's unsettling to see this moment, but I don't close my eyes. She's pale and lifeless on the forest floor, unflinching from the liquid raining on her.

The man lights a match and tosses it, setting her ablaze. While she burns, he takes the time to dig a shallow grave. Once he finishes digging, he uses the shovel to roll her charred remains into the hole, then buries her. He gets in his car, and she has a choice: follow him to the left or enter the welcoming light on the right.

She follows the black luxury car.

The images slide past me in my bedroom as if I'm flying alongside her as she follows the car. She's memorized the license plate number, but somewhere along the way, her thoughts have shifted to Tiffanie.

Unexpectedly, the scene morphs into Cassia's apartment. The blinds are open, and I can see a view of New York City. Tiffanie is in the kitchen making a green salad for herself. A Yorkshire terrier follows eagerly at her heels. Her phone rings, and she answers it.

It's her mother. "It's all done," she sings to Tiffanie.

I can feel the anger rise inside my chest, again unsure to whom it belongs. Probably both of us. The 360-degree vision morphs back into my bedroom.

All I can think is, *Oh my God*!

My heart is racing with an intensity I didn't even know existed. Time passes as Cassia lets me process what just happened. I think back through the vision and the other dreams. Cassia had suspicions about her stepmom and the lengths she'd go to to get her dad's money. She was going to find her mom, not just to reawaken a mother-daughter relationship she was beginning to realize she needed so desperately, but to talk about Tiffanie and the money. But she was too late. Her wicked stepmother hired someone to kill her.

How could she do that?

Cassia startles me by answering my thought. "All of my dad's money would have passed on to me in the event of his death."

So Tiffanie had the stupid stereotypical plan: get rid of Cassia and get her husband's inheritance. It's something you see on TV shows like *Snapped* all the time, but it's one of those things that still seems preposterous to me—the fact there're people in this world who actually do this!

Cassia continues, making a pretzel of my legs. "What Tiffanie didn't know, and *I* didn't even know until recently, is my mom is part of the inheritance too."

"Huh?"

"Tiffanie knows this now. It's only a matter of time before she does the same thing to her." She's flailing my right hand a lot, getting worked up, possibly wasting energy.

I blink. "Whoa. Wait. No way. That'd be *way* too suspicious. His daughter dies, then his ex-wife. I mean, who's next?" Now I'm doing the same thing, flailing.

"No one. My dad has no other family. But I worry after a few years of marriage, *he'll* be next. This is why she chose him. They don't make a good couple. They have nothing in common. He's having a mid-life crisis or something. I think, especially since I turned eighteen, he didn't want to be alone. He figured it was time he could remarry. There're only two people to eliminate, two people standing in her way to millions of dollars. My dad dabbles in other things, and he invests well. There's a lot more than one would think. I imagine she did her homework."

My mind is slow to keep up. I go back two steps. "Wait, how'd you find out about the inheritance going to your mom?" Nothing but crickets from Cassia. Her vault is open but not that open, I guess. "Is *that* where you go?"

"Yes, lately. Before that, I don't know where I was. There are still times where it's like I get lost."

Midway through her sentence, I fling my legs off the edge and start pacing my room. I can't help it. I need to know all that's in this vault. "Have you seen your dad?" I ask her.

Cassia sighs. "Don't be mad. Yes."

I wave my arm. "So why am I booking a trip to New York for you to see him?"

She gives the answer I was afraid of. "So I can stop her. Prove her guilty. Save my mom and dad. I think she's planning to act after Christmas, sometime in January."

My hand rubs my face from top to bottom. This is the "more" she was talking about before. "And what proof do you have?" I can't avoid the uneasiness in my voice. "Police are going to want some kind of evidence, Cassia. Not some girl from Utah claiming she '*just knows.*' I'll be charged. Or put in a psych ward." *Like I said before, "Asylum, here I come."*

"Shut your pie hole!" she interjects. "She's going to contact him again."

"How do you know?"

"I just do. That's why I need you to go there. I need to get it recorded somehow."

"Wait! What? What do you expect me to do? There has to be another way. Can't you enter your dad's body?"

"No, I've tried."

"Well, why can't you?"

"I don't know, Cam. It's not like I have a handbook on this stuff!" She's raising my voice at me. I don't care. I'm still desperate for someone else to figure this out. I'm desperate to *find* a handbook. Does *The Handbook for the Recently Deceased* exist? *If that's not a real thing, it should be.*

I stop pacing, close my eyes, and press my fingertips into them. I feel a headache coming on. Then, before I know it, I feel a tickle in my nose. *Ugh!* Another nosebleed. I grab tissues and pace again. "What about dreams for him?"

"I've tried to do that too. It's not getting through. It's not working."

"What about your mom or your friend Kate…or Travin?"

"Travin…" She shakes my head with a sigh. "Travin and Kate are no good. I can't get through to them. And I can't seem to find my mom." She's calmer now. "Maybe because I don't know her anymore. I have to visualize and concentrate on the person I want to visit. I'm getting better, but, like I said, sometimes I still get lost."

"Am I easy to find?" I ask, thinking how she can be with me so abruptly sometimes while other times, she doesn't come for a couple of days. I stop pacing and reposition the tissue in my nose.

"Yes. You're different from everyone else." There's a softness and sincerity in the way she says this. "There's a glow around you. A light. I'm almost drawn to you."

I think of the light that was in her vision just a minute ago and how welcoming it was.

"Yes! Like the feeling of that light. That's how you are for me."

Like so many other things, I'm not sure what the significance of this is. I don't spend a lot of time thinking about it now, either. Instead, I calmly ask, "What about the bucket list, Cassia? I'm not going to be able to afford anything if we go to New York." I can't believe I'm considering this. My head is suddenly pounding. I sit on the edge of my bed.

"I love feeling alive again with you," she admits. "But this is bigger than…" She trails off, seeming sad. "I'll miss that." She then chuckles. "I definitely can't help but want more when I'm with you."

I understand what she means. She *was* cut short. She *was* cheated.

"You're the only person I can do bucket-list stuff with," she says. "And you're the only person I can do this with." She means help her with the daunting task of getting proof for the police. And if she has to choose one, it's going to be the latter.

I hang my head, thinking. "Christmas is cutting it really close," I say.

"Well, I knew you'd need time to save the money. Plus, I thought you might go back to school for fall semester. Who am I to stop you? That's not right."

It's my turn to chuckle now. "Oh, but asking me to go to New York to somehow prove your stepmother is guilty of hiring someone to kill your mom *is*?" I get up, throw away the blood-soaked tissue, and shove another up my nose.

She gives a small giggle. "Exactly. But I did have the thought of trying for something sooner."

I rub my face again with both hands this time and sit back on my bed, thinking about money. I also think about fall semester and then back to the vision. "What about the license plate number?" I ask, feeling like I'm onto something.

"It was a rental car. He flew here after."

"Did he come here to kill someone else, or does he live here?" Either way, that's disturbing.

"I don't know. I ended up getting lost."

I gasp with a good idea. "What about leaving an anonymous tip?"

She hesitates. "I thought about that, but you don't have any proof yet. What if they track you and start hounding you? They'll charge you. Or put you in a psych ward." She's regurgitating my words back at me.

Her choice of the words "track" and "hound" makes me picture hound dogs tracking me through Salt Lake City. They catch me, biting my forearms and taking me down as police swarm me.

I blink. *Enough of that.*

I don't actually think that's how it goes, but I also hesitate with the idea of calling New York police because I *don't* know how it goes. So I agree with her in my head. *Yeah, that could be a nightmare.* If she's saying no to an anonymous tip, then she'll say no to me calling her dad. I tell her, "Planning a future murder won't be as harsh of a punishment for Tiffanie compared to proving she was behind *your* murder."

She hesitates, thinking about my comment. "It doesn't matter. What if they never prove anything about me? I don't know how to explain it, but I really feel like I have to let go of what happened to me and try to catch her planning this. Something is telling me I need to focus on my mom. Besides, I don't matter anymore. I'm already gone. My mom isn't, though."

I think about everything. I disagree. It does matter. *She* matters. The *truth* matters. But I'm feeling nauseated, so I'm not going to argue this point. "When are you thinking we need to go?"

"Well…I don't know. I need to spend some more time there. Then I can let you know."

My shoulders slouch. "How long does 'some more time' mean?"

"I don't know. I'll let you know as soon as I can. I'm really sorry about all this, Cam. I think, though, it's the whole reason you and I can do what we do. You're the one who can help me."

I exhale, a little bit frightened at that thought. "You're brave, Cass. Even in the afterlife. It's amazing."

"Well, I'm not done yet. I need you to take me the rest of the way." She holds out my right hand.

Yes, she does need me, and there are two kinds of people in this world: the ones who'll say yes to help a friend and the ones who won't. I want to be the former. So, yes, I'll do it for her. I grab my right hand with my left and shake it once.

"You should get some rest," she tells me. "You're not feeling well. Oh! And happy birthday. I'm sorry I missed it."

"Thanks. Maybe I'll share the memory some other time."

"For sure. Good night, Camry."

"Bye, Cass."

After she leaves me, I look up the number to call the police in New York City. Pulling out my phone, I start to enter it in, but I can't seem to bring myself to push the call button. I know an anonymous tip is the best thing to do. It's the most logical thing to do. But something is stopping me. What is it? *What is it?*

I can't put my finger on it. And analyzing it all seems to be making my nose bleed more, so I switch gears, deal with my nose, and go to bed.

<h1 style="text-align:center">Tuesday, August 17</h1>

After Cassia left last night, my nose bled for another twenty minutes, then I threw up. But I still go to work today. It's déjà vu; like yesterday, I can't stop thinking about what happened the night before. I mean, I have more answers, but the thoughts are still all-consuming. Go to New York, prove her stepmom guilty, most likely deal with the police, and who knows what else. All of this, essentially by myself. *So why does that seem like what I should do rather than leave an anonymous tip? Why is there this gut feeling...to go?*

Classes start next week, so Trisha is the extra person on shift, working in the back for a third time. She's dispersing the boxes to their appropriate aisles while Chloe and I handle the register and unpack the boxes. Chloe's being better about her phone this time. I finally probe, trying to get my mind off last night. "You're not on your phone as much today," I say, but I'm thinking, *How much is this "trip" going to cost*?

"Ugghh." She draws out the exasperation while rolling her eyes and fingering a zit on her chin. "Adam is such a bloody wanker." She says this in her normal American accent.

Adam isn't who I last knew Chloe to be dating. I'm pretty sure it was Cole, but I say, "Is Adam British?" *And how long should I plan to stay there?*

She peeks at me from behind the small mirror she's grabbed from her purse and is using to view her zit. "No."

"Okay, then. Are you trying to become British?" I start thinking in a British accent. *Are all New York City taxi drivers strange like you see on the telly?*

She shrugs. "It's just my new thing."

"What happened to Cole?" *Cole was a nice bloke, I suppose.*

She sets the mirror on the counter and leans into it with two fingers on either side of the blemish, ready to pop it. "He was like three months ago. I told you we broke up, didn't I?"

I accidently say in a British accent, "I don't think so."

Chloe looks at me with a quirked eyebrow.

I'm across the counter from her and halfway down the aisle of different copy papers.

I blink. *Enough of that.*

I add, in my normal accent, "Leave it alone. It's not ready to pop yet."

She yanks the mirror back, having already decided this. Then she points to the zit. She's red and angry, just like it is now. "This is all Adam's fault!"

I regard her with sympathy because underneath all her rage is sadness. I set down the ream and walk over to her. "Wanna talk about it?"

With a scrunch of her nose, she shakes her head, and I believe her. After all, I'm the one who brought things up, not her.

"Wanna help me with the paper?"

Her smile doesn't mean it, but she says, "Sure."

Later, when I take my break, I bring back two lemonades and two muffins from Starbucks. I need to save money, but Chloe needs a friend right now. As we enjoy the goodies, I tell her, "You should take a break from guys."

She side-eyes me. "Are you suggesting girls? Because I like Ashley, but I don't *like* Ashley."

I giggle. "No, I mean, don't date *anyone* for a while." I don't want to attack her lifestyle, but she's never without a guy, and I think she could benefit from, well, time without a guy.

She mulls over my idea. "Who are you dating right now?" she asks.

"No one."

"Ah, so you think everyone should be single and miserable?" she teases and takes a bite of her muffin.

"That's not what I meant. And I'm not miserable," I say a bit defensively but then throw in, "I mean, out of the two of us right now, who's the miserable one?"

Chloe considers this and jokes again, "You. Definitely you." We laugh, but then she offers a rebuttal. "But when it's good, it's so good. And how do you know who you like unless you try?"

I take a drink and shrug.

She drinks too, the straw in the corner of her mouth, and says, "I guess the perk of being single is I can—"

"Skip shaving your legs?" I offer.

She chuckles and agrees but doesn't finish what she was going to say. Instead, she asks, "What are you doin' after work?"

I nod in the direction of the gym. "Heading over to work out." (Not my normal day. I'm doing well with my inconsistent routine, right?)

She scratches her arm, not meeting my gaze with her next question. "Can I come?"

I lift a shoulder. "Sure."

After we close, Chloe and I walk over to the gym. I want to do a light version of my normal treadmill run and weightlifting routine, but Chloe doesn't have the stamina or the right clothing. I always bring clothes to change into, but she has to remain in her shorts and frilly top. So we're doing an extra-light version. Her being here is helping to keep me somewhat distracted from thoughts of Cassia and New York, though, so that's good.

She's weakly doing butterfly presses. "Isn't there something we can punch?" she asks after a while.

I regard her as I count squats. *Twenty-eight, twenty-nine, thirty.* A guy behind her glances at her, curious about her comment. I ignore him and put the dumbbells back. Tightening my ponytail, I step over to her. "You mean something you can imagine Adam's face on?"

She looks up at me, exhilarated. "Yeeesss!"

The guy now turns around, eyeing me and the back of Chloe's head. "There are punching bags over in The Vault," he suggests.

I laugh inside at the irony that the university gym has a room called "The Vault." Again, things that make me think of Cassia are everywhere.

Chloe's arms fling back as she drops the weight and twists to see him. My phone rings. Picking it up, I see it's my mom calling. *That's weird. She rarely calls me. I hope everything is okay.* I look back to

Chloe. She's already engaged in a conversation with Bronzy Muscle Man.

I step over to lean against the wall and answer, "Hello?"

"What the hell is going on, Camry?" she screeches. I don't have the worst relationship with my parents, but I certainly don't have the best either. She continues, "I mean, hi, honey. Are you all right?" The question is empty.

"I'm fine," I answer.

I'm about to ask what she's talking about, but she cuts me off. "I got my insurance statement in the mail, and it says you've been in the hospital! There're all kinds of charges here! Almost eighteen thousand dollars in charges, Camry!"

Ah! The bee incident. She's unquestionably more worried about the money than about me. She's screeching so loudly I have to pull the phone away from my ear.

"You could've at least called and warned me! Or told me two days ago when we called you!"

She's right. I should've warned her. I forgot she gets the insurance explanation before I get the bill. But, as far as the conversation on my birthday, there wasn't really an opportunity to tell them. They didn't even ask what was up with me or how I was doing.

"I don't expect you to pay it, Mom," I say calmly. If I begin screeching as well, it'll only escalate. I hear my dad in the background telling my mother to find out the reason for the hospital visit. I don't wait for her to ask. "I got stung by a bee and stopped breathing, passed out, and hit my head on the sidewalk. An ambulance had to come; that's probably why it's so much. Sorry. Next time, I'll just die." I can't help the snootiness in my voice at the end there.

"Oh, don't be ridiculous!" she says.

My dad asks what I said, and she tells him. He asks about my adrenaline shot and why I didn't use it. I answer his question again through my mom. "I didn't have it with me, Mom."

"She didn't have it with her," she says to my dad.

This little mistake is going to cost me money now. They're going to see it as half my fault. At least half, maybe more. "I haven't gotten a statement yet," I point out. "Does it say how much I'll have to pay?"

"Well, the deductible is ten thousand," she spits at me.

"Okay, so is that all?"

"Oh, I don't know! Frank! Frank, how do you read this stupid thing?"

I hear my dad again through the phone; he's irritated. Whether it's at her or me, I'm not sure. "It's right here! Thirteen thousand and thirteen dollars."

"Okay, don't worry about it. I'll figure it out, Mom," is what I say, but I'm thinking, *Holy hell monkeys!*

"Well, hang on." I hear muffled brushing sounds and picture my mother holding the phone against her breast to cover what she's saying to my dad. She speaks through the phone once more. "We have five thousand right now we can help you with."

"No, Mom. It's really okay," I argue. I don't want to be under their thumb because of this.

"No, it's fine. We're glad you're okay. I'll transfer the money as soon as I can. Then when you get the bill, you can pay a huge chunk straight away."

Or…I could go to New York. That's maybe a terrible thought. But it might also be the greatest thought in the history of my thinking. I consent. "Okay, thanks." With my thumb tapping the red button to end the call, I decide to book the trip; I won't be going back to school for fall semester. I'd been kicking the idea around in my head anyway, but thirteen thousand dollars has clinched it.

Walking back to where Chloe was, I discover she isn't there. Neither is Bronzy Muscle Man. My phone chimes signaling me I have a text.

Chloe: *Hey, I went with Chris over to the punching bags. You don't have to wait for me. I'll see ya later.*

Oh boy. Two thoughts wrestle to be the main cause for my current vexation One: *She couldn't even go one day without a guy.* Two: *She ditched me. Again.*

Me: *You sure you're okay?*

Chloe: *Yes.*

Me: *Text me when you get home.*

Yep, I'm a worrywart.

Wednesday, August 18

As Ashley and I help our long lines of customers, I'm successfully distracted from my earlier thoughts of going to the travel agency later today. I mean, I'm not going to go unless Cassia comes to see me first, but I want to. She didn't come visit at all yesterday, and I need to talk to her to confirm some things before I book the flight and hotel.

In between the waves of customers, I ask Ashley how things went with visiting the girl she likes at her work.

"I don't know," she admits. "I went there, chatted for a little while, and bought a shirt, but I can't tell what she's thinking."

"Did you ask to hang out again?"

"No. It was awkward. Her coworker was right there."

I nod, understanding. "Well, maybe you'll have another class with her fall semester."

"What classes are you taking anyway?" she asks me.

"None."

Her eyes widen. "Really?"

"Can't afford it," I tell her. "My hospital bill was a lot."

Her head sags to one side as her expression changes to one of sympathy. "That sucks. I'm sorry."

"Don't worry about it. Just give me all the shifts you don't want when classes start to get intense."

She chuckles. "You got it."

I sit in my car for a minute after starting it. Cassia usually joins me when I'm finished with work, but so far, she's not here. I start driving. On the way home, I veer off to a Chevron, noticing I'm low on gas. Still no Cassia. Back on the road, I swerve into oncoming traffic and merge back into my lane as she suddenly joins me, scaring the crap out of me.

"Jeez!" I scream, my knuckles white on the steering wheel. *Terrible timing, Cassia!*

"Oh man! I'm so sorry," Cassia quickly says. "Pull over. We need to talk."

I pull into the parking lot of an old house that's been turned into a dental office. "What's up?"

"Tiffanie and her mom made a trip up to Syracuse," she says. "I've seen her! My mom! I've seen her, and now I can go to her!"

I'm excited. This is great news! She didn't need to almost kill me for it, but…it's great news! I put my car in park. "Do you think you can…?"

"Yes. I mean, she has some issues with depression, but I've given her dreams the past two nights. I think I can get through to her."

"Why did Tiffanie go up there?"

"I think she's getting impatient. They're bouncing around ideas of doing it themselves. They wanted to see what she was like, her living conditions, what she drives. You know…things like that."

I turn the radio off. "Where's your dad?"

"In Philadelphia for business. The maid stayed and cleaned the first day, and then she went to stay with her mother in Queens."

"So what now?"

"Well, I think I need to stay with my mom and Tiffanie and see what's going on. Maybe Bella can help too. She seems to notice me."

"Who's Bella?" I ask.

"The maid."

"Oh. Why don't you get inside Tiffanie? See what she's thinking." *Have I asked her this before?*

"I've tried. I can't. Your parents are giving you money?" she asks.

"Oh yeah!" The thought of my mother and father's five thousand dollars must be somewhat on the surface of my mind. Cassia needs to be caught up. "Yeah, they called me about the hospital bill. They're transferring five thousand dollars to help me pay it down. I could book the trip if you want—"

"No, Camry. Wait for me to find out more. Maybe I can take care of this without you having to sacrifice so much. You've already done so much for me. Maybe between my mom and Bella, it'll all work out."

Before, I was desperate for her to find someone else to do this, and now it's possibly working out that she can do it on her own, and I'm feeling disappointed about it. I hate how wishy-washy I can be sometimes. I take a split second to analyze what I'm really feeling. I decide I *want* to go. I want justice for her. I want to be part of bringing that justice forward. Because I think she was right the other day; she and I have this gift so I can help her.

"Thanks, Camry. For everything." Her voice is sincere, but she doesn't acknowledge my previous thought about wanting to go, wanting to help her. Instead, she says, "I'll still visit and keep you in the loop, okay? Have fun at the concert."

She apparently doesn't plan to come back before Friday if she's telling me to have fun at the concert. "Cass," I say, confused. "I can't 'have fun at the concert.' What're you thinking? Stay. Talk to me more."

The familiar tingle rushes out of me. I glance in the rearview mirror, watching my eyes become hazel as she leaves me alone in the parking lot.

Thursday, August 19

After work, I drive to the bowling alley. I hope he's working and hope Cassia doesn't come. I don't think she will, given our conversation yesterday. *Okay, Camry. Quick. Like a Band-Aid.*

I make myself open the glass door and cross the threshold into the cool air and familiar sounds of the place I've become so accustomed to. Benson is assisting customers but sees me and stiffens. Without smiling, he blinks and holds up one finger.

It's almost as if some other force has pushed me here. I can't explain how I felt the need to come tell him this. It hit me so strongly this morning and gnawed at me all day at work. I wonder if part of it's me, wanting things to work out with Jake so badly, which can't happen if I don't do this.

I sit on the bench near the door, bouncing my leg to help with my nerves. It doesn't help. So as I wait, I try *not* to think about what I'm doing here. I focus on a flyer pinned to a board next to the door. It has an old advertisement for a musical at West High School a few blocks over. It's a classic: *Grease*. I'd have loved to play Sandy, but my high school never did that one. I hum a melody from the movie. It helps ease my nerves better than the bouncing leg.

When the customers move on, Benson holds up his finger again and disappears around the shoes. Coming back, he walks toward me with trepidation, fingers in his pockets with thumbs sticking out. Classic Benson.

I stand and motion to the door. "Can we talk outside?" I've decided if I can help it, I don't want to be in here with all the sights and sounds that'll jog my memory of Cassia.

"Uh, sure." We both squint from the intense light as we exit. "There's some shade over here," he suggests.

Around the side of the building, I sit on the curb of the sidewalk under the shade of a small tree and fold my arms atop my knees. He mimics me.

Looking forward, I exhale. Benson is waiting for me to speak, but I can't even look at him. *Why'd I think this was a good idea?* I open my mouth a number of times (seriously, like ten times), but nothing comes out.

He grabs my left hand with his right and kisses my fingers. I finally manage a gaze. He says with care, "What's up? I've only got fifteen minutes." Cue the crooked smile.

Squeezing his hand, I blink the entire sentence. "I'm *so* sorry about Friday." My voice cracks at the end. It's not what I came here to say, but still, it needed to be said. It's the most earnest apology I think I've ever made.

Lifting his eyebrows, he answers, "Well, that's a start. But that's where the good part ends, huh, hazel eyes?" We're back to the eyes-changing-color-with-my-mood thing. I don't need one of those cheap mood rings. One look at me, and he thinks he knows; I'm not as happy when I'm hazel, when I'm me. My eyes sting with the threat of tears. And he has more. "What? You gonna tell me you like this other guy better?"

Taken aback, I wrench my hand away. Immediately, he apologizes, knowing that was the wrong thing to say. I tell him with a bit of a backbiting tone, "You don't know the circumstances." I get flustered. "You can't—that isn't fair. And—you didn't listen." I look forward again, focusing on the red car in the parking lot with the license plate that reads RAERAES.

He shifts toward me a tad. "You're right. I'm sorry. That's not fair, but I did listen. I'm just still confused about why I'm supposed to be a dick."

I shake my head. *Unbelievable*. It's my own fault, though. My self-centered little moment of going along with his surprise date and...*oh, whatever*. Let's bounce past that and just get this over with.

I exhale. "I'm not..." *Ugh!* My forehead hits the palms of my hands as my fingers are lost in my hair. *Say it! Just say it, Camry! I'm not*

Cassia. He needs to know who I am if Jake is going to work out! I try again. "I'm not…"

The tingle is rapid, and I twitch as Cassia blurts out, "…staying here."

Benson becomes rigid. "What?"

My thoughts echo his. *What the hell is blue eyes doing?*

"I'm going to go back to New York," she says and twists toward him.

"W-when? Why?" Shock has taken over his entire expression. It even seems he's turned a bit pale.

I want to ask the same questions, but Cassia has pushed me so far back that I can't do anything but listen. I'm figuratively bound and gagged in the back of my own mind. *I don't know that this is helping.*

"Tomorrow," she answers.

Benson's surprise is blatant. "Tomorrow? Did you know this last Friday?"

I can't tell if she's serious when she says, "I was still thinking about it."

"Is that why you were acting so weird? Why didn't you just tell me?"

"I'm telling you now. Face-to-face. This is hard for me, but you deserve this much. Besides, it's not like I planned on meeting you and liking you so much and going on that date, for that matter. It's not like you asked me. We just went." *Is this me or her talking? It's odd how I can't tell sometimes. Am I ungagged, or do we just have the same feelings on this?*

"If I'd asked you, would you have said no?" he asks, proving a point it didn't matter. It *doesn't* matter. Neither Cassia nor I answer. "I'm sorry for being an ass. Stay. Please." He grabs my hand again, pleading. "This needs more time. I just—I just know it."

"I can't." She tries to take my hand back, but he won't let her.

"Why? Why are you going? You said you liked it here. Is it money? Is it…me?" His insecurity surprises me. And he's *so* not an ass.

"I can't get into this with you. I'm sorry." She stands up, succeeding in getting my hand back just in time to catch a tear.

He's up quickly and blocks her with his fingertips on my stomach. "Don't. Don't run away again. Just…give me a minute. Can we still talk? Will you be coming back?"

She shakes my head. "I won't be coming back."

"You say that so…definitively. Are you sure?"

She nods. *This isn't helping for a potential future with Jake.*

"Well, can I spend today with you?" He's grappling for anything he can.

"Why? What would be the point? You can't change what I have to do."

"To spend time with the girl I…like."

He hesitated. Was he going to say "love"? "You don't like me!" I spit. "You don't know me!" *Whoa! That was me who said that. Wait! Why am I free?* I feel the tingle. She's leaving! *Craaap!*

Appalled, he raises his voice. "Hey! You can't tell people what they feel. That's not up to you."

I argue back, "I'm not who you think I am." Benson deserves someone better. He deserves the real Cassia. I'm still tingling. *What's going on? Is she leaving or not? Are my eyes hazel or blue? One of each?*

He shakes his head and thinks. He thinks for a while. I try to walk away again, but he matches my side steps and won't let me. I give in and wait for him to settle with the fact that he just has to let me go. The shadow that crossed his face begins to disintegrate. He's calm when he speaks again. His shoulders have relaxed at least three inches.

Slowly, he says, "Yes, you are. And maybe I don't know everything about you…yet. But here's what I do know." He scans my entire face, then drags his finger along my jawline. "You're beautiful."

Now that I know Cassia looks a lot like me, that doesn't count.

"You're smart." He stops at my chin.

I'm not that smart, but I guess I'm not a total idiot either. And neither is Cassia. Still, it doesn't count.

"You're funny." He taps the tip of my nose with his finger and a smile.

I can be funny, but the funny he knows is from Cassia.

"We have the same interests." He steps closer to me.

That one is all Cassia. It's not a competition. Just proof I can't or shouldn't be with him. And I'm trying not to be rude; he's being utterly sweet and romantic. I suppose I could still try the truth. *Ugh! I want to scream!*

"And I can be myself around you," he says.

Well, good…for…you! I sure as hell can't do that!

"Completely myself. I don't have to put on any pretenses or…anything." Then he adds an afterthought. "And you're tall."

I give a quizzical scowl. *I'm not* that *tall. And when did his hand end up on my waist?*

"Seriously. I love that. Do you know how hard it is to find a tall girl with all that other stuff who's not already taken? It's *really* hard!" He chuckles, then adds, "I really feel like you walked into the bowling alley that first day…for me."

I'm *still* tingling. A tear drops from my right eye. If I had to guess, that's the blue one.

He pulls me toward him until our chests meet. "You're fighting with yourself, aren't you? I can see it in your eyes."

I shut my eyes tightly. *Damn it!*

Grabbing my face gently with both of his hands, he tells me, "Don't. If you really are leaving, I want to remember every detail about them."

The tingling stops. Cassia is fully with me.

Then Benson says something that changes *everything* in me. "Come on. Life is too short. *Be* with me today."

At this, I sigh inwardly and let go.

Completely.

For Cassia, but maybe even more so for Benson.

And the next thing I know, I'm sitting cross-legged on my bed, looking at all the articles that are spread out to cover it entirely.

I jolt as I come to. I can't recall *anything* between Benson's hands on my face and now. I ask with an edge of worry, "What happened with Benson?" I turn to look at my clock: 1:58 a.m.

Holy crap! Eight hours? I can't help but think of the possibilities. But one stands out above them all: *Did she spend eight hours with him in the backseat of a car in underground parking?*

Silence. Cassia's not with me. I think I can sense her in my room, though. My eyes then focus on a piece of paper in front of me. It's Cassia's handwriting.

Thank you for letting me have tonight, and don't worry, there wasn't anything past first base. I'm so sorry to ask this of you, but I need you to visit Benson and tell him everything. I mean EVERYTHING. Please, Camry. For me. I'll show you why in a few days. He's expecting you in two weeks.

I'm going back to New York for a while. This is the end of the bucket list. I can't keep doing this to you. I'm sad to leave and not spend time with you, but promise me you'll let me go and live your life to the fullest.

I love you,
Cassia

P.S. Also, promise me you will *think of me when you look up to admire the sky.*

There's real, actual, physical pain that pangs in my chest cavity as I read it. "Cassia?" I ask my room. "Please tell me what this is all about," I beg. *Tell Benson everything?* I mean, I was going to tell him my real name at least, but she's wanting *everything. Really?*

Silence.

I sigh and read it again. Whatever tinge of worry I had a moment ago about what she did with Benson has completely faded as I understand what this note really means, what her silence really means. She's not going to be with me anymore. I mean, she'll "show" me in a dream what she means by having me tell Benson everything, and she said she'd keep me in the loop with things, but it's not going to be the same; it's not going to be like it has been. Then again, things were changing anyway; the guys have complicated things between Cassia and me.

My eyes begin to water, and my throat hurts. I swallow as I realize I can't stop her from what she believes she has to do. And she believes *this*. I can't stop her from leaving any more than I can stop the Earth from spinning.

"Promise." I hear her beg a whisper in my ear. My bedroom light flickers.

Closing my eyes, I silently promise her that I'll talk with Benson, I'll think of her every day, and I'll let her go. I drop my head in my hands to cry. I feel the warmth of her love wrap around me like a hug, and eventually, something inside me shifts, and I can accept what she's doing. I *can* let her go.

My light flickers again, and then my room feels empty. *I* feel empty, like something's been drained from me, something essential to life. I didn't even feel this way when I moved here and first realized how alone I was. I feel worse than that right now; I feel not only hollow but without purpose. *What will I do if not this?*

Friday, August 20

I'm a zombie at work because I only slept an hour before my alarm went off this morning. And because of my zombie-like state, I decide to skip working out when I'm done here, pretty certain my arms will detach if I try to lift dumbbells. My imagination runs wild with this picture: me standing upright and dumbly looking down at my detached arms that are still gripping the dumbbells, sticking straight up in the air.

I blink. *Enough of that.*

But seriously, I'm surprised I can pull books out of boxes. As I weakly do this, one book at a time, I think of Cassia and Benson. A lot. Too much. I hate not knowing the details of their time together, but there's nothing I can do about it. I'm a little sunburned on my forehead, nose, and forearms, so they were outside for a while. But other than that, I'm finding no other clues as to what they did together. I just have to wait to see if Cassia will give me a dream. I didn't realize I needed to give her a curfew—didn't think they'd stay out that late.

I'm having anxiety about talking to Benson in two weeks. *How am I supposed to tell him everything? And why? Because I need more drama right now?*

I was going to keep the promise to Cassia. At the time, I thought I *could* let her go. Let it *all* go. I think she leaves more of an impression on me when she's with me than I realize, if that makes sense. After she gave me her ghostly hug, I was totally willing to let her go last night, which is a bit out of character for me. But as I woke up this morning, my brain was immediately thinking about going to New York and just doing what needs to be done without her consent. Last night was a lie.

The last time I lied was…well, technically, it was the other night to my friends. And all of the Benson stuff is a lie, but that's out of my control. Well, sort of. Have I lied to Jake? Suck. I have. I'm getting sidetracked. The point is I'm not usually a liar. In fact, I try really hard not to be.

I try to shift my thoughts to Jake. I was so excited to go out with him at first, but now it's only a few hours away, and I don't even have that nervous butterfly feeling. *Come on, butterflies! Where are you?* I slowly replay our date from last Saturday in my head, hoping it will happily fill up the last couple of hours of work and get me excited for later.

I'm so grateful I'm working with Zach today. He has tons of energy for the both of us, so he's picking up my slack. I'm a broken record telling him "sorry, thanks" over and over.

"Are you sick or something? You don't look good today," is what he said this morning. Then he felt bad telling me I didn't look good and tried to recover. "I mean, you look tired or sick or something. Are you okay to be here?"

"I'm fine. Just tired," I told him.

He teased me, saying, "You painted the town till the sun came up, didn't you? You're such a party animal, Camry." He shook his head at me with a wry smile, knowing I would never do that. Then he gave me the rest of his Starbucks coffee.

It helped. After all, I'm pulling books out of boxes. One at a time. So, obviously, it helped.

When I'm off, I drive to the travel agency. I don't care what the cost is; I'll figure it out. Well, hopefully, it's less than five thousand dollars. And I need to figure out a plan too.

Yeah, dingbat. That might be a good idea. Later, though.

Right now, I'm just focused on booking the trip.

The travel agency office is cool and quiet. *They need a radio or something.*

"Can I help you?" asks the woman at the front counter. I guess her to be in her early thirties. She has a pretty face with soft skin, and I like her makeup. Her eyeshadow matches her shirt. Peach. A good color with her dark hair.

"Yeah," I start. "I'd like to price out a trip to New York City." I step toward her.

"Sure," she says in a friendly way and motions me to follow her to another desk behind the counter.

I tell her how I tried to price some things on the internet, but (like a pro) she finds me a bargain: a weeklong stay is just under three thousand dollars. It's fortuitous and seals the deal for me. The only catch is the trip has to start by the end of August. I was sort of hoping to have a bit more time to plan things out. *Oh well. New York, here I come!*

I make a deposit of fifty dollars, which, more or less, saves what she started for me, and I plan to come back after the money is in my account from my parents. I'm going to leave knowing my tentative flights and dates and check-in times. She's given me several pamphlets on New York City and its sights, which I don't really care about. These will sit next to the post-concussion syndrome pamphlet on my passenger seat.

Back home, I fall onto my bed and manage to sleep for a couple of hours before I have to get ready for my date with Jake. Something about the nap makes me feel unreservedly refreshed. I sort of hoped Cassia would've given me a dream showing what she and Benson did for the eight hours I don't remember, the way she filled me in with the Subway conversation, but no images entered my mind. I simply slept well. Really well. Like, heavy.

I'm feeling better. And yeah, good rest is part of it, but it could be the fact I have things set in motion. Well, sort of. I think knowing even a tentative plan for New York is helping me to focus better on the date ahead of me. And it's helping me not to be so sad about what happened with Cassia last night and Benson before that.

Part of me wonders if something happened between her and Benson while they were out, causing her to want to leave so suddenly and decidedly, but I can't think what that'd be.

I make the conscious decision to wear my flat sandals; Jake isn't as tall as Benson. I goth up, wearing all black with capri leggings so if something happens and my dress flips up, I won't be giving everyone a peep show. I wear my makeup darker, make my ponytail high and poofy, and put on lots of black jewelry.

Walking into Jake's work, I see he's ready and waiting for me on the bench next to the drinking fountains…with *dead* flowers?

He jumps up, excited. He's wearing a Chevelle T-shirt. "Hey!" He hands me the dead bouquet with a lively smile. A couple of dry leaves fall to the floor in the exchange.

It's not until I take them that I remember what I said the other day about beautiful flowers. I giggle.

"I've been killing them since Sunday. No bee's gonna come near that bundle."

"How sweet of you. You shouldn't have," I say as we both laugh. "Thank you. I like your shirt."

"You're welcome, and thanks," he says, smoothing his shirt down and eyeing himself, then he gently pushes my back to walk me out.

Oh yeah, that shiver. *Ahhh.*

"You look properly ready for a rock concert too."

"Do I?" I ask, glancing down at myself now. "Like, I'm *really* asking because I'm not sure. At all. I did my best."

He laughs and answers excitedly, "Yes! You look great! How was your birthday? What'd you do?"

Follow-up questions. What a guy! "Spent the day with some friends from high school. It was fun."

He nods. "What'd you do?" he repeats, wanting details.

I share about Olive Garden and seeing the movie with Kayla, Sienna, and Lindsey. "I like Julia movies," I confess.

"Hmmm. I like *Ocean's Eleven.*"

"That's not a Julia movie," I argue.

He laughs. "How come? She's in it."

"Hardly."

"Fine." He thinks for a second. "*Hook.*"

Now I laugh. "*Tinkerbell*?" I shake my head. "That's still a stretch."

He shrugs, still smiling. He's parked at the end of the lot, but as we near his truck, he asks, "So where are we eating?"

"Yeah, I was thinking about that and…I'm sort of having a pig-out-on-pizza kind of day. What do you think?"

He cocks his head at me. "Hmm. Didn't see that one coming. I think that's great."

Most pizza joints don't have dine-in, or they're so crowded and loud they're terrible to try to eat in. I've thought of this also. "At the park? Not the one with all the homeless people." I scrunch my face. "A different one."

He laughs. "I know one we can go to. That's a great idea." He opens the door for me to climb in and stares at me with a striking smile. "Pizza in the park it is."

After getting the twenty-inch full-of-meat pizza with drinks, we sit on the grass of the beautiful and (more importantly) homeless-less Washington Square Park. Jake even fetches a blanket he'd shoved under the seat of his truck. It's a bit dirty, but I don't mind. And in the shade of the old locust trees, it's all quite pleasant. I mean, the day is still hot, and there are no clouds in the sky, but there's a slight breeze.

Until now, we've been talking about our workdays and the music on the radio. But things turn a little more uneasy when Jake asks me, "So why are you having a 'pig-out-on-pizza' day?" He's sitting cross-legged next to me, I notice (not across from me), and hands me a few napkins.

Suck! Why'd I say that? Recoiling, I say, "Well, that ties into the other story I'm still not ready to tell you. Just go with it."

He thinks for a second. "Ya know, you're gonna have to tell me eventually. Why not now?"

My eyes shift away.

"Let me get this straight," he goes on. "You wanting a pizza day ties into you not really wanting to go to a rock concert that you were going to buy a single ticket for?"

I continue to avoid his gaze and answer, "Yeah. Well. I mean, there are some things you don't just jump into…and this…is one of them. Can we talk about something else?"

He takes a bite. "It sounds to me like you don't want to go. You sure you don't want to do something else? I don't want to take you if it's stressing you out."

"I *do* want to go. I'm just…" I wish he'd stop. I have yet to bite into my delicious-looking slice. I stare down at it, lost in thought about what might happen tonight. Not only about things with Jake, but will Cassia maybe come? I hate to think of what she's going through back in New York. Things are coming to a head two thousand miles away, and here I am—on a date.

Ridiculous!

"I'm sorry," Jake says, pulling me back into the moment, the one where I'm on the blanket in the park, eating pizza with his gorgeous self. "I didn't realize it was a sensitive subject." He's being sincere, and I realize my eyes are watery.

I blink and swallow. "No. I'm sorry. I promise I *am* a normal girl, normally. But you've met me at a strange time. There's a lot going on and…and I don't know." I say most of this to the pizza instead of Jake.

"Okay. Never mind. Let's just pig out on pizza." He shoves half of a new slice in his mouth, and I finally take a bite.

Things go much better after that. Like at the restaurant last week, we talk effortlessly. We learn about each other's family, work, and school. His life parallels my own in some ways. He's an only child. He dated someone in high school, but she moved away for college. He loves music. He lives on his own, no roommates; except he has a house, and I have an apartment. I think he has more friends than I do, though, especially since Cassia doesn't really count. Even my high school friends don't really count anymore.

A few small crust pieces litter the inside of the pizza box, and I'm fit to burst. I worry I'll need to pee soon, so we hit a sandwich shop across the street to use the restroom before we head over to the concert. *Am I crazy for telling him I still want to do this? I mean, a rock concert? I imagine the dangers of a rock concert and wish Cassia were here.*

A dim setting along with a cigarette stench welcomes us as we enter for the concert. The crowd is loud, excited for the show to begin. There's an insane amount of energy in the air here. We're a bit late, but the opening band has yet to start. Our tickets are for upper seats to the left of the stage. As I peer down at the mass of people on the floor, it's easy to imagine a mosh pit breaking out. The house lights dim, and beams of colorful stage lights reach out to all of us. The boom of bass notes fills the building, followed by a cloud of fog from the edge of the stage. Members of the opening band emerge as the crowd cheers wildly and bodysurfing starts.

I think of Cassia and *will* her to come for just a minute. Just *one* minute.

The individuals here are of a certain breed. Mohawks mix with hippie hair and tattoos and gauged ears to become a rough sea of people. Their movements crash like waves upon themselves.

As I pan over all the people, I think, *Why do they waste their energy on the opening band?* I also think, even though I've chosen black clothing, I don't belong. And even though we have assigned seats, people all around stand and move about as they please. I also stand. They bump into us, and I try to keep my ground. I'm not a jumper or a screamer; I find this type of music hard to dance to. I mean, if I had space, I could whip up a modern/jazz routine, I suppose, but this is *very* different from dancing to the radio in my living room. I imagine myself doing that and internally laugh.

I blink. *Enough of that.*

Then I see a guy behind me with bloodshot eyes and realize he's stoned. He doesn't have a seat. He's just in the large walkway behind us with a bunch of other people who are high. I'm nervous I'm going to get secondhand high. I've never been stoned before, never had the desire to lose any sort of control; plus, no singer (or even dancer) in their right mind would smoke anything. I went to a party in high school where marijuana made its appearance, and yes, people were having fun, but they also were acting like idiots. I can act like an idiot all on my own, thank you very much. No need to inhale smoke to do it. I know this world of "getting high while rocking out" exists, but I never enter it, so…*interesting.*

The smell of the drug is becoming thicker as the songs play on. Jake stays close to me. He cups his hands around his mouth to carry his cheering as far as possible with the rest of the crowd.

I try to soak in every detail just in case Cassia does come visit me, so I can share the memory at least. The crowd is generous with applause as the opening band walks off stage. I sit to rest and close my eyes to will Cassia here one more time.

Jake grabs my shoulder and leans in so I can hear him. "Are you okay?"

I nod, and he sits next to me. The crowd is still loud, and I'm sweating. There are so many people here. I wipe my forehead and fan myself. Jake notices and seems as though he wants to ask me something but doesn't. The stoner who was behind me is now on the other side of Jake, offering him a joint, but Jake declines. Again, no singer in their right mind would smoke anything, but I still wonder if it's because he's with me. Then the stoner offers it to me, and I decline but wonder if Cassia would've accepted. *Is that on her bucket list? Has she ever been high?*

Chevelle takes their time coming onstage, and the crowd is beginning to grow restless. A fight breaks out behind us. Jake pulls me up and out of the way of the two men shoving each other and entering our space. He's then separated from me as the conflict pushes between us. But then the lights start, and the first song of the band we all came to see starts to play. This breaks up the battle. *Thank goodness!*

I'm out of the fight zone and decide to stay put, hoping Jake will find me. I glance excitedly down at the stage. I actually don't mind this song. After a minute or so, Jake makes his way over to me. I look at him, seeing the relief of finding me on his face.

I grin and wave him to me while singing along. *"So send the pain below…"* Of course, he can't hear my mezzo-soprano amongst the competition, but he sees my lips move and laughs.

Halfway through the second song, another fight breaks out behind us. *Did we pick a bad night to come? Is it just this particular crowd? Maybe this is how all rock concerts are.* I turn my head to see what's going on just as a pack of people shoves into me. Several of us fall, and

I'm squished by the weight of a man who needs to lose fifty pounds. *Ooof, pretty sure that was two hundred pounds I didn't need on top of me.*

Finally, I hear Jake yelling over the music and the fight. I'm on the floor on my stomach, but I start to push myself up after the heavy man finally gets off me. Someone other than Jake helps me up, holding on to my arm. I'm about to thank him until I notice the drunk look in his eyes. He looks me up and down and nauseatingly licks his lips. I try to twist and search for Jake, but he squishes his body against mine and tries to dance with me. He stinks of alcohol and sweat.

O, Jake, Jake, wherefore art thou, Jake? At long last, Jake is beside me, grabbing my hand to rescue me. But somehow, this drunken loser has catlike reflexes and throws a punch straight into Jake's beautiful face. Jake amazingly holds his ground even as his head snaps back from the blow. He doesn't reach for his face to ease the pain. Instead, he keeps a grip on my hand and blinks hard.

I glare at the drunk. "Hey!" I shout at him, then shove him hard with my other hand. He doesn't move much, but he notices Jake's hand clasped in mine and turns away after a flick of his wrist, giving up.

Jake leads me, and we make our way through the crowd. He pulls me out onto the large terrace and into the cooling night air of Salt Lake. I don't think we needed to completely *leave* the concert, perhaps just relocate, but I start to hobble; my ankle hurts. And I realize I'm wet; someone spilled a drink on me, and now I smell like alcohol. Jake looks me over.

Okay, maybe it was good we left.

He stops at the top of the waterfall steps and orders me to sit down. The last few steps force me to walk on the toes of my right foot. It's the same ankle I sprained earlier this year. The swelling has started, and the straps of my sandal are digging into my skin.

As I sit to undo the little buckle, I explain, "I sprained my ankle." No doubt he's already noticed this, but I felt the need to say it anyway.

"Here." He motions for me to give my foot to him. "Let me see." He scoots a step lower and gently tries to move my ankle around a little bit while pressing his thumb into the swelling. I pull back in pain. "Are you sure it isn't broken?"

"I don't think so," I say.

I'm not about to go to the emergency room. If it doesn't get better, I may go to the doctor, but I'll be damned if I'm paying the expense of an

ER visit again. I think he wants to say more but doesn't. Instead, he pulls my bangs aside to reveal a goose egg on my forehead.

He winces and looks into my eyes. "Are you sure you don't want to go to the emergency room?"

I feel the bump; it's on the opposite side from my scar. It all happened so fast. I don't remember hitting my head…or twisting my ankle…or someone spilling their drink on me. A flash of post-concussion syndrome enters my thoughts. *What'd that pamphlet say about a second injury before the first one has healed?*

I answer, "I'm sure. Are you okay?" I gesture to his nose, which now has a drop of blood coming out of one of his nostrils. Seeing it, my hand reaches for my own nose out of sympathy pain. "Oh jeez. I'm so sorry."

He dabs at the drop, then sniffs. "Don't be," he tells me. "It's not broken. It was a lousy punch." He pauses. "I think someone spilled on you too."

I look down at myself and chuckle. Even though Cassia's not up there, I tilt my head to the night sky and smile as if she is.

Jake's smiling, too, and offers a chuckle back. "Do you see why I thought you were crazy to come to something like this by yourself? Korn would've probably been worse."

I burst into complete laughter now. Partly because my ankle hurts like hell, and I have a headache from hell, and if I don't laugh, I'll probably cry. And partly because Jake is right; that was *crazy*. "Cassia would've loved that," I say and immediately regret it.

"Who's Cassia?" Jake asks.

I have to go with it. "Just a friend who would've loved that."

"The one you bowl with?"

I nod.

"Well, why didn't she come with you?"

"She…had to go back to New York."

"Oh. Well, what about your other friends?"

I shake my head. "Not their thing. At all."

He squints at me. "I'm gonna figure out this whole you-going-to-a-rock-concert-alone thing. Just you wait."

I scoff. "Oh. Ya think? I don't know. It's a tough one."

He's silent for a moment, thinking. Finally, he says, "We need to wrap your ankle." He stands and turns his back to me. Looking over his shoulder and gesturing with his hands to his sides, he tells me to jump on his back, and he'll give me a piggyback ride to his truck.

"No," I protest. "It's okay. I can walk." I stand and hobble one step, which hurts like hell, as Jake tells me not to be ridiculous.

I give in, standing with difficulty, then climb onto his back. He's strong; I can feel his back and shoulder muscles working easily. After the first of three blocks, I feel bad and tell him I can walk. I didn't really think about how far away we had to park, and with each of his steps, my head throbs.

"No way," he replies.

"I feel bad," I admit.

"Oh please! Would you be put out if you had to carry a puppy down the street?"

I scoff. "Puppies don't weigh as much as I do."

"Okay. How 'bout this by way of argument? My mom would kill me if she found out I made you walk three blocks on a sprained, possibly broken, ankle."

"So don't tell her," I argue. But I believe him; his mom seems like she'd give him a hard time about that sort of thing, being a nurse and all.

"I can't not tell my mom about this date. She's gonna be all nosy about it."

"Really?"

"Well, yeah. I mean…"

I wait, but he doesn't finish. I tilt my head to get a look at him. He sighs and halfway rolls his eyes. I realize and tease him, "Oh. You mean there's something you're not ready to tell me just yet?"

He breathes a small laugh.

I want to know what it is, but I don't make a big deal of it because I understand. I change the subject. "Thanks. For taking me."

"I'm sorry it wasn't better."

"And carrying me," I add. "You can stop to rest if you need to." His breathing has quickened.

"Eh. We're almost there."

The last block, I savor each breath of him as the slight breeze blows his scent back to me. Jake skillfully opens the passenger door of his truck while still holding on to me and sets me gently in the seat. He pushes the button that moves the seat back. I see him reach for my foot, then stop himself. Instead, he tells me to rest it on his dashboard. It needs to be elevated, I know. I do as he says but think I'd have liked the touch from him.

He gives me some ibuprofen from his console and tells me, "We'll go to my house. I have all the stuff we need there."

I'm sure he does, probably courtesy of his mother, the nurse. Still, I say, "I don't want to take your stuff. We can go to the store."

"Three blocks was one thing. I'm not going to piggyback you around the store." He laughs.

I chuckle too, picturing that. "I could wait in the truck. I'll give you my money."

"Or you could just come to my house," he reasons with a casual tone. "We'll wrap it up, get some ice on it…Maybe we could hang out, watch a movie or somethin'. What do ya think?"

I'm okay with not going to the emergency room, but am I okay going to Jake's house this soon? I'm starting to feel like crap, so I don't know. I can't think. I'm not about to complain about my condition; the medicine will kick in, and I'm sure it'll be fine. "All right," I tell him, and he drives to his house in the Avenues.

Jake jokes as he carries me to his front door. "Second date, and I got you to come home with me."

I whistle as if to say he's smooth, and he laughs.

Maples and locust trees line his block, lifting the sidewalks as their old roots spread through the soil. His house is old as well. The trees maybe shared the beginning of their life with the first owner of the red brick house. It's well maintained. I note the weeded flower beds flanking both sides of the three-step porch. Marigolds and petunias alternate and share the space evenly. I wonder to myself if this is all Jake's doing or if his mother had something to do with it. She seems like the type to impose her thoughts of gardening upon her son too. The grass is cut, and the bushes along the approach are trimmed also.

As we enter, it smells clean inside, like fresh laundry, and I can see it's been remodeled and updated. I wonder about this as well, if it's his doing or if he bought it this way. He chooses to set me on the chair in the living room to rest my foot on the ottoman, then disappears down the hallway.

He owns a large flat-screen surrounded by speakers that take up his entire front window. I suppose he doesn't care to ever look out it. Signed posters of bands decorate his walls, along with signed portraits with personalized notes.

I want to stand to read them all, but obviously, I won't. Instead, I slouch and rest my head on the cushy back of the taupe chair. I close my eyes and patiently wait for Jake, thinking how I won't make it through a movie. Once the pain lessens, I could easily just fall asleep.

After a minute, I hear him in the kitchen making banging noises and talking to himself. When he comes back to me, he explains, "I couldn't find the cold pack at first. I had to take all the food out of my freezer."

He kneels, and his hands move quickly and skillfully as he starts to wrap my ankle. It seems as if he's done this many times. His touch is gentle and empathetic. Whether he learned this from his mom or school, I don't know, but whoever it was, they've taught him well.

After he places the cold pack over the top of my foot, he explains that even my toes will probably have bruising.

"I know. I sprained this same ankle in January."

He looks from my toes to my eyes and raises a brow. "Dance?"

"No. I fell down the stairs on campus."

He blinks and chuckles.

"Thank you. It feels good," I tell him, meaning the wrap. The amount of compression is perfectly comforting.

He smiles and stares thoughtfully at me, long enough it makes me a little uncomfortable.

"I like your posters," I comment lamely and gesture to some of them.

"Look at the light," he orders me, ignoring my comment. He doesn't take his eyes off mine, only points to the ceiling light in the center of the room.

I glance at it and quickly look back at him. I don't understand why I'm looking at his light fixture. He leans over my legs toward me and stares at me again so deeply I feel hypnotized. *Is he going to kiss me?* The pressure in my head builds, and the butterflies are going crazy again.

He orders me again to look at his ceiling light.

I look again, longer. *What does he want me to see?* I squint.

"Okay," he says. "Look at me."

I meet his green eyes with mine. *He's not going to kiss me. His face is too serious.*

"I think you may have a concussion. Do you feel sick?"

I think about the butterflies. *Is it nausea instead?* "No." But there's a question and hesitation in my answer.

Jake jumps up and leaves the room. Another cold pack accompanies him when he returns. He grabs a pillow from his sofa and lifts my foot even more, then places the cold pack gently on my goose egg as he kneels next to me this time. "You're stayin' here tonight."

I throw an apprehensive glance at him; I don't want to be a burden. Deep down, though, I'm completely touched and taken with him.

"Don't even sweat it," he remarks easily. "Are you dizzy?"

"No. Just a headache. How's your nose?"

He shrugs. "Fine. No worries."

I reach to take over and hold the ice on my head in place.

"No, I got it." He holds it and looks at me, a mere six inches from my face. "Best date ever!" His eyes grow wide, and his smile spreads across his face, showing all of his perfectly straight teeth.

I laugh. The motion makes my head hurt more. *Is this my third concussion? Fourth? What happens to the brain with too many concussions again?*

He also laughs. "I mean it."

I cover my eyes, embarrassed and tired. Tears rush to them underneath the lids as I hide my face. *Is it because I'm laughing, or am I about to cry?* I can't decide.

Jake continues. "I mean, I'm already excited for our next date. I feel like every time I see you, it's such an adventure. And I'm a thrill seeker, so, you know…we're meant to be together, it seems."

I open my eyes and wipe the corners of them. I play off the tears to be laughing tears, but I think I *am* on the edge of losing it. I look at him. His eyes are green and pure and sincere. They tell me, *You're okay, Camry.*

If he were to grab my hand and lace our fingers, I'd melt just as I did with Benson. *Is that a girl thing?* I mean, would any good-looking guy warm my heart with a sincere look or a handhold?

No. I'm convinced, no.

I like Jake. I like how he didn't push the topic of why I wanted pizza. I like how he didn't disappoint me by accepting the joint. I like the way he looks at me like how he is right now, all deep and genuine. I'm glad I like Jake. I wanted to like him; we have so much in common.

The words "so much in common" make me think of Cassia and feel guilty. *Why do I feel guilty?* I don't know, but it's enough to pull my gaze away from Jake.

"No. Keep looking at me. You need to stay awake. For a while, at least."

He means because of the possible concussion. Then I have a sudden thought and ask, "Where's your studio?"

"Downstairs," he says simply.

I move to sit up but think better of it. Jake quickly stops me anyway. "I wanna hear your song," I tell him.

"Yeah?" he asks, excitement reaching his voice.

I nod. "Of course."

I grab hold of the cold pack on my head, and he disappears to get his laptop and comes back upstairs with a folding chair too. Sitting next to me, he balances the laptop on the cushy arm of my chair, then clicks the icon to open the song while explaining he sang both parts but will tell me when it's supposed to be the girl's part.

I try to conceal my worry that I won't be a good fit or quite the mezzo-soprano he's searching for. I feel like he's banking on me too much. He seems eager.

"I haven't let anyone listen to this," he admits, and I wonder if I misinterpreted him as being eager just now. It could be he's anxious. "But I feel like you…" He looks at me thoughtfully.

"Like I what?"

"Never mind." He clicks the play button, and soft piano music starts.

"You play the piano?" I ask.

"I play a lot of things."

I think how that makes sense, and I shouldn't be so surprised. All the instruments he can play have never come up in our conversations. He's not one to brag, though, I'm noticing. It's a beautiful melody. After eight measures, new synthesized sounds begin, still soft, though. If Coldplay and One Republic had a baby, it would be Jake's song. And then Jake's deep voice comes through the laptop speakers, and it's as beautiful as he is.

I think my voice would match his nicely, or at least, it wouldn't be the worst combination. I don't know if my radio-singing-in-the-car voice is the same as when I'm actually *trying* to sound good. I haven't tried to sound good for a year, so I could be totally wrong. I push this thought aside and try to focus on Jake's voice and lyrics. I watch his voice move up and down on the screen as the time rolls it by.

I thought I'd be scared to fall in love,
But you lead me; you make it easy.
I don't want any secrets, no regrets.
You're the one, the one for me.
New sounds join the piano, and Jake informs me the girl would sing:
I thought I'd be scared to love like this,
But my dreams are good when I'm with you.
And all my fears, they disappear.

I feel it still; can this be true?

The beat and piano pick up for the climax. Jake says both would sing this part, the chorus:

And I feel so close to you right now.
It should be no surprise.
It won't be long; we'll take our bow.
You and I.

The fire at the funeral has begun.
The ache is no surprise.
But forever, we will be unbroken.
You and I.

Jake wears an unsure expression and watches me listen to the piano solo. "Back to me," he says.

When you have to say your last goodbye,
Just please, please take your time.
And please, please don't fade away.
There's only so much I can take.

He points to the computer, meaning it's back to the girl again.

Trust, my love, it's hard to say goodbye.
I'll try, try to take my time.
I don't want, don't want to fade away.
There's only so much I can take.

Both would sing the chorus again. "On the next verse, I get the first two lines," Jake explains, "and the girl gets the last two."

I'm standing on the edge; my eyes are open.
We had it all, thought we'd never fall.

And even if I fade, fade away,
I'll make sure a piece is there to stay.

The chorus runs one more time with a couple of tweaks. When the song finishes with a soft piano fade, I stare at him, wide-eyed. My mouth is open, but I'm not sure how to say all my thoughts. I finally sort them out and say, "You're amazing. That was really beautiful."

He doesn't say anything. Instead, he closes the desktop window that held the beautiful song and shuts the laptop.

I mean it, and I want him to know I mean it. "Jake, seriously."

He shyly says, "Thanks."

We stare at each other but not for long because he looks away from me. I've never seen him unsure of himself. He always seems so confident—humble, but confident. Music is his strength and his weakness. He's passionate and talented yet vulnerable to criticism and even praise.

I assume the song is about his previous girlfriend. He said she moved away to college. "What was her name?" I ask.

He softly chuckles to himself, but I don't know why. "Nicki."

I think the funeral is probably just a metaphor for the death of their relationship. But if I'm wrong and the song isn't about his ex-girlfriend at all but a best-friend-since-childhood girl who died of cancer, then I better wait for more from him. So I watch him and wait. I watch him fidget with his hands, feeling his fingernails and cracking his knuckles.

He finally says, "We mutually broke up; it's not like I'm sad about it still. It's just…a little weird having someone else hear it."

Whew! Not cancer. "Because it's personal. I get it. Do you guys still talk?" I shake my head at myself. "Never mind. That's maybe not my business."

"No, it's fine." He shrugs as part of his answer. "Sometimes. It's getting less and less."

There's so much he's not saying because I'm me. If I were his mom or some other neutral party, he'd be admitting more. Probably something like how he still cares about her, misses her, is upset they're growing apart.

But I really do get it.

Like the song says, he doesn't want her to fade away. His memories of the two of them are too precious for him to lose. He always wants to have a piece of her. This doesn't bother me. I understand.

Then he does say more, in an embarrassed tone. "I haven't dated anyone since she left. That's why my mom"—he inhales with rounding eyes—"is going to want all the details."

I smile but decide against commenting on the amount of pressure he didn't mean to just put on me. Instead, I tap the cold pack I'm holding on my head and say, "Well, you have quite the story to tell her."

"Yes, I do," he agrees. He sets the laptop on the floor. "Let me know if you want to do the song."

"Hmmm. I don't think I'm as good as you, but would you be willing to burn me a copy? I could practice at home."

"Sure. How you feelin'?"

I shrug. "The ibuprofen is helping."

We stay up until one in the morning talking. He mentions more than once I'm showing good signs of not having severe head trauma. That seems sort of like a miracle, considering I bonked my head and got stitches, what, two weeks ago?

I manage to hop to the bathroom, which gives me a chance to straighten out and clean myself up a bit. I look awful, but I'm not embarrassed about it. I feel comfortable with Jake, like I've known him a long time. Or possibly, it's because this isn't the first time he's seen me look this awful, and he still wanted to go out with me. That's a miracle too.

Saturday, August 21

After sleeping a few hours, I hear the front door open. Tiredly, I peel open my eyes and lift my head. Jake has fallen asleep in the folding chair, leaning over with his head on the pillowy arm of my chair. I welcome the comfort of the blanket he's placed over the top of me.

There are two kinds of people in this world: the ones who will sleep uncomfortably next to you in a folding chair and the ones who won't. I smile at the fact that Jake is the former. Silver lining of spraining an ankle? Sleeping next to a nice and handsome guy.

A ray of sunshine has blasted in through the half-open door, along with the person letting themself in: Jake's mother, Caroline. She stops suddenly and yelps. The yelp is what wakes Jake.

He rubs his eye and groggily says, "Mom, what're you doing here?"

I wipe from my lip a small amount of drool that had embarrassingly trailed from the corner of my mouth. I attempt a grin for his mom as she stares at me with unhidden surprise.

"I brought your mail," she answers, looking at my ankle, which hangs out of the bottom of the blanket.

"You've got to stop just letting yourself in. I'm starting to regret giving you a key. What if I were walking around naked?"

"Oh please! I'm a nurse. I've seen it all," she answers with a flick of her wrist, not even fazed.

She closes the door, and Jake shoots me a look as if to say, *It was worth a try*. Then after rubbing his eyes again and yawning, he sleepily gestures while saying, "Mom, you remember Camry. Camry—"

"Of course. How could I forget?" She turns to me, all her deep laugh lines on display. "I'm so glad you went out with my Jakey." She then points to my ankle. "Looks like it was a wild concert…or a wild night."

"Mom!"

I look at Jake and offer a sheepish grin. *Is she suggesting what I think she's suggesting?*

A slight blush crosses Jake's face.

Yes, she is, I decide.

"Is it sprained? What happened?" She hands Jake his mail.

"Yeah," I say and push myself up a bit.

Jake cuts in. "It was a wild concert. Let's just leave it at that."

Caroline quickly puts up her finger. "I have a crutch!" she says with round eyes. "In the car. Only one, but it'll be better than nothing. You can have it. I'll be right back." Before either of us can respond, she's out the door in a flash.

Jake starts to make an apology, I assume for the bluntness she exhibits.

"It's okay. She's a funny lady."

"She means well," he offers.

"I know. It's nice you have a mom who cares so much."

Jake glances at me with sympathy. I shared with him last night how my relationship with my parents is.

I rake my fingers through my hair and straighten my clothes before she comes storming in again. I look at Jake and see his hair is squished on the side he was sleeping on. It's not much crazier than how he normally styles it, but he tries to fix it anyway, just as I do.

After adjusting the crutch and trying it out upon Caroline's insistence, she starts with small talk about why Jake isn't working today.

"I told you I wasn't gonna work today," he answers, "because I figured I'd be tired from the concert." He stands with the front door open and a hand on the knob. Leaning down to her, he gives her a half hug with a kiss on the cheek. "I'll call ya later," he tells her and manages to gently push her out.

I hang back a little, next to the TV, and wave as she and I say goodbye to each other.

"Good luck with that ankle," she hollers to me from the porch.

"Thanks," I say.

Closing the door, Jake says, "Man, she was pained, not being able to ask details." I laugh, and he asks if I want a glass of water.

"Please." As he disappears around the wall, I remember something. "Your TV turned on in the middle of the night," I say.

"Oh really? Must be Sam," he says indifferently. I hear the water turn on and off.

I look at him expectantly as he brings me a glass with the kind addition of Tylenol.

"He's a ghost. He hasn't come around for a while, though." Jake looks me over while taking a drink. "Maybe he likes you." He smiles as if it's a jolly joke, but I know he's semi-serious.

"You believe in ghosts?" I ask, interested and a little weirded out.

"Yeah. I mean, this is an old house, right? Don't you?"

Of course, I think of Cassia. "Yeah." I glance at the TV, feeling a bit like I'm in *The Twilight Zone*. The classic theme music runs through my head. "How do you know his name is Sam?"

"I don't. I named him that. I figured it could go for a boy or a girl, but I find when I talk about him, I say *him*, so maybe that was dumb."

"No, I like Sam." I swallow the pills with a gulp and thank him. My head still hurts, but not as badly as last night.

He indulges my curiosity. "When I moved in, it was kind of a dump, so my dad and I started remodeling. I don't think Sam liked it. Lots of banging. Tools would go missing. I had bad dreams for a while. You know, stuff like that. But I think when all was said and done, he must like it now. He still messes with the TV and the lights from time to time. I think it's just to let me know he's still around."

"Weird," is all I can think to say. I've finished my glass of water, and he takes it back from me to the kitchen. I reposition myself with the crutch. "Dreams, huh?" I ask.

The glasses clank in the sink. "Yeah," he hollers. "Like, I'd dream I'd have accidents with the saw or the nail gun. One time I fell off the roof."

"And that didn't bother you?" I'm thinking of Cassia. She has to try the dreams again. If she could just get through to her dad with dreams, or maybe she could scare Tiffanie out of following through with it all.

Jake comes back again with half a grin. "Well, if I said yes, then I'd seem like a wimp. This is only our second date. I can't have you thinking I'm a wimp."

I watch him for a moment, then peek at the clock on the wall behind him. "When does it become the third date?"

He turns, also glancing at the time. "Now. If you wanna go get some breakfast."

I glance down at myself and think about how I still smell like alcohol and my ankle still hurts along with my head. I'm sure my makeup has worn off and my hair is a mess too.

He chuckles. "Wanna borrow one of my shirts?"

I nod.

The waitress takes our order and leaves. We're sitting across from each other this time. Jake tells me to rest my foot on his lap. I do so, then he asks me, "So what's your ghost story? You must have one if you believe." He sets his hand on my ankle.

I look at him, unsure. In a way, I want to share what's happening to me with Jake. *Do I test this out on him before I have to tell Benson?* Knowing Jake has a ghost experience of his own *does* make me feel like he'd understand, but still, I hesitate. I feel like I need Cassia's permission.

"Maybe some other time," I say. "This is only our third date. I have to make sure you know I'm not crazy before I tell you."

"So far, I'm…impressed with you." He sucks an ice cube from his water and crunches it.

My elbow is on the table with my hand holding my head up. I joke, "You make it sound like I'm interviewing for a job."

He smiles. "No. You know what I mean. You've been tallying me up too. Everyone does it when they date."

My eyebrows slowly draw together. *So are we officially "dating?" I suppose we're going on dates, so I suppose one could be tallying.* "I guess," I say.

"You've got five, almost six pros and only one con. That's pretty damn good."

I choke on my water and chuckle. "Who says stuff like that?" *And what's the con? That I won't tell him my secret? That my car is two different colors? That I'm accident-prone? Jeez, I could potentially have several cons now that I think about it.*

He laughs. "Me. Come on. What about me so far?"

"Oh, crikey. Putting me on the spot? Okay." I think for a minute.

Jake taps his fingers.

Scowling at the tapping, I say, "You can just stop that. It's not like I've been adding them up as we go, like you. I have to think back."

"Six, for sure. Maybe seven," he says.

This distracts me. I blink but sneer. Then I close my eyes and go back to counting on my fingers. Pros: Attractive. Saved my life (that's a big one). Thoughtful. Gentleman. Should I count that he has a job, has a vehicle, has a goal in life? Good with an ace bandage and noticing a concussion. Good sense of humor. Same interests. *Ugh!* That one makes me think of Benson. Con: Benson's cousin (*that's* a big one)! All my fingers are open, and so are my eyes now.

He says with round eyes, "I hope that's the pros list."

"Well, I don't know if I should count some of them. I don't know what you're counting."

"Hey, everyone has different things that're important to them. How many cons do I have?"

I study him for a second. Holding up a finger, I say, "One. But it's not your fault, so maybe it shouldn't count."

He shifts his position, curious. "Hey, I told you I didn't want to take you if you didn't really want to go."

I raise my eyebrows and hold up a second finger. "Don't assume. That's not it."

He holds up both hands. "Okay. I'm sorry. You're right."

I put my second finger down, and he returns his hand to the top of my foot.

"You're not gonna tell me, are you?" He narrows his eyes at me.

"Are you gonna tell me *my* con?"

He thinks for a long second, looking up to the ceiling. "Technically, it's not your fault either. So…I guess we don't count the cons?"

But mine for him is so big! I don't know if I can't count it.

The waitress brings our delicious-looking pancakes, eggs, and bacon. "Thank you," we say to her in unison.

The distraction of food makes it so I don't have to really answer him. *Whew! Good. Because what if I don't count it? What if it's not a con? Then what?* I don't want to think about that now. One day at a time. Hell, one *date* at a time. And the last one was a bit of a doozy, so let's not gunk this one up.

Jake wants to drive me home, but I insist I need my car. I finally persuade him I'm perfectly capable of driving with a bum ankle. I did it before. He comes around the truck and helps me out. We stand next to my car. The morning is heating up as August weather usually promises.

"I wanna call and check on you later. Is that all right?" He raises a hand to block the sunlight blasting in his face.

I haven't even given Benson my number. I can't feel bad about that, though. Him blowing up my phone is a stress I don't need. Okay, let's be honest; he'd send one polite text and leave it at that. But still, that one text would loom over me everywhere I went for days on end.

Jake is waiting. "Yeah, that's fine," I tell him.

"Did you put my number in your phone? Just text me."

Duh! What a great idea. I reach for my phone and text him the brunette girl emoji who's waving. His phone chimes in his pocket, but he just stares at me.

Cassia pops into my mind as I stare back, replaying last night and this morning in my head. I'd never have gone to the concert if it weren't for her, but I did have fun, on the one hand. And if she hadn't wanted to do that, I'd never have met Jake.

The night didn't go as I'd pictured it. Spending the night at Jake's house and breakfast was far better (even with the sprained ankle) than going to a concert I'd figured I wouldn't like and a kiss I'd imagined might happen.

What am I waiting for? Because I feel like Jake likes me for me. And I'm *just* me around him. I can't be me with Benson; I have to be Cassia. But I can give all of me to Jake. All my glory this morning is my alcohol-smelling dress in my hands, no makeup, and bacon breath, not to mention that I'm a hobbling cripple. And yet, Jake's studying me with that thoughtful stare of his. I don't need to guard myself or hesitate anymore.

I'm about to move in to test the waters for a kiss when he grabs my shoulder as if to steady me. "You all right?"

Wow! Did I seriously misinterpret that whole scene? It's not a thoughtful stare in the way I thought? Either that, or my alcohol-smelling dress, no makeup, and bacon breath are off-putting to him. Not to mention, I'm a hobbling cripple. Who wants to kiss all that? All my glory this morning is…I'm a smelly, ugly idiot.

"You seem a little lost in thought," he adds.

"Yeah." I chuckle. "I guess you could say that." He helps me plop into my car with some difficulty, then reaches in his truck for something while I roll down my window to say goodbye.

Not knowing what to think of things now, Jake adds to my confusion by poking his head in and kissing me on the cheek, the way he kissed his mom. "I'll call you later," he says, also the way he did with his mom. He passes his CD through the window to me. "Almost forgot."

What the hell am I supposed to make of all this? I like you like I like my mom? Here's my CD so you can sing for me because that's all I really need from you?

After my confusing drive home, I clean myself up and try not to sleep. It'll mess me up if I sleep now. But all my recent thoughts of Jake are bugging the crap out of me, so I let my eyes grow heavy as I watch TV in bed, and I'm out after fighting it for only a few minutes.

A dream begins…

I'm outside the bowling alley with Benson. He's holding my face, looking into my eyes. His eyes are the color of the ocean. Camry always describes them as ocean blue. And she's right; the lashes pull you in, and you just want to be in his waters. That's how I feel now. I want to be in Benson's ocean right now. And forever.

Camry has let go. Completely. It's a miracle. She's given this time to me; I cannot waste it. I will not waste it. I tug Benson's shirt and pull him down for a kiss. His ocean is smooth and warm and comforting.

We separate, but he keeps hold of my face. "Yeah?" he asks with a grin. It's in response to his question earlier about spending the day with him before he thinks I have to go.

I joke by shaking my head no, then I say, "Yes."

His eyes scan me, and he laughs. He pulls me back into the bowling alley while explaining he has to let his boss know he won't be returning to work.

After he comes back from telling Chip, I ask, "Are you going to be in trouble?"

"Nah. Chip's cool. Plus, I called Nate to come work for me. He'll be here in twenty minutes or so. It'll be fine."

I've never seen a Nate there, but okay. We make our way over to his truck. I have no idea what he has planned, but I definitely need to respect Camry's body. Not that Benson is thinking that, but…

"What do ya want to do?" he asks me.

I glance around at nothing in particular. Then I look up and down the street. "Umm. I don't know."

"Never mind. I know a place to go," he says with finality and grabs hold of my hand. "Want a really good shake?"

Benson's hand is obviously bigger than mine—er, bigger than Camry's—but still, as our palms are pressed together, as the life lines and love lines of our hands match up, we fit. I answer with a squeeze of my hand in his. I've grown accustomed to squeezing in answer to questions. I chuckle to myself and remember to actually speak. "Yes."

We end up at a small, hole-in-the-wall-type joint, which has amazing shakes. We only sit for a minute before Benson stands back up and says, "Wait. We don't have time to sit. I have to fit like three dates in one here."

I look at him with a raised brow.

His forehead wrinkles with his big eyes. "Yes. I had plans. For dates with you. Come on." He motions for me to get moving.

"Oh. Uh, okay." I grab my shake.

He walks quickly back to his truck, and I can't help but laugh at him a bit as I try to keep up. He waggles a finger at me. "No, no. This is no laughing matter."

I open the door. "Are ya sure?"

Meeting face-to-face in the truck, he says, "I'm so sure. I've never been more sure."

"Okaaay." I draw the word out. "Where are we going, Mister So Sure?"

"Have you been to the zoo yet?"

I think back to the day Camry and I were talking about going to the zoo, but I stopped her. It was one of the first things we talked about doing—once she finally understood who I was, what I was, what we could do and be together. I stopped her because I'd been to the Central Park Zoo a hundred times. We went for a hike instead that day. Being in the mountains, on the trails, was so much more amazing. Who knew there was so much to see on a silly little hike? I'll never forget it.

Even though I've been to the zoo in New York, and I swear most zoos have got to be the same, I've never been to a zoo with Benson. And honestly, I don't think I could refuse him anything today. "I have not," I tell him with a smile.

We see the giraffes first and ride the train. Benson starts taking photos of us with his phone. I leave that to him, not wanting Camry's phone filled with pictures of her and Benson. That seems...problematic.

It takes him a while to work up the courage to ask me again, but after we finish watching the alligator and move on, he finally says, "Why are you going back?" His voice is soft and lacks confidence.

I huff a sigh as we stop and watch the orangutans move about. The vague truth isn't so bad when you subtract all the "I'm-dead-and-borrowing-this-body" stuff. "There's some family drama that I just...need to go back for." I contemplate telling him there has been a death in the family but don't want to have to keep up with a bunch of lies.

He leaves it at that, maybe sensing I don't want to talk more about it or just being his typical nice self. But he does say, "I want you to come back."

I turn and study him. His face is almost pained, so I pull his shirt, bringing him down to kiss his wound better. "Please don't—" I stop myself; I don't want to accuse him of ruining the day. It's not his fault I'm hiding something big. It's not his fault he likes me enough to be curious. I try again. "I don't want this day to be sad. Can we just pretend I'm not leaving?"

He gives this a lot of thought as he glances emotionlessly at the orangutans. I feel like he wants to say no, but he's trying, trying to do what I'm asking of him. He relents, brings his eyes back to me, and says with a slow blink, "Sure."

We make all the stops down and back up. We make sure to see the bird show and the sea lion show, but we miss the elephant show. Still, we admire the large gray creatures, and I think of Camry. They're one of her favorite animals. I know this like I know everything else about Camry: I have access to her mind and feelings.

Camry's likes and dislikes are easy to know; I just feel them. She likes elephants. When we came upon the elephants, I could feel a smile in my heart, and somehow, it had a "Camry" feel about it. I can feel the difference between her and me. She struggles with this sometimes (actually, often), but I don't.

Her memories are a bit more difficult. There has to be a trigger, then I have to dig a little to fully see and understand. It's easier if she thinks of it, then I see and feel it clearly, without all the work. All the work exhausts me, and then I can't stay as long.

Benson and I approach The Beastro, a restaurant within the zoo, and without even discussing it, we enter. Hunger was eating at both of us, apparently. Air conditioning cools my skin from the heat of the August sun. (It definitely can get hot in Utah. And dry. Camry moisturizes every day, but it's still not enough.) The smell of cooked meat drifts through the building, making my mouth water.

Other than Benson's question earlier, I've managed to keep the conversation about the animals. But after we order, Benson hits me with, "So may I ask what the family drama is?"

I glance out the window, thinking. There are gift shop items on a few racks outside the windows, and I watch a brother and sister argue about what's fair to purchase. I ponder twisting the different truths for Benson, wondering if that would be good enough to keep more of his questions at bay. There are about three options I quickly come up with, but when I look ahead to the end result, it's like a magic eight ball telling me, "Outlook not so good."

I hear him sigh, and I glance in his direction. He has his arms folded in front of him as he leans on the table. I feel like he's struggling to maintain himself. Finally, he surrenders, looking down. "Never mind."

I encourage him to tell me more about his family, and he obliges me with stories of his little brothers and sisters, some of which I know already; I follow him often. But his stories help fill the time and keep the topic off me. He's a good sport about it, and he's accomplishing the pretending I asked of him well.

Dinner hits the spot, and we make our way to the exit. "I need to hit the restrooms first," I tell him.

"Good idea," he agrees.

After using the toilet, I stare at Camry's face and body in the bathroom mirror for a long time. She's taller than I was by an inch or so, her fingers are longer than mine were, and her teeth are different but still straight. She had braces once, just as I did. Our noses are different from the side, hers being more straight-sloped and mine more ski-sloped. Otherwise, we're nearly identical. We're slender and fit. She dances, but I played tennis. Our hair is the same, only she keeps it straight most of the time and has thin bangs, whereas I prefer to give it a curl and no bangs. Our other facial features are so alike it's...uncanny. It's so bizarre, to see me and yet...not quite me. I'm like a copy of a copy, not quite the original. I've wondered what the significance of our looking so similar means. I know Camry has as well.

I love her so much for doing this for me. I don't know how I can ever repay her. I need to think on that more.

"Cassia?" Benson hollers into the bathroom. "You still in there?"

I've lost track of time and been in here too long. "I'm coming!" I holler back.

When I come out, he admits, "I was worried I'd lost ya. You okay?"

"Of course." I smooth my dress and glance at him. I'm ready to go, but it seems like he's not. He's rubbing one hand with his other thumb and biting his lip. He wants to say something, but he's holding back. "What?" I ask.

"I don't have your number." His entire body language says he was worried about me and wanted to call me but couldn't because Camry's never given him her number.

I'm about to say, "You don't need it," but change my mind and try to joke. "I'm not gonna ditch you."

It turns out this was still the wrong thing to say because he comes back with, "But you are. You're leaving tomorrow."

The ocean is getting rougher, and I'm weighing my options. Somehow, I end up with, "I have your number." It's weak and nowhere near good enough for Benson.

He retorts, "I don't believe you're ever gonna use it."

Well, he's correct on that one.

"I'm wracking my brain, Cassia. Trying to figure out what it is you're not telling me," he says, trying to remain calm in a stormy sea. "I'm trying to figure out ways that I can move to New York, for Christ's sake." He runs his hands through his hair, a sign of frustration. But when his hands drop back to his sides, he's amazingly composed when he speaks again. He's almost pleading. "I really wish you'd just open up about whatever is going on."

I've hung my head now because the tears have begun to sting. He pulls my chin up with one finger, but I step back. "I can't, okay?" It doesn't come out as strong as I want it to. It's weak and edged with anger. This is the first time I begin to regret coming with him. I should've known it'd turn into a Q and A about why I'm leaving, about my secret.

I'm aware of a little girl at a table next to us. She's watching me, and I suddenly have to get out of here. I begin walking.

Fast.

Benson follows, of course. He tries to grab my shoulder, but I yank it away and start jogging. The exit isn't far. I'm out of the zoo within seconds, but then I don't know where to go, so I stop. He catches up with me quickly but has the good sense to keep his distance and not touch me; he stays a couple of feet behind.

He ends up stuttering, not knowing what to say, "W-what...I-I—"

I wipe the corners of my eyes and sniff. "Can we just go?"

After what seems like forever, he's finally by my side, grabbing my hand and leading me to his truck. He opens the door for me, and I climb in. I've mostly collected myself as he rounds the back and steps in also. He starts it up so we have air conditioning, but he doesn't begin to drive. Instead, he sits with his hands in his lap, waiting expectantly.

I shove my embarrassment aside and try to think of a compromise. The best I come up with is, "I'm sorry." I don't look at him. I stare at the glove box in front of me. "I can't tell you. But...I can give you today. And I'm sorry that's all, but"—I brave a look at him—"it's all I've got. Believe me, I want it to be more so bad, but it's not up to me."

This makes him squint with confusion. I can only imagine what's going through his mind.

He takes a long time, then says, "Who's it up to?"

I open my mouth but close it again, not knowing how to answer.

"Your dad?" he guesses. He's still in this small, little world where dads control their daughters who have run off to Utah, forcing them to come back and not have any contact with any possible boy they've met there. He has no idea the complexity of this, no idea this is beyond anything he could guess—anything anyone could guess.

I reach, grab his hand, and squeeze it. "Can we please go to our second date?" This is what I ask with words, but my expression implores him to drop it and go back to pretending as we were before.

Benson thinks as he rubs his mouth and chin with his other hand. He looks down at our locked hands and adjusts his fingers. He's been thinking long enough that I begin to worry he's going to say no. I pull his hand up to my lips and kiss it, then set it on my lap. He turns away from me, looks out his window, and begins biting his thumbnail. I've never seen him bite his nails; he must also be biting down on whatever it is he wants to say.

The silence stretches and is killing me. I give him another option, feeling insecure. "Or...you can take me back to my car."

His head whips back to face me. A lack of understanding consumes him, then he shakes his head as if to clear some jumbled-up thoughts and says, "Do you want me to take you back to your car?"

"Not the slightest bit," I answer, confidently looking into his ocean eyes. We study each other for a long time. I'm dying to know what he's thinking.

"Okay then," he says. He shifts the truck in gear and drives to a different bowling alley on the other side of town.

I look at him curiously as we park.

"Yep." He answers my look. "If I could play against anyone in the world, it's you."

I can't help it; I grin from ear to ear, remembering our conversation from before.

"Get ready to get your butt kicked," Benson says, bouncing, fists up like a boxer. He's loosened up and is back to pretending for me. Also, he's paid, and we have our bowling shoes on. I'm selecting the ball I want and laughing at him. He looks like a fool since he's in his bowling shirt from where he works on the other side of town.

Benson starts the play and gets a spare. He's good. He comes over, fists up again, but all smiles. He points to me—my turn.

I grab my pink ball, and out of nowhere, he says, "You look pretty today."

I'm ready for the play, but this stops me, and the butterflies stir in my stomach. "Are you trying to throw off my game?" I ask him with a scowl. Camry is wearing, of course, a cute dress, one with flowers on the top half and a soft pink from the waist down.

Benson smiles crookedly and shrugs. "I realize I haven't told you that, but I've been thinking it all night."

"Thanks," I say softly, then I bowl. I bowl a strike! My mouth drops open. I jump and do a little victory dance, thankful I can. I don't have to save energy like when I bowl with Camry.

Benson is laughing at me. "I'll let you win if you keep that up."

"No," I whine. "You have to actually try."

"Yeah, yeah. Okay." He stands and goes for his ball. He throws and gets a strike. He turns, bowing to nobody, left and right, then faces me and bows again.

Show-off!

Next turn, I get a spare.

Benson is up. He winks at me before turning on his heel and throwing another strike. He walks up to me. Close. "You sure you still want me to try?" he asks in a villainous tone.

"Yesss." I draw the word out.

He steps aside and lets me grab my ball. I get three pins down, then six. I'm a bit upset.

He matches my nine.

The game is neck and neck, and I feel like he's doing it on purpose. If he wanted to, he could take me down.

I never shared with Camry that the whole bowling thing was just a stupid and meaningless bet between my dad and me. I actually couldn't have cared less about playing because I realized after about five games that I was never going to hit three hundred. But I let Camry keep taking me because of Benson. I wanted to see him. It became something I needed, every chance I could get. Just as the glow around Camry draws me toward her, there's a similar pull toward Benson. Like a magnet.

Benson seems to make sure his last roll is a gutter ball. My last roll equals seven. I barely beat him.

"You stopped trying," I accuse him as I walk back over to the chairs.

There's that crooked smile.

I sit sideways on his lap and wrap my arms around his neck. He welcomes me with arms around my waist. As I stare at him, I begin to drown in the ocean blue. I bring my hand up to caress his face. His beard stubble is rough like sandpaper. "Thank you," I say sincerely. I mean it for so much. For taking me out. For dropping the issue of my secret. For being amazing. And maybe even for letting me win.

He simply stares back into my eyes, blinking slowly.

I kiss him softly, with meaning, and I watch him close his eyes and inhale the kiss. Pulling back, I stare at him some more. I want to tell him I've fallen in love with him. I want to tell him I know him deeper than he thinks. I know he's sweet to his brothers and sisters. I know he admires his parents and wants a relationship just like theirs. I know he's a careful driver and loves dogs, and he likes raw carrots but not cooked ones. And so much more. But I can't.

Obviously, I can't.

It sucks.

So instead, I say, "Where to next?"

It's dusk, and the evening is cooling off. The sunset has turned the sky a pinkish-orange, and the mountains have a purple hue. Walking into the planetarium, we check out the showtimes for the dome theater, and Benson purchases tickets for The Birth of Planet Earth. *We have almost an hour to kill before the show starts, which Benson tells me is perfect. There's apparently enough to see and do here for that time frame.*

We watch the Foucault pendulum knock down two bars and talk about how people used to believe Earth was the center of the universe. For hundreds and hundreds of years, they were wrong. It makes me feel small and as if we still perhaps don't know anything.

We play the interactive game of landing a lunar module, and I fail miserably, but Benson actually doesn't do much better. We walk through the makeshift Mars and take goofy photos. We head over to the scales and see how much we weigh on the moon, on Mercury, on Jupiter...all of them. We watch the big marbles make their way through the roller coaster. Huh, Benson was right; there was plenty to do before the show started.

Sitting on Benson's left, I hold his hand with my right and lean my head on his shoulder while the employee announces tonight's sky and its constellations before the show starts. I breathe him in and admire the dome.

I straighten up when the show starts. Even though it's only forty minutes, I know I'm going to get tired in the comfortable seats. The thought of Camry coming back in that relaxing state perks me up a bit. I can't miss any of Benson. She can't come back yet.

We hold hands the entire time. The show's short, but it's amazing. And again, after watching it, I feel so small and like we don't really know anything. Like nothing really matters. Life is so short. We aren't even a blink in the history of everything. And yet we're still part of it all. Benson's a part of me, and I'm a part of him.

And it does matter.

I mean, it matters to me. This, today, matters so much to me. It means the world to me.

Standing between Camry's car and Benson's truck, he holds me. It was a quiet drive back, not only because it's getting late and we're getting tired, but we're nearing the end of the dates and nearing the awkward goodbyes of it all.

"I can't believe you're leaving," he says faintly. "And I can't believe you're just cutting me off like I never existed."

I can't read his tone. I mean, it's sad, but I can't tell what he's getting at. I'm the one who should've never existed in his world. "That's not true," I tell him softly.

"Well, it sure does feel that way." It's amazing how he can be so calm and nice when I know he's frustrated and confused beyond belief. He's been managing it all night, and it makes me love him even more.

I begin thinking about a type of compromise because I start thinking about the fact that he could easily run into Camry after today. Not even because of the whole Jake thing, but they could run into each other at the gas station. The grocery store. School. Why didn't I think of this before? Oh yeah, because I was trying to save Camry from completely ruining everything. And jumping into her body and saying I was going back to New York was the only thing I could think of at the time. I look at him, trying to form my words, ready to speak any second now.

"What?" he asks, noticing my inner tussle.

"Uh," I start. I hate to ask so much of Camry, but I have to make her promise this for me. For him. "I..." I try again. "This is going to sound weird."

He gazes at me hopefully. He's been waiting all night for something. But it's not going to be what he wants to hear.

"One day," I breathe, trying to find the best words. Words that don't sound completely insane...only halfway insane. Words that'll make sense to him. I finally think of something that might work. "One day, my friend Camry is going to come visit you, and I promise she'll explain everything."

He cocks his head, completely perplexed. And disappointed. "Why can't you explain it to me now?"

I shake my head and move past his question. "It'll be totally confusing to you at first, but I promise if you listen with an open mind, it'll make sense. And I promise it's all true." I stare at him deeply to be sure he's following me, believing me.

Benson chuckles in frustration, tilting his head heavenward. His Adam's apple bounces up and down as he swallows. "That's so—" He stops himself, not knowing what word to use. He gives up and says, "I don't understand."

"You will...after she explains it." I want him to know she and I are separate. I want him to know me. Not the "Camry" version of me, but the real me, if that makes sense. And only she can do that.

He sighs and visibly decides to go along with this as he's gone along with everything else this evening. "Okay. When can I expect this Camry?"

"A couple of weeks, maybe." My answer comes out unsure...because it is.

He huffs out another sigh, not liking this at all. But he shrugs. "What choice do I have? Okay," he says, rubbing an eye. "I'd feel much better having your number, though," he adds, trying again.

I offer nothing but silence and a stare.

"God, what is it about that look you give me? I just—it makes me crazy!"

I don't know what look I'm giving or how to take this. Crazy good or crazy bad? I pull him down to me and kiss him deeply. This will be the last time, so I want to make it good and long. I want to remember his lips and tongue and taste and the way he holds my waist and pulls me into him. I want to remember his warmth and the way my heart flutters when I kiss him. But then I start to feel bad. This is all for me.

Oh God, what am I doing? This is so selfish and mean. This is so unfair to him. I'm the worst girl he's ever known. I don't care if there's an unseen pull toward him. I know right from wrong. And this is wrong. Just like Camry said.

Why is this hitting me now?

I feel myself slipping.

Oh no! If I slip, Camry comes back. I've got to get back to her apartment. Like, now. *I pull away from Benson.*

He makes a disappointed sound.

"I…" I want to tell him I love him, but I say, "I have to go." I dig for Camry's keys.

"Well, what time are you leaving? Do you need someone to take you to the airport?"

I shake my head and lie like a pro. "I called a taxi." I've found the keys and unlock the door with the button.

"Cancel it. Let me take you," he begs and squeezes my hand.

I shake my head again.

"So…this is it?" he asks.

This stabs my heart, and I begin to sob. Because I realize this is actually it. I can't keep doing this. Not only to Benson but to Camry as well. Benson immediately pulls me into a hug. I squeeze him, tucking my head into him. I thank him through my sobs. For tonight. For making a difference in my life.

He doesn't say anything, just holds me. It's after midnight. People have come out of the bowling alley. They seem like they're on a double date. Their car is next to mine, so I try to quiet down. They notice us; they notice me, crying like a baby. And I don't like it.

I reel it in and pull away from Benson. I can't look at him. I turn and open Camry's car door to get in.

"Wait," he says.

Of course, he'd tell me to wait.

"I can't let you go without telling you…" He waits for me to look at him. "I love you." He blinks. "I know that seems fast, but…" He puts his hand to his chest. "I feel it. And you don't have to say it back. I just thought you should know."

Tears fall freely down my cheeks because I know he means it, and I can't stand doing this to him. Pain stabs at my heart, and I feel like I'm dying all over again. I hate this. I hate this moment. And I hate that I hate this moment. This moment should be the most fantastic thing that's ever happened to me. The man I love just told me he loves me. But if I say it back, it'll only hurt him more.

He shoves his fingers in his pockets with his thumbs sticking out. "Better to have loved and lost than never to have loved at all, huh?" He has come to accept I'm not going to give in. I'm not going to call him. I'm not going to come back.

But it's just a couple of weeks, *I tell myself.* Just a couple of weeks he'll have this pain. Then Camry will come and explain it all. Won't that make it better? A little bit?

I grab his face. "She'll explain everything. I promise." Then I do one of the most difficult things in my life. I turn, get into Camry's car, and drive away from the man I love.

After dreaming of Benson for several hours, I wake up slowly. I'm crying. Overwhelmed doesn't even begin to describe what I feel in this moment. I don't think a word exists in the English dictionary for what I'm feeling right now.

She had me looking through her eyes, thinking everything she was thinking and feeling, and I'm so confused about my own feelings now. Because she was right; I *can't* tell the difference sometimes. I struggle with that where, apparently, she doesn't.

I roll over and curl into a ball. I want to forget it all; it was too much at once. Yet I want to remember it all; it was *her* in such a deep way. And it was Benson in such a deep way too.

She might be here, in my room, but I can't focus. And I can't bring myself to call to her, to try to see if she'll join me. It's still too much. I have all of my own feelings for Jake, even if they're muddled a bit, and now all of mine *and* hers for Benson. And even though they're good feelings, feelings of love, I'm having a hard time with them. I need her to take her feelings back. She can leave the memories, like I watched a movie, but the feelings are too much.

I'm thankful she told me, though. And I appreciate that she truly was respectful and thoughtful of my body. I'm also glad she was respectful of my privacy, not using my phone for pictures, not giving him my number, not letting him come to my apartment. And it's nice to have some insight as to how it is for her to be with me.

Then I remember her note, that she couldn't keep doing this to me. I understand it better now. I feel so sad for Benson, but I try to focus on the fact that he's right: "Better to have loved and lost than never to have loved at all." And she's right: "Just a couple of weeks he'll have this pain." So I settle with the fact I should do this, talk to Benson like she asked me to.

I lie in my bed for a long time, sifting through *my* memories and feelings and *her* memories and feelings. I'm trying to sort them. I'm trying to discard the Benson ones. Because even if I do kind of like Benson, it's way too complicated now to do anything about it. I could never be with him without thinking of her. Or thinking that he's only thinking of her when he's with me. Yep, too complicated.

After an hour or so of that, I make myself a sandwich. It takes me five times as long as it should because my brain is so distracted. My ankle is hurting too; I need to elevate it. I sit at my small dining table and rest my leg on top, next to my plate. Cassia came back to let me know about the time she spent with Benson, just like she said she would. I try to focus on whether or not I feel her presence. Toward the end, I was getting better about sensing her in the room.

I set the sandwich back down on the plate. "Cassia?"

I know it's really only been like a day, and she's been gone longer than that before, but I did view it as "the end," and now I can't help but be all excited she might be back for good.

But my apartment feels empty.

I decide she's not here.

I'm alone.

I eat my sandwich and think about New York. Thinking of the airplane gives me anxiety; an unsettling feeling accompanies it. Probably because now that I've sprained my ankle, I picture myself hobbling through the airports, awkwardly getting into taxis, and limping on the busy streets and sidewalks of the city. Then I think of Jake's song. I want to practice, sound good for him, and hopefully record it before I leave.

I've finished my sandwich and am refilling my glass of water when my phone scares me as it rings and vibrates on the dining table. I hop over to it by the third ring. The display tells me it's Jake. A man of his word, calling to check on me. I answer.

"Hey, how you feelin'?" Jake's deep voice is sweet and caring.

"Good. I'm good." *Do people ever really say how they are? Because I'm pretty not good.* "How are you?" I ask.

"Hungry," he says. "I was thinking Chinese sounded really good, and I thought I could get some takeout and bring it over." He becomes more and more unsure of his idea as he gets closer to finishing his sentence.

"Sure," I say without thinking. I backpedal, realizing I just finished a whole sandwich. "Don't get too much, though. I just had a sandwich."

"Oh, okay. Where do you live?"

I tell him, and he says he'll be here in about thirty minutes.

I take this time to check my bank account. The money is there from my mom and dad, so I make a call to the travel place and pay the rest of what I owe for the trip. The excited, nervous feeling gets me as I hang up the phone. *I'm going to New York!*

I shove those thoughts back and painfully make my way over to the radio I have in the corner of my living room, it has a CD player also. I practice Jake's song before he arrives. There aren't a lot of highs or lows in this song; it's smooth.

I thought I'd be scared to love like this,
But my dreams are good when I'm with you.
And all my fears, they disappear.
I feel it still; can this be true?

But I've got to get the tones and timing right, not to mention the overall feel of its sadness.

Trust, my love, it's hard to say goodbye.
I'll try, try to take my time.
I don't want, don't want to fade away.
There's only so much I can take.

When I hear the knock, I don't bother with the crutch. I hobble over and open the door. Jake stands there in comfortable shorts and a Foo Fighters T-shirt, his backpack over his shoulder with the Chinese sack in the other hand. His smile sends my butterflies fluttering. I think I must have sorted out the feelings well. Him looking amazing doesn't hurt, though. His beautiful face isn't even bruised. That must have been the lousiest punch in the world. It didn't seem lousy at the time. Then again, I'd just hit my head pretty hard.

I'm suddenly aware I'm not put together at all. After my shower, I donned yoga pants and a T-shirt advertising Logan High School (*Go, Grizzlies!*). My hair is in a messy bun, I never put any makeup on, and my ankle wrap job is definitely not as good as Jake's.

"Were you practicing my song?" he asks with a smirk as I let him in.

I smile, somewhat uncomfortable that he heard me.

He glances down my body to my ankle. "How are you?"

I glance down my body as well. "Um…not as good as you, I guess," I answer, looking at him by comparison. Then I add, "You don't even look like you went to a rock concert." I touch my nose, implying his nose is perfect.

He shakes his head and smiles, then walks over to the dining table and sets the food and backpack down. His eyes search for the crutch as he asks me if I took more ibuprofen or Tylenol.

"No," I answer.

He finds the crutch in the kitchen and brings it to me with a scowl. He's too late; I'm at the table already. After all, it's only five hops away.

"It'll be easier and heal faster if you use this," he says, then asks where my medicine is.

I tell him, and he brings me some, noticing (for the first time) my bare living room behind my shoulder. He furrows his brows at me, confused. "This is where I dance," I explain, leaning the crutch against the table.

"Oh, you practice *here*?"

I'd told him I've danced since I was little, but I guess I didn't tell him I practice here a lot. "Yeah," I answer.

"Well, do you have a TV? I brought my Xbox." He pats the backpack.

"Oh. Yeah. It's in the bedroom." *We're going to play games?* I don't know why I thought it'd just be food, and then he'd go home.

We sit, and he hands me one container while keeping two for himself. "Your voice is delicate. It's nice. I like it."

I squish my eyes shut, self-conscious, then reach to open my Chinese container—ham fried rice.

"What? Don't be embarrassed. I seriously like it." He grabs his food as well. "You're holding back, though."

I scratch my scar. "I have neighbors," I tell him.

He agrees with a quick lift of his eyebrows, then tells me about his day of running errands. He finishes with, "Thought about napping, but then I wouldn't sleep tonight."

"Yeah, I'm all messed up now. I slept all afternoon." *Or did I?* The dream was fairly exhausting. I actually don't feel very rested. I could totally fall back asleep if I got all cozy again. *All cozy again, this time with Jake.* I don't have an oversized comfy chair with big, pillowy arms for Jake to get cozy too, though. I think of Jake and me cozy in my bed.

I blink. *Enough of that.*

"And I wanted to check on you," he admits with his thoughtful stare.

"You said you'd *call* to check on me. You didn't have to come over and bring me dinner."

He lifts his shoulder in a half shrug while taking three quick bites of rice with the little plastic fork.

"Thanks, though," I say.

"Of course. How's it lookin'?" He nods to my ankle.

"Like a cankle," I answer.

He drops his fork into the empty container and sets it down, laughing at me. "Let me see."

I cross my leg on my knee and take off the wrap. It's bruised down to my toes, just like he said it'd probably be.

He sucks in air through his teeth. "That's a good one." He gently presses his thumbs into the swollen tissue without comment. "Want me to wrap it back up for ya?"

"No, I got it."

But he reaches to help anyway, repositioning my leg on his lap. When he finishes, it's good and tight and better than I'd have done. He kisses his fingers and presses the kiss on my ankle as if to make it all better. Then his eyes grow wide, and he reaches for his backpack. "Do you play?"

"I haven't in a long time. We'd play with my best friend's brother, but that was like three years ago."

Jake rubs his hands together with a scheming look on his face, like beating me is going to be easy as pie. He still has some chicken left in the other container. He stuffs his mouth but can't fit the last one. Forking it, he extends his arm out to me. I hesitate. "Come on. I'm full," he reasons.

I'm discovering everything about Jake is easygoing and straightforward, from his appearance to the way he walks and talks. He's laid-back with his choices and uncomplicated with his actions. I lean forward and take the bite.

"It's good, huh?"

I nod, and he cleans up the trash and tosses it for me. He then grabs his backpack, and I point him to my bedroom, staying in the hallway, though, to use the bathroom.

I'm forgetting all the "treating me like his mom" stuff. *Or would he feed Chinese chicken to his mom?* I don't know; I don't care. I'm choosing to forget all that and smile at the fact that he's here, in my house, in my bedroom. *Whoa.*

When I crutch back to my room, I stop in the doorway. My inner smile drops like a heavy weight to my gut. Jake has taken the picture of Cassia off my wall and is holding it. He's standing on the other side of my bed near the desk. The Xbox rests on the floor at the foot of my bed and in front of my TV. I can see he hasn't finished hooking it all up, as wires are strewn all about.

"Is this—?" he starts, pointing to it.

I'm frozen with big ol' round owl eyes. I completely forgot that was there! Jake, here, in my house, in my bedroom, suddenly isn't so appealing to me anymore. He's looking at me, waiting for the answer he must already know. He's no fool. I mean, it says Cassia Simonsen right on the bottom. I've got no answer for him.

"She looks just like you," he says. "I mean, you guys could be sisters, maybe even twins." He picks up the other papers, the articles I printed. They were on my desk, just below the picture. "She's been missing for months. You said you went bowling with her, and she just went back to New York."

I take a step forward with my free hand out. "Don't think I'm crazy," I say, because that's what not-crazy people say, right?

Crazy is the cue word. "Is *she* your ghost story?"

"I'm trying to help her," I tell him, squishing my face.

He gazes thoughtfully at her picture, then back at me. "If you had blue eyes, I don't think I could tell you apart."

"They turn blue when she's with me."

"What? Okay, that's eerie." He thinks about it for a minute, looking into my eyes. The light in my room is bright enough. "So she's not here now?"

I don't clarify I meant when she's sharing my body. Instead, I just say, "No." I watch him skim the articles for just a few moments.

"But you can sense her?"

I nod with a bit of a shrug.

"Like…a sixth sense? Have you always been like that?"

"No. It's just lately. It's just her."

He thinks about that then returns to the articles. "Are they still searching for her?"

"I don't think so."

"You know where she is, don't you?"

"Not exactly."

"But you know what happened to her?" he presses.

I rest the crutch against the wall, limp over to him, ignoring his disapproving look, and take the picture, staring at it. With tears blurring my vision, I sit down on the edge of my bed.

"This is what you meant when you said you had a lot going on." He's putting two and two together and getting four. "Camry, this *is* a lot." He gestures to all the papers. "Are you losing sleep over this? How much…Does anybody else know about this?"

Do I tell him? Will he understand? I don't like thinking about the dream she gave me showing her being murdered, and now I'm considering telling it. I reach and grab the box of tissues from my nightstand. "No," I answer.

"How did this all start?" he asks.

I feel like that's a loaded question. "It's complicated."

Jake sits on the bed next to me, wordlessly and still holding the articles. He's reading them. All of his excitement about playing games has faded; he's engrossed in this a hundred percent. Part of me wants to tell him to go home because part of me doesn't want to talk about this. But a larger part of me wants to know what he thinks about it all, so I let him read on. Finally, he says, "Was it a ransom gone wrong? Sounds like her dad is well off."

Wiping my nose, I decide I can't tell him the details. I just can't. Instead, I shake my head and tell him the super-summed-up version. "Her stepmom hired someone to kill her. She wanted to be the only one to get her new husband's money." Tears fall down my cheeks.

Jake's head snaps to look at me. "Seriously?!" He soaks that in for a second. "Oh my God. That's…" He trails off, but I know what he means. It's so completely awful, there isn't a word for it. "How do you know that? How do you communicate with her?"

"We talk. She shows me things." I close my eyes and shudder in a breath, thinking about her murder. I start to cry more. "And those images…they don't just go away. And I *feel*. I *feel* her fear. She was so scared."

Jake rubs my back, and I apologize for my ugly crying face. "Don't be sorry," he says, full of compassion. He gives me a minute while I use and toss three tissues into my trash, then starts again. "So I don't get it. How does she show you things like that?"

I sniff. "Dreams."

He nods almost immediately. "Can you see her too when you talk to her?"

I shake my head and swallow my spit. "It's not like that." I hesitate. "This is where it gets a little crazy"—I roll my eyes at myself—"well, craz*ier*."

Jake's attention is fully on me, his gaze intense.

I inhale, prepping myself for the next statement. "She shares my body and talks through me."

Jake can't bury his surprise at that one. His eyes grow wide, lifting his brows to wrinkle his forehead.

"I know!" I slap my hands over my face. "It's absolutely crazy!"

"Like a possession?"

"No!" I quickly answer, hands out. "I share my body with her and…" I struggle with how to explain the way things are with Cassia and me. "She still wants to experience life and"—I shrug—"I let her. She's the reason I went to Zion, the reason I went bowling, the reason I bought a single ticket to a rock concert. She was supposed to be with me—"

"Like a bucket list?"

"Yes." I exhale. *Good, he understands.* "For the longest time, she refused to tell me anything about her, but then things started to get complicated, and things in New York were escalating…"

"Escalating?"

"She thinks her stepmom is planning to have her mom killed too. She thinks it's only a matter of time."

Jake inhales and blinks, probably trying to deal with the mental overload. With a confused expression, he asks, "So *how* are you supposed to help her?"

"She asked me to go to New York to help her prove her stepmom guilty." I don't bother with the fact that she's since told me not to—that she's just trying to figure it out on her own. None of that seems to matter because of a gut feeling I have telling me she can't do it on her own. She just can't.

Jake's eyebrows rise again with surprise he can't conceal. "Are you going?"

I look at him, nervous, and nod.

"When?" He sounds alarmed.

"I have a flight booked for Friday. For a week."

Now Jake gapes at me like I *am* crazy. I can't *stand* the look on his face, and I feel like he's right. He's confirming a deep fear I was trying to ignore—I was *successful* in ignoring it until this moment—that it's too risky to go, that the dangers are plentiful. I was determined to do the right thing and be brave while doing it, but his look tells me he thinks it's a terrible idea.

I fling myself back on my bed and cover my face. "I know! I'm crazy, huh?" My eyes are swimming in tears again. The drops dive into my hair before I can wipe them away. I'm shaking.

Jake grabs a pillow and shoves it under my head for me. He turns onto his side and leans back on one elbow. He's looking down at me with that thoughtful stare he does where his eyes search mine; for what, I don't know. There's the start of a sincere grin like I've pleasantly surprised him, although I have no idea how I could have done that just now. This isn't like surprising him at work with Life Savers; it's surprising him with the fact that I'm completely bonkers. *Does the asylum have visiting hours?* He waits for me to compose myself again. Tissues pile up as I use them and dispose of them by my side.

After a minute, he says softly, "I don't think you're crazy. Stop saying that."

"I can't not go. I just…can't."

He nods understandingly. "Do you want to know what I think?"

My expression has the answer all over my face. *Yes.*

He brings his hand up to wipe away a tear that's heading for my ear, then leans into me. He whispers against my cheek. "I think," he begins, looking into my eyes, "you're pretty cool."

I chuckle and argue, "You should think I'm crazy."

He gently kisses my cheekbone, eyeing me with a glare. Moving down just a bit, he argues back, "Good crazy."

"No. Certifiably crazy," I whisper. "You should be wanting to leave."

He's now kissing my cheek but eyes me again, answering with a small shake of his head. He turns my head toward his with one finger on my chin so our lips are barely touching. It tickles as he begins to talk again. "I don't want to leave. I want to kiss you."

"Then you'd be crazy too," I whisper.

"You want to help someone. That's not crazy."

"It is when that someone is dead and you use all your money to go to New York to do it, not knowing that it's even going to work or—"

"Can I kiss you now?" he interrupts.

I study his expression and features, his lips. I close the gap between us. His lips are as warm and soft as I thought they'd be. His fingers trace my jawline and wrap behind my ear. I begin to melt as we kiss softly, but it's not long enough. He pulls away, startling me. "But," he says louder than before, "it's stupid to go alone. Didn't you learn anything from the concert?"

"I-I won't be alone," I stutter. "Cassia will be with me."

Jake gives me another glare, one that says, *That doesn't count.*

"What? You wanna come?" I ask, half joking. Actually, mostly joking. Actually, I don't know why I said that.

"Yeah," he answers quickly.

I sit up, pushing him up with me. "No! Why would you want to come?"

"Why wouldn't I want to come?"

"Um, lots of reasons. I can't believe you're still here. I can't believe I just told you all that." I squint at the floor in front of me, pressing on my temples to try to gather my thoughts. This conversation shifted so quickly I have to recover from its whiplash.

"Um," he says, mimicking my tone. "No. Not lots of reasons. And…I'm glad you told me. How long have you been dealing with this on your own? It probably feels good to tell someone all that."

He's right, and he's wrong. A weight *has* been lifted, but now it's like I'm exposed. Naked, somehow. "Since April," I answer.

He blinks wide eyes and then, after a couple of breaths, gives me validation. "I can see why you didn't want to tell me." He clarifies, "In the beginning." He holds up his hands at my shocked side-eye. "*Not* saying you're crazy. At all. Just, I agree with you that there are some things you don't just jump into. And this was one of them. Okay?"

I purse my lips at him, then go back a step. "Technically, I think we're still in the beginning," I tell him. He shakes his head. "I don't even know your favorite color," I try to argue.

Jake doesn't hesitate. "Red. And we're totally past the beginning."

I glance at us on my bed.

He laughs. "Not because of that. I mean, yes, I am smooth," he jokes again, then thoughtfully continues, "but because I feel like I've known you…a long time. Because…I let you listen to my song."

I regard him. He's exposed, too, naked because I've heard his song—a deep piece of him. I can't acknowledge I feel like I've known him forever too. If I acknowledge that, then what? I pinch the bridge of my nose. "We're getting sidetracked."

"Okay, think about it, Camry," Jake says, picking up where he left off. "There's a reason you met me. I'm meant to help you."

Is this really his argument? Maybe. After all, I think the same thing of Cassia and me. I'm meant to help her. *Aren't I?*

He goes on. "You're gonna need help. And what about your ankle?"

"It'll be fine. And I *have* thought about it. That's why you can't come. Just because you're with me doesn't mean things couldn't go bad. It just puts you in jeopardy also."

"Jeopardy of what? I think I can manage a trip to New York."

His face would make me laugh if I weren't upset in this moment. He thinks I'm ludicrous; I'm almost positive.

"And no, it's not really fine," he continues. "Your ankle will still be weak. How are you gonna carry luggage, hail taxis, walk the streets of New York, *and* stop the evil stepmother?" He points his thumbs at himself with bulging eyes.

I haven't told him my plan, and I can't bring myself to tell him now. I'm speechless. I stare at him incredulously. *Can't we go back two minutes to his soft lips on mine?* I *would* like someone to come with me. I'm scared as all hell. And I *have* thought about Jake and me going to New York. Like a daydream-type thought. I *know* things could go badly. I could be arrested. If they think I have anything to do with Cassia's disappearance, I'm sure they wouldn't hesitate. I just can't involve Jake.

I open my mouth, then close it. I can't even think where to begin with more protest. The expression on his face tells me I've pretty much lost this battle. He reaches for my hand on the bed, but I pull away. I'm sort of angry.

"Camry, don't."

I stare down at my feet on the carpet. Tears flood my eyes again, and I grab another tissue for my runny nose. At least it's not bleeding. *Is it?* I look at the tissue. *Nope.*

Jake scoots right next to me, one arm behind me so his body is twisted toward mine. He cares. "I appreciate you worrying about me, but I don't think you're thinking about what good it can be to have someone go with you. You're only thinking about the bad."

I don't look at him. I can't.

"If there're any issues, I'll be there to back you up." His hand moves up and down my back. "Not only that, but you're young, you're pretty and"—he points to my ankle and chuckles—"handicapped. You're totally a target if you're alone. I'll be your support. Figuratively and literally." I hear him smile.

This isn't much of an argument.

I start to refuse, but he stops me with his fingers on my forearm. "Just…think about the odds, please. What're the odds?"

What's he getting at?

He goes on like a lawyer pushing his case. "I can *totally* go to New York next week. I've got nothing stopping me. Okay, I have some plans. But I can easily change them. Who else can go to New York, basically on a whim? Plus, I can *afford* to go to New York. Been saving for a trip to Cancun, but New York is cool too. *And*"—he pauses for effect—"I *totally* believe and *love* your ghost story. Now, how many guys can say all that?" He then remembers something to add. "Oh! Oh! And I'm pretty good at most medical things. Since you seem to have that kind of luck, I can help with that too."

I scowl at him but end up smiling. I *am* thinking about his argument. *Is he correct? Does he make a good point?* Possibly. I need to think about it more.

"Camry," he interrupts my pondering. "You've been on your own for a while. You've been conditioned to do things on your own. But with something like this…you shouldn't have to. You *don't* have to. Let someone help you. Let *me* help you." He's looking deeply into my eyes, all jokes aside. "Let me in." He says this hardly begging, but more so in a way that shows me he sees through me. He sees that I have my guard up, and he's asking me to put it down. For this. For him. For the beginning of us.

I don't know if I can.

He's still studying me, waiting for me to give some sort of response. "I'll think about it," I answer.

He presses his lips together in a hard line. "I can convince you by the end of tonight," he says with confidence.

I point to his game console on the floor in front of my TV. "Do you wanna clean up?"

"No," he retorts, snapping his brows down. "I'm not leaving. Not after our first—was this a fight?" I can hear him smile again, and I laugh. He pulls me into him, and I rest my head on his shoulder, right next to his neck, in that comfortable little spot. He rubs my arm. "We're still gonna play. It'll be good to think about something else for a while."

"What game are we playing?"

"I have a few. You can choose. Fair warning, though; loser has to kiss the winner."

This makes me chuckle. Our lips meet again, and I think how genuine he is. Maybe it *would* be good to have him come with me.

"Fourth date, and I'm kissing you on your bed." He waggles his eyebrows up and down. "I *am* smooth."

I whistle.

"And *you* are the most interesting girl I've ever known."
Hmm. That feels better than being the strangest *girl anyone's ever known.*

Friday, August 27

Jake was able to get on the same flight but not sitting next to me. I look seven rows back at him and grin before I sit and buckle up. We have an hour-long layover in Chicago but should be in New York City by their dinnertime. The time change is a two-hour loss, which sort of bums me out.

As I gaze out the plane window, waiting for takeoff, I think back through the week that has been so utterly dreamlike, like how I imagine paradise to be. It's amazing how close Jake and I've become in the past six days. I think I feel closer to him than I do to my best friends, Kayla, Sienna, and Lindsey. Closer in a completely open way—we think on the same wavelength and can anticipate what the other is going to say or do, he's seen me without makeup and looking completely awful and I don't even care, and he knows my deepest, craziest secret and supports me 100 percent.

We spent all of Sunday together. He read the articles I had on Cassia and had lots of questions. I answered what I could. I've told him everything, from how things began with her until now. Well, not everything; I left out all the Benson stuff. I'm just not ready to have that conversation yet. But I did divulge the latest about Cassia *not* wanting me to come to New York. At that point, Jake had the same idea I did about calling anonymously.

"I don't think she'll be coming back to me for a while," I had told him. "I need to go there to find her, see what the latest is, and help her in a way she's okay with." This was a strong feeling for me I didn't really know how to convey because I hadn't really figured it out myself.

He frowned. "But what if you can't find her?"

"She'll know I'm there," I said with confidence. "I'll find her. I know I will."

After work on Monday, we went to the travel agency and adjusted my trip to accommodate two people instead of one, then we went on a date to the movies.

Throughout the week, we tried to come up with a plan while researching Cassia's father, Terrick Simonsen. There's a fairly long article about him on Wikipedia but no website for him. I couldn't even find a contact number or address, so I'm going to have to rely on Cassia for that when we get there. Jake kept talking about going to the police, but I was heavily hesitating on that. Again, I'll need to find her first and see what she's okay with. Jake doesn't agree but will support me.

Also, throughout the week, he and I loosely practiced his song, mostly in the car as we drove to and from our date activities. He told me we could wait until after we came back from New York to record it, but I pushed him to do it before we left. We recorded it yesterday, and, despite my nerves, it turned out pretty amazing.

While recording, I refrained from suggesting Jake tape a sheet up to cover the window that separated us.

"Closer," he said.

I brought my lips within millimeters of the mic. "Testing, testing."

"Good."

The music started, then Jake's recorded voice rang out the first part, and my part approached. Although I was nervous, I vowed to do my best. I completed the entire verse, only a little self-conscious about him watching me, before he stopped me.

"Hold on a sec," he said with sounds of static.

I exhaled with growing nerves. *Was it a technical thing? Did he hate it?*

Opening the door to the booth, he grabbed my face and planted his lips firmly on mine.

I guessed he liked it. I tried to ask him as I pulled my headset down, but all I got out was, "Um." Then he was kissing me again, so I kissed him back.

We finally broke apart, but his hands remained cupping my face. Staring deeply, he said, "Thank you for doing this. That was…remarkable."

"Really?" I was skeptical.

"Trust me. I've worked with people not even half as talented as you. You were holding out on me in the car." He side-eyed me.

He had me feeling embarrassed, with his staring into my eyes and giving me compliments. I didn't like so much attention. He looked thoughtfully at me and opened his mouth to say more but changed his mind.

"What?"

"I'll tell you later. Let's finish." Pecking me on the lips, he disappeared back to the other side.

I sang the chorus and the other parts that were mine. Silence from Jake. "You there?" I asked.

"Camry?"

"Yeah?"

"Where have you *been* all my life?"

"Um."

He laughed. "Do you want to hear it?"

Did I? "Yeah."

"Just leave the headset in there. Come on over."

I went over to the other side with all the knobs and dials and switches. Sitting next to him, I hunched a bit with my legs together and my hands shoved under my thighs.

He swiveled his chair, grabbed my knees, and twisted me so we faced each other. "Thank you."

I simply said, "You're welcome."

Again, he opened his mouth but didn't say anything.

"What?"

"Nothing. You ready?"

With a single, certain nod, I said, "Yes." I'd heard it a hundred times with Jake's voice, but I was about to hear it with mine, and I could only hope it was as good as he was making it seem.

Jake's beautiful piano started, and his beautiful voice followed, and suddenly, there I was. My voice came through the speakers sounding as good as any duet I'd ever heard. Our voices sounded better together than I thought they would.

"That's you!" Jake yelled excitedly.

He was watching me, watching my reaction. I smiled as he reached for my hand, relaxing in his chair as the song finished.

When it stopped, he hit a couple of buttons. "I have some things to tweak, but I love it. Thank you." He looked at me deeply again, like he wanted to say something but couldn't.

A thought entered my mind. "Do you have more?" I asked.

With a smirk on his flawless face, he said, "You know it! Did you have fun?"

I nodded.

We worked on more songs until my voice was hoarse.

A young woman bumps into my bad ankle as she sits next to me, bringing my thoughts away from Jake and his songs, back to the plane on the tarmac about to take off. It's not her fault. It's not like I'm wearing a medical boot; she doesn't see the wrap under my long skirt. I grin at her and look left out the window.

Yes, I'm still a bit of a cripple, but my ankle has healed surprisingly well. I mean, there's no way I could run away from someone trying to kidnap me and kill me in the woods, but as long as that doesn't happen, I'll be okay, especially with Jake's help. I realize now that Jake never told me whatever it was he was going to tell me the day of the recording.

Taking deep breaths, I meditate and mentally prepare myself for takeoff. Having never flown before, I only have movies to guide me with what I should expect. My palms start to get clammy. After the pilot and flight attendant give their announcements and we're lined up on the runway to go, the plane picks up speed, and the force that shoves me into my seat surprises me. The liftoff isn't so bad; it's not until we level off that my stomach churns its contents uncomfortably, not unlike a roller coaster. *Okay. That wasn't so bad. What was I worried about?*

The young woman next to me turns out to be quite annoying. She not only hogs the armrest but also leans into me. I don't understand why she can't lean the other way, at least sometimes. She plays the music from her phone too loud until the flight attendant asks her to use her earbuds. And she makes this annoying clicking sound with her tongue; I'm not sure if it's a scratchy throat/allergy thing, or a way of dealing with anxiety about the flight, but it bugs me. Then she nods off and jerks awake, throwing her arms up in the air, knocking into my tray, and spilling my drink all over me. Thank goodness it's Sprite, so I won't have a big brown spot on my white top. Still, it'll harden if I don't rinse it. Instead of apologizing, she laughs.

I stand and don't say sorry as I accidentally step on her toe getting past her to go to the bathroom. I dry myself off as best I can and head back to my seat. Jake notices me and gives a baffled expression. I roll my eyes toward my seat, then do a double take, noticing she's taken my spot.

"I just love the window. Do you mind?" Her teeth are big and strikingly white. She'd be cute except for how obnoxious she is.

It's not worth it. "No," I say.

She smiles but doesn't thank me.

She hogs the armrest again the rest of the flight but doesn't lean into me. Instead, she looks out the window. Still, I'm glad to land and be rid of her. Landing gives a different sort of tumble in my stomach, but again, not unlike a theme park ride. I'm not sure what I was nervous about.

Jake and I share a delicious pizza from a café in the airport. "I love that you love pizza. I should give you a tally for that." He draws a line in the air.

Our suitcases are next to our legs as we sit across from each other at a two-person table. "Doesn't everyone love pizza?" I ask.

Jake glances around at nothing specific. "Mmm, I'd argue there's more salad girls out there then pizza girls."

I shrug. "I like salad too."

His face tells me, *You're missing the point.*

Just then, I see the annoying woman sit down a couple of tables away with a salad. Jake follows my gaze, seeing her as well. We both laugh at the irony.

"I'd never date her. I'm done with salad girls," he says. Then he asks, "What happened with her anyway?"

I don't answer Jake right away. We're both distracted by watching her. She tries to scoot her chair in and ends up knocking her drink over. On the way to get more napkins, she trips on seemingly nothing and falls on all fours. After cleaning up, she tries to enjoy her salad, but her phone rings and scares her. She's in the middle of pouring her dressing and ends up with it all over her front. She cleans herself up and goes to get more dressing. I'm anxious to see if she can actually eat now.

I look at Jake. "I feel like that says it all."

"Oh. My. God."

"I know, right? I mean, she's really pretty, but damn."

She moves to scoot in again, trying to get out of the way of passing people, but somehow manages to get *in* the way. A teenage boy trips on her chair. She laughs and gives him an awkward smile. No apology. She never apologized to me either, but I guess I can see why. If she did, that's all she'd be saying all day long.

"She's *way* worse than you," Jake points out.

Cocking my head, I wonder, *Is she?* I mean, she's definitely accident-prone. But they're all little accidents. Mine seem to be big ones. *Which is worse?*

Jake adds, "It's like, I can't stop watching her. She's like reality TV, but better."

I reach over and flick his shoulder.

"What?" He laughs. "You can't stop either!"

It's true. I just *have* to know how this episode ends.

She does manage to finish her salad without any further delays, but she leaves her cell phone on the table, and a good Samaritan returns it to her. When she throws her salad garbage away, she drops half of it on the floor. I give her props, though, for cleaning up her messes. She knows how she is, and at least she tries to make up for it.

Jake exhales. "That…was exhausting."

"Try sitting next to her on a plane for two hours," I say.

After the layover, we're ready to board the next plane. Again, we got the same flight but don't sit next to each other. I'm in the middle, and Jake is two rows ahead and across from me. He sits next to the window and keeps peering over the seat behind him to make goofy faces at me.

Then the unimaginable happens. Another episode of our *Flight to New York* reality TV show begins. I spot the same annoying young woman, and she finds her seat next to Jake. I can't help but laugh as he notices her and seems worried beyond belief.

This is going to be a long two hours.

She's different, though, sitting next to him. She's loud and laughing and hitting on him. I shouldn't blame her; he's a good-lookin' specimen. It's comical at first, his awkwardness, but then he starts laughing, and I have to tell myself not to be jealous. He even said there's no way he'd date her.

Then I hear him say, "Yeah, we didn't get seats together, but that's her back there." He points me out.

She turns, and I smile awkwardly. Her face shifts into something between annoyance and jealousy. She doesn't return a smile, even an awkward one, but Jake waves at me.

The Big Apple doesn't welcome us. It attacks us from all sides and engulfs us like a python circling and squeezing its prey. I feel claustrophobic from not being able to see a view. Salt Lake City has tall buildings, but they don't compare to this. But it's not just that. The number of cars and people is crowding me as well. We're in a jungle here, where I can't make out north or south, only tall and small. And we're definitely small. We're the bugs about to be squashed by the baddie of New York City.

Perhaps I shouldn't say *we* so much as *I*. *I'm* the one struggling. I feel completely and totally out of place and out of my mind. My anxiety is higher than any one of these skyscrapers.

My leg is bouncing as we ride the shuttle to our hotel. And even though Jake gently puts his hand on my knee to try to help me, I think Cassia is the only one who can right now. If she'd just find me, I think I could settle down a bit. I remind myself to be patient.

I let Jake sit by the window in the shuttle since he seems completely stoked about the visual overload. Under different circumstances, I might be stoked too. He pulls me closer to him to look at this building and that building out the window. I look but pull back.

"You okay?" he asks.

I tighten my grip on the strap of the small duffle bag I have resting at my feet. "Yeah."

He puts his arm around my shoulder and kisses my forehead. "It's gonna be fine, Cam. Just fine."

The carpet of the Salisbury Hotel is a dark and depressing green, but the white linen on the king-size bed greets me well. My nerves have been on such high alert that I want to fall into it and sleep for twenty-four hours straight.

"One bed, huh?" Jake says.

"Why do people make a big deal about one bed?" I say, squishing my eyebrows together. "There're still two sides to one bed."

He looks me up and down. "You know why."

I ignore his implication. "Hey, what were you going to tell me yesterday when we were in your studio? I keep forgetting to ask you."

We've dropped our bags on the floor by the TV. He grabs me and pulls me into him. "That you're the most amazing person I've ever met. And..." He pushes my bangs to the side a bit.

"And what?" I ask. "You're doing it again. What is it you want to say?"

He narrows his eyes. "Do you come with a catch?"

"Is that what you were going to say?"

"No."

I purse my lips at that but move on. "What do you mean, a catch?"

"You know, when something seems too good to be true, there's usually a catch."

"Yeah. I do come with a catch. You'll probably be arrested within the week."

He smiles. "No. Seriously. Because I think I—"

"Wait," I interrupt, squeezing my eyes shut. Rubbing my forehead, I sigh. "I do have something else to tell you. About…all of this." I'm grave because there *is* a catch, and I don't know if there's ever going to be a good time to tell him, so…

"Ahhoookay. Serious?" He cocks his head and studies my face.

I nod apprehensively.

His face falls. "I thought you told me everything there was to tell."

I fiddle with my earring. "Well, there's one more thing you should probably know." I try to downplay it. "It's maybe not even that big of a deal to you."

His head cocks the other way. "Camry. If you didn't think it was a big deal to me, you would've told me before now."

Worry is written all over my face.

He sighs and backs up, pulling me along with him and sitting on the end of the bed. I stand between his knees, and his hands hold the backs of my thighs as his head falls onto my stomach. My fingers run through his crazy hair, and he pulls back, looking up at me. Blinking slowly, he asks, "What is it?"

I caress his face, feeling a touch of stubble, then drop my hands to his forearms. "I'm sorry. I just didn't know how to tell you this, but I can see there isn't a good way…so I'm just gonna say it. Benson is in love with Cassia."

His face twists in confusion. "Benson? As in my cousin Ben? From the bowling alley?"

I nod.

Jake thinks for a split second. Then the realization hits him, and his face relaxes. "You were bowling there with Cassia."

I nod again, even though it's not a question.

He eyes me. "Doesn't that mean Ben's in love with *you*?"

I exhale a breath that I apparently was holding and shake my head. "Everything he knows is Cassia."

"What do you mean?" There's an edge to his voice.

"Every time I went bowling, she was with me. She did most of the talking."

"Wait. Did you guys…Were you dating?"

I scratch my forehead, feeling my scar. "There were a couple of dates, yeah."

"A couple? Do you like him?" Now there's an impatience to his voice.

"It doesn't matter." I move my hands to my hips.

"Yes, it does."

"No, it doesn't. He loves Cassia. Not me. Again,"—I fling my arms out—"*everything* he knows is Cassia."

Jake replies with more anger than I'm comfortable with. "Not your body!"

He's correct, but he doesn't realize… "He thinks I *am* Cassia." I wince.

Jake stands up without breaking our stare down. "And who told him that?"

"I was talking to her, and he overheard me. I just…never corrected him." The repercussions of this mistake are hitting me in full force now. Jake scoffs. "Yes, it was a huge mistake," I admit, looking at the ugly carpet. "I…Let me back up." I'm so bad at this kind of thing. "It was all such bad timing." I'm using my hands a lot, but I don't know what else to do with them other than pull my hair.

Jake pulls my chin back up. Maybe he's not angry; his face *has* softened. I hope he isn't angry. But he's definitely resolute. "Do. You. Like him?"

I shrug. "I did. Then I went out with you. I don't know."

"Did you kiss him?" Jealousy veils him. I open my mouth, but he stops me. "Not Cassia. Did *you* kiss him?"

I nod.

His face doesn't waver.

"I tried to tell him the truth," I try to explain. Now his expression shifts to confusion. "But then that didn't really work." *Ugh! I don't want this to lead to how I let Cassia have eight hours with him.* I end up with, "Cassia was taking it too far."

"Cassia? Or you? Because Cassia can't really do anything without you letting her, right?"

Hmmm, there's some gray area there.

"Ben's like my brother," he explains, a significant level calmer than he just was. "I had no one when I was little. My parents worked all the time. Ben's family *was* my family. We went to different high schools, but I still…" He shakes his head, taking a step back from me and rubbing his face with one hand. "I need to think," he says, then sidesteps me, heading for the door.

I grab his sleeve. "You're leaving?"

"I'm gonna take a walk. It's fine. I'm glad you told me. I just…need a minute." He pulls his arm away.

As I watch him turn and leave, I worry it's not as fine as he's saying. I suppose I could use a minute as well. I feel like there's more I could have tried to explain, though. Normally, Jake is reasonable and rational. He must be stressed out. Or maybe he's the jealous type, and I haven't ever picked up on that. Or maybe he's just jealous when it comes to Benson. *Ben's like my brother* rings in my ears. *Ugh!* How would I feel if I were him? I have no answer to that.

I open the draperies to see our view. Surprise! Another tall building looms above me. *What's wrong with me?* I should be a *little* excited. Mostly edgy, jumpy, and panicky, considering what has to be done, but…a *little* excited. I'm in New freakin' York! I do what I've been wanting to do since I walked in the door: fling myself onto the bed, sink into its fluffy white duvet, and fall asleep.

Cassia visits me in a dream…

We're in the hotel room.

"Cassia!" I cry from the bed as she walks in the door. This is the first time I've seen her full-bodied and normal. All the other times she's given me dreams, I was seeing through her eyes. "You found me."

She smiles, and I feel warm. She wears an expensive-looking blue blouse with flowing black pants and, comically, bare feet. Her long brown hair falls in big beach waves around her face and is worthy of a commercial, one with a slow-motion hair flip. She's gorgeous with her flashy blue eyes and brilliant smile. "Of course, I found you," she says, walking toward me. "But why did you come?"

"Because I couldn't stand knowing you're here trying to do this on your own. You need a body, Cassia! You need me. Remember? I'm the only one you can do this with." Then I add, "And I want to. I want to help you, Cass."

"Aren't you scared being here?" she asks, climbing onto the bed.

"No. I'm not alone." I smile. "Jake's with me."

"I noticed." She offers a mischievous smile. We regard each other for a bizarre moment as she sits cross-legged with me. It's crazy how much we look alike. It's as if I'm looking in a mirror, a mirror with a fancy feature of dolling up my reflection.

I wince. "He's mad at me right now. I told him about Benson and—"

"He's not mad at you."

"Huh?"

"He'll come back. He's fine. He just thinks better when he's alone. He's...falling for you."

I grin. "You think?"

She nods, her curls bouncing a bit. I think how I should curl my hair instead of always keeping it straight.

She reaches over to me and rests her hand on top of mine. She closes her eyes, but I'm not sure what she's doing. After a minute, she asks, "You have no real plan, do you?"

I scoff at her mind reading. "I just wanted to find you and see what you're okay with."

"Well, you'll be happy to hear I was able to get Bella to help. I can't do what I do with you, but she remembers the dreams I give her. She has an audio file on her phone of Tiffanie and her mother talking about hiring someone to kill my mom."

My eyes pop open. I'm unequivocally elated at this news.

"But..." she continues, and the way she says "but" brings my elation down several notches. "I feel like it's soon, sooner than I thought, and she's blocked me. Something has changed. I can't seem to get through to her anymore. I've been trying to get her to give it to my dad, but she doesn't seem to be making any moves toward that. You might have come at just the right time." She lifts her brows.

Okay, getting Bella to give the recording to Mr. Simonsen isn't the worst thing in the world. I exhale, still excited, and almost giggle with relief because this won't be as difficult as I first thought. But wait... "How soon? Why has she blocked you?" I ask.

"I'm not sure. She...I don't know. I feel like there's something I've missed. It might be you have to get the file from her."

So I have to get her to email it to me or something? I'm having a hard time picturing a conversation with this lady I've never met, asking her to send me the file. It doesn't seem to be a plausible future. "Okay," I start. "Say I get the file. We should turn it in to the police," I tell her, thinking Jake was right. "We can't risk giving it to your dad and having Tiffanie find it. And how would I even give it to him anyway?"

Cassia gives a fleeting look toward the door. "I'm going to think on that. I'll figure something out. Don't worry." She's rushing now, and I'm not sure why. "Listen, rest for now. We have time. Tomorrow you can get acquainted with the city a bit and find my apartment building. It might be good for you to see. Thank you for coming, Cam."

"Wait. I have more questions. Where—?"

But Cassia leaves me. Not by way of getting off the bed and walking out the door. She dissolves directly in front of my eyes. And in my dream, I lie down and sleep.

I'm not sure how much time has passed when I feel a weight on me. It's not bad. I wake nice and easy. It's Jake. He's climbed onto the bed and is leaning over me. Putting most of his weight on his elbows, he pushes my bangs aside. "Hey," he whispers.

I squeeze my eyes to get the sleep out of them. "Hey." It comes out hoarse. I clear my throat.

His eyes seem greener than normal, if that's even possible. Then I realize the white part is a little pink, making the green stand out. He must be tired.

He asks, "Are you mad?"

I bring my hand up from my side and poke him in the armpit. "No."

He squirms, then gets me in the ribs. We go back and forth until I can't take it anymore and beg him to stop. I've laughed so hard that I've even snorted. He mocks me with his own snort but stops. On top of me, his nose tickling mine, he kisses me.

I ask, "Are *you* mad?"

He side-eyes me as if to say, *Really*? "Obviously, no."

"Were you?"

He sighs. "I just…think better when I'm alone."

Déjà vu. Did Cassia follow him before coming to me? "Can I explain?" I ask.

"No," he says quickly. "No. You're right. It doesn't matter."

"You bet your booty I'm right." I grab his face.

He laughs, then gives me another gentle kiss.

I add, "I want you to know I'll always tell you the truth." My thumb feels his soft lips. "Always. Okay?" I look at him deeply. I've never made eye contact with anyone this way before.

He nods, and we kiss deep and long.

When I sleep for the night, it's not restful by a long shot. I'm Cassia, and she's taking me through all the streets of Manhattan. Okay, not *all* the streets, but definitely a lot of them. And I have memories of places along the way. They're Cassia's memories, like the Chinese restaurant where she liked to eat and the statue in Central Park that she and her dad used to go to sometimes. I wake just enough to toss and turn and then fall right back to it. More memories of the Empire State Building and her going to work with her dad. I'm feeling exhausted.

I know she's trying to help, but if I don't get a good night's sleep, I won't be very useful to her. I feel like I'm flying low through the city rather than walking or driving. I'm like Superman. And I feel like I forget some of it right after she shows it to me. She's moving on to the next memory so quickly. But somehow, there's a feeling I'll remember *what* I need to *when* I need to.

She finally lets me rest just before I wake in the middle of the night to Jake having a nightmare. Groggily, I try to gently nudge him with my elbow to wake him up. It doesn't work. I squint at the clock on the nightstand. My inner clock is all thrown off. I'd have guessed 3 a.m., but it's 5:30.

"Jake." I shake him again. "Jake!" He's not having it. Reaching over, I turn on my lamp. His face is distorted. "Jake! Wake up!"

His eyes pop open as he gasps and jumps. His wide eyes meet mine like he's scared out of his mind, then he stumbles out of bed.

I sigh. "Some nightmare, huh? Are you all right?"

He continues to stare at me like he's seen a ghost.

Holy cannoli! He has!

Cassia!

I scoot and scoot and scoot to escape this monster-size bed. "What—?"

"You burned!" His eyes are as big as grapefruits.

Oh no! She didn't show him that, *did she?* "No, Jake. That was Cassia." I try to hug him, but he starts pacing and breathing loudly out his mouth. He shakes his head and digs at his eyes, rubbing them hard.

I grab his hands to make him stop. *Stop digging. Stop walking. Just breathe.* He can barely look at me, so I grab his face. "Jake, it's me. I'm here."

He shuts his eyes tightly, then goes to sit on the edge of the fancy chair in the corner of the room. He sits with his elbows on his knees and his face in his hands.

I kneel in front of him, not knowing what to say; I don't know all that she showed him. "I'm sorry she did that. I don't know why—"

"I know why." He brings his hands down to his chin.

"What? Why?"

He still can barely even look at me. "Because…I was doubting you. Her. Everything." He breathes. "Even coming here with you." He looks at me, finally. Disgracefully. Dreadfully. "I'm sorry," he says, a glisten of possible tears starting.

His confession stings me, prickling at the strings around my heart. But I can understand, and I don't blame him. But I have to wonder… "Was that the only thing she showed you?" I ask.

The slightest shake of his head tells me "no," but the way he turns from me tells me he's not ready to share what else there was. The light of the lamp shadows half of his face, hiding half of him, just like he's only sharing half with me. He's keeping some of the darkness, processing it.

I glance back at the clock. "How about we get an early start?"

After a few seconds, he nods.

"Is it okay if I take a shower? Then we can talk about it?" I figure, since he thinks better alone, it may be good to leave him with his thoughts for thirty minutes or so.

He somewhat nods. Enough that I think he means yes. I stand up, but he grabs my hand before I turn. "Wait." He stands and pulls me in for a tight hug. Really tight. With his face turned into my neck, he murmurs, "I don't know how you manage…all this."

"Jake, I'm sorry you saw how she died, but—"

"No. *All* this." He pulls back and considers me. "Everything."

I squint at him, confused.

"And you're right. I *feel*. Like you were saying, I *felt* everything she did. Everything she *does* when she's with you. And everything you feel too."

I remember when I had feelings overload. I offer a (hopefully) comforting smile. "That's a lot of *feeling*," I say, trying to make a joke. I'm a little uncomfortable. If he's talking about literally *everything*, does that include Benson?

"You hated Ben at first."

Yep. Literally, everything. "I wouldn't say *hated*."

"Well, you sure as hell didn't like him."

I open my mouth but don't know what to say, so I shrug. *Cassia was trying to prove a point for me.*

He smiles, showing all his teeth. "You liked me right away."

I feel excess blood rush to my face.

He adjusts his hands and is back to serious. "I'm sorry I doubted you. You told the truth. Like you said."

I chuckle. "Jake, I couldn't make this stuff up if I tried."

Pressing his lips on mine, he keeps his eyes open, so I do too. With our eyes locked and lips together, he says, "Love you."

I pull back just a hair. Looking into his eyes, I think about everything, from the bee sting, to telling him about Cassia, to recording the songs, to being here with him. "And I love you."

Saturday, August 28

At breakfast, which ironically is at a Subway just a couple of buildings up the street, I tell Jake about what Cassia said when I'd taken a nap yesterday.

"That's not a very clear plan," Jake says.

I sigh. "I know."

"And where does Bella live? We're just supposed to wait for Cassia to point us in the right direction? Where is she?"

"I don't know. She said we should find her apartment building today. So let's start with that. Maybe she'll come later." I'm hoping after seeing Cassia's building, I'll feel more at ease to possibly do some sightseeing with Jake. *Just some. Let's not get carried away.*

As we exit Subway, although I have no idea where to go, I have the urge to hail a taxi. I do so, knowing how, not because of television and movies, but because it's somewhat familiar to me, even though I, personally, have never done it.

Jake steals a glimpse, astonished, and asks, "Where are we going?"

"One forty East Sixty-Third, please," I spit out as we settle in the cab. I look at Jake. "That was weird. I didn't know her address until now. And yet, she's not here to tell me."

He takes my hand and holds it in his lap.

That feeling returns. The one that tells me I'll know *what* I need to know *when* I need to know it.

I trust her.

The driver nods and merges back into traffic. I'm impressed with the cab, actually. It's nicer and cleaner than I thought it'd be, or maybe we just got lucky this first go-around. Not only that, but it's fairly high-tech, with a little TV showing the news, a credit card machine ready to go, and a digital map of the city.

"*We're* in a *taxi* in New York *City*," Jake slowly says, amazed, then lifts a brow at me. "That's pretty cool."

I smile at him.

"We are in"—he peers at his phone—"one of thirteen thousand, two hundred and thirty-seven taxi cabs."

Jake and I look out our respective windows, with the exception of him pulling me over to see something grand or eccentric. Being in the most populated borough in New York City, you wouldn't think I'd be surprised about the number of people and amount of traffic, but to see it live and in person really is something else. It's mind-blowing this many people can exist in one area, this many people can survive and endure this type of environment. Then again, I guess they don't know any different.

Feeling *at ease* was the wrong expression, I suppose. Because as the taxi stops and we step onto the sidewalk, I feel overwhelmingly emotional looking at the familiar brick archways that line the second floor of Cassia's building and begin hyperventilating.

But maybe it's more of a "Cassia-memory." I realize she used to work out at the gym on the second floor here. Maybe I'm not hyperventilating, just breathing heavily from a "Cassia-workout-memory thing."

Oh, who am I fooling?

I notice our reflection in the silver of the front doors. I can't quite put my finger on why I'm so emotional, though. All I know is this is going to be a long trip if I can't get a grip. I try not to make a scene, but that's sort of what I'm doing. I'm sobbing on the sidewalk in the middle of the day.

Jake wraps me in his arms, muffling my sobs into his shirt. "Breathe, Camry. Breathe." He strokes my hair.

"I don't know if I can do this," I admit.

"*We* can do this. We *are* doing this. Okay? It's going to be fine."

I try to let the rumble of Jake's voice in his chest cavity lull me.

"Should we walk away from this building?"

Nodding and wiping my tears, I say, "Yeah. That might help."

With his arm never letting me go, we begin to walk toward the Starbucks where the one-way street meets another one-way street. We've seen enough "one way" signs to make a skyscraper of our own.

It helps—the farther we get, the better I feel. I utilize a tree for leaning on, giving Jake a rest. The humidity of a New York August is feeling heavy in my chest. It doesn't help the whole claustrophobic sensation I already have.

Where's Cassia? Why was she thinking it'd be good for me to see her building? I was sort of hoping she'd find me here. Then again, maybe she *is* here. I try to focus on whether or not I feel her presence.

I don't.

But maybe the bustle of the city is distracting me. Maybe I'm just too flustered to notice. Maybe there's nothing here for me. Maybe, maybe, maybe. *Ugh!*

"What're ya thinking?" Jake asks, hands on his hips.

I stare at him, wondering how long I left him there as I got lost in my thoughts.

"Do you want to keep walking?" He gestures down the sidewalk. "Just see what we see? See if Cassia comes?" He looks at me again. "How's your ankle?"

I shrug. "It's good."

"I think you could use a break from *this*." *This* means "all this Cassia stuff." He continues. "You want to go…to a museum? Oh!" He grabs my hand. "Let's go to the zoo." He smiles big.

I know he's thinking about how Cassia said we had some time today, but I don't know if I agree. I'm feeling impatient like we can't waste time. I can't bring my lips to curl for a smile.

His face grows pained as he steps closer to me. "Anything new from Cassia?"

I shake my head.

"You need a distraction. You're really stressed out. I can see it all over you. And you know what? It's okay if we don't finish this on day one."

Suddenly, an address pops into my head. I blurt out, "Four twenty-five East One Fourteenth."

Jake blinks at me.

"That's where Bella lives," I explain.

"Is Cassia here? How do you know?"

"I don't know. I just…suddenly know. It's weird, right?"

"You sure you want to do this now?"

"She's home. Yes."

"Wait. Let's think. Does Bella know Cassia? Personally?"

I nod. I know what he's saying. It's the same thing I want to spare Cassia's dad from—the fact that I look just like Cassia, only with hazel eyes—but I don't care. I don't care about Bella. She's hiding something. Something that'll bring peace for Terrick Simonsen, father of an innocent girl who was taken, strangled, burned, and buried. "Maybe Bella needs to see me," I protest. "Maybe seeing a ghost is exactly what she needs. We need that file."

Jake stares at me as if what I said was too harsh.

I realize that *was* a bit harsh of me. I take a moment with a couple of deep breaths. "Listen, let's just see if we can talk her into doing the right thing."

Jake thinks. "You sure you're okay?" He glances at my ankle again, then peers deeply into my eyes as if he's trying to find the answer there somehow.

I nod, certain. "Yes."

He smirks. "Can I hail the taxi this time?"

On the fifteen-minute drive there, Jake and I try to come up with a plan, ending up with not much at all. The ideas of pretending to be a delivery person or a neighbor who can't find their keys are just…not good. If the taxi driver is listening, I can only imagine what he thinks of us. We arrive at Bella's apartment, a four-story red brick building smashed between other red brick buildings. Garbage cans and garbage bags line the front of the building on either side of the steps to the doorway. I've never thought about how much garbage a big city like this has. It has to be tons per day. *Gross.*

I curiously glance around at the neighborhood. Jake does too. Across the street is Jefferson Park, or so the map on his phone says. A random shopping cart sits across the street on the sidewalk. On the other side of the black iron fence, kids are playing in the field, and people are getting their exercise on the track that circles it. The trees around the park are old and tall. I'm pretty sure they're sycamore trees; we have them in Utah too. I shake my head from the random stupid thought about trees and turn back. Noticing a ladder for the fire escape that hangs above the garbage cans, I can't help but think how "New York City" it is. I sort of love it.

I ring the buzzer next to the glass door for Bella's apartment. Jake reaches to stop me, but he's too late. "Whoa, did you decide what to say?" he asks.

I don't answer, and he fixes me with a worried look.

A lady—I'm assuming Bella—answers warily, "Hello?"

"Bella?"

"Who's this?"

"I'm a friend of Cassia's." I pause to let that sink in. "Do you have a minute?" Too many seconds pass; I begin fidgeting with my earring.

"For what? To talk about her? I really don't want to." She has a foreign accent I can't place.

"No! Wait. Please. Yes. To talk about her." I'm fumbling but think of something that might work. "More specifically to talk about how you can help her."

"What do you mean? I've already talked to the police. There's nothing more I can do."

"The police aren't doing enough. I'm trying to do more. Will you help me? I just have a few questions."

Jake's gaping at me with wide eyes as if I'm blowing it. I hope I'm not.

"I'm sorry, what's your name?"

"Camry."

"Camry what?"

"Camry Jacobs."

It takes a while, but she says, "Okay, but I only have a minute."

"That's fine. I understand."

She buzzes the door open.

"Don't think you're leaving me out here," Jake says.

"Not at all," I say. "You're coming with me." I probably should've mentioned to her that I have a plus one.

We climb two flights of stairs to apartment 2A. Bella opens the door after Jake knocks. The shock of seeing my look-alike features works to our benefit. She lets go of the door and backs up as her face pales. She's a short woman of thirtysomething carrying excess weight through her torso. She wears a simple T-shirt and denim shorts and has her thick black hair tied up in a messy bun. She begins mumbling in her native tongue at an incredible speed.

I hold my hands out innocently while taking a step into her apartment. Jake is close at my back, closing the door quietly behind us.

"I'm sorry! I know I look like her; it's weird. Just give us a chance, please—"

"Who are you? What is this?" she asks with wide eyes. "And who are *you*?" She looks Jake up and down. Jake holds up his hands to display his innocence as well.

"I'm Camry, and this is Jake." I introduce us, talking like one would to a small, scared child.

Her petrified stare slides back and forth between the two of us. She must know I'm not Cassia but still seems incredibly freaked out. "Are you really a friend of hers?" She holds a hand over her chest.

I wince. "Sort of."

"What does 'sort of' mean?"

Her apartment is small; we're squished in her living room, sharing space with a loveseat, coffee table, and small television in the opposite corner. "Can we sit and talk?" I ask, gesturing to the couch.

She repeats, more sternly, "What does 'sort of' mean?"

Okaaay. Not gonna sit then. "Well," I start, "I've been dreaming a lot lately, just like you."

More color drains from her face, which had just begun to look normal. I wish she'd just sit so she doesn't pass out from lack of blood to her head. She begins to pace and mumble again.

I tell her, "We came to talk to you about the audio file you have. We need to do the right thing, Bella."

She stops, scowls at me, and plays dumb. "I don't know anything about a file."

My eyes narrow at the nerve she has to say those words.

"But we know you have it." Jake almost laughs, unconvinced.

I adopt a suppliant tone, with my hands in prayer fashion. "Bella. We're talking about justice for Cassia. Don't you want that? And saving an innocent life. JoAnna will die if we don't stop this from happening."

Bella's face shifts into something I can't entirely read at the mention of JoAnna's name.

"If you don't want to turn it in, please give it to us. I won't say anything about you. It'll be like you were never involved." My face pleads with her. *Please!*

Her body language shifts as she folds her arms across her chest and says, "You're too late. I don't have it anymore."

"What?" Jake and I say together, incredulously, Jake more forcefully than I. I suddenly wish I'd been recording this conversation. *Stupid me.*

Just like other things in the past twenty-four hours, an understanding pops into my head. "You made a deal?"

Bella lifts her chin as if to challenge me.

"For money?" I feel Cassia's presence now.

Strong.

I can hear her say in my ear as clearly as if she were here speaking to me. "She has no intentions of turning it in. It's still on her phone." This is the part Cassia didn't understand, the part she was missing. She gets it now and is sharing the information with me.

The niceties are going out the window. Because there are two kinds of people in this world: the ones who have a file of evidence of a planned murder and turn it in to the police and the ones who use it for blackmail to get money. *Argh!* Bella is the latter! She doesn't know who she's dealing with. She'll probably be next after JoAnna.

I spit out, "How could you?!" while stepping toward her. Jake grabs my forearm. I glower at him in a way I've never glowered at anyone before. My blood is beginning to boil. I haven't been this angry in a long time, since…I don't know when; I don't usually get angry.

The light in Bella's living room flickers, then three things happen within milliseconds of each other. One: Bella spits, "Get out!" Two: Jake's face turns to astonishment as he sees Cassia quickly join me. And three: my right fist connects with Bella's left eye.

I've never punched anyone before. Well, technically, Cassia punched her, but still, it hurts all the way through my forearm. Bella has stumbled back, tripped over the coffee table, and fallen on the floor.

Jake pulls me back. "Camry! Get a hold of yourself!"

Cassia wrenches my body free of him and covers my mouth with our shaky hands. She's incredibly angry at Bella for this. I'm angry also, but I feel Cassia's rage mixed with hurt from Bella's betrayal too. Trying to speak calmly, she apologizes to him, or maybe Bella; I'm not sure. Jake lowers his head to look at my face and watches as she leaves me, changing my eyes back to hazel. I blink hard at the sensation, take a deep breath, then wipe my mouth with the back of my hand. My hands are still shaking. Cassia left, but the adrenaline stayed.

I watch Bella; her shirt is bunched up, and she's on her hands and knees, trying to get up. Jake and I move toward her but for different reasons. He reaches to help her up at the same time as I quickly grab her phone, which had fallen out of her back pocket onto the floor.

Jake glances at me curiously. Bella doesn't make it to her feet. Instead, she sits on her loveseat, her black hair falling out of the bun and hanging in her face. She holds her left eye and says nothing. Since I don't have any pockets, I slip her phone into his while she's not looking.

"I'm sorry," I say with a voice so shaky I'm surprised I got out any words at all.

Jake moves past me into her kitchen. I see him grab a towel and open her freezer for some ice. I begin pacing to help flush out the adrenaline. He wraps up the ice and brings it over to her. He can't help but be a nurse.

She takes it and holds it to her eye. Peering out of the good one, she looks at me and admits, "I need the money. My mother…my mother is sick."

I halt and try to have sympathy for her, but…I shake my head. "Not at the expense of someone else's life, Bella."

She looks down. "Just give me some time. I'll do it. I'll turn it in. I just need another payment."

"JoAnna may not have time. Do you know when all this is supposed to happen?"

"I don't know, but I know I have time for one more payment."

Jake and I look at each other. He's faster than I am. "When is the payment scheduled for?" he asks.

She sighs. "Monday."

This is all possibly way sooner than I thought. Bella has to realize, though, she can't keep the money. She also should realize all I have to do is call the police on her. I don't want it to go down like that, but is she really so set on this money that she can't see these probabilities?

I start to realize the bottom line is we can't really trust her and we can't really wait for her, but I play along and firmly say, "Okay. We'll be back on Monday." I turn and briskly walk out. Jake shadows me, jogging to catch up. We're up the street and turning the corner when I reach into his pocket and take her phone out. My hands are still shaking.

Jake pulls on my arm, stopping me, and grabs the phone back. He also grabs my hand to examine the damage. My knuckles are red, but they're fine. I flex my fingers. He seems frustrated, either with me or the way things happened just now or something, but the first thing out of his mouth is concern. "Are you okay?"

"I don't know." I rub my face. My adrenaline is still pumping through my veins; I'm a little sick to my stomach. "It's fine. I'll be fine."

Now a bit of the frustration comes out. "So, so far, we have assault and battery and theft. What's next?"

"I'm sorry, but we need that phone," I say defensively.

He puts the phone back in his pocket and eyes me expectantly.

"You heard. She's made a deal with Tiffanie for money, Jake. But I don't believe she'll ever turn it in. There's always going to be the temptation of another payment." I sigh. "There's a copy of the file on her phone. Let's just try to find the file."

He thinks for a minute, then grabs my arm and starts walking me. Farther away from Bella's building.

"Jake?"

"Okay, okay," he says. "But me. Not you. We're getting a cab and going back to the hotel. I'm not taking the phone out of my pocket until we get there." I begin to protest, but he holds up his finger in my face. "*I*—and only *I*—am going to look through the phone to try to find it. *You* need to rest. Chill out. Take a break. Whatever. If you keep going like this, you're gonna break. And that's not why I came with you. I'm here to help. Remember?"

Suck! He's right.

Back at the hotel, I'm holding Bella's phone and pacing again. Of course Bella would have a passcode to get in. I don't have one on my phone; I don't have anything to hide. I don't know what the number is, and Cassia isn't coming to me. Then again, it could be she doesn't know it either. I really thought if I held it for a while, it would come to me—just like the addresses earlier popping into my mind. But so far, I've got nothing. Jake is sitting in the fancy chair, watching sketchy videos on his phone for a way to break in to Bella's phone.

It's been twenty minutes and I'm flustered to no end. I toss the phone on the bed and rub my forehead.

Jake pauses his video and stands up. He carefully grabs my bruised hand. "Why don't you go down the hall to get some ice? You could use a distraction. I've got something to try anyway. Just go take a breather. Maybe it'll come to you. Or maybe Cassia will come to you."

On the way back from the ice machine, Cassia startles me, and I drop the bag of ice. I watch it scatter across the hallway, bouncing as if happy to be free.

"Sorry," she says.

I begin to pick up the ice chips. "Where have you been?"

She doesn't answer. She says instead, "I'm sorry about your hand."

"Yeah. And what was that about? I mean, it was kind of badass, but I'm trying not to make things worse, remember? And that was the first time Jake's ever met you. Not the best way to meet someone for the first time, I'd say."

"What do you want me to say? I'm sorry."

I shake my head. "Do you know the passcode?" I stand up and head back to the ice machine. Even though it's in a bag, I don't like the idea that it touched the floor. I want new ice.

A pause. "No. I just know that Bella has it on her phone. Listen, I know you don't agree, but I need to see my dad. Sometime before you leave."

"Yeah, do you remember my idea about taking it to the police?" I dump the ice in the little sink and start to get a fresh batch.

"I see what you're saying, but…if you go to the police, they'll hold you for questioning. I don't want any of this to escalate to where you need a lawyer. How are you going to explain how you got the phone? Just give it to my dad and let him turn in the evidence and leave you guys out of it."

She makes good sense, on the one hand. On the other hand, I loosely wonder if she's trying to convince me of this to sway my choice. "Is dropping it off at his office an option?" I ask.

She stops me from getting ice. After a moment, she says, "Camry. I don't know how to explain it, but…I need to see my dad through you. I just need to."

"Cass, I don't think that's a good idea. I look just like you. Especially when you're with me. You saw what happened with Bella."

"You know how some people think ghosts have unfinished business or something?"

Yeah.

"Well, I think maybe that's true. I feel like I'm stuck here. I feel like I have to make this right. I have to save my mom." She hesitates. "And I need to see my dad. Then after that, I think I can go."

Cassia is very persistent about me *seeing* her dad, and I'm not liking the idea very much. I tell her, "I don't understand what it is my body can do for you *or* him other than upset him."

"He wants to find me. Can you understand that?" Her voice is borderline whining.

I manage to finish the ice. Someone walks by, and we both shut up. The older gentleman grins and nods at me, so I do the same. I *do* understand; finding her remains will help Terrick Simonsen heal.

Lightly, I think in the back of my mind that when I turn in the file, I could also tell the police where to find Cassia's remains. But that'd require her telling me where her body is buried. And I'd look suspicious, so I don't know if that's the best idea.

I begin walking back to the room since I've got my new ice. As I turn the corner, I ask, "You really don't have any idea what the passcode could be? What's her birthday?"

I'm forced to stop because Cassia breaks down sobbing. She slides me down the wall to a sitting position on the floor.

What's going on? I think to her since I can't speak through the sobs.

"He feels so bad about the last conversation we had when he yelled at me. I…I could give him the chance he needs to say he's sorry. To have some closure."

*But you know that he's sorry about that and he loves you and…*My thinking trails off.

"He would *know* that I know. And it's not just that. I never had the chance to tell him goodbye. If I could just touch his hand, it would be so much."

Be *so much?* I question. *Cassia, think about all the people who die unexpectedly and never get to say goodbye…or resolve a fight.*

"Yeah. And think about all the living people and how their lives would be different if they had one more chance."

Cassia leaves me unexpectedly.

"Camry?" a voice calls from down the hall. It's Jake. He begins walking fast as he sees me crying on the floor. "Are you okay?" He takes my hands to help me up.

Hmm. He spooks Cassia away, I'm noticing. "Yeah, *I'm* fine." I wipe her tears. "Cassia's not."

Jake is sympathetic, but there's a light in his eyes. "I think I found the file."

I gape at him, excited. *Glory, Glory, Hallelujah! Evidence!*

Then the light fades as he wrinkles his nose. "But it prompts a password. Do you know what it is?"

Another security check?! I blink and shake my head. We both hurry back to the room even though my ankle tells me to slow down. I'm hoping once I see it, the password will pop into my head or Cassia will whisper it to me.

Jake picks up the phone and taps on the audio file. It disappears. "What?!" we both yelp.

He taps back out and back in and scrolls around to find the file. "It's gone!" He says, still scrolling. "You've got to be friggin' kidding me! It was right here!"

Tap, tap, tap.

Scroll, scroll, scroll.

I'm pretty sure Bella knows we have her phone and has removed the file, probably using another device tied to her phone. We're screwed, basically.

"Aaagghh!" Jake snarls and pulls his hair. He almost throws the phone across the room but thinks better of it. Thank goodness.

"What about text messages or voicemail? *Any* incriminating evidence?"

"No. I checked."

I sit on the edge of the bed. "Okay. What're our options?"

Jake is pacing and squeezing the phone with such force, I hope he doesn't break it. "Go back to Bella's or call the police on her."

I sigh. "There's no way she'll let us in, and—"

A very TV-New-York-thing happens, cutting me off. We hear sirens right on our street. Jake and I look at each other. It's almost as if the universe is telling us something.

"We should go to the police," Jake says, following the cosmic suggestion.

But I don't know about the universe. The universe seems somewhat backward to me right now. Plus, Cassia's words ring in my ears. I say, "Cassia had concerns about that. We shouldn't get ourselves into a situation where we'd need a lawyer. I do *not* want to get stuck here."

"I don't think that's how it works."

"How do you know? Have you ever given a tip about a murder plot before?"

"Why are you so nervous to go to the police?"

"I wouldn't say I'm nervous. I just…I don't know. I can't put my finger on it."

"So, is Terrick on your radar?"

Nervously, I nod.

"You don't think that'll somehow turn into a crazy mess that might get us stuck here anyway? In need of a lawyer anyway?" Jakes says, then adds curiously, "What happens to the guy who gives a tip? I need to watch more crime shows."

I think for a minute, wishing I were smarter, and ignoring the idea that Cassia might be trying to influence me. "I might be able to get through to him. Mr. Simonsen," I clarify.

Jake's expression is unsure. "How? What're you thinkin'?"

"I should say, Cassia might be able to get through to him." *Yep, you got it. I'm thinking about what Cassia has been wanting to do all along.* I wonder if she is close by, near enough to put thoughts like this in my head. I'm not sensing her though. Perhaps somehow her presence has become so much it's as if my thoughts *are* her thoughts.

No. That's not what I mean. It's deeper than that. *Has she left a part of her with me permanently? Am I one-quarter Cassia?*

One-third?

More?

Jake moves quickly and sits next to me on the bed. "Cam. I don't..." Shaking his head, he says with certainty, "No."

"As much as I've been trying to avoid going to him, I think it might be the best way."

Jake shakes his head again. His styled-messy hair shakes a split second longer.

I add, "And Cassia keeps saying she needs to see him."

"What? Why?" Jake's green eyes search my face.

"She says it's because he'd have the chance to apologize to her. The last time they talked, they argued. He yelled at her." I pause. "And she'd like to be able to say goodbye since she obviously didn't before. I'd like to give that to her. She thinks she can go after saving her mom and seeing her dad."

Jake thinks about that.

"She's acting sort of funny about it though."

"What? You think there's something she's not telling you?"

"Hmmm, I don't know. I don't think she quite knows either."

"What about Tiffanie? Where is she?" Jake asks.

"I don't know. Cassia hasn't said anything about her."

Jake thinks for a minute, then says, "Think back to what you do know about her. Tiffanie, I mean. Where does she work or usually hang out?"

I try to think, but I don't know anything. "Cassia didn't share that kind of stuff with me." We sit in silence for a few moments. "Scroll through her texts," I tell Jake. "I want to see the messages between Tiffanie and Bella."

Jake pulls it up while shaking his head. "If there were any, she's deleted them." He shows me an empty text screen for Tiffanie. "There's nothing on 'Mom' either. Well, I mean nothing that leads to anything." He shows me, but he's right. It's just texts about needing milk or the time she thinks she'll be home. "I've looked through all of them."

I trust him but still take the phone and glance to see for myself. I tap on "Terrick Simonsen." We didn't get the file, but the silver lining here is at least we can reach Cassia's dad.

Jake gently grabs my hand—and the phone. "What if we contact him anonymously?"

"We can't anticipate what he'll do. If I'm someone he trusts, then we're in. Right? Jake, I didn't come all this way to leave it halfway done." And I realize that's really the biggest thing. I don't want to leave a note or make an anonymous call and then return to Utah having to wonder if it all worked out. I need to be *sure* it all worked out.

Jake asks, "Are we sure there isn't a better way?"

The smallest of nods, but I sigh too. Because here I am again, lying. I'm pretending to be Bella; I'm tricking Mr. Simonsen. Looking through their conversation history, it's mostly her texting him to let him know she's done with her cleaning duties and then him thanking her. It seems to be a weekly occurrence. Jake watches me tap all the letters for a very different text message from little miss Bella, a.k.a. Traitor.

Me: *Are you available today? I have something I need to discuss in person with you.*

Three anxiety-filled minutes later. Mr. Simonsen: *Can it wait until tomorrow?*

I think I understand what he's getting at; he most likely has tomorrow off, or at least it's a less busy day than today is for him. This gets me feeling bad. If he's busy today, I'd hate to interrupt him with such disturbing news and throw off the rest of what he needs to do. Then again, is there ever a good time for something like this? I glance at the time: 11:38.

Suddenly. Mr. Simonsen: *Or can you discuss it with Tiffanie? She'll be home around 4:00.*

He most likely believes this to be a cleaning issue. Me: *No. This is a personal matter I'd like to discuss only with you and in person.*

One minute later. Mr. Simonsen: *Is everything all right?*

Well, that's a loaded question. Me: *No.*

Mr. Simonsen: *Meet me in my building lobby at 1:30.*

I hunch in relief. He's squeezing her into his busy day. It's very kind of him. It tells me they probably have a decent relationship, and he respects her. I can't believe she'd turn on him like she has.

Me: *Thank you.*

Jake rubs my back. "You sure you're ready for this?" he asks.

"No, but I have to be."

He pulls me against him for a side hug. "We should eat. I bet that's what he's doing, allowing himself time for lunch, then he'll meet us."

Coming out of the Salisbury, we turn right and head to the corner. Across the street is the Carnegie Diner that'll do just fine. Over our hamburgers and fries, Jake and I try to come up with a loose plan while admiring Carnegie Hall. Cassia's building isn't like Bella's where we can buzz the tenant and we're granted entrance; there's a doorman. A doorman who's going to be just as freaked out as Bella was when she saw me. We were lucky, I realize, not to have run into him when we were there earlier.

I haven't shared my fear with Jake yet about the doorman possibly being the same one from the articles, the one who last saw Cassia alive, Antony Masterfield. Jake's talking and has skipped over the part about how we get in the building and jumped to the part where we talk to Mr. Simonsen. I guess, in his mind, we just walk in. I don't stop him; he's thinking out loud, brainstorming ideas. So far, he's thinking the best option is to leave me out of it completely.

"I don't believe Cassia will go for that," I tell him.

Jake and I go back and forth on this and other things until he finishes my fries and I suck down the last of my soda.

Even though I don't want to talk to Mr. Simonsen in his building lobby, that's where he's chosen. I contemplate texting him again to see if he'll consider meeting at a different location, then decide against it. With the disturbing news I'll be giving, it may be good for him to be in a familiar and comforting place.

We have almost forty-five minutes until we have to meet him, which is good for allowing my greasy burger to settle—less chance of upchucking from nerves causing my stomach to go haywire. So many things depend on so many things: if Cassia is or isn't with me, if the doorman is or isn't Antony (and if I would even know if it were him), if we happen to be walking in at the same time as Mr. Simonsen, resulting in a very awkward moment on the sidewalk, and I'm sure other things I can't even imagine right now. We're just going to have to wing it.

We arrive fifteen minutes early, getting out of the taxi half a block away. The temperature is climbing into the eighties now, and the humidity is really starting to overwhelm me. I try not to lose focus, but I don't make it farther than the visual distance of seeing the tall dark-skinned man in uniform. Cassia isn't with me, but I guess some of her memories are. And it would appear they have triggers now. I recognize Antony. He's standing on the curb, hailing a taxi for a short and prim older woman.

I stop abruptly, yank Jake's arm, and turn around. We throw off a few people who were behind us, causing them to split and go around us. "That's Antony!" I whisper yell. My fingers rub my forehead.

Jake has an idea, and because I have the sudden desire to arrive *before* Mr. Simonsen, I go with it. With my hand in Jake's, he walks us straight up to Antony and extends his arm for a shake while saying, "Good afternoon. I'm Jake, and this is Camry. We're here to meet Mr. Simonsen on Bella's behalf. She couldn't make it. May we wait in the lobby?" Jake was so fluid he left no chance for Antony to intervene.

The doorman smiles, though, while shaking Jake's hand and listening, up until he gets a glimpse of me. I was trying to hide behind Jake's shoulder a bit, but there's really no hiding. I'm as obvious as King Kong on the Empire State Building. Antony falters and stutters as his eyes examine my face.

I go for it; I meet his stare with my hazel eyes and smile.

He only stumbles a second more. "O-Of course, sir," he replies, then opens the door for us. "Miss? Your name again please?"

"Camry," I say, and he nods.

"There're some chairs across the lobby," he offers, letting the door close behind us.

I don't know about Jake, but I exhale in relief as we enter. Then I absorb the elegance of the lobby with all my senses. The glow of the lighting sparkles through the chandeliers. The fragrance of the enormous flower display on the table in the center of the floor hovers in the air. And the echo of our footsteps on the shiny tile floor bounces off the walls and ceiling. The feel of it is…home. All these things push through the part of my brain that holds a small permanent bit of Cassia. I take a second to acknowledge this with a small grin to myself, then I pull Jake across the room to park ourselves on some chairs.

I sit rigidly at the edge of a comfortable cream-colored chair, waiting for Cassia's father. Jake sits in an identical chair, leaning forward with his palms on his knees. There's a small lamp table separating us, and I don't think Jake likes it. He scoots his chair a couple of inches but still can't reach me. He seems to give up, asking me instead, "Are you sure you're ready for this?"

I glance at my lap. I think I might be feeling Cassia nearby. "Yes," I tell Jake, though I'm not at all sure. I'm up to my neck in anxiety; I'm pretty sure I feel a lump in my throat from it. I hold up a finger to Jake, telling him to wait a minute.

Cassia's not joined with me, but I try to concentrate on her. I think I feel her energy. It's full of confidence, almost a type of excitement. It could be for herself, but I think it could be for me too. She may be trying to pump me up without joining me; I feel it circling me. I'm reminded of the Zion jump. I'd encouraged her then to take the leap, to fall into the canyon with only the safety of a thin rope, and now she's doing the same for me. Can I take this leap? Can I fall into this unknown with only the safety of a strand of hope? Hope that Mr. Simonsen will understand. Hope that he won't call the police. Hope that everything will turn out fine. Together, Cassia and I made it through the jump at Zion—granted, I ended up with a broken nose, but still…

I add to the hope list: I hope I don't somehow break my nose today.

The door opens, and a boisterous voice echoes throughout the otherwise serene foyer. "I don't know a Jake or Camry, Antony. I don't appreciate her changing things when she insists on meeting me in person." It's Mr. Simonsen, and, from his tone, he seems extremely irritated.

This isn't a good start.

Jake jumps to his feet, but my gaze remains on my lap. My hair is pulled back into a basic ponytail, and I'm wearing a soft pink top with a knee-length black skirt. I don't think these are the type of clothes Cassia would wear or how she'd style her hair. I cross my fingers that I don't look like her to him.

Antony's footsteps seem to follow Mr. Simonsen's as they round the table of flowers. "Sir, I need to warn you—"

The clicks of the dress shoes belonging to Mr. Simonsen and the doorman cease as, I assume, Mr. Simonsen sees me. Suddenly, he rushes over to me. "Oh my God! Baby?" He kneels and puts his hands on my knees. "Baby?"

My heart hurts as it skips a beat and I cry inside, *No!* I force my head up. My hazel eyes glance slowly over his expensive shoes, up his expensive suit, and meet his "Cassia-blue" eyes. They tell him the sad truth that I'm, unfortunately, not his "baby." Despite the strength I was trying to build up, my eyes water as his face changes to disappointment with this realization.

He swiftly rises to his feet, looking as if he feels like a fool. He clears his throat and composes himself quickly like he's had a lot of practice. Before I know it, he's back to professional businessman Terrick Simonsen after a simple apology for the misunderstanding.

Antony stands behind and away from him, staring at me oddly. The tall and barrel-chested Mr. Simonsen looks to him, then back to us with a scowl. "What's going on here?" He directs the question to Jake, so Jake stands too. Mr. Simonsen's voice, along with his presence, is intimidating, but I have strength; Cassia is right next to me. Jake, however, I don't know.

Lastly, I stand.

Jake extends his hand to Mr. Simonsen. "I'm Jake, and this is Camry."

Mr. Simonsen glowers at Jake's hand and makes no move to shake it. In fact, he inspects every part of Jake, from his styled-messy hair to his T-shirt sporting The Killers to his converse sneakers, with what I'd consider disgust.

Jake takes back his hand and tries for more. "We—"

"Where's Bella?" Mr. Simonsen barks. "How do you know her? Is this her way of quitting?"

Ignoring his questions, I answer, "She has something very valuable to you. We're here to talk about it—"

Mr. Simonsen's eyes shift to me. "She's stolen from me? How would you know…?" He stops as my shaking head has told him his assumption is incorrect.

"I didn't say she stole from you." I talk slower than I normally would because he's talking so fast. I need him to slow down and understand my every word and just how serious I am. "She possesses something very valuable, very important to you. Can we go somewhere to sit down?" My expression is stern. I can see in his hard eyes he's not one to mess with, and I'm pushing it. But I need to hold my ground.

"Did you stage this?" Mr. Simonsen looks between the two of us then steps in front of me. "How do you have my private number?"

Argh! Is he listening to me?

I not only feel tiny in this nerve-racking moment; I literally am tiny compared to Terrick Simonsen—even Jake is small. He towers over us and is as wide as both of us put together. "We need to talk," I continue.

"Preferably not in the lobby and not in your apartment. We can't risk Tiffanie coming home. She can't know about this. Okay?"

"No. This is ridiculous. Who are you? How do you know my wife and Bella? You've got about five seconds." He sounds mad, but there's a hint of wonder in his eyes. I know I remind him of Cassia, and he's trying to be strong. Logical. After all, I'm not his daughter. My eyes told him that instantly.

"My name is Camry Jacobs." I then glance at the floor and take a small step forward. Mr. Simonsen doesn't step back; he doesn't feel threatened by me. "But," I whisper to the floor, then invite Cassia to join me. *I think this is a mistake, but she's been whispering it in my ear, and I feel like we're losing him, so here goes.* My other foot matches my step, and I meet Mr. Simonsen's gaze again just as Cassia joins me, turning my hazel into her familiar blue right before his eyes. "It's me, CJ," says Cassia. I didn't realize Cassia Jane has the same initials as my name, Camry Jacobs.

She slowly reaches for him. But he begins blinking rapidly, and his chin quivers. He quickly covers his mouth with one hand and steps back as his eyes flood with tears, then he begins to shake his head violently.

Antony's eyes grow wide as his dark complexion pales.

"Cam?" Jake reaches for me, twisting his neck to find my eyes.

I don't give him anything. I can't; Cassia's driving. I tell her to stop, though. Three seconds is long enough. She relents enough I can repeat, "We need to talk. Time is something we may not have a lot of right now."

Mr. Simonsen suddenly steps forward into my bubble. Every muscle in his face speaks of his anger. He's turned to rage, probably to avoid the chance of breaking down. It takes everything I have not to step backward from his intimidating presence. My head tilts severely to maintain eye contact. Cassia leaves me, and I inhale deeply.

He watches me with furrowed brows, narrowing his eyes to slits. "Tell me now! Who are you? What are you doing here?" His unruly voice echoes in the foyer. "And don't be vague, goddamn it! Or I'll have you thrown in jail for—"

Jake cuts in, loud, but not yelling, "Whoa!" He holds out his hands to each of us. "Let's maybe go somewhere we can *calmly* talk about this."

We stand in silence, the echoes lost in the fancy ceiling and chandeliers. Mr. Simonsen scans the lobby, stealing a glance at Antony as well.

Antony carries a look agreeable to Jake's suggestion but then says, "Sir, would you like me to contact the police?"

Cassia's father thinks a long moment, our eyes locked on each other's. He's demanding when he asks, "Does this have anything to do with my daughter's disappearance?" His attempt to stay composed is obvious.

I can't answer his question. He might allow the phone call to the police. I can't lie to him either. So I simply continue to stare, afraid of him yelling at me again. Mr. Simonsen turns around and begins pacing, hands on his hips. I glance at Jake without moving my head.

Mr. Simonsen is taking so long that I start to imagine telling him his daughter is dead. I hate I have to do this to a man who's already been through so much. Mr. Simonsen stops pacing and squints back at me just as I blink a tear down my cheek.

His expression twitches, then it's back to negotiating businessman Terrick Simonsen. "You say Bella has something?"

I nod.

"Tell me what it is." He's demanding, walking into my bubble again. "And I won't press charges."

Jake moves, reaching his hand to support my back. "Press charges for what?" he starts, frustrated. "We're here to help."

Mr. Simonsen ignores Jake, his stare fixed on me. I choke down some of the chilling fear of him being in my face with those icy eyes. I wonder if Cassia can have that same look when she's angry or if it's just him who's capable of this. He's waiting.

"Like I said, not in the lobby," I tell him. "And not in your apartment."

As much as I disagreed with Cassia doing that, it was probably necessary. It kept Mr. Simonsen interested enough to give us more time. It's keeping him from calling the police right now. "Antony? Find a room for us to convene."

Antony nods and bows a little before rushing off to fill the order.

Jake and I exhale, and we both adjust our clothing. His wide-eyed look tells me he's on edge. He grabs my hand and laces our fingers together but maintains his posture and stares up at the unflinching Mr. Simonsen. I can't help but peer down at his hand connected with mine. Then I look back at Cassia's dad. He's trying hard to figure this whole thing out, but there's almost no way he can yet.

Antony halfway returns with a calling for us to "come this way." Mr. Simonsen turns to the side and holds out his hand in a gesture for us to go first. We do. We cross the foyer to a room next to the elevators. Antony holds the door open for us, and Mr. Simonsen follows a few steps behind. He whispers something to Antony. Antony nods and closes the door as he leaves.

The room is some sort of classroom, though I'm not sure what for. Possibly, meetings or trainings. There are two rows of three tables each. The tables are large enough to sit four chairs behind them. All chairs are facing the front of the class, which is complete with a whiteboard and projection machine. Extra chairs line the edges of the room in stacks of four. They must have to cram quite a few people in here sometimes. It smells old, and there are stains on the ceiling. It's a stark contrast to the elegance of the foyer.

The door clicks shut, and I turn around to face Mr. Simonsen. I can only imagine what he must be thinking. Jake still grips my hand. The three of us stand there, the silence dragging out. I can feel Cassia close by and mentally tell her not to enter my body. I don't know if her dad can handle that again. I don't know if *I* can handle her dad again.

Mr. Simonsen starts, "What does Bella have?"

"You might want to sit down." Jake suggests, pulling out a chair for him.

Frowning at him, Mr. Simonsen turns to me. "What happened back there?" he says firmly, curiosity taking over the object I keep insisting Bella has for him. But then he speaks again, and it comes out quite soft. "You looked just like her, but you're not her." This is the only thing keeping him even halfway believing anything I have to offer. There's no doubt in my mind he'd have kicked us to the curb by now if it weren't for that crazy stunt she pulled. He swallows and begins to crack. "Where's my CJ?"

The icy fear from before shatters, and my heart breaks into a thousand pieces for him. For Cassia. For what I have to say next. "She's…gone." Tears fall from both my eyes. "I'm so sorry."

He stares at me, then denial or anger or both start. He shakes his head vehemently. "No! No!" His hands clench into fists, knuckles white. A roar: "*No!*"

I flinch.

He paces once. Twice. Then says, "How do you know anything?"

"I…your daughter's spirit found me. I can talk to her, and she can talk to me," I say.

He scoffs. "I don't believe in ghosts."

I don't know how to respond to that. Something tells me I need to be quick with the rest of it, though. It's an unsettling feeling because I don't want to rush this. Jake's hand squeezes mine tightly. I reluctantly give in to the feeling and tell Mr. Simonsen, "Bella has an audio file in her possession that proves your wife is hiring someone to kill JoAnna." I'm not finished, but I'll let him absorb that much.

The white knuckles disappear as Mr. Simonsen becomes stunned. "JoAnna?"

I continue, "Tiffanie is paying Bella to keep quiet. She…did the same thing with Cassia."

"That's impossible. How could she…?"

"She just wants your money. Her mother is helping her."

Mr. Simonsen falls into the chair Jake had pulled out for him. I'm not sure if he's unable to handle it all or is just pondering what his logic is telling him about all this. His face rests in his hands, elbows on the table. Jake relaxes the squeeze on my hand and pulls out a chair for me, then himself, away from the table. We sit.

"Mr. Simonsen," I begin. "You need to get Bella to give you the file. Take it to the police."

"Who *are* you?" The question is deep. Not just that I'm Camry Jacobs, but how exactly do I know what I know?

"I like to think I'm someone who can help," I say, then think of something that'll resonate with him. "I'm someone who dreams."

He blinks and slowly turns to me. "Dreams?" he questions.

I nod.

His eyes scan the dirty carpet as if he's watching something unravel before him, helpless to stop it. He's thinking. Remembering. Remembering he's been dreaming too.

I let him think for a long time. Let him remember. He's a busy man and likely doesn't remember his dreams. Minutes pass, but I think he must remember something because his face contorts, and tears slip off his cheeks to the floor.

"She," I start, and he peers up at me, "wants you to know that she knows you're sorry about the fight you had that day. That it's all okay. That she knows you love her." I let that sink in and swallow my tears. "And she loves you too."

Mr. Simonsen whispers, "She tried to tell me."

I move to kneel in front of him. "And she's trying to tell you again. Through me. It's okay to let her go. JoAnna needs your help now."

Cassia joins me, and I dip my head, not wanting him to see her eyes. She reaches my right hand out to him, placing it gently atop his, and peers up at him.

I feel a rush of profound love and deep memories. It's mostly their love and memories, but she includes my love for her and my memories of her too. I feel a warmth flow through the center of my being and into her father. Then time slows. It moves in a gentle, relaxed sort of way, swaying and allowing for a connection not any of us are capable of describing. I feel her dimension expand, swelling into mine, growing and allowing for other-worldly colors to pour into me and overflow into him. And I feel gravity shift. It's a sonic wave that wrinkles the universe, making my reality blurry and unclear.

I'm Cassia, *and* I'm me. But different than before. We are one in a deeper way, a more profound way.

Mr. Simonsen freezes, probably in a state of shock. His bottom lip twitches as if he's going to say something but is cut off by the sound of the door opening behind us.

"In here, officers," Antony says.

Jake and my body both turn back to see two police officers come in with their hands ready to draw their pistols.

Jake jumps up before I do. "Whoa!" he says loudly. He looks at me, completely freaked out.

I've stood and physically separated from Mr. Simonsen. I'm me, and yet, I'm still there holding Cassia's father's hand. Somehow, I'm in two places at once. *Have I stepped out of my body?*

The physical me looks at Mr. Simonsen with despondency and disappointment. *That's what he whispered to Antony, for him to go ahead and contact the police. That's why I felt the need to hurry.*

I can't read his expression. *Is he still lost in what Cassia is doing to him?* "If I could just touch his hand, it would be so much," she'd said back at the hotel. She couldn't get to him. He wasn't open to her dimension. She needed me to make that connection. And a piece of me must stay for the connection to continue. Not necessarily a physical piece of me. Part of my soul will do. She couldn't find the words to tell me this, but with our souls like one in this delicate moment, I understand now. Things have fallen into place.

One of the officers is saying something, but there's a rush in my ears, and I can't hear. I don't know who he's talking to, but I feel the officer gently grab my arm. Jake begins protesting, saying something about us being here to help.

I'm torn. I don't know if I should stay with Cassia or remain in my body.

I don't fully understand what Cassia is doing to him. I can guess, but I don't know. I'm not seeing or hearing anything from her, and Mr. Simonsen is in a daze. I decide to try to stay, to give her more time with him. But my body is being taken away, and I find, even though I try to fight it, even though I try to split or stretch, I'm being dragged with it as a whole.

By the time I'm sitting in the back of the police cruiser, I come to. I'm fully me again. The distance is finally too great. I blink and realize we're being taken to the police station, but I'm not in cuffs. We aren't being arrested. We're in separate cruisers, though. I can see the back of Jake's head in the police car in front of us. We're being taken separately "downtown." *It'll be fine*, I tell myself. *It's probably just for questioning*. I can't seem to find my voice to ask the officer any questions.

The drive is disconcerting. I know what happened, but it's so *unbelievable* that my brain is having a hard time accommodating it; it's next to impossible. I assume the connection was lost when I fully became myself again. I hope it was enough time for her to do what she needed to do. I hope Mr. Simonsen is all right.

I glance at the clock on the radio which reads 2:33. We were there, in that room with Mr. Simonsen, longer than I thought—at least half an hour. It felt like half that time.

Once we arrive at the station, I push all the "unbelievable" to the back of my brain and try to focus on the here and now. I've found my voice and begin asking about Jake. I don't see him anywhere. The potbellied officer tells me they're going to question us separately. He takes my purse after collecting my identification, my phone, and Bella's phone separately, then leads me to a room.

The questioning room is small. There's a single table with a chair on either side and a camera in two of the corners. Otherwise, it's barren. He hands me a water bottle and small bag of chips then instructs me to sit; a detective will be in soon.

"Soon" feels like two hours. Not joking. Two hours. Then again, time might still be messed up. Still, I wonder many things during what feels like two hours. I wonder if they're questioning Jake first. I wonder if they're watching me. I wonder if they do this on purpose to freak us out and wear us down. I wonder if I need a lawyer. I wonder if I *have* to stay here or if I can just walk out. I wonder if they're researching me. I wonder how much longer; I need to pee. I wonder if Jake will still love me after all this; I'm putting him through hell. And, of course, I wonder where Cassia is; I feel nothing from her.

Finally, the door opens and startles the wonders out of me. The detective isn't what I expected. She's a woman, for one thing; I didn't realize I'd stereotyped detectives. She's short and petite with an A-line haircut sporting unnaturally red hair. I watch her every move. She's gentle in the way she sits, setting a file on the table in front of her and lacing her fingers together.

"Hi, Camry," she says, slow and soft. "My name is Detective Carol Greenly." She pauses, and I'm not sure why. *Am I supposed to* say, "*Nice to meet you?*" "I'm sorry to keep you waiting," she continues. "Do you mind if I record our conversation?"

I glance at the cameras in the corners.

"I prefer my own for my cases. Better quality."

"Okay. Can I use the bathroom before we start?" I bounce the empty water bottle against the table twice while holding onto the top.

She obliges, awkwardly accompanying me. When we return, she turns on a handheld video recording device and sets it on the table, positioning it to view me perfectly. "For the record," she begins, "please state your full name."

"Camry Jacobs." Saying my name starts me jittering. My palms get clammy, and I begin to fidget.

"And you're here because you have information regarding the disappearance of Cassia Jane Simonsen, is that correct?"

That's not all, but it's a yes-or-no question, so I say, "Yes."

"You're from Salt Lake City; is that right, Miss Jacobs?" she asks, lacing her fingers together again.

"Yes."

"That's a long way from New York. Do you know Cassia?"

"Before she died? No." I feel like that's a stupid question.

"How do you know she's dead, Miss Jacobs?" Detective Greenly asks, still so calm.

I feel like everyone should know by now she's dead, but I remind myself they don't have her body yet, so of course, they don't assume she's dead. *Suck! Was that a bad thing for me to say?* I don't know how to answer. I think for a while. "Because…I know her now. Not before," I try to clarify.

"What do you mean by that? Can you elaborate?" She moves her fingers in a circle to encourage me to tell more.

"It's like I told Mr. Simonsen. She came to me and told me everything. I'm not crazy." This is the first time I begin to get irritated.

"No one is saying you're crazy, Miss Jacobs. This is very serious. And we want—"

"I'm aware this is serious," I interrupt. "That's why I spent all my money to come to New York. That's why I'm here. *Cooperating.*" My tone is impatient, and I raise my voice a little bit. The fear of getting stuck here and needing a lawyer is creeping in. *Breathe, Camry.*

Detective Greenly inhales slowly and thinks before speaking again. "Do you have psychic abilities, Miss Jacobs?"

I dumbly glance around. *How am I supposed to answer that?* I think about how I just know things, but only things that are related to Cassia. It's not like there are spirits other than her. I think Cassia and I just have a connection, and she's getting really good at communicating with me. I mean, she doesn't even have to be with me for me to know things. I shrug as my answer.

"Are you a clairvoyant? Medium? Do you know what these things are?"

I shake my head and shrug again. "I just…can talk to her. That's all," I admit.

She opens the file folder and flips a page. "Do you hear other voices, Miss Jacobs?"

This question gets under my skin. This isn't how I thought things were going to go. "I'm not a schizo," I say defensively. "I don't hear voices. Listen, Cassia's spirit came to me; I don't know how, but I know why. Bella has an audio file with evidence. Can we please focus on Cassia and JoAnna instead of my…credibility?"

Detective Greenly's eyebrows raise just a hair as she considers what I've said. "Very well," she consents. "What about JoAnna?"

"She's next," is all I say.

"We didn't find any evidence on Bella's phone that suggests she knows anything of Cassia's disappearance or a plan to murder Ms. Simonsen."

"It's not on her phone anymore, but she has it somewhere. You need to bring her in for questioning. There's a file with evidence that Tiffanie and Tiffanie's mother are planning to kill JoAnna Simonsen. Tiffanie is paying Bella to keep quiet about it. Look at her bank statements. I don't know. There's got to be something. Get Tiffanie and her mom in here." I realize I don't know *all* the things relating to Cassia; I don't even know Tiffanie's mother's name.

"Have you heard the audio, Miss Jacobs?" Her calm tone is beginning to scratch at my nerves.

"No. I haven't." I rest against the back of the chair. I can guess her next question.

"Then how do you know what's on the file?"

I look her directly in the eyes. "Because Cassia told me." I should have asked Cassia more questions, but since all this has snowballed, she hasn't been around enough for me to get this sort of information. And I guess I don't know what to ask. It's not like I've done this before.

Detective Greenly changes the subject. "How'd you get Bella Cardoso's phone, Miss Jacobs?" She doesn't cover the fact that her eyes have shifted to the knuckles of my right hand. They betray me, all red and slightly swollen. *Is she hinting they're about to charge me with something? Oh why did Cassia have to punch her?*

She opens her mouth to speak, but I interrupt, directing the conversation back to where it should be. "I'd really like to focus on Cassia and JoAnna. Is JoAnna safe? Please tell me you've done something to make her safe. They've already made a trip up there to check things out. I need you guys to do the parts that I can't."

Detective Greenly exhales. "JoAnna is safe. Local police arrived there about an hour ago."

I relax my shoulders with relief, then lean my elbows on the table and rub my forehead. "Thank you." We sit, silent for a short minute. "Where's Bella?" I ask.

"I can't discuss Bella right now."

I scoff. "I'll take that as a good thing. Where's Tiffanie?"

"Tell me about Jake."

My expression becomes pained at the thought of Jake going through what I'm going through. What a terrible way to begin a relationship. "Is he okay?"

She looks at me, but her expression is as empty as space.

I shake my head, annoyed with myself. "He's…just here for me. So I wouldn't be alone."

She finally nods, understanding. I hope she believes me. This makes me think of a point to prove. "I have no reason to lie. About any of this. Believe me, I realize how it looks. How I seem. I just want to do the right thing. And I really hope I don't get arrested for it. I want JoAnna to be okay. I want Tiffanie and her mother to pay for what they've done. I want Terrick, I mean, Mr. Simonsen, to be okay. I mean, he'll never be 'okay.' But to have some…peace." I breathe. "I'm sorry I couldn't get you actual evidence. Bella has it though. I promise."

"What else can you offer, Miss Jacobs?" Detective Greenly asks, closing the file. "About Cassia? You say she's dead. Who killed her? Where's her body? What happened to her?"

I rest my head in my hands and squeeze my eyes shut. I think of all the images Cassia showed me. *Do I have to tell it?* It's the most dreadful thing in the world to think about compiling the words that tell that story. I've relived it in my head so many times; it's unbearable to think about telling it to Detective Greenly. But after all, in a way, it's why I came here.

My voice cracks and breaks with my first word. "Um." I open my eyes and blink several times to stop the burning tears from coming. I blow out through my mouth and then swallow, ready to try again. But before I start, I feel her.

Cassia is here.

I exhale, a tad bit sad to sense her now, sad she has to hear this part.

"Camry?" Detective Greenly says. "Are you all right?"

The lights flicker, and my gaze shifts around the room. Detective Greenly glances as well. A comforting warmth wraps around me—it's Cassia. I answer with a small grin, "Yeah. I'm fine."

Cassia surprises me by telling her story through me. She's careful to say "she" instead of "I" as she talks about her taking the bus to find her mother, the stop at Castle Creek, and herself being murdered. She also tells the detective how to get to the area where she's buried, which I wouldn't have been able to do. I wonder if Detective Greenly noticed my eye color change. And I wonder how Cassia is making it through this so powerfully. I thank her for sparing me. I mean, I'm still here, and the words are still terrible, but I'm somewhat numb to it. She's spared me the pain of it. And I love her. I love her *so* much.

When Cassia finishes, Detective Greenly says, "I think that's enough for today. We see that you have a flight back to Salt Lake City on Friday, is that correct?"

I nod, wiping the tears from my cheeks.

"Very well, Miss Jacobs. We'd like to ask you not to leave before then. We may need to speak to you or Jake again. Would that be all right?"

I nod again. "Of course," I say. It's more than just speaking to me, though. She could call me in Utah. It may just be my paranoia, but I'm nervous I'm a "person of interest," and she wants me to stay in case they decide to arrest me. At this point, I realize this will follow me home and be part of my life for a while. Possibly months. Possibly even years.

She reaches into her blazer pocket and hands me a card with her name and contact information on it. "I'll walk you out," she says, standing and grabbing the file folder.

I resist the urge to stretch my muscles after I stand. My rear is sore. I feel like she thinks I'm crazy, but I try not to care. Jake is waiting for me in a dirty, scratched chair near the front doors. His leg is bouncing with his arms crossed over his chest, accompanied by an overall apprehensive appearance.

He immediately pops up out of the chair when he sees me. I watch as relief relaxes every muscle in his body. Cassia is still with me, but I have most of the control. His arms open for me, and I go to him.

As I get closer, his brows furrow. "Cassia?" he mouths.

Nodding, I hug him. "It's me too," I tell him.

It's a quick hug. Detective Greenly reiterates for us to stick around town, then tells us we're free to leave the station. An officer motions for us to approach the front desk. He then retreats to another area, searching for our belongings. Jake turns to me, curious. His eyes search my face. What he's looking for, I don't know.

Cassia smiles softly. "Hi," she says.

"Hi," he says back, then blinks. "Wow. This is…odd."

"I know. Don't overthink it. Just—I just want to thank you for everything you've done for us. Me and Camry," she clarifies. "And everything you said. To the detective, I mean."

"Of course," he says genuinely.

Cassia makes a twisty face. "And I'm sorry. About the dream."

Jake shakes his head. "I needed it."

She considers that. Then she considers him. "I think things are going to be okay now," she says.

Jake squeezes our hand and smiles.

With a smile back, Cassia says, "Go enjoy your time here. I'll try not to bother you guys anymore." She stands on tiptoe and kisses his cheek.

The officer returns, and Cassia leaves. He gives us our identifications and phones back. They've kept Bella's phone, though. After that, Jake meets my eyes again—my hazel eyes—and seems dejected, so I offer a half smile. He grabs my hand as we exit the station and try to hail a taxi.

"Well, that was an experience," Jake says as we wait for one.

"I'm so sorry, Jake," I tell him. "Are you okay? What'd they ask you?"

He rubs my hand with his thumb and looks at me. "Don't be sorry. We figured on going to the police, right? I mean, that was sort of the original plan. And it could've been a lot worse. At least we're not arrested. How are *you*?"

"I'm fine. I think." I haven't really permitted myself to consider how I'm truly feeling about it all. My internal dialogue has been shut down, in need of a reboot.

Jake opens the door of a taxi that's pulled up, and I climb in. He looks at me expectantly after we tell the driver where to go.

I add, "I think things are going to be okay."

He leans over and kisses me, then rests his forehead on mine, looking into my eyes. "She's amazing," he says.

Thursday, September 2

Jake and I are admiring the massive blue whale at the Museum of Natural History when my phone rings. It's not a number I know, but it does have the New York area code 646. It's not Detective Greenly; I put her number in my contact list so I could immediately freak out if she called, not just wonder if I should freak out. We leave tomorrow, so I wouldn't be surprised if it still *is* the detective or someone on her behalf. I answer, "Hello?"

"Miss Jacobs?"

I know that strong voice. *How did he get my number?* "Mr. Simonsen?"

"Please. Call me Terrick."

"Call me Camry. Hi. How are…you?" *Ugh. That was an awful question. Note to self: When someone has just found out their daughter died, don't ask them how they are.*

"Well, that's difficult to answer. I don't think I know yet. But listen, I know you two are leaving tomorrow, and I'd really like to invite you to dinner before you go. My treat."

"Oh. Tonight?" *I didn't think he'd ever want to speak to me again, let alone see me.* I'd leaned the phone out a bit so Jake could hear also. He'd moved closer to me but missed half of it. I mouth, *Terrick. Dinner. Tonight.*

Jake nods like he understood that much but then mouths, *Really?*

"Yes. Tonight. I have a private table reserved at Le Bernardin. How about seven o'clock?" Terrick Simonsen is technically asking, but in such a Mr. Simonsen way. There's a command in his tone. I can't say "no." Not that I was going to, but still, I have to make sure…

"Is everything all right?" I ask.

No hesitation. "Of course. Many things need to be said, Camry. But in person, okay?"

There's a sincerity in his voice, so I agree, "Yes, okay."

"Dinner at seven? Will you two come?"

"We'd love to, Mr. Simonsen," I say.

"Terrick," he reminds me.

"Terrick," I return. "We'll be there at seven."

"Excellent. But Camry?"

"Hmm?"

"I'll have my driver pick you two up at your hotel at five for a surprise. Again, my treat."

I look at Jake. He's got nothing but a swift glance at his watch and a shrug.

Mr. Simonsen presses, "Does five o'clock work for you?"

"Uh, yes, Mr.—uh—Terrick. Five is great. Thank you."

"Bye now."

"Bye." I hang up and stare at Jake. "What do you think that's all about?" There's been only silence from Cassia and obviously nothing from Detective Greenly either. I have no idea how the investigation is going. Jake and I've been enjoying the sights of the city since Sunday.

In that time, I've been able to relax in a way I haven't for months. Everything feels right, the way it's supposed to be. The wrinkles Cassia and I created in the universe have smoothed out, it seems, and time has returned to normal.

"Maybe he just wants to see you again before we leave," Jake offers.

"That's weird. I look like his dead daughter," I say.

"Well, maybe he wants to apologize. I mean, he did kind of pull a dick move last time we saw him."

"That's true." I begin to play with my earring as my anxiety grows thinking about dinner. *And what the hell is the surprise? A two-hour joyride in a limo? We think it's all good until it ends at the police station with little Detective Greenly standing there waiting for us, a set of handcuffs in each hand? Dinner is actually gross grits and hard biscuits served behind bars?*

Jake grabs my hand, pulling my fingers away from the comfort of fidgeting. "Stop worrying." He looks me in the eye. "I'll be right there. And there's no way he can pull the same move. I doubt cops are going to be there waiting to arrest us."

I blink. *Enough of that.* Detective Greenly would've already made that happen if that's the direction this was all going. I'm freaking out for no reason.

Jake and I are waiting at the front of our hotel at five o'clock. I've chosen a long navy-blue skirt with a white top, and Jake's managed jeans and a polo, which is as dressed up as his suitcase wardrobe will allow him.

A sleek black Lincoln pulls up, and the driver steps out, sharply locking eyes with me. He's fortysomething, clean-cut, and fit in his black suit and tie, and…familiar. Instinctively, I look down.

He asks if we're Mademoiselle Jacobs and Monsieur Clark.

Jake answers, "Yep, that's us."

I didn't think about the driver being familiar. Like this isn't weird enough.

He comes around the front of the car for us, smiling as he stops and opens the door. He says in his French accent, "I'm Luke. I'm Monsieur Simonsen's driver, here to take you for your 'surprise' and dinner."

Jake lets me get in first. It's like something from a movie, except we're severely underdressed. Jake can tell something's up with me. He leans in. "You okay?"

"Yeah." I smile. He doesn't buy it but takes my hand and doesn't pry.

Luke settles in and begins to drive, explaining Monsieur Clark will be treated first.

"And what is it we're being treated to?"

Smiling at us from the rearview mirror, he says, "That would ruin the surprise, now wouldn't it, Monsieur Clark?" He continues to eye me in the mirror. "I must say, mademoiselle, the resemblance is remarkable. Monsieur Simonsen warned me, but I still was a bit stunned. My apologies, mademoiselle."

"It's all right, Luke," I reply. "I understand. How much did Mr. Simonsen tell you?"

He thinks as he looks at me through the mirror once more. "Enough."

Arriving at a suit shop, we both begin to understand the "surprise." Jake is catered to, finding just the right fit without having to tailor a suit for him. He tries on four of them before he finds one he likes. I take lots of pictures. It really is just an ordinary-looking black suit and black tie, but he's waggling his eyebrows up and down at me, doing James Bond poses. And he's so handsome, I can't stop smiling and clicking photos.

Jake asks for the price.

"It matters not, Monsieur Clark," Luke explains. "Monsieur Simonsen will spare no expense for the two of you tonight."

After finding shoes as well, Luke goes to pay for the suit, and we leave with Jake's old clothes and shoes in the store bag.

"Your turn, I assume," Jake says to me as we walk out.

"Right you are," Luke answers.

The dress shop is completely ridiculous. I can't help but stand there wide-eyed. Again, I feel like I'm in a movie.

No.

There's a memory.

Mr. Simonsen used to send Cassia here when she needed a gown.

I want Cassia here now. This is so incredible.

I don't know where to begin. But I guess I don't have to know because two ladies come to me, recognizing Luke. They hesitate and glance at each other, I assume noticing who I look like, but compose themselves quickly. They measure my waist, my chest, and my height from armpit to floor, then flitter away and come back with several gowns on each of their arms. Being swept toward a dressing room, I steal a look back at Jake. He's smiling big and gives me a little wave.

The dressing room is large with an entire wall as a mirror and a four-panel changing screen. The ladies introduce themselves as Michelle and Jenny. They start me with a red dress and direct me behind the screen. It doesn't fit badly, and Jake approves with a thumbs up as I show him, but I don't love red, necessarily. I shake my head.

"Wait," Jake says, stopping me from returning to change.

Luke has my phone. Jake stands next to me, and we smile for a photo.

The green one matches my eyes and skin tone really well but shows way too much cleavage. I still show Jake, but my hands are atop my breasts, and my face is as red as the other dress. All he has for me is a chuckle. A quick photo, and I flee back to the dressing room.

The purple one is a nice color but a little too poofy for me. Jake shakes his head at this one, not only looking left and right to accommodate the poofiness but to tell me, *No, it's no good.*

The blue one is amazing in every way. It's Cinderella perfect, but I can't bring myself to say yes to it. My hazel eyes clash with it, and it reminds me too much of Cassia. I can't do it. And yet, I can't take it off. I stare at myself in the mirror for a long time. Even the ladies helping me seem to see Cassia in this dress. The one called Jenny blinks tears away from her eyes. Michelle rests a hand on my shoulder with a look of sadness. I don't know how much they know about me, who I am to Mr. Simonsen, but like Luke, they seem to know enough.

"Camry?" Jake asks through the door. "Are you all right?"

I realize the noise of me getting ready has been replaced by sniffing sounds. I clear my throat. "Yeah," I tell him, but it's evident in my voice that I'm not quite all right. "I can't show this one," is all I say, and I begin taking it off.

"Okay," Jake says, understanding.

I gather myself, skipping over the peach one and reaching for the ivory one. The top part is lacy, and the straps are thick. The bottom flares out only slightly, beginning at the waist. I try it on and know it's right. It fits all my little curves and isn't too provocative. It's classic.

The ladies helping me gasp and bring their hands to their mouths. I peek at the price. Of course, it's the most expensive one, twice the amount of any of the others. My face says what I'm thinking. I consider the blue one again. Maybe the red one? I reach for the peach one. They're all cheaper.

"No," Michelle says to me, a hand on my forearm. "Mr. Simonsen would want you to have this one. No worrying about price, my dear. This one is made for you."

I grin and keep it on. Jenny brings me some ivory heels to match, and it's almost seven o'clock. Blushing, I come out to show Jake and Luke. Jake is pacing but freezes, looking me up and down.

Luke smiles and walks over to the counter to pay for the dress.

"You…look exquisite," Jake says, fake fanning himself.

I bring my arms around his neck, and we kiss. It isn't until I pull away from him and happen to catch our reflections in the mirror that I realize I look like a bride. We look like we're getting married.

Luke interrupts my thoughts of marriage to take our picture. I don't tell Jake that I *wish* I were his bride. I wish every day could be like this. I know I'm young, but he feels so right, so absolute. He's as suitable for me as his suit is for him. And I'm convinced I'm as fitting for him as this dress is for me. We are perfectly perfect in this moment. And I feel whole—as if I've been completed.

The restaurant is busy and full of spiffies just like us. Dim light comes from the chandeliers above and candles on each table. Flowers are on all the tables as well, adding a pop of color against the overall gray design. We follow the hostess, weaving through the chairs as she leads us to Terrick's table in the far corner. It's somewhat partitioned off from the rest of the room, allowing privacy that I wonder if I should be grateful for or worried about. *We're not being arrested, Camry. Not in a dress and suit that cost more than my bi-colored car is probably worth.*

We're five minutes early, but Terrick is earlier. He's waiting and looking like he's been there awhile. He's accompanied by a woman. I slow and squeeze Jake's hand as they stand and the hostess leaves us.

My hands have now reached up to cover my mouth of their own accord, and tears spill down my cheeks.

I cry way too much.

"Miss Jacobs. Mr. Clark," Terrick begins. "I'd like you to meet—"

"JoAnna," I whisper.

She wears a silky green dress. She has Cassia's small build, her nose and lips and hair, but her eyes are a chestnut brown. Terrick gave Cassia the blue eyes. She clasps her hands in front of her as Terrick rests his hand on the small of her back.

Before I know it, I've rounded the table and am hugging her, embracing her openheartedly. We're both a hot mess of tears and runny noses. And suddenly, as I hold her, I know everything. Cassia's not gone yet. I know she's been in her mother's dreams. Cassia has been guiding her in so many ways. And because of that, JoAnna has been able to guide Terrick. And I suspect, from whatever Cassia did to her dad, he's been able to guide JoAnna as well. They're deeply connected now, linked by a bond no one else will ever fully relate to or understand. It's surreal.

I pull away and stare into her brown eyes. "That's why she hasn't been around. She's been with you."

JoAnna nods and tries to smile, but her crying barely allows it. She cups my face the way only a mother can do. "Thank you," she says.

And I realize too that Cassia has told her everything I've done for her. JoAnna understands *everything*. It's amazing, considering it's only been four days. Then again, it *is* her daughter. Mothers and daughters are supposed to have a deep understanding, a connection that reaches into the soul. I have a fleeting thought of how I *don't* have that with my mother. The thought of me being a "mistake" enters my mind again. Not that my parents are bad parents, just…indifferent.

My throat is tight with emotion, so I nod in response to her. I look to Terrick. Jake has finished shaking hands with him, and we trade places. I hear Jake say what a pleasure it is to meet JoAnna as I hug Terrick. I don't think he was expecting a hug, but I don't care.

Terrick adjusts and embraces me, whispering in my ear, "Thank you. I'm sorry I didn't believe you at first. I'm sorry for my behavior."

I chuckle just a tiny bit. "I don't know if I'd have believed me either," I say, then pull back. I keep hold of his wide shoulders and look into his Cassia eyes. I understand he wanted to say that to me in person, and I appreciate the apology, but I say, "You don't ever have to apologize to me. Ever." My eyebrows lift to be sure he understands.

A grieving father should have no apologies.

He nods just the tiniest bit, and I see he's taking me in, making sure he remembers this moment forever. And I want to remember it as well.

I step back to my chair, wipe my tears away, and change the subject. "We can't thank you enough for the 'surprise.' This is really…very kind of you, Mr. Simonsen," I say, then correct myself. "Terrick."

"I couldn't agree more," Jake puts in, rubbing his hands down his suit and puffing his chest out a bit. "Thank you, sir."

"Of course. Of course," Terrick says, smiling generously.

JoAnna adds with a sparkle in her eye, "You both look so beautiful."

"Please," Terrick says, gesturing. "Sit down. I took the liberty of ordering." Just then, a waiter comes over and pours JoAnna and Terrick some champagne while Jake and I are given an alcohol-free beverage of some sort.

Terrick holds up his champagne glass to make a toast. "To the both of you," he starts. "For everything you've done for us and our Cassia." He, amazingly, makes it through that well. He opens his mouth for more but seemingly can't find the words. Clearing his throat, he lets it be, just like that.

Jake shakes his head and thumbs at me. "It's all her."

Grinning, Terrick considers the two of us. "Respectfully, I disagree, Mr. Clark." He motions his glass higher in the air.

"Call me Jake," Jake says, I think realizing if he doesn't, Terrick will continue calling him Mr. Clark all night.

Terrick nods. We all raise our glasses and drink with him. "They contacted Bella. She went to the station and has turned over the file."

I straighten up and steal a glance at Jake, who's done the same. "I'm so glad to hear that."

"She was worried. For herself and her mother. I guess threats had been made." He looks down as if he's ashamed of Tiffanie's behavior. There's a lot he's not saying regarding this, but I get it; he doesn't want to dampen the mood any more than it already is.

I have sympathy for Bella. I probably shouldn't have decked her. But where would we be now if we hadn't gotten her phone? I mean, we didn't get the file, but that's how I got Terrick's number. I can only assume he heard the audio. But I wonder something else. "Terrick? Did you watch my conversation with Detective Greenly?" I ask.

"I did," he answers. "Police are searching the area you described." He stares at his glass and rubs his thumb over it. It's difficult for him to say these next words. "They haven't found anything yet. But I have hope." He inhales deeply. "Tiffanie and Beverly have been arrested…" He begins to crack, having to clear his throat again. "But JoAnna is safe." He grabs her hand and holds it in her lap. "Thanks to both of you."

Again, Jake thumbs at me. I grab his hand and shove it down. "I couldn't have done this without you," I tell him.

I'm impressed with how put together Terrick and JoAnna are for this evening. They've had so much to contend with over the past few days. If Terrick could see on the video that it was actually Cassia describing the location, he doesn't say so. Neither does he give any more details about how Tiffanie and her mother, Beverly, managed to evade the police. And I don't ask. There's a time and place, and this isn't it. But actually, I don't really need those details. Terrick perhaps does, and so do the police, but I don't.

Dinner is brought out to us, and we begin to eat. Jake and I talk about the basics of our lives back in Utah upon their asking, then he tells the story of how we met. I have to agree, it's a great "how we met" story.

"I was thinking, 'Who does she think she is, going to a Korn concert alone? This girl is crazy. Beautiful. But crazy.'" Jake does the crazy sign, circling his fork around the side of his head. I nudge him playfully. Terrick and JoAnna listen closely with sincere smiles as he goes on about the bee incident and how he waited in the hospital to see me the next morning. "By the time she came to the store the second time, I knew I was done for. That was it. Her pros list just kept growing." He smiles in my direction.

I'm about to stop Jake from embarrassing me when JoAnna says, "That's really sweet. You guys found each other because of Cassia."

I smile at her, agreeing. "And I thank her every day for that." I really do. It's a subtler, deeper thought in the subconscious part of my brain, but it's there. Just like the fact I have to thank Jake for every day I'm alive.

Jake swallows a bite. "I should too. I didn't think of it like that. What about you two?" He moves his fork slightly, motioning to Terrick and JoAnna. "How'd you meet?"

Terrick takes the lead. "College sweethearts. Columbia University. We had a business class together. She'd missed some time and needed notes."

"I missed a lot of time. My appendix had burst, and I was held up in the hospital for a week. I missed two weeks altogether."

Terrick finishes, with as much of a smirk as he can do. "I took pity on her and helped her study what she'd missed, and we just never stopped spending time together." He gazes upon his lady in green. "It was so good then." Again, he's holding back on saying more. But maybe he doesn't really need to. The look of awe for her says what it needs to.

A solemn veil falls upon her. "Everything changed when Cassia was born. My depression slowly worsened, and before I knew it, I…" Her tears come quickly, but she's just as quick to lift her cloth napkin to catch them. Terrick rests his hand on her shoulder, and we all give her a moment. "Since Cassia's dreams started, I feel so much better. I feel like my old self."

I'm sure JoAnna has a long way to go, but I can see she's healing. She'll be well…soon. And so will Terrick. I think they'll stay together. Which is good. It's great, actually. I think they need each other. I mean, I can't imagine going through what they are, alone.

JoAnna starts with something else. "Did you really jump off a cliff for her?"

All three of them look to me. I burst into laughter. "Well, she did the actual jumping, but yes. Scariest thing I've ever done! Would not recommend it!"

Dinner doesn't fill me up. Because why would a hundred-dollar meal do *that*? But it *was* delicious.

"Don't be a stranger," Terrick orders me as we stand on the curb, waiting for Luke.

The night has turned dark, and a breeze cuts through my dress, chilling me just a bit. Jake has given me his suit jacket and holds me close, arm around my waist, which helps.

"I want to hear from you," Terrick continues. "You have my number."

I nod.

JoAnna nods.

"We can have dinner again, my treat. Always," he says. Then he pulls an envelope from the inner pocket of his jacket. "This is for you. Don't open it until you're on your flight home."

I take it because I know it's the polite thing to do, but my face says I don't want to. From the way he's talking, I'm slightly concerned it contains money. *He doesn't owe me anything. Especially money. Especially after tonight.*

Luke arrives in the black Lincoln. Terrick's return expression says, *It's okay. Just take it.* He opens the door for Jake and me. "You go," he says, nodding toward the car. "We'll catch a cab."

We all hug once more, and even though Terrick wants to keep in touch and seems to be planning more visits for dinner, I can't help but feel like this may be the last time I see him. So I hug him tight and kiss his cheek and stare into his Cassia eyes. It's difficult to let him go. But I have to, so I do.

We sit in the car, and Luke begins to drive. I look to Jake. He's grinning from ear to ear, which makes me smile.

"We did it," we both say.

I laugh and repeat, "We did it!"

He's laughing, too, then he squeezes my hand. "I love you."

"I love you too," I say.

Back at our hotel, just outside the door to our room, Jake looks me up and down again. He picks me up like a bride and carries me through the door. I laugh and hold on tight as he spins me around. We kiss, and he sets me down.

He chooses a song from his phone and sets it on the dresser to play: "Evermore" by Hollow Coves. We begin to dance and sing along. I feel like the song is meant for us. I feel like it could be *our* song.

It's the most romantic thing I've ever been part of, and I feel indescribably whole. We dance slow, and we kiss slow, and we make love slow. And I don't want morning to come. This is true paradise, and I want to stay in this moment "evermore."

<h1 style="text-align:center">Friday, September 3</h1>

Morning does come, unfortunately. It comes with the sound of my phone ringing. I roll away from cuddling with Jake and answer groggily without looking at the display.

"This is Detective Greenly. Is this Camry?"

I quickly sit up and rub my eyes. "Yes. Detective. Hi."

Jake perks up and arranges the pillows so we can rest against them.

"I know you're leaving today, and I just wanted to thank you for your help with the case." She falters. "We've…found Cassia's remains."

I sit erect and inhale. Jake duplicates my motion; he can hear her through the phone.

"This morning," she clarifies. "JoAnna and Terrick Simonsen have already been notified. It's a little unconventional for me to call you, but…I thought you should know."

I swallow hard. "Yeah. I mean, yes. Detective, thank you so much. So what happens now?"

Detective Greenly breathes and says, "They'll try to get what forensics they can. To help prove she was drugged and cause of death. Then I imagine a funeral or ceremony of some kind will take place, which, if I were to guess, Mr. Simonsen would like you to attend. He told me about your conversation last night."

"It was a good one," I admit.

She's silent on the other end for a while. Then says, "I deal with lots of missing persons, Camry. A lot of the time, we never solve the case. A lot of the time, we never find the body. A lot of the time, I don't remember the details because they all mix together. All the cases. But I don't think I'll ever forget this one. I don't think I'll ever forget you. Please, if you ever visit the city again, call me. I'd love to chat with you again."

"Unrecorded?" I joke.

She huffs a small chuckle. "Unrecorded."

"I will," I say. "Thank you again."

We say our goodbyes, and I turn to Jake. Resting against the pillows, he embraces me, and I sob.

Does this mean she's gone?

In the taxi on the way to the airport, I tell Jake how Cassia wants me to tell Benson everything.

He asks, "What does 'everything' mean?"

"Like, *everything*." I tell him what Cassia said to Benson at the end of their date, the night I let myself go and let her take over. "She said for him to listen with an open mind and it would all make sense."

Jake drawls out, "Okaaay."

"God, I hope he can do that." I'm imagining this future conversation with Benson.

"Do you want me to come?"

I ponder this. "No," I say decisively. "But just know…that's going to be a rough day for me."

He lifts my hand and kisses it. "We can pig out on pizza after if you want."

I try to smile. I try to nod. But I can't. I look out the window instead. There's been nothing from Cassia. Not that I really expected anything. I don't know what I expected, actually. I guess I just hoped. Hoped she would come say goodbye or…something. Leave some sign she was okay now.

Jake senses my thoughts and says, "It's okay, Camry. She's okay."

I swallow my tears, so *sick* of crying, and nod.

Boarding the plane, Jake and I sit together this time, but I switch seats with him, putting him next to the window and giving myself the aisle because I'm not feeling like the window, and I know Jake loves it. It's a direct flight to Salt Lake City this time, which I'm grateful for, sort of wanting to get home and back to familiar things. I scroll through all the photos on my phone to help distract me; I'm nervous about flying again. Jake leans over to look at them with me. I think I've taken hundreds. We went to Central Park and the zoo. We went to the Empire State Building and the National 9/11 Memorial and Museum. We went to Ellis Island, the Statue of Liberty, and the Museum of Natural History.

"You need to give me copies of these," Jake says. He took some but not as many as I did.

"I'll give you access," I tell him and tap through the process to share my photos.

Then there're the photos of last night. I pause at the one in the dress shop after I'd chosen the ivory dress. Luke captured one I didn't know about, when I thought he was paying for the dress. I'm kissing Jake. The ivory flows down, barely resting at my heels. Jake is holding my waist so gently. My arms are draped around his neck. Both of our eyes are closed. It's the most beautiful picture in the world.

"I didn't know he took that," Jake says.

"Me neither."

"I like it," he admits.

"I love it."

He chortles. "Yeah. I love it too."

Once the plane takes off and my nerves settle down, I pull the envelope from Terrick out of my purse. There's another envelope inside and a tri-folded letter to read first, I presume. We read Terrick's sharp cursive together.

Camry,

To say I'm grateful to you for everything you've done for Cassia, JoAnna, and me is an understatement. To say you are a wonderful, amazing, and beautiful soul is also an understatement. Words simply cannot express the thoughts and feelings I have for you and all that has happened. I thank you from the bottom of my heart.

To be able to see and speak to Cassia one more time was something I would've given literally anything for, and I was able to do that more than once because of you. It has made all the difference. I will cherish that forever.

One thing Cassia insisted upon (and I agree) was to repay you for the medical and travel expenses you incurred on her behalf. I would also like to assist you with whatever financial needs you have for your schooling.

I'm confident we'll find her and would like you and Jake to return for her services once that happens. All expenses will be covered. I'll keep in touch with you about this.
Warm Regards,
Terrick Simonsen

P.S. Jake, your role in all this is not overlooked. My feelings of gratitude extend to you as well. Please accept my gift and take care of your beautiful dame.

I shake my head. *Unbelievable.* "I can't," I tell Jake and hand the other envelope over. I can't open it. I can't believe he did this. I can't believe Cassia had him do this. I just can't. It's one of the kindest things ever, but I don't know if I can handle it.

"Whoa," Jake says. "Yep, that'll cover things."

I groan. "Really? It's a lot?"

He twists the checks to show me. The check written to Jake Clark is for ten thousand dollars, which is jaw-dropping enough, but the one written to Camry Jacobs reads fifty thousand dollars. I think my eyes are going to pop out.

"How would it be to have that much money?" Jake asks rhetorically as he admires the dollar amounts.

I don't want to accept it but thinking about how much fifty thousand would help me is hard not to do. It'd pay off the hospital, replenish my savings, and cover probably four semesters. Jake replaces it in the envelope and shoves it into my purse for me.

The flight is pleasant, but I begin to get a very anxious feeling as we approach the Salt Lake City landing strip. I unexpectedly remember my dream about the plane crash, and I'm feeling extremely uneasy.

"Are you okay?" Jake asks, noticing me tensing.

I don't meet his eyes. "Something's not right," I say.

The plane begins its descent, and suddenly, an explosion blasts from one of the engines, and people start screaming. The plane tips to the side, but the pilot manages to level out relatively quickly. Jake grabs my hand just as a second boom echoes through the cabin, and the plane begins to shake violently, dropping and tilting again. My buckle breaks, my grip on Jake breaks, and I'm thrown across the cabin.

I don't know how long it's been, but I know I hurt. I fade in and out, catching blurry glimpses of figures moving around. I see flashes of light when I close my eyes, and I don't know if I can stay awake. The muffled screams and cries I hear become clearer after several moments, one standing out above them all.

Jake.

I hear him loud and close now.

He grabs my head, calling my name.

I didn't realize I hadn't taken a breath, so I do. That hurts too. A lot.

"Camry!"

I wheeze and cough. Something wet and warm comes out of my mouth. Then I taste it: blood. *That can't be good.* There's the flashing light again in my darkness. I can't move.

"Oh God! Camry! Stay with me, stay with me." I feel Jake's forehead meet mine. I feel his breath on me, and his hands wrapped around my head, holding my face. Desperation consumes him. "It's okay. They're coming. You're gonna be okay. Stay with me."

I breathe shallowly and wheeze again but manage to open my eyes. Jake breathes a sigh of relief but doesn't relax very much. He's blurry to me, but I can make out that he's dirty and has blood oozing from a cut above his eye.

"That's good. Look at me. Just look at me. I got you. Okay? You're gonna be okay. They're coming to get you."

A sharp pain stabs my left lung when I try to breathe, so I hold my breath as much as I can. Tears run down to my ears, and my vision tunnels out.

"Cam! Breathe! Cam! Cam!" Jake's voice fades.

Then blackness.

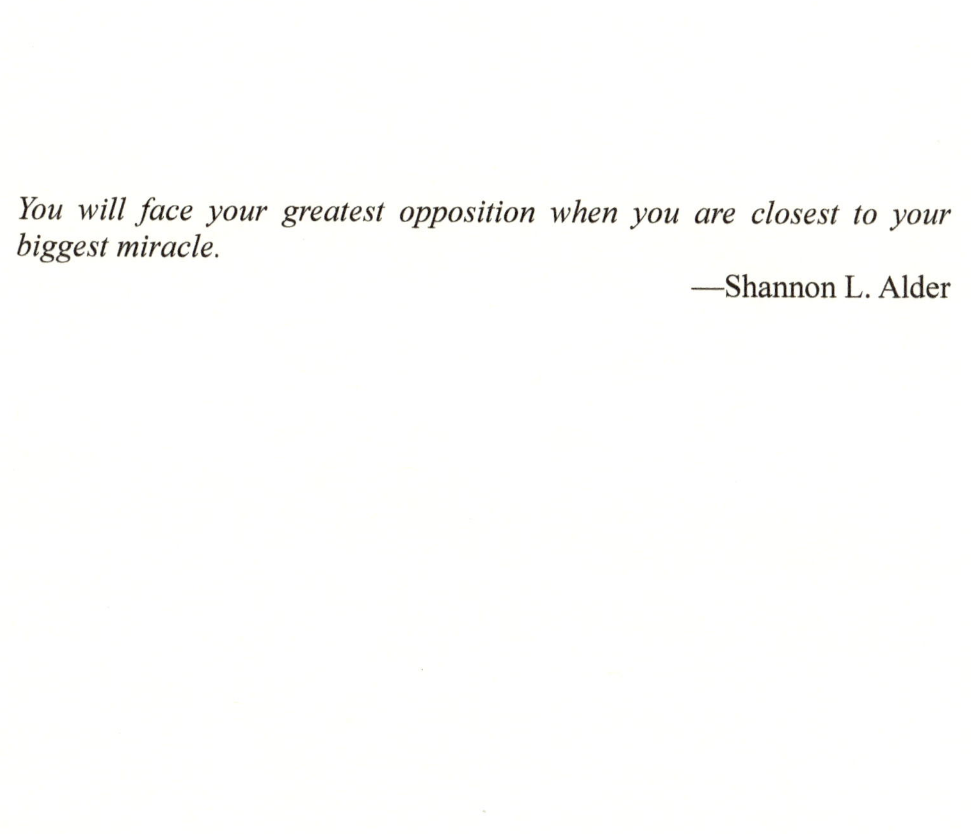

You will face your greatest opposition when you are closest to your biggest miracle.

—Shannon L. Alder

Do you believe in miracles? Is it a miracle all 188 passengers of Flight 1354 survived and no one on the ground was killed either?

I see it clearly now. Yes. This was the universe ensuring things would continue on a safe path; it was keeping the balance. It could've just as easily been that everyone died if that's how it was supposed to be. But according to the universe, none of those people were meant to die. The chain reaction from that would've been too much in this time for those individuals. The plane failed, but the universe kept them alive with a series of small occurrences. One being the pilot who was called in just before the flight, who had more skill and knowledge about that particular aircraft.

Everything happens for a reason.

The universe is always actively playing a role in the process known as "self-correction." And we're all part of that process, we're all part of that miracle, even if we can't see it. But again, I see it clearly now.

I also can see another miracle here. Some (not all, but some) of the people aboard Flight 1354 will go on with their lives after this experience with a change in their perception. They'll love in a way they never have before and create more miracles in their own lives and others'. They'll see, with that love and those miracles, that anything is possible and love is the only real thing.

Back up, though. Not all 188 passengers of Flight 1354 survived.

The universe presented an opportunity for one of them to be a miracle for another, for one of them to die.

Me.

Camry Jacobs.

The news, however, won't report a death. Only a handful of people will ever have the viewpoint to understand. Because my organs still work, my heart still beats, still pumps blood and sustains life for *someone.*

That someone is Cassia Jane Simonsen.

She fought me tooth and nail. The entire time we were in surgery, in fact. Surgery was the perfect time to do what needed to be done. It allowed a connection between here and there, and her and me, all at the same time—something the universe was struggling to create before then. I tried to make her understand, but she couldn't see what I could see. In my darkness, there was a light, and once I could focus on it, I could see *so* much. I could see everything I was meant to. I could see Cassia wasn't supposed to die. It was a mistake. A cosmic, collective, colossal mistake. The universe *had* to correct the error.

The universe looked and looked, and it found...me.

Monday, September 6

I'm waking up. Or, at least, I'm trying to. Sleep pulls me back. Pain makes me let it.

Tuesday, September 7

I'm waking up. Or, at least, I'm trying to. The pain is less today. But the pulling sensation of sleep isn't.

Wednesday, September 8

I'm waking up. Or, at least, I'm trying to. The pain is significantly less today. Sleep doesn't pull me back. At least not hard enough. This time, I succeed in staying awake. This time, there's a hand in mine. I test myself by squeezing my fingers. There's a squeeze back.

"Camry?" a hopeful voice asks.

Opening my eyes is like lifting a thousand pounds. It's shockingly difficult. But after several attempts, I succeed in this as well. The lights are dim, and I hear the beeps of the machines now as they confirm I'm alive.

I'm alive?

I see Jake. He's leaning over me. I close my eyes again; they're sore.

"Camry. Look at me," he says, caressing my face.

I try again and blink him into focus. Our eyes finally lock, and he freezes. He pales. He stops breathing.

"Jake?" I croak.

He withdraws a hair. "Cassia?"

And then I remember! Oh *God*, I remember. Oh no, I *remember*. How could she do this? No, no, no, no. *No!* This isn't right! This isn't how it's supposed to be! I *hate* her for doing this! I hate her so much! I told her! I told her over and over and over!

I cough a sob, and I cry, "Jake. I'm so sorry. Oh God. I'm so sorry." My throat hurts. My voice hurts, but I keep going. He *has* to know. "I tried," I cry. Saliva accumulates in my mouth, and tears are like rain down my cheeks. "I tried, Jake. I tried. Please know that I tried."

Jake trembles at my words and struggles to breathe. He sits back down, taking my hand in both of his. His forehead dips until it meets our joined hands, and he sobs. He weeps until he's exhausted. And so do I.

Friday, September 10

It's been a week since the accident, and even though doctors are impressed with my improvement, I still have a long way to go. This body was broken. I should say *her* side was broken: fractured left tibia and fibula, fractured left ankle, fractured pelvis, three fractured ribs on the left side, punctured lung on the left side, fractured left wrist, fractured left collarbone, left orbital fracture, internal bleeding. And, of course, yet another concussion.

Twelve screws, three plates, and two casts help hold her bones together now—well, my bones, I guess. My heart and soul I'm afraid will never heal, however. The doctors say I'll need rehabilitation for a long time, and I'll probably have to learn to walk again. Camry's parents are here. Jake hasn't returned. I can't blame him; I know he's hurting just as much as I am.

I've tried to reach her. Camry, that is. I've tried the only way I know how: the way I used to push myself to her. I push myself out. I try all directions, but she isn't there.

I can't find her.

I'm lost.

And I'm so wrecked.

Saturday, September 11

My nurse steps in. "You have a visitor," she says, almost singsongy.

I think of Jake, but it's not Jake who enters. A tall and handsome man with ocean-blue eyes and dark lashes steps through my door with one of the largest bouquets of red roses I've ever seen.

There's a slight hesitation as he takes in my appearance, a pause in his breathing or something. I trust I'm a sight for sore eyes, for sure. But he's graceful in recovering and gently sets the roses on the counter by the door. He thinks better of it and brings them to my bedside, scooting a chair along as well.

I wonder how he's here, but I can't form the words to wonder aloud. After the time with Camry's parents and all the doctors yesterday, it feels as if speaking would exhaust me. I want to grab him and squeeze him tight, not caring how much it might hurt.

He sits on my unbroken side, takes my good hand, and rubs it with his thumbs, then kisses my fingers softly. He smiles. It's not an attempt at smiling; he's genuinely smiling. He's not afraid of what all this means for me or us as a couple. He's genuinely full of bliss about seeing me, about being able to come here. "We've got to keep you away from birds," he says.

I realize airplanes are sometimes referred to as "birds" and recall the bird at Zion National Park. I laugh, then cough. It hurts, forcing me to wince. "Well, you should see the bird," I whisper hoarsely and with difficulty.

He laughs, and it's music to my ears. Then he holds my hand up to his warm cheek and says, "I can't let you go. I can't let the most beautiful girl I've ever met walk away." He's repeating the words he said to Camry that night, the night she left him without all the puzzle pieces. It seems so long ago. He glances at my leg all casted up. "Oh, wait. You couldn't walk away even if you wanted to."

I laugh again. I love his sense of humor. Camry loved it as well. "Shut up," I groan.

"Are your lips broken too, or can I kiss them?"

Smiling, I shake my head ever so slightly. "They're not broken."

He leans forward and carefully presses his lips to mine. My heart flutters, and my pain is gone for just a brief moment. Tears fall freely down my cheeks. It's like heaven in his kiss, and I'm so glad he's here. I don't know how, and I don't care how, but he's here.

Pulling away, he wipes my tears and winks at me. "You'll be at three hundred in no time," he tells me, all smiles.

EPILOGUE
Seven Months Later

There are two of me in this world: the me inside this body that is all of Cassia and the me inside this body that is all of Camry.

I *am* Cassia. I look like I used to, for the most part.

I'm Camry as well, though. The tiny bump on my nose from the bird fight reminds me. The scar on my forehead from the bee fight reminds me. And the way my bones on the left side—her side—of my body ache, depending on the weather, reminds me also.

But more so, I have her memories. Except for the Jake-in-New-York-City memories. She took those when she left me. I'm thankful for that; she should have something that's just hers. Otherwise, I remember when Camry was little. I have memories of Christmases and birthdays and friends, including her old boyfriend, Ashton. Even intimate times with Ashton, which is, to say the least, a bit strange.

And I'm Camry when I work at the University Bookstore. I'm Camry when her parents call to check on her. I'm Camry to Mrs. Halman next door.

But I'm Cassia to my mom and dad, JoAnna and Terrick. They're together now, and I've explained everything to them.

I'm Cassia to Benson. I love him so much.

It's more complicated with Jake. He truly loved Camry. I haven't seen him since that day in the hospital. Jake told Benson where to find me. Jake told Benson everything. It was supposed to be Camry who did that. Benson told me most of how that conversation went but not the details of how Jake was handling things. He only said as much as, "I've never seen anyone that broken. He was completely destroyed."

It's been seven months, and I'm walking normally now. I have a tiny limp in the cold weather; my leg aches sometimes.

Camry's parents moved back to Florida about three months ago, just after Christmas, after Benson convinced them I'm finally okay on my own. Plus, he's here to help me. I could tell they were itching to go back. Camry was right; they're nice but…disconnected parents.

Benson has moved in with me. There's a sofa in my living room now. I'm a little sad about this—I loved watching Camry dance. I've learned from her memories and practice at the gym, but she was, by far, so much more graceful and elegant.

I'm nervous to see him. Jake, that is. I've texted him often in these seven months. Benson has too, and he's called and gone over to his house, but Jake's never answered until now. I walk into the restaurant, and the hostess guides me over to where he's waiting at a table in the corner. He stands up and smiles. The smile doesn't reach his eyes, though.

He wears his usual T-shirt sporting a band (this time, the White Stripes) and has his hair in the same messy style as always. Although these things are the same, there's something different about him, and I can't put my finger on it.

I've got on my skinny jeans and a yellow blouse. Camry would've never worn yellow…or skinny jeans. My hair is curled and down, and my bangs have grown out. I'm hoping I don't remind him too much of her.

We sit and order sodas for now.

"You look…" Jake hesitates and struggles to find the best words. "You look all better. How *are* you, Cassia?"

"I'm…" I struggle also. "I'm really good. But I'll never be 'all better.'"

He surely knows what I mean. Some wounds are too deep, so deep they scar your soul. He and I have the same wound.

"How are *you*?" I ask. "I heard your song on the radio the other day."

He smiles sadly. "Yeah?"

I nod and smile back. "It's beautiful."

"Thanks." Jake clears his throat. "Yeah, things are going really well that way. I'm spending a lot of time in the studio. Well...*you* know. She and I did several songs together."

"Yeah. I know."

"I've saved some for the next album, but..." He grabs something at his side and sets it on the table, sliding it over to me. It's a wrapped present, but it's the shape of a CD.

It's his CD.

No.

It's *their* CD.

Smiling, I thank him and tell him I've already bought the single, holding up my phone. I take the present, though, and hold it to my chest. I hold *her* to my chest.

He swallows. "When I got home. After...everything," he clarifies. "I was so lost. I dove into my music. It was the only thing that numbed the pain." He holds on to his drink but doesn't take a swig. "It sounds weird, but...everything has been easy. The music I make comes easy. The lyrics come easy. And it was totally a crazy way that I met Scott, my music manager, and everything from there on out was...easy. Before I knew it, I was in the studio, and the song was on the radio, and I can't help but think..."

"Camry's helping?" I ask.

He nods.

"That sounds like her, doesn't it?"

He smiles more genuinely now. "Yeah. It does." He's thoughtful for a moment, then snaps out of it. "Open it," he tells me, pointing to the present.

I hesitate, then gently pull the tape, and unwrap what I know to be the most precious gift anyone has ever given or will ever give to me.

The cover is a photo of Camry and Jake. They're kissing and dressed as if it's their wedding day. This must be one of their days in New York. I have no memory of it. And I haven't allowed myself to look at her phone pictures yet, fearing it'll hurt too much.

My mouth opens a bit in awe, and my hand comes up to cover it. It's one of the most beautiful photos I've ever seen. My eyes water. "Jake," is all I can manage as I look to him.

He smiles woefully.

I open the case and read what he's written on the back of the inside. *Cassia & Ben, #9's for you. Love, Jake.*

I find the title for number nine: *Once in a Lifetime*. I try to form words, but it doesn't really work. I end up with a tight throat, saying only, "Thank you."

Jake nods, then changes the subject. "So how's it going for you? Is it like you're living a double life?"

I tell Jake about how it is now. I tell him how Benson calls me "Cassia" at home but "Camry" when he needs to. I tell him Benson misses him. I tell him about the time with Camry's parents here and about work and how I started school. I tell him how I think Camry helped me too; all my doctors were impressed at my recovery. And I tell him how Camry took away her memories from the time they were in New York together.

Jake looks at me, confused. "You don't remember...anything?" he asks.

I shake my head. "I mean, I remember visiting my dad at the hotel and the questioning with Detective Greenly, but then...nothing. Until I woke up in the hospital. Well, just before that," I correct myself, thinking about how I argued with Camry.

Jake grins, to himself more than me. "You don't remember that?" He points to the CD, meaning the photo.

I shake my head. "Oh gosh!" I realize and feel stupid for not realizing it before now. "Have you been thinking...this whole time...that...I knew about your guys' time together?"

Jake blushes.

I giggle. "I mean, I can guess what happened during that week."

Now Jake is finding this funny as well.

"But I don't actually remember any of it."

He nods, smiling and looking out the window. The branches of the young trees play in the wind. It's still cold, but spring is starting. New life is budding and blooming.

I set down the CD and begin, "Listen. I want to explain more. About that time. In between." *Does he follow me?*

He thinks for a minute. "When you tried?" he asks. "When you tried to get her to stay?"

I nod. "I didn't remember everything there at first. It's taken me a long time, actually. What I remember most was fighting with her. I was so *mad* at her. But I think I understand now."

Jake is waiting patiently.

"She was trying to tell me it was a mistake. My death. There's a whole other layer we don't understand. She said she could see that layer, and my death wasn't supposed to happen. She said that *I* had never reached that layer. But *she* had…because she was the one who could make it right for me. She was the one who could correct what happened to me." I wait for Jake to absorb this.

He clenches his jaw and sniffs as tears fill his eyes.

"I don't know what it's from, but she wanted me to tell you that you were her 'evermore.' Does that make sense to you?"

A sob releases even though he tries to stop it. His fist comes up to cover his mouth. He nods.

I have one more thing I *have* to tell him. "I have a memory of you telling her that she met you for a reason." I pause. "And I *know* she felt she couldn't have done all that without you."

He clears his throat and tries to gather himself.

"Jake." I wait for him to look at me.

He finally does.

"It's not what I wanted either, but there's something out there so much bigger than us. You were right; she met you for a reason. Because she *couldn't* have done all that without you and…I'm here not only because of her but because of you. I need you to know I don't take that for granted. I know I've got a second chance here." I chortle, knowing how insanely ridiculous that is. I've come back from the dead! My voice cracks. "And even though *every day* I wish it were the other way around, I'm not going to blow this chance." I pause. "And I really don't want to spend this life only seeing you every seven months."

He meets my eyes better now. "I'm sorry," he says with a pained expression.

I swallow and shake my head. "Don't be. I didn't mean…I know you needed time. And I'm glad you have your music. I'm *so* glad that's helping. But—" It's my turn to look out the window now. To try to escape this moment for just a moment. Things aren't coming out quite right. *How can I tell him I need him?* "There are times when…even Benson can't understand." A tear threatens to fall, and I wipe my nose. My voice betrays me, cracking again. "There are times when it's really difficult, times when it'd be really nice to talk to you. And I think you probably have that happening too, yeah?"

His eyes wander at nothing specific, thinking.

I clear my throat. "Like I said…I'll never be all better. And neither will you, I suspect." I sniff. "But I think if you could see me as an entirely different person, as just another friend of Camry's, grieving like you are, it's possible we could heal a little bit more. Especially if we have each other."

I reach across the table and rest my hand on top of his. He stares at our hands. It takes a while, but he finally rolls his hand over and holds mine. Then he nods. And I feel—no, I *know*—things are going to be fine with Jake and me now. Because this moment is a change in perception. This moment, the fear is gone, and love is all that remains.

This moment…is a miracle.

9 781956 932355